THE GRASSHOPPER

Sasha J.M.

To the victims

Part I: Eve

Chapter 1

The Grasshopper, wearing a black uniform without any insignia, tall and slim, with a long narrow face, fair hair neatly combed back with gel revealing his tall forehead, watched with the perpetually serious and contemplative gaze of his gray-green eyes, as the body of the president of Earth fell onto the medallion that was woven into the middle of the oriental rug, in fine, regular knots in the color of old gold.

Blood seeped in a thin stream from a small wound on the president's forehead, down the root of his nose, past his opened eye and down his cheek, creating a new irregular ornament on the rug.

The Grasshopper bent down to return the revolver to the holster on his thigh.

Vice President Erivan passed by the Grasshopper, sat down in the naturally velvety leather armchair, and placed his large fists on the massive desk, made of five different types of wood: mahogany, cherry, chestnut, walnut and Carpathian elm.

The front of the desk was decorated with a relief of the planet Earth.

The wall behind Vice President Erivan was interrupted by a long string of large windows, currently covered by heavy dark red curtains. Hanging on it was the state flag, depicting a blue planet on a black background.

Erivan's large round head, sitting atop his bull-like neck, featured fat cheeks, a large nose, bulging eyes with no eyelashes, and thinning eyebrows.

Positioned between the relief and the blue Earth, it created a perfect symmetry of three orbs.

"Mr. President," said the Grasshopper, interrupting the silence.

Erivan raised his eyes from the cramped body before him and looked at the Grasshopper.

"You, Grasshopper, are the person to first have the right to call me by that name," he said, with a slight smile.

"Thank you, Mr. President."

"With this act... on this night... starts...," Erivan stopped, contemplatively, searching for the right word, "...a new era in the history of mankind. You are now going on your most important mission ever. Are you aware of that, Grasshopper?"

"I am, Mr. President."

"Are you aware of all the things that depend on you, what responsibility you are taking upon yourself? The responsibility of protecting the Constitution, the responsibility for the survival of the State, the survival of civilization?"

"Yes, I am, Mr. President. Fully."

"Do you know that I would not entrust anyone else with such a mission? Do you understand the trust that I have in you?"

"I understand Mr. President and I am grateful for it. I will justify your trust."

"I know you will, I know. When do you leave?"

"Immediately, Mr. President."

"Alright. In that case I won't keep you. Good luck, Grasshopper."

"Thank you, Mr. President," said the Grasshopper and left the office at a fast pace.

Chapter 2

Pulling back the drapes, Erivan watched the silhouettes of the Grasshopper and his lads moving at a running pace towards the helicopter awaiting them on the lawn in front of the residence. Beyond the rotating blades sparkled the lights of Capital City, the capital of Earth, and on the rise above it the castle of Mr. Kaella, the owner of the Kaella Cosmic Energy Corporation. The night was dark, without a single star in the sky.

"Except mine," Erivan thought. "Mine is the only star out tonight. Finally and irreversibly."

Having seen the helicopter take off, he spread his thumb and index finger and released the drape. It swayed slowly and returned to its place, preventing the crystals from the grandiose chandelier from continuing to struttingly gleam in the window pane.

He turned slowly and heavily, seemingly tiredly but actually magnificently, towards the desk, and turned on the intercom and summoned Alpha, the leader of A Squad, the squad in charge of protecting the president of Earth and his family.

Alpha was delighted to see the body of his former president laying practically in the middle of the large oriental rug. All it would take was to roll him up in the rug and take him away.

"Mr. President, where will you sleep tonight?"

"In my room."

"In the vice president's or..."

"Yes. The presidential part of the residence should be cleaned out and prepared for me without any hast. I'm in no hurry. Not anymore."

Chapter 3

Having entered his chambers Erivan immediately called Mr. Kaella.
"Mr. Kaella"
"May I call you President of Earth, Erivan?" Kaella asked.
"You may, sir. I thank you for your trust."
"No, no...," Kaella said. "I have you to thank. If only I had listened to you earlier..."
"Mr. Kaella, don't trouble yourself with that anymore, please. Perhaps it is better that the situation escalated. That also created the opportunity for us to once and for all deal with this gang of Non-Consumers. You, Mr. Kaella, as a great humanist, I dare say the greatest in history, also took it for granted that other people are also humane. But they are not. They took advantage of your humanism for their evil ambitions. And that is why we will punish them. Mercilessly."
"That's right, mercilessly! Mercilessly!" Kaella shouted excitedly.

"Mr. Kaella, be prepared, before the cameras, at exactly 6:07 p.m., your time," Erivan continued after a brief pause.
"I will be. I can't wait for that moment," Kaella calmed himself.
"You have made an excellent choice of location for your interview, Mr. Kaella. You will be far from... events. We cannot allow for even the faintest suspicion among our Consumers regarding the perpetrators. As soon as you learn about the heinous assassination of the president, immediately officially declare war on the Non-Consumers. I mean like..."
"Ominously, I will do it ominously, Erivan. Don't worry."

"Mr. Kaella, your son, Mr. Prince, is he aware of...?"
"Of course, Erivan. Fully, with all the details."
"Well... does he agree...?"
"Of course. The interview and the location were both his ideas. He too has the utmost respect for you. You have nothing to worry about. You will be President even after my passing."
"Mr. Kaella!" Erivan said excitedly. "That's not why I ask! Something like that didn't even occur to me! For me the position of President represents the opportunity and honor, in line with my abilities, to

serve the State and your family. And don't speak about your... about your departure. I don't want to think about that. There are many years before you, Mr. Kaella."

"Thank you for your kind wishes, Erivan, but... you'll see for yourself... When you are far into your eighties like me... then you draw a line. But I will leave in peace. Because I am leaving the Company and the State in good hands. To my son and you, Erivan. And now, it is already very late, we have to all get some rest. You get some sleep too."

"I will, a few hours. I want to supervise every detail of tomorrow's operation."

"Yes. I ask that you personally run the operation. I can no longer trust anyone else."

"Have no worries, Mr. Kaella. Everything will go smoothly."

"Yes, it will. Good night, Erivan."

"Good night, Mr. Kaella."

Chapter 4

Mr. Kaella, having finished his conversation with Erivan in the Royal Suite on the last floor of an elite hotel, turned towards his son. Prince Kaella sat in an armchair and placed on the club table in front of him the oval glass of cognac that he was enjoying, after a truly magnificent dinner.

"So the first act was concluded successfully?" he asked his father, who was slowly lowering himself into his armchair, holding on to the wide armrest.

"Yes it has, son. Unfortunately we have to use all available means to protect Humane Capitalism. You know, I'm very sorry..." Mr. Kaella's voice trembled. "It is very difficult for me... that you, my only son, will have to face such people, to fight against them. I wanted to enable you to peacefully focus on preserving our wounded planet and saving mankind from the ruthless nature. That is the mission that you had chosen, son, as a young man. And that was no coincidence, son. That is quite the logical continuation of our family tradition," Mr. Kaella's voice became firm once again. "You are actually continuing what your great-grandfather started, with the discovery of Cosmic Energy. And your grandfather and I were forced to dedicate our lives to organizing human society. He – by creating the State of Earth, and I – by creating the Association of Companies.

"And trust me, son, there is no job more difficult, more prickly and ungrateful that this job. While doing good for people, instead of gratitude, you are slapped in the face ceaselessly by human envy, stupidity... hatred. It is obvious that I have lived all this time in an illusion that you can change that by persistent goodness and nobleness. And I didn't listen to the persistent advice and warnings of my faithful Erivan. But now I know, on the eve of my death it is finally clear to me, that with such deviant creatures, such as the Non-Consumers, you can only do away with them by force!" Mr. Kaella raised his voice and slammed his weak hand on the armrest.

"Please, father," Prince Kaella interrupted his elderly father. "Don't trouble yourself with that. Everything will be alright in the end. You will rule the world for many more years, and I will calmly continue with my work. The way that you've always wanted it to be."

"I'm not some naïve dreamer who doesn't understand what is going on around him. All these years I have been aware that you are hiding from me the real problems of the State and the Company, that you wanted to spare me these ugly, unpleasant facts. However, the Non-Consumption evil is present and together we can meet it head-on and defeat it. We finally have a real operative as president. He will do this... prickly job, for us."

"I know. And I knew all this time that it was clear to you... but I still dreamt that... Perhaps your three beautiful children will rule a better world? Do you know, son, how proud I am of my grandchildren? How happy I am that they are beautiful and smart, excellent students... that they love each other, that they get along well. Son, they are our greatest treasure. And their wonderful mother. How she supports you in your efforts..."

Prince was no longer listening to his repeated elderly lament. He also wasn't thinking about the Non-Consumers, or about his children or the world that they would rule. He was thinking about something else. About someone else. Just as it had been every moment since he first saw her.

"...I'll be at peace, son, only when that damned Pascal Alexander is no longer among the living."

That name interrupted Prince's train of thought.

"That man, father, that beast, is the only thing that is troubling me!" said Prince while sitting up in his chair. "He drives me crazy, to be completely honest." Prince's eyes were full of hatred. "The fact that he dares to hold his election speech in Magapolis, the largest city on Earth, which I have created, from the very first street, from the first building, over twenty years, day after day..."

Prince slammed his fist on the club table, which was not sturdy enough to quietly absorb the exerted force, and leaned it over a little. The oval glass fell over, rolling through the spilt cognac to the very edge, then slipped of it and fell on the carpet. Due to table's low height and the considerable thickness of the carpet, which is appropriate for a carpet in the salon of a Royal Suite - the glass did not break.

"...twenty years of work, creative thinking, late nights... Megapolis, my Megapolis, a city far from any shore, unburdened by the rising ocean level, beyond the reach of tsunamis, in an area with the fewest storms, hurricanes... best protected from viruses, epidemics..."

"I know, son, I know everything…" Mr. Kaella whispered.

"…with drinkable tap water," Prince got up and started violently walking around the Royal Suite, "…parks, avenues green with trees… Every person on Earth dreams of living in it. In my Megapolis! And that worm will hold his speech in the square that I created, in the largest and greenest square on the planet, a square that bears the sacred name Consumer Square. He's spitting on my entire life! On everything that I am and everything that I exist for!"

Prince suddenly became quiet and went to the window. He watched the lights of the city beneath him and breathed with difficulty, trying to calm himself.

When Mr. Kaella finally managed to raise his feeble body from the deep armchair, he approached Prince and put his trembling hand on his shoulder.

"Just a little more, son, and we'll defeat them."

"I know that, father," Prince answered in a much calmer voice. "But that speech will be held. It is clear to me. We have to allow this, in order not to arouse suspicion. But even after our victory, that act will…" he spoke softly, full of bitterness and despair, "will always be a open sore on my heart."

After several moments of silence Prince turned from the window towards his father and looked at him tenderly.

"Forgive me, father," he said. "Instead of unwaveringly supporting you in these historic moments, I'm burdening you with my actually irrational, solely emotional outbursts of anger. Forgive me."

"No, you forgive me, son… for not doing this ten years ago. Had I done so, no scoundrel would have gotten close to your Megapolis. But I didn't. It is difficult to make such a decision. It's contrary to the convictions, efforts and results that our family had achieved over four generations. Actually, that wasn't my decision. The Non-Consumers themselves made the decision. I will just very considerately give them what they want."

"I understand, father."

"Now go, son. Sleep, get some rest."

"I will. Good night."

"Good night, son."

Chapter 5

At that moment Svetlana came out of the bathroom into the modernly, tastefully and functionally furnished room in the hotel located on the edge of Consumer Square in Megapolis, adjacent the magnificent building of the television station. This slender girl with symmetrical facial features, long brown hair, leaned over to pick up her thong and bra off the floor.

"Leave it," said Pascal Alexander.
Svetlana stood up and looked at Pascal, who lay naked on a large bed.
"Why?" she asked.
"I want you to stay with me tonight... I want to tell you something."

Svetlana lay down next to Pascal, placing her head on his shoulder, her eyes following the tips of her fingers while she gently passed them across his chest.
"You know, until I met you I didn't believe that a man in his forties can still have such a muscular body and smooth, tight skin."
"I want you to leave Megapolis early tomorrow morning," said Pascal.
Svetlana trembled but didn't say anything.
"You don't ask why?" Pascal was surprised.
"Tell me," she whispered.
"What is going on with you, Svetlana? You didn't even ask me what I had discussed with Mayor Seneca and Raul."
"Tell me... if you want."
"Seneca received shocking news from the Company Sector for Marketing and Public Opinion Polls."

Having said that, Pascal looked at Svetlana waiting her reaction. And she continued to silently caress his chest.
"You're not interested in what this shocking news is?" Pascal became angry because of her unexpected indifference. "Well, I'll tell you anyway. According to the latest polls, I will win the elections by a landslide, with sixty-two percent of the votes, becoming the president of Earth."

He lifted her chin and made her look at him.

"President of Earth, do you hear me? Aren't you pleased? You've been working tirelessly for my campaign for two years... and now... nothing... you're silent."

"I'm pleased. Congratulations." Svetlana said quietly and again looked down.

"You have nothing to congratulate me for. This is the official information that Kaella received. And he is surely in shock now, thinking frantically. No one expected such an advantage. Seneca believes, and I think that he is completely right, that Kaella has two options at this moment: either to fake the elections and reelect President Xing, or to kill me. All three of us agreed that an assassination is more likely. And Raul is almost convinced of this. He is convinced that Prince Kaella will not allow me to hold the speech tomorrow in his Megapolis."

"So why do only I have to leave Megapolis? Doesn't the Mayor..." Svetlana whispered.

"And as far as Mayor Seneca is concerned," Pascal continued, "for him the most important thing is to preserve peace and order in this city. And that is why he wants us to leave it immediately. But he doesn't want to force us, to drive us out, escorted by the inspectors. Actually, it was more like he asked Raul and me to leave, rather than demand. I have great respect for Seneca... and I am grateful to him for everything. But Svetlana, despite this, I will hold that speech. I've made up my mind. If they kill me, they will make me a martyr, an icon of resistance to Humane Capitalism. I could be more useful to the cause dead than alive. That's why I told Raul today for him and his team to decide on their own whether they will stay or leave Magapolis. And you, Svetlana, I am ordering to leave."

Svetlana was silent for quite a while. Pascal knew how difficult it was for her, which is why he didn't interrupt the silence. Finally Svetlana sighed and said:

"You were absolutely right to not allow Raul and the campaign staff to get marry you off for the sake of the presidential campaign. It would be truly an injustice for only one woman to enjoy you, Pascal."

"What are you talking about, Svetlana?" Pascal was surprised by such a reaction from her. "What does that have to do with anything? I want you to leave here, you understand?" Pascal asked, turning towards her.

"I understand," Svetlana replied. She lay on her stomach, leaned on her elbows and looked at him. "I understand everything, Pascal. It's all clear to me."

"Alright, if that's true..."

"I understand that I have to leave Megapolis, I understand that Seneca will take down your stage, I understand that despite all that you will take to the streets and wait for the sniper's bullet. Pascal, I also understand that after almost two years... of our relationship, let's call it that, you can calmly tell me your decision and don't even ask me what I think, what I feel..."

"Forgive me, Svetlana, forgive me... but I... it cannot be any other way. This is how it has to be, Svetlana."

Svetlana suddenly flipped onto her back and covered her face with her hands, trying to hold back the tears. When she calmed down, she lowered her arms next to her body and without opening her eyes, she said

"We both know that you will not go into the square tomorrow."

"I will, Svetlana, I will go."

"You won't, because Raul won't let you."

"Raul? How can Raul stop me?"

"Raul, Margot... Liam. Liam will stop you. The security guys."

"Don't be ridiculous. They wouldn't dare."

"Perhaps they wouldn't... Raul will call Seneca... His inspectors will arrest you, drive you out of Megapolis."

"Seneca could have already done that. I clearly told him today that I would hold a speech to the gathered people. Regardless of how many of them there are."

They both lay on their backs in silence, each in their own half of the bed.

"You know what, Pascal?" Svetlana suddenly spoke out, loudly. "I really don't care now. It isn't at all important to me. These are now your things, right? I'm not involved anymore. But all this will be happening tomorrow. And this is my night, Pascal. My last night with you. and it will be the way I want it to be," Svetlana turned over again, propped herself on her elbows and looked at Pascal. "You didn't thank you PR for all the votes," she said with a sad smile.

"You? Of course I'm grateful to you... And not only to you, to all our people, the entire staff..."

"No, no, primarily to me. My large screen at your speeches brought you the votes."

"Well, I see that you're joking now."

17

"It wasn't enough for people to see you from afar, Pascal. I told the cameraman to shoot only your face for the big screen." Svetlana removed a lock of hair from Pascal's forehead. "For people to see your dark hair... gentle waves... the lock that falls on your intelligent forehead... and you brush it away without any concern, with a swift movement of your hand... or head. You pull the long hair... on the collar of your shirt... behind your ear. And those lips..." Svetlana ran the tips of her fingers over Pascal's lips, "beautiful lips, very beautiful... full, juicy... and the chin, the round chin, not aggressive... it is charming, amiable. And you know what actually secured the votes of the women?"

"Svetlana, please."

"Be quiet... just be quiet... This is my night," Svetlana whispered. "You never thought of it, admit it. That very slightly pug nose of yours. Like that of a boy. It awakes motherly instincts. And your eyes. Dark, deep... 'Eyes, get the eyes!' I told the cameraman... because when they look at a person... it is so, like... Every person feels that you are focused on them, that you respect them, understand them... that you know everything about them. And they don't notice, captivated by those eyes of yours... that at one moment your gaze went through them. It didn't wander, it didn't. But it went someplace... only it knows where. Uncatchable, untouchable to anyone else..." Svetlana started to cry.

"Don't, Svetlana, please," Pascal held her to his chest.

"And then your gaze, Pascal," continued Svetlana without daring to look at him, fearing that she would see acknowledgment in his eyes, "did in fact stop on someone. It didn't pass through someone. It reached its place... that it loves. From where it doesn't want to go... anywhere."

"Please, stop cry, please," Pascal kissed her hair.

"Tell me... tell me... has your gaze stopped?"

"Stopped? My gaze? I don't understand a thing you're saying, Svetlana, really. You're too upset. But don't worry, calm down. I'm sure it will be as you said. Seneca will arrest me and won't let me go to the square. Raul also would never allow me to. You're completely right. And this is not our last night. And stop sobbing," Pascal smiled and raised her face towards his. "I just don't want to you be in any danger. Tomorrow is a critical, uncertain day."

Chapter 6

Having come out of his father's suite, Prince Kaella did not go to his room. He took the elevator to the hotel lobby, nodded to the inspectors who were watching the hotel, and walked to the reception.

"How can I help you, Mr. Kaella," the receptionist said.

"I'm interested in whether the members of the television crew were still working or whether they had gone up to their rooms?"

"Most of them are still working, sir. Only the editor-in-chief and Miss Babe are in their rooms."

"Very well. Thank you. Good night."

"Good night, Mr. Kaella."

Prince got off the elevator on the third floor and walked down the hallway looking for room 314. The head of Babe's television station, Capital City TV, had booked the same hotel, following Prince's instructions, and informed him of Babe's room number.

He stood in front of her door for a while. There was no sound. Slowly, indecisively he raised his hand as though to knock, then unexpectedly lowered it, turned around and walked back to the elevator.

Chapter 7

Pascal managed to calm Svetlana down.

"Let's go to sleep," he said.

"I don't want to. I talked about you, now I want us to talk about me," Svetlana said.

"OK. You want me to talk now, how beautiful you are?"

"No. I want something else. You said that you don't want me to be in danger."

"Of course I don't."

"Don't you think that I put myself in jeopardy two years ago, when I started working for your campaign?"

"I do. But that was just the beginning. We didn't even dream that I would become a presidential candidate. Now the threat is much greater."

"At the time, when your team was being created, I had just gotten my Master's degree. I could always choose boys, but you were the man that I wanted. I was fascinated by the legend of you, your good looks, intelligence, courage... your huge libido. Your refusal to be tied down by one woman."

"Refusal or perhaps inability?" said Pascal.

"For me you were a challenge. With my knowledge and my youth I could have chosen any well-paid job. And I chose to work for your campaign. A life-threatening job with paid food and rent."

"I didn't know that. I thought that you were with us out of conviction?"

"I guess love and passion are also a type of conviction, Pascal."

"Yes, one could say that. But all that is not important now. We will talk about it when we meet again. Don't hope that I will change my decision. You are leaving tomorrow. I'm firing you. No more food and rent."

"Remember when I took some time off a year ago?"

"Svetlana, please, get serious."

"And I sent my friend from university as a replacement. Do you remember?"

"No."

"Before she came to your headquarters I deceived her a little. I told her that even after a one-year effort I hadn't succeeded in getting you in my bed. I'm sure you'll remember her. Her name is Norma."

"I don't remember that name."

"Probably not. But I'm sure you remember her body."

Pascal didn't answer.

"Norma immediately reported proudly to me that she slept with you already on the first night."

Pascal was still silent.

"On the seventh day of my vacation I called you up and asked what you wanted: for Norma to continue working or for me to come back. You said that I should come back, as soon as possible. I heard something in your voice then. Something... that I needed so badly. At that moment there was no happier girl than me."

"Svetlana, you yourself say that you knew what I was like. That I was just a challenge to you."

"I was happy, because you weren't with me only because of the inability to move around, the cramped space, the small number of people that you had been surrounded by for a long time. I gave you a choice and you chose me; between two girls, both much younger than you. I wasn't afraid of older women. I believed that I could successfully take advantage of your midlife crisis and your age, and forever capture your age with my youth."

"What are you trying to tell me, Svetlana?"

"Pascal, have you ever been with married women? With the mothers of another man's children?"

"I've never answered such questions. Even in much less important moments. Do you understand at all what might happen tomorrow?"

"Have you, Pascal?"

"I have."

Svetlana brushed the hair from his forehead. Holding herself up, she leaned her pear-shaped breast on his biceps and gently kissed his lips, getting his face wet with her tears. After that she got up, picked up her thong and bra from the floor, and said:

"I'll take your advice and I won't put myself at risk. I'm leaving... tonight."

Pascal wondered whether it was the last time that he would be seeing Svetlana's naked body or any woman's naked body.

Chapter 8

Alpha was going down the stairs, walking behind Bear and Iceman, two members of his A Squad, who were carrying the body of former president Xing, rolled up in a carpet. Having reached the garage, they passed by the parked state cars, ready for tomorrow's escort and security of the presidential motorcade.

Leaning on one of the support columns, Alpha silently watched as Bear and Iceman lowered the carpet next to the lifeless bodies of Xing's wife and two children, who lay neatly arranged on the floor of the garage, wrapped in sheets.

"They were killed in their sleep?" Bear asked the colleagues who brought the three bodies.
"Yes," one of them answered.
"Why did they have to... the entire family?"
"Xing would have given his last election speech tomorrow. It was logical for his wife and children to be at his side on the stage. In any case, it is not up to us to discuss this, Bear. It is our job to protect the president," Alpha said.
"I see. We've successfully protected him."
"I won't allow such sarcasm. It's our job to protect Erivan. We were just carrying out his orders and allowed the Grasshopper to do his job."
"As though we could have stopped the Grasshopper even if we tried to," Iceman said. "I was relieved when they left, I must admit."

The team silently nodding their heads in agreement.
"Forget about that Grasshopper," Alpha said angrily, and then continued with a milder tone. "I understand you. It wasn't easy for me either. We've been protecting presidents for years, and now... It's as though we've betrayed ourselves. That's what high-level politics is like. What can we do? Come on, people, let us... I mean, before rigor mortis sets in... let's get them in the car."

The team reluctantly approached the bodies.

"In an upright position… Everything has to look like… normal… you understand? And fasten them somehow… I don't know how…"

Chapter 9

The Director of the Tourism Sector was always very cross, but kept it to himself, whenever Mr. Kaella wanted to go for a ride in his submarine, with the large portholes and powerful floodlights, down the streets of one of the many submerged cities.

Then the Director would have to cancel the excursions of all the tourist submarines to that city, which always caused an outcry among visitors. There were also fewer and fewer people prepared to pay the quite hefty price for such trips, because the submerged structures, exposed to the high level of acidity of the increasingly saltier and warmer seawater, had started to decay and left an unpleasant, almost sickening feeling.

Once upon a time the tours of the submerged cities were really enjoyable. The buildings were still intact, and the sea life had already been destroyed. There was no seaweed, algae, and whatever it had been called, to stick to them. If some mutant fish happened to swim past the portholes of the submarine, it would not conceal the tourists' view of the city.

This time, due to Kaella's submarine ride the following day, the Director was overcome by a completely different feeling. A feeling of content, for onboard the submarine Kaella would be giving his interview, which would be broadcast live by all the television stations in the State. This means that people, mimicking their ruler and idol, would scurry on excursions to the submerged cities.

The Atlantis tourist program would most likely generate profit this quarter. Maybe even the next quarter, considering the fact that Kaella would be interviewed by Miss Babe. And after that he would suspend Atlantis. The maintenance costs of the submarines in this acid soup of an ocean were enormous. He would sell the dilapidated submarines to the Inspectorate, for any price. Better than nothing. But not yet, not as long as the marketing effect of the interview still existed. Men would be the best clients, the Director was certain, judging by himself.

Because just on this night, while making his way along Kaella's route for tomorrow, he imagined Babe sitting next to him in the submarine, and not Erivan's squire Charlie, in charge of Kaella's personal security.

The sight of Charlie interrupted the Director's hot fantasies and he got back to work.
"Mr. Charlie, the cameras will go on and the interview with Mr. Kaella, according to the program director's wishes, will start at the beginning of this street..." the Director explained.

Charlie pointed the searchlights into every side street and at every opening on the decrepit buildings large enough to conceal a submarine in. The inspectors had checked this long ago but Charlie had to see for himself too and report to Erivan that there were no intruders in this city.

Chapter 10

Svetlana and Pascal stood fully dressed in the middle of the hotel room. Pascal truly didn't expect such a agonizing parting with her. It wasn't becoming, nor did they need it after two years of shared struggle for freedom, after two years of intimacy, tenderness in these grueling times.

"Svetlana, don't leave like this, please. I'm not pushing you away. I'm afraid for you. Don't you get it? The mayor also wants you all to leave the city."
"It's alright Pascal. Speaking of the mayor, let's tell each other... everything."
"What everything, Svetlana? What does the mayor have to do with anything? I really don't understand."
"You don't understand? Pascal, who brought you sixty-two percent of the votes?"
"Who? What do you mean 'who'? You said you did... and your screen on the stage..." Pascal tried to joke.
"Megapolis gave you the lead, Pascal. Megapolis. Mayor Seneca placed at your feet this city of a hundred million people."
"Perhaps... Yes, you're right. But I still don't understand..."
"Have you ever wondered why Seneca did this?"
"Because he understood that we were right. He accepted our ideas. He felt the thirst, the hunger for freedom."
"Did he? The man that Prince Kaella appointed director of the most important television station in the State and mayor of his flagship, his Megapolis. The regime man of the greatest confidence suddenly realized that we were right?"
"That's not strange, Svetlana. During all these years, how many people in high-ranking positions from all sectors of the Company or from the top of the Inspectorate have crossed over to our side? Without such people who understood, who opened their eyes, we would have ceased to exist long ago. Seneca is only one of them."
"You would have convinced me with this explanation if I didn't know Seneca. He has not accepted our ideas. He also never accepted the ideology of Humane Capitalism. He is not a man of ideas. He doesn't think about them. He's an operative, a top-notch operative.

You appoint him to a certain position and he develops the best possible system, without ever questioning its fairness, morality, correctness. He is only interested in the optimal functioning of the system. He is a man of assignments. And as such at one moment he refused to carry out the assignment that the regime had given him, and he started carrying out a different assignment, which he was given by someone he trusts, someone he loves."

"I agree. You described him very well. Perhaps he has not accepted our ideas, but he is aware that Megapolis is mainly inhabited by the intellectual elite, and this is where the largest university in the world is. The city is full of young educated people. If he were to oppose us, there would be riots. The man is a pragmatist. And you're going into philosophy. Someone gave him a new assignment, so Seneca changed. What does that have to do with the two of us?

"You surprise me, Pascal. I never though that you... that you are afraid of... that you can't even admit to yourself what has happened to you."
"What has happened to me?"
"Alright. How long have we been here in Magapolis?"
"Well... I don't know exactly. We're not always here. We go away... and come back."
"But our base is here."
"That it is."
"Since when?"
"What since when?"
"Since when have our headquarters been in Megapolis? We used to go from city to city. We didn't have a permanent base. Wasn't it like that?"
"Yes, it was. It's almost a year, I think, since we settled down in this hotel. Why are you interrogating me like this, Svetlana? Tell me already, what is it that I cannot admit to myself? What has happened to me?"

"You're incredible, Pascal. It's not that great a sin that you should hide it even from yourself. So say it, where do you go... you and Raul... or you take Jagdish and me too, as soon as we get back... I mean the very moment... you don't even unpack... when we return to Megapolis from another city?"
"Well... I'm not sure... that it's the same instant..."
"Where, Pascal?"
"To see Seneca. Is that so strange?"

"Strange? It's not strange to me, Pascal. Tell me, why do we go to Seneca's house? And not only on such occasions. Almost every second, third day."

"Well… because Seneca wants that. He doesn't want to receive us officially on television or at the Mayor's Office. He wants to keep his neutral status."

"OK. And he also wants to be informed, to be up-to-date…"

"Yes, of course."

"And you inform him. You, Raul, me…"

"Not only that. He does a lot for us. He gives us wise advice, connects us with people…"

"Alright, alright… I agree. Of course Seneca is exceptionally important to us. I told you myself that he brought us victory. But I'm interested in why we go to his house? Can't he meet with us, can't he come secretly, in a regular car, to the hotel garage?"

"It's more isolated there, and safer. Here, at the hotel, we can never know who is coming or going. Who is watching or listening."

"The coffee probably also isn't as tasty."

"This is becoming ridiculous. What coffee…"

"Well exactly. What coffee?! You'd rather have a cup of real green tea! Isn't that right, Pascal?!" Svetlana's eyes started to fill up with tears.

Pascal was silent.

"But you… You, the great Don Juan, don't dare ask even for one cup, but keep ordering coffee, which Seneca's butler bring you, you tell the mayor how you feel uncomfortable drinking alone, and that he should have something too. And when after your third coffee Seneca finally decides to have something to drink, he asks for green tea. And how does he ask for it, Pascal?"

Svetlana's tears started trickling unstoppably down her face and her shrieking voice trembled. Pascal stared at the floor and was silent.

"And then he tells the butler 'Please tell my wife to prepare some green tea for me.' And then you stare, without breathing, as Mrs. Seneca, in one of her kimonos, brings a cup of green tea, humbly holding it with two hands. She approaches her husband, with her small steps, looking at the floor the entire time. She puts the tea in front of him and when she sees him bring it up to his lips, she glances at you for a moment. That moment, those glances of yours, I can't stand them, Pascal. I would stand for all other women my entire life. As long as I was the first. But I don't want to nor will I be second. Not even for you."

28

Svetlana then opened the door to the hotel room with one brisk move and ran out into the hallway. Pascal did not follow her. He did not see Svetlana running, slamming her body, bouncing off the walls of the hallway. But he heard the night's silence shattered by her moans and piercing groans. The moans of a young soul, hurt for the very first time.

Chapter 11

That night Mr. Kaella could not sleep. He tried yet again to explain to himself how it was possible that this was how this ugly world was repaying him for everything that he had done for it.

Having inherited his father's company, Cosmic Energy Kaella, and having acquired companies for the exploitation and distribution of drinking water, as well as the companies for the production and distribution of food, he provided the great majority of the people on the planet with a decent life.

Unemployment was minimal, the loans comfortable. The water distribution system was extensive and efficient. Food was expensive but readily available. And that was what was most important. Cosmic Energy made all this possible.

In order for such a level of prosperity of the State to be sustainable, people had to fulfill only one condition: they had to spend. This is why at the beginning of his rule he ordered the President of the State to enter into the Constitution, into the first article, the following definition and obligation:

"The social order of the State of Earth is Humane Capitalism. The fundamental value of Humane Capitalism is consumption, because one person's spending provides work and income for another person. This is why consumption is the constitutional obligation of each and every citizen of the State of Earth."

It was not by chance that he called his social system Humane Capitalism. In the entire history of mankind only he had the right to do such a thing. Because he was the most humane ruler of all times, there was no doubt about it.

"Who else provided his people with water, food, cooling, transportation, education, healthcare, jobs..." Mr. Kaella thought to himself. "Everything, absolutely everything that a civilized person needs. And without any discrimination, on any grounds. What else can you give a person? What? Thanks to Cosmic Energy and my family, there haven't been any wars in a century."

"And what does this Pascal Alexander want? He wants freedom, the right to choose, he says. To buy what he wants or to not buy at all. To spend when he wants or not to spend at all. Is that it?" The fuming Mr. Kaella shook, alone in the enormous bed in the Presidential Suite, with his entire elderly body.

"And what about those people... what about those companies whose products Mr. Aleksandar and his Non-Consumers don't want to buy, whose services they don't need? What will happen to those people and their families, Mr. Alexander?! I ask you this! How will they earn money and pay their bills for energy, water... What will they give their children to eat when their companies go bankrupt because of you? What?! You soulless selfish animal!"

"I have to stop doing this," Mr. Kaella said out loud. "My poor body can't take it anymore."

For years he had tortured himself by trying to understand the villains. Good cannot understand evil. This was a simple fact that he must accept. But he can and must fight against evil. And he will fight. Starting tomorrow, until the final victory.

Chapter 12

Prince Kaella was obviously wiser than his father, at least on this night.

"Events are taking their course," he thought. "The right course. Capable and loyal people are in their positions, prepared to act."

Why should he trouble himself with that anymore? Especially now, when she was finally there, just a few floors beneath him. He could decide tonight, at any moment, to get out of bed and to knock on her door within a few minutes.

Who knows, he might even do that. Because this desire, this passion... he has never felt... anything similar... so powerful. It was as though he had only now awaken from some monotony, from some mist, nothingness, senselessness... in which he had spent his entire life.

Her body, her seething flesh... exactly in the right spots, exactly where it should... simply forces a man to lose his mind... to go mad!

But no. Not only that. There are such female bodies on every step, alright not exactly like that, but similar. But there is no journalist, host, editor that looks like that, while at the same time creating an evening news program with record-breaking ratings.

How much good she actually did for his father, him, the Company and the State. She exposed irregularities that occurred in society, invited to the studio the persons responsible from all sectors of the Company and the Inspectorate and clearly, without any reluctance, before the millions-strong audience, demanded that they stop non-consumption and mercilessly punish the Non-Consumers.

Those responsible would promise that before the cameras and soon after, in some cases already the following day, they would carry out arrests and raids of well-concealed, secret Non-Consumer outlets, full of goods from past seasons. Such successful actions by the Inspectorate were always immortalized by Babe's camera crew. In the next show she aired with great pleasure the footage showing outlets ablaze and Non-Consumers with their hands handcuffed behind their backs, surrounded by shapely inspectors and their grayish uniforms, humbly entering Inspectorate vehicles, heads hung low.

Prince was pleased with himself. He had decided that from now on he would always give in to his desires, urges and instincts. His rationality would never allow him to simply get up after one of Babe's shows, to go to his study followed by his wife's gaze, and to call the director of Capital City TV and announce his official visit to his media company, with the request that Miss Babe describe to him the entire process of creating her show In the Eye of the Storm. Had he not acted on the cries, the shrieks of his soul, had he not listened to the real him, he would have never learned... he would have never seen, felt how Babe looked at him, how her breath stopped from his nearness, how this fearless journalist become confused, only in his company...
How she bowed her head and trembled.

This is why he organized this interview in the submarine, far away from Capital City. Here, where he and Babe would be alone, where he could knock on her door...
No, he would not disturb her tonight, his instinct clearly told him. He would not allow her to feel uncomfortable when she stepped out before him, half-asleep, in just a plain nightgown, without any makeup. Let her prepare for the interview in peace. Tomorrow she will look...
He would make it another night without her, just one more night. Just one more. And after the interview, when they return to the hotel... then nothing would to stop him. Nothing!

Chapter 13

That night Pascal Alexander also did not sleep. After Svetlana left he stayed up for a long time looking down from his window into Consumer Square, where the occasional passerby scurried home, without paying attention to the magnificent fountain, the statues of Mr. Kaella's grandfather and father, or the stage prepared for Pascal's speech the following day.

"The stage will be taken down in the morning," Pascal thought. "I didn't tell you that, Svetlana. Seneca will not arrest me tomorrow. He told me that I am a free citizen who has not committed any violation. I didn't want you to worry, to suffer even more, Svetlana, because tomorrow I will go into the square. I will, Svetlana."

He finally forced himself to sit in the armchair, to take the tablet from the table, place it on his knees and start watching footage of his speeches. He wanted to distil from them what is best... no, not the best, but the parts, the words and ideas that people reacted to the most, with shouts. His thoughts that the people understood.

He started every speech with the words:
"Hello, free people!"
He skipped the usual initial shouts and his waves and thanks.
"We will win these presidential elections. For the first time since the founding of the Company, the State will have a president who will be the president of the free people, and not Kaella's puppet."
There, that is where the people shouted out in approval. It was clear to them who governed them.

"On the first day I will slate free elections for Parliament. And when we finally get representatives of free people in their offices, we will do away with the first article of the Constitution and all the others that limit our freedom."
Just a few voices could be heard. What do people know about Parliament? Most of them don't even know what the Constitution is. He won't mention that. He mustn't confuse the people.

"I will immediately carry out an investigation into how the companies for energy, water and food were acquired at the time by

34

one single family. I promise you, here and now, that the Company, which this family is using to enslave us, will be again listed on the stock exchange and its shares will be handed out to all the citizens. Cosmic Energy is cosmic and it cannot be the property of one dynasty. We will all be owners."

Now there was a surge of shouts. This can be expanded, emphasized. Repeat several times that all the people will be owners.

"When we resolve the issues of satisfying our basic needs for energy, water and food, we will go back to ourselves, nature, evolution – because all life, just like us, was created through evolution. And it represents nothing other than a struggle in the free market. We will inscribe democracy, free market and protection of competition in the first article of our new Constitution."

Nothing. Silence. It isn't the people's fault. Kaella writes the history textbooks, censures the Internet. How would people know what the world looked like a hundred years ago? He mustn't confuse them with that. They will slowly, gradually learn this, over time.

"How much of your monthly income goes towards energy, water and food? How much do you pay per month to his son Prince, for the loan for you overpriced apartment, your entire working life? Or rent? Why do we work, why do we live? In order to give Kaella everything that we earn? Is that why we live? Will our descendants also live only to fill the pockets of Kaella's descendants? No! Its enough!"

Catharsis. That's the real deal. Telling people about their daily lives, about their bills, through which they overpay for basic living costs.

"And what happens to the remainder of your monthly income? You are required to spend it on things that you don't need. New clothes and shoes are mandatory every season. Every year a new dishwasher, a new car every two years. And if you don't buy them the Inspectors take you to prison, take away your apartment, expel your children from school... We refuse!"

The crowd roared "We refuse! We refuse! We refuse!"

"We will spend as much as we want and when we want. We will purchase goods and services that we want. From companies that are capable of offering, through fair competition in a free market, a product that we need, one that we like, one that we want. At a price that we are prepared to pay for them, and not the one that Kaella sets."

Here the people were shouting more against Kaella's name than...
One should not complicate things with products and services.

Pascal got up suddenly, stopped the recording, angrily threw the tablet on the armchair and frantically walked around the room. After a while, when his steps became slower and his hands dropped by his sides, he approached the window. Closing his eyes, he leaned his forehead on the glass.

Chapter 14

Once again Prince Kaella's instinct was not wrong. Babe actually was in a nightgown, carefully laying outfits for tomorrow on half of the double bed in room 314.

She would wear the first outfit in the morning, when she meets Prince and Mr. Kaella for breakfast, in order to discuss the final details before the interview. For this occasion she chose a beige knee-length skirt and a white nontransparent broad blouse, which she would button up high.

She will tickle him with her modesty. Let Prince only get a hint of things at breakfast, let him imagine, let his desire grow. Wearing that same outfit she would leave the hotel immediately after breakfast, while he watches. Let him think that she would appear before him like that for the show. And in the afternoon, when Prince raises his eyes as he enters the submarine's salon, having let his old father enter first…

Like two weeks ago when he was on an official visit to the television station. She didn't realize immediately that he had come because of her. She knew of course that he had come because of her show. He had told the editor-in-chief so himself. But she didn't know that he had come only because of her. Until the moment when everyone from the editorial board had left the studio and when she said, with her back turned to him:

"And it is only then, Mr. Kaella, after a whole day of constant work, that I go into the studio, that the cameras and lights are turned on…" and showing the familiar set with a broad gesture of her hand, she turned towards him, looked at him and stopped.

In Prince's look she saw, like only a woman can see, that from that moment on he was only hers. She had always felt that she would achieve a lot in life, that she would go very far, but she had never considered such heights, the throne itself. Babe wasn't at all interested what it would be like: official or unofficial, public or secret. She simply knew that from that moment on, she, Babe, was queen of the world. The Princess of the planet Earth.

Prince Kaella did not even consider the possibility that Miss Babe might not open the door to him if he decided to knock on it even tonight. And she wouldn't have. Of course she would not allow for him to see her in plain nightgown. At one time, later, when she is safely anchored as Princess. And considering his great desire, if he were to knock right now, which was certainly possible, then she would...

Babe smiled, creating in her head an entire scenario of what it would be like. Like, she was just ironing out the creases, bent over the bed, when she heard a knock.

"Who is it?" she would ask, with a seemingly surprised and frightened voice, like one would expect of a girl alone in a hotel room, if a stranger were to knock on her door in the middle of the night.
"Prince Kaella," he would whisper.
"Oh, Mr. Kaella!" she would shout out, in a voice that would lose the tone of fear, but would contain a stronger note of surprise, with a mild, initial note of typical female excitement.
"You're not sleeping, Miss Babe?", Prince would ask.
"I was just about to, Mr. Kaella".
"May I come in?"
"Come in? What do you mean? I'm not dressed. I always sleep in the nude, Mr. Kaella."

Babe giggled out loud, imagining him panting in the hallway, completely shocked by this statement of hers.
"I understand... well... put something on."
"Why, Mr. Kaella? Has something happened? Is your dad feeling unwell?"
"Hm, no, no... I just wanted..."
"What? Tell me."
"Well... I must see you."
"We'll see each other in the morning, Mr. Kaella."
"I know... I know that, but... I can't wait."
"What can't you wait for, Mr. Kaella?"
"I... I... long for you so much."
"Mr. Kaella! Tomorrow is an important day. Millions of people across the Earth will be watching the interview with you and your father. I have to be focused and I cannot give in to... Go now, please."
"What can't you give in to?"

At this point she would be silent and with that silence she would show Prince how much she reprimanded herself for foolishly betraying and revealing her immense feelings for him. Of course he would repeat the question.

"What can't you give in to? Tell me... please."

"Mr. Kaella, this really isn't the time for such conversations. In any case, someone might hear us and tell your dad. We cannot upset him in any way before the interview. I'm sure you agree with this, right?"

"Well... yes," Prince said gloomily.

"And after the interview, Mr. Kaella..."

"What after the interview? What? Tell me... tell me..."

"I mean, if you want to, at all..."

"If I want to?! If I want to?!"

"Quite. Quiet, Mr. Kaella."

"What after the interview? Tell me already!"

"Then I will open my door to you and allow you to come in, Mr. Kaella."

"It's a pity that he is so shy and intimidated, and he doesn't dare knock. Boy, what I would do to him."

Chapter 15

That night the new president of Earth, Erivan, did not sleep either. As soon as he went to bed he lay on his side and tried to go to sleep. But it didn't work, he was too excited.

"Finally..." he thought, raising his large body and leaning back on the arched backboard, "...finally... after twenty-five years of being vice president."

During that period he had also held the office of President, on several occasions, when Kaella would get angry enough and stopped being surprised that these grown men were taking their function of president seriously, and they would start thinking on their own and making decisions.

Then under order from Kaella, Erivan would eliminate the incumbent President, making use of media campaigns and court cases, and in line with the Constitution he would take his place pending early elections, and after that he would again retreat to the position of vice president. Into the shadows of the loyal guardian of Humane Capitalism.

But this time it wasn't so. And it would never be again. In the past several years Erivan had been under a lot of stress and it took its toll on his health, because Kaella did not take his warnings seriously. From time to time Kaella would not even read his reports on Pascal Alexander's activities and would tell him that he was exaggerating. Alexander had succeeded in creating a strong Non-Consumer movement. They had taken power in entire cities and on all the continents. They had taken factories, started their own production of goods.

When he realized Alexander's strength, Erivan stopped realistically and truthfully reporting to Kaella. It was probably his smartest, one might even say his ingenious decision. He allowed Alexander and the Non-Consumers to produce their own weapons and waited for the right opportunity. He waited for the moment when Kaella would no longer have any choice and when he would have to chose to finally put an end to the Non-Consumers. This sixty-two percent support for Alexander, which Erivan had shown to Kaella only now, on the eve of the elections, had finally sobered up the old and naïve ruler. He accepted the proposal for them to carry out an assassination of Xing, when he goes tomorrow by car to give his election speech, here in Capital City, and to blame the Non-Consumers for it.

And he had done well to have already killed the Xings. Zodiac, the pilot of the stolen Non-Consumer plane, told him that their rockets were not a hundred percent accurate. If the first projectiles were to miss or only graze the presidential car, one of the Xings might run out and escape. Why should he take such a risk if the family was within his reach the entire time?

"Now it's really enough, Mr. President," Erivan said to himself out lout, smiling because of the "Mr. President". "Don't torture yourself with things that are no longer important. Rest. Starting tomorrow numerous statesman and wartime duties await you as President and Supreme Commander of the Inspectorate.

He got up out of bed and went to the bathroom. He got a box of sleep medication from the cabinet, took one pill, greeted himself in the mirror with a dignified bow, and returned to bed.

Chapter 16

"What am I doing?" thought Pascal Alexander, removing his forehead from the window. "I'm watching footage as though I don't know what I will say tomorrow? After all these years I don't know what I will tell the people?

"Well I won't tell them anything more! Let them kill me tomorrow! I want them to kill me. Please, Kaella, don't steal the elections, kill me... please. If you won't, let your son kill me. He won't give me his Megapolis. Your Erivan will kill me... if you won't, Kaella. Kill me... anyone... please."

"I didn't do this because of the people. I did this for myself. It was I that couldn't stand you. I need freedom. Why did you challenge me? Why did you make me into a leader? Why did you bring me to this damn Megapolis? Why did you make me meet her? Why did your Seneca listen to her and place Megapolis before my feet?

"You are right, Svetlana. About everything you told me tonight. Forgive me, Svetlana, but I'm so in..."

"Do you see it, Manami... do you see it with you brief look? And why do you look at me at all? Why do you torture me, when you cannot be mine?!"

Pascal ran out of the room and took the elevator down to the reception.

"Mr. Alexander, what has happened?" a scared young man and young woman at the desk asked.

"Nothing, nothing... I'm just a little tense... do you have any alcohol?"

"Of course, we'll get some from the bar. What do you want?"

"Tequila. Get me a tequila. Bring the bottle..."

"Immediately," said the girl and ran off towards the bar.

"And three glasses," Pascal shouted after her. "You'll have some too, please," Pascal told the young man. "I simply can't be alone tonight."

Chapter 17

"I'll go up to my suite to rest," Mr. Kaella told Prince and Miss Babe, already leaning with both shaky hands on the armrests.

Prince nodded to the two bodyguards who rushed up to Mr. Kaella, held him under his arms, pulled back his chair and helped him up.
"See my father to his suite and stay in front of his door," Prince ordered them.
"Both of us?" one of the bodyguards asked.
"Yes. I won't be needing you, and in any case – there's a lobby full of inspectors."
"As you wish, Mr. Kaella."

Prince and Babe remained alone, sitting across from each other at a large oval table set up in the middle of the completely empty hotel dining room. They had barely touched the variety of food served in silver dishes. Prince summoned the waiter without taking his eyes off of Babe.
"Yes, Mr. Kaella?"
"Please, take this away..." Prince made a circular motion above the table, "and bring us... Are you for coffee?... or perhaps some juice, Miss Babe?"
"No, thank you, nothing. I've had too much of everything. It's time for me to go."
"Go? Already?" Prince looked at the waiter, who was waiting for his order. "Bring us two coffees."
"Immediately, Mr. Kaella."
"But, Mr. Kaella..." Babe protested.
"Miss Babe, I really don't see any reason for you to rush... unless you feel uncomfortable in my company."
"I'm not uncomfortable in your company," Babe answered seriously, without any coquetry. "However..."

Babe was silent, while four waiters, under the watchful eye of the maître 'd, took away the dishes, plates, cups, glasses, silverware and napkins from their table.
"Please, continue," said Prince, once the waiters had gone.

"You know, this breakfast of ours has gotten pretty long. I didn't expect that."

"I know. But you saw yourself.. my father wanted to go through all the questions with you once more. Please understand him."

"I understand, I understand... certainly. But I have obligations."

Prince waited for them to be served the coffee and then asked:

"But what obligations? Now everything is being done by the members of your team: technicians, cameramen, the director... Miss Babe, I listened very carefully when you explained to me how your show is produced. All you need to do is get to the studio fifteen minutes before the show time. What are you hiding from me?"

"I obviously don't have a choice. I have to tell you, otherwise you won't allow me to leave, right?"

"I won't allow you. You can be certain of that. Now just admit everything."

Babe sighed and said:

"Mr. Kaella, an entire team of people of various profiles have been waiting for me in the adjacent hotel for an hour already."

"Why?"

"Well... to touch me up for the interview."

"Really? I thought that you will... that you're already touched up. Although it seemed a little too, how would I say it... conservative. But I thought that you chose such a style for my elderly father. Although, on the other hand... your viewers are not used to seeing you like this."

"Mr. Kaella, I'm leaving this instant," Babe said, already getting up from the table. "Some procedures, treatments take some time. Forgive me, please, I'm getting nervous..."

Prince also got up, and looked at her with a smile.

"With all due respect to your father... and today I don't really care what my viewers are used to. I'm getting touched up for you, if you really want to know! Now I've lost the element of surprise and I'm very angry because of that!"

Babe abruptly turned spun around and started walking briskly towards the dining room exit. Prince ran after her, got around her and stood in front of her.

"Miss Babe," said Prince, eating her up with his eyes.

"Yes?" Babe asked angrily.

"I have reserved a superb restaurant, I mean the entire restaurant, just for the two of us, tonight... with candles. Will you..."

"If you wish so after the interview."

"If I wish so?!"

"Mr. Kaella, you know how to rule the world but you have no idea how much time it takes a woman to prepare for... please, let me pass."

Prince watched as her curves strained the fabric of the slim conservative skirt, as she walked away, at almost a running pace.

Chapter 18

"Pascal, wake up! Pascal!" shouted Raul Bukowski, the head of Pascal's electoral staff, while pounding on the door of his room.

"Here, here... take it easy, Raul," said Pascal, getting up from his bed, fully dressed and hung over.

He went to the door and unlocked it. Raul, a small stocky man nearing sixty years of age, stepped into the room.

"Where's Svetlana?" he asked.

"She's gone," Pascal responded, while locking the door.

"Without goodbye?"

"Don't be angry at her."

"You got drunk because of Svetlana?" Raul questioned him.

"Yes... everyone is probably talking about it... What time is it?" asked Pascal, passing his hands over his face.

"Nine."

"Nine? Why are you waking me so early? In any case, why are you still here? You haven't decided to stay in Megapolis, have you? You have no obligations to me anymore."

"We have no obligations to you anymore?" said Raul staring furiously at Pascal. "Shame on you! You think that we did all this because of some obligation to you? At any rate, how do you dare say something like that? I don't allow you to insult such wonderful people from our team."

"Forgive me, Raul, forgive me, please... I didn't mean it like that... you know that I didn't... my head hurts... Wait here. Let me wash my face... to get... to come to my senses. You burst in like that..." said Pascal in a hoarse voice, while closing the bathroom door behind him.

After ten minutes, washed and shaven, he came up to Raul, who was standing at the window watching the workers taking down the stage in the square. An echelon of inspectors in helmets and carrying shields prevented angry protesters from approaching the stage, the hotel and the television station.

46

"Get away from the window," Raul said, turning towards him and pushing him deeper into the room. "Sit on the bed. Here, in this blind spot," he said pointing at the pillow.

"You're overreacting, Raul," said Pascal, who sat on the bed anyway.

"I'm not overreacting. This window might already be in the sights of one of Erivan's snipers."

"It might..." Pascal whispered.

Raul sat down next to him and patted him in a friendly manner on the knee.

"Come on, Pascal. Our entire team is already in the lobby. They're waiting for me to bring you down. The mayor will send a bus which will take us safely to the airport. And there's an airplane waiting for us. We can fly away wherever we want. I recommend a smaller city, one that is completely in our hands. An old decrepit one, one that Prince Kaella is not interested in. We can't provoke him anymore. Hmm? What do you say?"

"There, there... I agree. That's wise... go."

Raul took a deep sigh, got up off the bed and looked at Pascal.

"We should go? Without you?"

"Yes. Why are you torturing me again, Raul? Do you think its easy for me to part with all of you? I told you clearly that I would hold that speech."

"How? The stage is being dismantled, people are being driven away. Who will you speak to?"

"I don't know. I'll go out into the square and speak. To the inspectors if need be."

"Pascal, in all these years, how many times have we been driven out of some city?

"Countless times."

"And what? Nothing. We continued on. And we returned to those cities a few months later, a year later, when our movement gained strength in them, when our people took local power. So what's the difference?"

"This is Megapolis."

"I don't believe you, Pascal. I don't believe that you are being stubborn against Prince Kaella because of Megapolis. Those that want power are stubborn. And Pascal Alexander is not like that. I don't believe you, Pascal. There's something else going on. Svetlana, right? You're disappointed and miserable because of her?"

"Yes, because of her."

"Why? What happened? Liam reported to me that his guard in the lobby saw Svetlana leave the hotel, suitcase in hand, at dawn."

"She left me."

"Left you?" Raul was surprised, and then asked "Did you tell Svetlana what happened at Seneca's place yesterday?"

"I did."

"And you told her that you were still going to hold the speech?"

"Yes."

"And it didn't occur to you that she left only in order to make you go with her? To get you out of Megapolis?"

"That's not why she left."

Pascal stared at the floor the entire time, with his head hung low and speaking softly. He did not look up even once at Raul, who stood in front of him.

"Pascal, excuse me, but I have to tell you. You too are not as young as you used to be. Svetlana is probably the first woman to leave you?"

"Yes."

"You are actually in shock now. I can understand that. But you'll realize that it is normal, natural. Time does its thing, Pascal. We're getting old. And Svetlana is young. She has the rest of her life to live. Someone her age probably caught her eye... but... where did she meet him? She's been with us the entire time... Is it someone from the campaign? No, no... someone would notice it. OK, OK... you're in shock. Svetlana could have waited a bit longer, she could have chosen a better moment. Not like this... to disable you. I did notice, I really did, that she's been kind of quiet lately... restrained. And you, Pascal, when you calm down you can finally find yourself a serious woman your own age. Well, not exactly your age... just a little younger. And you can have children, create a family. As befitting a democratically elected president. That's what I've been telling you all these years. Now you see for yourself that I was right... Admit it."

"I admit it."

"There, you see... You'll be better, I'm not worried... But hey, let's not talk about women now. We'll go somewhere. We'll hide out until the elections, even if we have hide in a foxhole. You won't appear in public. We don't need any more speeches. Think about it. You're the rival of Kaella's current president. Officially. Your name is printed on the ballots. People take their telephone and circle it. Sixty-two percent of the people. And what do they need you for at that moment? They don't need you. And after that... we'll wait for Kaella's move, and then we'll decide. You can set up your office in any city. Wherever you are will be the capital of Earth. Understand?"

"You're right," Pascal said softly.

Raul was delighted, with a huge smile.

"Of course I'm right. When was your Raul ever wrong? When?"

"I'm old. I'm very old… and tired."

"I didn't say that you were old for president. You're tired… Its normal to be tired. We all are…"

"Raul, I had no idea… I never thought that it was possible to be this old."

"Don't be ridiculous. Look at me. I'm fifteen years older than you. But our struggle has made me a young man. I'm full of energy, life. Come on, pack up so that we can get going."

"I'm not going anywhere anymore."

Raul walked to the door, grabbed the doorknob and turning to Pascal he asked:

"Will you at least say goodbye to the staff? The bus for airport is almost here. We're leaving, Pascal."

"I can't."

Chapter 19

Julius Seneca, the mayor and director of Megapolis TV, watched from his office on the last floor of the tall building as a torrent of people converged on the square from four avenues.

He ordered the Megapolis Inspectorate to use force only in extreme, isolated cases. For example, looting, torching, the breaking of shop windows. This would in any case be done only by delinquents.

The citizens of Megapolis would not. Nor would he ever use force again them. Megapolis was not made up of its magnificent buildings, avenues and squares. Megapolis was made up of its citizens. They are Megapolis. And he is their mayor.

The ring of the telephone pulled him from his thoughts. He picked up immediately.

"Yes, Raul?"

"Mr. Mayor, as we expected, he is not giving up. He will hold his speech," Raul said, breathing heavily, while walking down the stairs from Pascal's room to the hotel lobby.

The mayor didn't respond. He wasn't surprised. "Each of us is fighting his own battle," he thought.

"Mr. Mayor, do you hear me?"

"I hear you, I hear you."

"He's in a worse mood than he was yesterday. Svetlana has left him. It seems that it has completely crushed him. The man simply won't accept any arguments."

"What Svetlana? What does that mean now?"

"Svetlana... you know... she sometimes came with us to your place for meetings."

"How? She is a very young woman."

"She is. And that is what has crushed him. He feels terribly old and tired, he says."

"But these are things not becoming a presidential candidate. Such a gentleman. I am very surprised."

"You didn't know that? He's been chasing women his entire life. That is to say, they've been chasing him. And now he has been dumped."|

"Alright, alright... leave that. These are Mr. Alexander's personal affairs," Mayor Seneca interrupted the conversation on this topic.

"Perhaps it is better like this. The two of us have an agreement, Mr. Mayor."

Mayor Seneca didn't answer.

"Mr. Mayor, you promised me," Raul was concerned because of Seneca's silence.

"Alright, Raul, we'll do it..." Seneca finally spoke.

"Thank you, truly," Raul sighed a sigh of relief.

"What did Mr. Alexander say, when will he go to the square?"

"He didn't say anything. The stage is gone. Your inspectors have surrounded the hotel. They are appealing to the people to disperse from the square. Pascal is in a strange state, Mr. Mayor. He's very nervous. He's going to take a shower, get dressed and go to the square as soon as possible."

Seneca was silent.

"Mr. Mayor?" Raul was uneasy again.

"Listen to me carefully, Raul. I will not send the bus to take you to the airport."

"But, Mr. Mayor...":

"It's too risky. Many people would be involved. I'll send you my airplane."

"Your airplane?"

"Yes. My airplane has a wide opaque tube, like a large hose. For the event of an emergency, for evacuation. The airplane will hover over the hotel and lower the tube to the roof. Your people have to attach its opening to the door that leads to the roof, so that nothing can be seen. Do you understand what I mean?"

"I do. So that no one can see who all is entering the tube."

"That's right. In the tube there is a conveyor belt. There are straps that you use to attach yourself to it and it raises you into the airplane. You can also attach your suitcases."

"Excellent, Mr. Mayor."

"I'll send a squadron of fighter planes to protect you," Seneca said and hung up.

"It's better that it turned out this way," Raul thought. "Much better."

Chapter 20

Pascal lay in the bathtub with his eyes closed. "What was it that you said to me, Raul?" he recalled their conversation. "To find a woman my own age... just a little younger. To have children... There is such a woman, my friend. I'd marry her immediately, trust me... immediately, immediately..."
"Immediately!" Pascal shouted out loud.

Then he sighed and submerged his head. When he ran out of air he came up and rested his shoulders on the edge of the tub. He barely visibly shook his head.
"But no. You would never be satisfied, Raul. You would think that a wife that already has two children is not becoming of a democratically elected president. And do you know what I would tell you, Raul? I'd tell you that I didn't care at all what you thought. And what was becoming and what was not. As long as she's mine.
"And I'll tell you that I'm not going anywhere from Megapolis anymore. I cannot leave without knowing... my Raul. And I always knew. We're going to that city for three days, then there... for five days... never longer than five days. I couldn't stand not seeing her for more than five days. How could I?
"And you were cross, Raul. 'Since we're already here, why don't we just stop by over there,' you said. 'What's a few more days? Better than going back to Megapolis and then hitting the road again.'
"You didn't get it, why we always went back to Megapolis. I didn't either. Actually I did, but I wouldn't admit it to myself."

"And now... I'm not going anywhere from this city, Manami. I'll die in it. Here, close to you, my love. And what if they don't kill me? Hmm? What do you think? I make it through today, no one shoots me... The people disperse from the square. Raul and the team have flown somewhere far away... and I'm left alone.
"Do you know what I would do? You wouldn't believe it. I'd climb that chestnut tree in front of your house immediately, tonight, like a teenager. I'd watch the lit windows. I'd see you go into Peter's room. Kiss your son on the head, tell him good night, turn off the light and leave. And your husband's not home. He's at his office, on

TV or at the Mayor's office... or somewhere... wherever. So you enter the room of your little Eir. And she's uncovered herself. You cover her up and caress her. And then you go to your room."

Pascal opened his eyes and abruptly rose up. "That isn't only your room, Manami! You share it with your husband!" he shouted. He covered his face with his hands and rested his forehead on his raised knees.
"Why isn't there an 'our room', Manami? Why?" he whispered. After some time he lowered his hands into the water, raised his head and looked at the bathroom wall.
"My friends are gone. What am I waiting for?"

He got up out of the tub. "I'm going out. I'm going to get killed. Immediately. A bullet to the heart, the head. Aim wherever you want, wherever you please. Just as soon as possible! As soon, please..."

*****

"I won't wear something... just usual... like always... Pants, unbuttoned shirt, sleeves rolled up," Pascal thought, standing in front of the open closet. "I'll dress elegantly. I'll wear this dark blue suit... and a tie. This one, with the wide dark blue and dark red stripes. Like blood... But they are diagonal. They will intersect with these gray lines on the suit. Do they go together? I guess they do... these lines are discrete... you can hardly see them. But the shirt must be plain white. Or perhaps that light blue one? No, no, white it is. I'll unbutton the jacket so the blood on the white shirt is visible.
"So that you can clearly see how my heart bleeds for you, Manami.
"And the shoes... these, yes... black, shiny... Like for a evening dance in some lavish hall.... You in a kimono... a gold kimono... in my arms. A huge orchestra... just the two of us. And no one else... in the whole world."

Chapter 21

Having received his orders from Erivan, Alpha left the President's office and reached the elevator with fast, nervous steps. But he didn't enter it. He first just stood there and then walked down the hall, looking around, leaning over, crouching, getting up and hitting his fist against the wall several times.

When he finally calmed down he took the elevator down to the garage. Once he got there, without saying a word he nodded to his subordinate White, he passed around the presidential car and made sure that the interior was not visible through the tinted windows. He then took his telephone from his jacket, took a deep breath, glanced once more at White, and called the driver who worked as a member of the residency staff.

"Please put on your uniform and come immediately to the garage," he said without saying hello, after the driver of the presidential car had picked up.

"Yes, of course, Mr. Alpha," the driver responded.

"Why are you calling the chauffer, Alpha? Won't the care be remote controlled?" his unit member asked.

"Be quiet, White, just be quiet. Don't ask anything. That's the order."

"Erivan's?"

"Yes."

"But..."

"But what?"

"Well, I think... the chauffer will see them... as soon as he opens the door."

"He won't open the door, White."

"How won't he? You don't mean... I can't do it, Alpha! Call someone else. Why didn't the Grasshopper also... the chauffer..."

"I will do it, White. I have to. This is what it's come to. Life and death struggle. We have to be up to the task."

Alpha slowly unbuttoned his jacket and pulled it back. He took out his pistol from the belt holster, raised it and aimed towards the elevator door.

Chapter 22

Pascal, dressed in the dark suit, stood in front of the window watching the square filled with people. "You're not taking the shot?" he spoke without any fear to the imaginary sniper. "Very well, I understand. Who would see that you've killed me? They would show my dead body on television. It is better to wait for me to leave the hotel, and then, in front of the crowd... For it to be shocking, to scare them... for them to scatter. It works better for me that way too. Let her see me fall, on her beloved husband's television channel..."

"Will you cry when you see me lying in the square with a bloody stain here?" He raised his hand and placed it on his chest. "No, you won't. Because you can't. So that your husband and children wouldn't notice. But tonight... when he goes to sleep, will you at least shed one tear? At least shed one tear for me, Manami."

Pascal slowly got up and went toward the door. He left the room and walked towards the elevator with brisk, decisive steps. Then he stopped in disbelief.

The elevator was at the end of the hallway. Between the elevator and the first rooms was the stairway, from where Mayor Seneca was walking towards Pascal.

When he saw Pascal Alexander stop in his tracks, Seneca slowed down his pace, waveringly went up to the door of the first room and also stopped. The two men, on opposite sides of the hallway, watched each other in silence.

"Why is Alexander just standing and not saying anything," Seneca thought. "Does he suspect something? No, surely not. Why would he? I could have arrested and banished him by now. And I haven't. It's probably clear to him that I don't pose a threat? It's probably logical that I just want to welcome him and escort him through the echelon of inspectors?"

"I have to be careful" Pascal thought fervently. "How stupid I am. How is it that I haven't thought of this earlier? That the man will come and take me through the cordon. Now for the first time I have to look him in the eye and speak to him... while I'm aware of... well yes... That's why I'm not... of course, that is the only reason why I haven't admitted to myself earlier... how much... I'm in love with your wife, Seneca."

"Don't be crazy," Pascal commanded himself. "Stop thinking about her. This instant. Do you understand? What do you want? For him to see in your eyes... and for him to pester and torment her for the rest of her life. Is that what you want? Come on... calm down. Everything is over. Let the man nicely escort you to your death. Be at least a little afraid of dying, you fool! OK, there... I'm afraid. That's what I'll look like. As though I'm afraid of dying. I'll be desperate. How will he know why I'm desperate?"

Pascal hesitantly stepped towards Seneca, and then continued with a firmer and stabler stride.

"Mr. Mayor," he said while approaching him.

"Mr. Alexander, it's as though you were surprised to see me. I just wanted to escort you through the cordon."

"Yes, yes, of course," said Pascal, already nearing Seneca and putting out his hand.

The door to the room that they stood in front of suddenly opened. Pascal turned around and wide-eyed in shock he looked at Raul, who stuck a needle into his outstretched arm through the sleeve of his jacket, and with his thumb he emptied the small injection. Pascal's body went limp the same moment. Raul and Seneca caught him, not letting him fall to the floor. Without saying a word they dragged the unconscious Pascal Alexander to the elevator.

Chapter 23

"There, son, you see how everything is going well today. Even that which we did not plan," Mr. Kaella told Prince, who was sitting across from him in the limousine driving them to the dock.

"Yes, really. It's a good sign. But it won't save Seneca," Prince responded.

"Certainly not, son. He must be held accountable for his crime. Like all the mayors and other officials that have crossed over to their side. We must punish them mercilessly. To make an example of them."

"I never thought that Seneca could be so stupid. He panicked, and drove Alexander out of Megapolis," Prince responded. "Well, he stopped his speech. That is why I will reward him with a quick death. You know, father, Alexander is the enemy. But one worthy of respect, I must admit. And Seneca is a traitor. He betrayed us, and now Alexander too. He is a despicable guy."

"I'm not sure that he betrayed Alexander. It seems to me like some maneuver on his part. Erivan says that Seneca gave him his airplane. And a squadron to escort him."

"What maneuver, father? Seneca wants to be sure that Alexander has left and that he will never return."

"Yes, you're probably right. The important thing for me is that he didn't give that speech. Because I couldn't sleep all night because of your words."

"What words? Why didn't you sleep? If I have upset you with anything, father, any time... you must tell me immediately. So that I can explain, if need be. And not for my father to worry and not sleep.

"Well... you said that even after our victory, there will always be a sore on your heart."

"Yes, I did. But let's forget about that now. There will be no wounds on our hearts. And on there's – I'm not exactly sure."

Father and son smiled wholeheartedly as their limousine slowed down, approaching the submarine tied to the dock.

"Here we are, " Prince said.

When the bodyguard opened the door, Prince got out of the car and helped his father out. He held him under the arm as they crossed the gangplank, entered the submarine and went past the room where the television crew had improvised a studio control room. All the way to the doors of the grand salon.

Then, having seen Babe, who was already standing with her hand resting on the backrest of one of the black leather armchairs, he let go of his father's arm, his eyes and mouth wide open. For Babe was wearing Earth's flag... She was draped in the flag... No, no... She was... she... Babe was the flag itself. The symbol, the meaning of everything... his work, his creation... his achievements... The reflection, the image of his... being.

Chapter 24

In the mayor's airplane, which took off from Megapolis with Pascal Alexander's entire electoral staff, everything was quiet. No one was talking to anyone. And previously it hadn't been so. When they had to leave a city, Pascal would walk among his associates smiling and say

"What is it? Why are you moping, my nomads? I couldn't wait for them to throw us out. It was a really boring city."

Then everyone would laugh, throw in their jokes, wisecracks and anecdotes about the particular city. But this time they had left Megapolis. And in it certainly no one was bored. They felt the intensive taste of defeat. As though the defeat was definite and irrevocable.

Even Pascal wasn't there to joke. He was in the mayor's salon, in the forward part of the airplane. He was getting over a hangover from last night. He was disappointed because of Svetlana, who had left him. That is at least what their boss Raul said, when he came out of the airplane salon. And after that he too wistfully sat in silence on the front seat, next to Liam, the head of Pascal's security.

The other staff members spread out throughout the large airplane. Only the secretaries sat together, as they always did. All five of them in two rows, behind their boss Margot, Raul's experienced long-standing associate. And Jin, the assistant to the head of PR, sat alone, far behind them.

Gloria, a dark-skinned girl with a lavish Afro, one of the five secretaries, got up from her seat and sat next to Jin, who looked out the window without paying attention to her.

"Well?" said Gloria.

"Excuse me?" said the surprised Jin. "Well what?"

"You're pretending that you don't know anything."

"Excuse me?" Jin was annoyed by such behavior. "What are you talking about, Gloria?"

"What am I talking about? Well, alright... Tell me, what happened to your boss?"

"To Svetlana?"

"Yes."

"Didn't you hear what Raul said? She left Pascal and quit the campaign," Jin said angrily.

"Well she didn't," said Gloria, when she saw that Jin's surprise was genuine and that she didn't have a clue.

"What do you mean 'she didn't'?" Jin shouted.

"Psssst! Quiet, Jin. They'll hear us. You see that Raul is hiding it from us."

"Hiding what? What's going on?" Jin whispered anxiously.

"I saw her last night."

"What are you saying? What did you see?"

"You know how it is. I came back late from the club last night... it's not important. I went to bed and I was falling asleep, but I still hadn't fallen asleep..."

"Well, and?"

"And I hear the elevator. It stopped on our floor. I jumped out of bed. And I thought 'He couldn't wait. He's coming for me.' And Dorika is sleeping next to me. How will we...? We can't in our room, get it...?"

"I get it, and?"

"I got to the door to tell him to wait while I got dressed... And the steps went past my door... and they weren't men's steps. I mean, its carpeting so you can't hear heels... but I guess I know what men's steps are like and what women's..."

"And?"

"And I heard, it seemed to me like the person was crying... weeping. Quietly... but I heard it."

"OK, OK, cut to the chase. You think that Svetlana was crying last night?"

"I don't think so, Jin. I know so. I pried open the door and see her unlock her room. And she noticed me. I don't know how. I was absolutely quiet. She felt me, I guess, in that deserted hallway and she looked at me."

"And?"

"Eyes red, makeup smeared. Distraught... she looked distraught. I mean not only physically, because of the makeup. But... how should I describe it... psychologically, mentally... desperation in her eyes, desperation on her face... you couldn't recognize her. You know yourself what she's like. Beautiful, dignified... all important next to her Pascal.

At that moment Margot walked towards the two of them, on her way to the toilet.

"Margot!" Jin rose from her seat.

"What's wrong with you, Jin?" Gloria got scared when Jin called her boss. "I told that only to you."

Margot had already come up to them.

"Yes, Jin?"

"What are you hiding from us?"

"What do you mean? We're not hiding anything."

"Gloria saw Svetlana last night, all in tears and distraught."

"No... it was dark... I'm not sure... Jin, really... Margot, please..."

"Is it possible?" Margot was surprised and concerned.

"No, no... I probably thought I saw something..." Gloria stuttered.

Margot wasn't listening anymore. She also didn't continue to the toilet. She briskly turned around and with vigorous fast steps went towards the first row, towards Raul.

Chapter 25

The shortest street in Capital City, only a hundred and twenty meters long, was not only referred to as Short Street – it was also its official name. It was located in the very center of the city. It connected Cypress Avenue and Olive Avenue, in the part where the two streets were closest to each other. This is why Short Street was always full of pedestrians and cars.

It was also narrow. It only had one lane going in either direction. The sidewalks were not very wide either. The few restaurants and cafes could only put two small tables outside.

Shops selling the most exclusive and most expensive were the norm on Short Street. Anyone who bought anything in any of the shops on Short Street could be certain of seeing envy in the eyes of people they knew. This is why Prince Kaella kept the highest price of rent in all of Capital City for offices on Short Street.

Short Street also had another characteristic. Motorcades carrying important individuals from the State or the Company very often took it, in order to shorten their route, and therefore the time that they were exposed to potential attacks. It was not always required to cheer and wave these motorcades and the important individuals in them. Only on State Day, on Company Day and of course on the birthdays of Mr. Kaella and his son Prince. Of course, there were exceptions. Today was such an exception, due to the electoral speech. It was necessary to wave to President Xing's motorcade.

Short Street was ideal for this purpose. The television crew needed only one crane to shoot the crowd of excited admirers which looked even larger in this small space, with wide and sincere smiles, children on their fathers' shoulders waving balloons painted like the planet Earth, two young people happily handing hands, a grandpa holding his arm around grandma's shoulder, while the love for the important individual sparkled in her old wise eyes. And of course, unavoidably, in a space specially cordoned off for them in the middle of Short Street – the pupils from one of the elementary schools.

Chapter 26

Having reached Raul, Margot said:

"Liam, please give us some privacy."

The head of security got up from his seat and went towards the middle of the airplane.

"Why did you lie to us, Raul, that Svetlana had left Pascal and that he had gotten drunk because of her?"

"I didn't lie, Margot. That is what Pascal told me."

"What is happening, Raul? Something much more serious is going on."

"No. That's it," Raul looked away.

"Gloria saw Svetlana in tears and distraught last night. And you're lying to us that she left Pascal."

"Every breakup is difficult."

"What are you hiding from me, Raul, from us? What right do you have? Why do you think that you have that right?"

"This is getting torturous," Raul thought. "What am I actually waiting for? To land, and for all of them to disappear somewhere and not see that…"

"Let me by," said Raul, passing by Margot who also got up. He then turned to the staff and said loudly

"Pascal is not with us!"

Chapter 27

Atop of Babe's head, with the nape shaved high, created out of her remaining hair, which spanned from a strong deep blue to the light blue color of the sky, without the unnecessary frills on the yellow-green continent, stylized, ultra modernly, and crystal clear – was a depiction of the planet.

Around here eyes, too. Two Earths, created in a thick layer of blue eye shadow, the poles of which touched her cheekbones and her forehead above her eyelashes, which were completely removed specially for this occasion.

From the piercing through her... from this distance Prince could not clearly see, but somewhere there... just beneath the corners of her beautiful large blue eyes, dangled two little chains, at whose ends, two little Earths were swinging, lined up with her full, tempting upper lip, covered in thick black lipstick.

The third little Earth swayed at the end of a little chain hanging from a ring pierced through the center of her massive, heavy lower lip, with blue-gray lipstick which extended towards the protruding, defiant chin.

"On the mark," Babe congratulated herself in her mind, blinking once again with the blue and black eyelashes at the stunned Prince.

She rushed over, with emphasized care, to the old Mr. Kaella, and gently lowered him into the armchair prepared for him, like any good daughter-in-law would.

"Thank you. You are very kind, Miss Babe," the old man said while sitting down. "And you look wonderful today. Like our flag. Wonderful."

"Thank you, Mr. Kaella. That's how I feel. Proud, inspired, honored, because you choose precisely me for your interview, out of all the excellent television hosts."

"Excellent, excellent... and none of them can hold a candle to you, Miss Babe," Mr. Kaella sincerely complimented her.

And while she had her backed turned to Prince, he watched that cascading blue-dyed hair of another woman, which started from the very bottom of her shaved skull, like from the edge of some tall mountain cliff, cascading down her back, along her metallic black leather short-sleeved jacket, and covering the upper hem of her short skirt, it reached the beginning of her strong, femininely protruding provocative spherical buttocks. And a sliver of lace from her fishnet stockings, remissly revealed by her slightly raised light fluttery blue-black skirt.

"Mr. Kaella, Mr. Kaella," the hasty and professional director of the interview nodded twice, greeting both father and son, while entering the salon. "Please, take your seats. We have to do a sound check."
"Certainly, certainly," said Prince, sitting in the armchair that the director waved to. Opposite the sofa, where apparently Babe would be sitting.

"So, I'll be able to watch you unobstructed the entire time," Prince thought, as far as he managed to gather his thoughts. "That is why you immediately placed my father in the armchair to the side. You're dangerous. Dangerous..."

Chapter 28

"Where is Pascal?" the agitated staff shouted.

"Calm down! Quiet! I'll explain everything to you," Raul tried to outshout them.

"Quiet!" Margot shouted. "Let's hear Raul!"

When the voices finally subsided, Raul said:

"Pascal is in a secure place and he is safe."

"How is he safe?!" the head of security shouted. "How do you know that he is safe? How can he be safe if we are not by his side?! Who is protecting him now, anyway?! What do you think, Raul? Who are you to assess the level of his security? Not only you, how can Pascal know whether he is safe? What do the two of you know about that? You've been under my protection for years, shielded by my guys and you think that it is a given. I demand that you immediately take us to Pascal! Turn this plane around!" Liam started towards the pilots' cabin.

Margot got in front of him. "Back off, Liam! Back off!"

"What's with you Margot? So you've known the entire time! You lied to us too! How could you?! How can you leave Pascal to someone else?!"

"I didn't know, Liam, I didn't. I too am hearing all this for the first time. We're all very upset. And scared. We all love Pascal. We all equally care about him. But we're not the only ones. Millions of people love him. That man means a lot to millions. And neither we here, in this campaign, in his team, nor all those people would know about him had it not been for Raul. Raul motivated him to start the struggle for freedom for all people, to become our leader, to become the meaning, the hope. No one in this world knows Pascal like Raul does. No one respects and loves Pascal like Raul does. None of us understand what Pascal actually represents, and what is the scope of this... like Raul does. That is why I'm ordering you... yes, you heard well, I'm ordering you to sit down and to listen quietly to what Raul has to tell us."

"What is he eating now? Who's cooking for him?" wept Citra, Raul's distant cousin and Pascal's personal cook. "He's picky... he can't eat just anything..."

"Citra, calm down, Citra... Don't overreact," said Raul. "Pascal isn't a child. He'll eat something. You cook for him... I mean, of course you cook the best and he likes it best when you prepare something for him. But... that's primarily for security. So that we're sure that no one has gone near his food... that no one's touched it, you understand?"

"There!" Liam exploded again. "And now, Raul, how can you know now who all is near his food? How?!"

"People, people... friends... Do you think it's easy for me? But that is only until the elections, and after..."

"Why until the elections?" Margot was surprised. "Isn't the most important thing that we are together and that we make appearances, that we are present publicly every moment until the elections?"

"Margot, allow me... I'm trying to say what happened... Why we made this decision."

"OK, OK... I apologize, Raul."

Everyone was quiet. Only Citra was still sniffling.

Chapter 29

Babe was extremely pleased with herself. Having transformed herself into the flag of Earth she reminded Prince of what he had grown accustomed to since he was a child. What was implied. She reminded him of who he actually was:

Prince Kaella, heir to the most magnificent throne in the history of mankind. Ruler of everything that exists. Having reminded him of his infinite power she injected him with the strongest dose of aphrodisiac. Directly into the vein. Judging by his reaction she had exceeded even her wildest expectations.

Babe started her interview with this great feeling of self-confidence.

"Dear viewers, it is my great honor to host on my show two men, father and son, two of the greatest persons today," said Babe, looking directly into the camera.

After that introduction she turned to Mr. Kaella.

"Mr. Kaella, good day."

"Good day to you too, Miss Babe, and of course, to your viewers," Mr. Kaella said with a great smile.

"Greetings to you too, Mr. Prince Kaella."

"Good day," Prince greeted her too.

"Dear viewers, as you yourself have noticed, we are in the Kaella family submarine and we are sailing towards one of the numerous submerged cities. You can send your answer to the question which city it is to the number appearing at the bottom of the screen, along with the price of your message. The selected viewer that gave the correct answer will win a submarine trip for two."

Babe looked away from the camera and looked at Mr. Kaella.

"Mr. Kaella, you like this type of outings?"

"Yes, but before I answer your questions I'd like to say in front of the audience that you look truly marvelous today, symbolizing our State, our planet. This is why I would like to invite our dear Consumers to follow in your footsteps, Miss Babe. Dear ladies, show in your appearance what you carry deep in your hearts."

"Thank you, Mr. Kaella. I am truly honored."

"To answer your questions. Yes, I enjoy these outings. This silence underwater relaxes me in a way. It allows me to think more clearly, to understand even better the progress that we have achieved compared to the society, well actually compared to the former, fragmented, constantly clashing human communities. Sailing down the avenues of these submerged cities, throughout our planet, I wonder how it is at all possible that in the not-so-distant past man's level of awareness was so low."

"Incredibly low, Mr. Kaella," Babe agreed.

"If they had worked so diligently on developing the greenhouse effect and increasing the temperature on Earth, why then did they invest so much, why did they live in coastal towns and why did they defend them for so long, unsuccessfully of course, from the ocean by building futile damns? Why didn't they realize that the waves of every following tsunami and super storm would easily get over those ridiculous walls? And my son, completely oppositely... I mean, I hope... that your viewers are aware that my son has dedicated his life to the struggle to save the planet and mankind."

"Of course," said Babe. "We are all immensely grateful to Mr. Prince for this. Mr. Prince, can you please tell us briefly what is the essence of your struggle?"

Babe was sitting in the middle of the couch with her legs tightly together, her body turned towards Prince. Only her head was faced the old Mr. Kaella. Being aware that during this introductory part he was being constantly on camera, Prince struggled with himself and held his eyes fixed on Babe's face, as was becoming of a respectful interviewee. The two little Earths that dangled from Babe's face wouldn't let him be. Even from this distance, a lot closer, he could not see where the chains were anchored. He couldn't see any rings. "They must be covered by the thick blue eye shadow around her eyes," he concluded, and stopped thinking about it.

But when Babe looked at his father he noticed something else. A tattoo behind her right ear. The tattoo was very discrete. Like a chain of barely visible symbols, in a color that was just a shade darker than her skin, arranged in an arch that followed the contour of her ear, which was completely covered in golden star-shaped rivets.

Chapter 30

Pascal was waking up. But he didn't open his eyes nor did he move any part of his body.

"I won't move. Let them think I'm not awake. Maybe they'll talk. Maybe I'll hear them." But he didn't hear anything: no one's breathing, movement, clothes rustling... nothing.

He recalled Mayor Seneca at the end of the hallway. "He was just standing there, waiting for me to approach him. And I was just thinking about... not revealing myself... for him not to notice, not to suspect anything. And I didn't pay attention at all... It can't be! That wasn't Raul. No, Raul would not join up with Seneca against me. Not only with Seneca, with anyone. Except... to save me from... myself. Raul knows me. He saw... it was clear to him that I actually wanted to die. That I was practically committing suicide. And he didn't allow it. He saved my life."

"I really can't hear anything. Silence. Absolute silence. How long have I been unconscious?" Pascal wondered. "I can't hear the rotors of a helicopter, airplane engines... I don't feel any vibrations... shaking. I'm not in a car, in some trunk. Or maybe I am? Just that the vehicle is standing still, that it isn't moving. Am I still in Megapolis? Or did Raul take me with them? And we might already be there... in one of our cities. Or are we waiting for the airplane to take of? But... this silence... is so absolute. If the vehicle is stationary... it isn't an airport or a parking lot... no one is passing by... there's no sound of the wind... no sound at all. No smell. Smell?"

Only then did he realize that he smelled something. Stale, right next to his nostrils. "There is some kind of cover beneath my cheek. I can feel it on my skin. It's soft... I'm lying on a bed. On my right side. It isn't the cold floor of some cell. And it's completely dark. If there was any light I'd see it through my eyelids. I'm sure I would. But the darkness is absolute... Is this a grave?"

Pascal abruptly opened his eyes. And it was as though he hadn't. The darkness truly was absolute. He pushed himself up on his elbow. He felt a pain in his arm and thought of Raul again.

"Raul, who gives you the right to decide about my life? Who are you to save me from myself? Not even you, Raul, after all these years… the struggle, everything… you don't understand. Freedom is above everything else. Not only freedom from Kaella. The freedom to live as you want and die as you want. You don't understand… Don't get me wrong, I'm not angry at you. Nor at Seneca, or anyone. You can't learn these thing, that is something you have to be. I would never prevent you from dying, my friend. For any reason. Regardless of whether I knew the reason or not. Regardless of whether I understood your reason or not. I would never in any way limit your freedom. To decide about you instead of you. I'll explain it to you. You'll set me free. When you come… to bring me food and water."

Chapter 31

"Why are you asking me, Babe?" Prince thought to himself. "Talk to my father, let me watch you in peace."

And he told Babe in front of the camera:

"Well... I wouldn't... I really wouldn't want to take valuable time from my father and you. There will be other opportunities for those topics."

"You know, Miss Babe, my son is very modest," Mr. Kaella explained. "He never wants to talk about himself and his achievements. Not only in public. He is the same within the family. And he always has been, since he was a child."

"That is the characteristic of great people, I think, Mr. Kaella."

"That's right. That is why I will sing some praise for my son, if you permit."

"Of course, of course. Please, Mr. Kaella."

"Through his struggle with the ruthless nature my Prince is saving humanity, while we await the arrival of the ice age. And one day when it comes it will be much milder than ignorant people fear, precisely thanks to the greenhouse effect. It will be like a slightly colder winter from the past. And we will easily adjust to it. Industrial production will turn to making heating appliances instead of cooling appliances. Transportation means will adjust to snow and ice instead of sand and rocks, and there will be countless, I mean countless, other changes and adaptations. And what is the main thing that this new industrial drive will bring?"

"Jobs and preservation of the Balance."

"Bravo, bravo, Miss Babe. And let someone try and tell me again that beauty and intelligence don't go together. Of course – the Balance. That is my greatest achievement, the pinnacle of my life."

"Mr. Kaella, the Balance that you have established in society, which you yourself say is the pinnacle of your life, is such an important topic, the most important topic. I would like to give it more time. Actually, I would like for you to tell us your life's journey. Please describe how you made it possible of us, people, Consumers, to live peacefully in a balanced community of man."

"I will. I agree with you, Miss Babe, here..."

"Just one moment, please, Mr. Kaella. I would like to first briefly ask Mr. Prince how he succeeded in protecting people from such a fate, from the forever lost settlements, like the ones that we can see outside the submarine? What is your intention when you selflessly invest, building modern poleis and making it possible for people to resettle?"

"Alright, I'll answer you. But really shortly. Unfortunately we inherited from our ancestors the greenhouse effect. Due to the climate changes food production and sources of drinking water inevitably relocated. Had food and water have had to be distributed to remote old human settlements under such conditions, it would have caused huge and completely unnecessary additional expenses. The development of modern poleis in the vicinity of food and water will allow people to satisfy their existential needs at the lowest possible price. We live in such a historical time. After the ice age, the mild one, as my father explained, the Earth will be once again become soaked and deserts will become fields, there will be plenty of drinking water throughout the planet. And then, once again, our descendants will be able to build their settlements wherever they want. I am only using basic logic for us to adapt in the most rational manner to the conditions that nature has imposed on us during this period."

"You are right, Mr. Kaella. Your son is too modest," said Babe.

"That is what he is like. There's nothing we can change about it," the proud father said.

"But we can admire him," said Babe and nodded slightly, looking at Prince with eyes full of admiration. "And now, Mr. Kaella, I'd like to ask you to describe your life's journey to our viewers. Before the interview I received countless messages, emails, letters, in which Consumers demand that I ask you this and that, so… and I think that you will answer all these questions if you tell us as many of your memories as possible."

"Alright, Miss Babe, I will. Well …"

Chapter 32

"As you know, Seneca yesterday prohibited Pascal's speech. You saw that they dismantled the stage this morning," Raul explained the newly-created situation to his team.

"He stabbed us in the back ahead of the elections. That was all planned long ago. And we naively believed that he had crossed over to our side, that he had turned against Kaella," said Jagdish, head of the analysts.

"It's not like that, Jagdish. Seneca yesterday received reliable secret information from Kaella's Company that Pascal was winning by a landslide with sixty-two percent of the votes."

"Bravo!"
"Victory!"
"Sixty-two?!" the team were jumping out their seats with excitement.

While he watched them, Raul slightly shook his head and smiled. At the same time he calmed them with a hand gesture indicating that they should be seated.

"First of all I would like to congratulate you. Without you, without us, this would not have been possible. On the other hand... Margot is right. I have known Pascal the longest and the best. And Pascal is... Pascal. He is different than us, than other people. In his own world... in his ideas. No, no, not ideas... in his dreams. You know what I mean... The Third Renaissance that he is dreaming of. After Tuscany and Northern California... a dreamer. But that is why he is Pascal. That is why he moves millions... he teaches people how to dream. It's true that he says what we prepare for him, what we write for him. Specifically, these are the bills you are paying to Kaella, your children will pay them... He speaks in our ordinary words. But he speaks them. People aren't ignorant. They know all that even without our speeches. But they don't know, they don't believe that it can be any different... That their children can live a better, freer life than theirs is. A life filled with meaning, purpose. Only when Pascal tells them, only then do they believe. Only Pascal can give raise to people's hope, after an entire century of slavery."

"Raul, we know this. Where is Pascal?" Margot asked quietly, seeing how difficult it was for Raul.

"Pascal is under Seneca's protection."

"Under Seneca's protection?!" Liam shouted. "Who is Seneca protecting him from? From himself? From his inspectors? How do you know that he hasn't already handed him over to Kaella? The mayor of Megapolis, Prince's Megapolis, is protecting Pascal! Raul, you're out of your mind, man!"

"Perhaps. That was what I decided. That is what we decided."

"Who is we?" Margot asked.

"Seneca and I... and Pascal," lied Raul. "I can't tell them everything. I have to lie to them, I have to calm them down," he thought feverishly.

"Pascal too? Are you sure, Raul?" Margot sensed Raul's insecurity.

"Well, Margot, do you think, can you even imagine Pascal staying against his will? That I took part in his arrest?" Raul lied more convincingly.

"I can't. I'm sorry," Margot said.

"When we heard this information, these high percentages in the polls, all three of us came to the same conclusion," Raul continued.

"That Kaella would have Pascal assassinated?" Jagdish asked.

"Yes, that's right. And we assumed that he would do that during his speech. In front of the entire world. Seneca was convinced that it would be the Grasshopper that does it, their most bloodthirsty killer."

"Why? How did he draw that conclusion?" Liam asked.

"Because he received information that the Grasshopper had disappeared off the face of the earth. No one, not even the top state leadership had any clues as to his whereabouts for past five months. Seneca assumed that the Grasshopper was in Megapolis the entire time and that he was waiting for his opportunity. In his style. To strike suddenly."

"So the three of you concluded that the Grasshopper was in Megapolis and that he would kill Pascal, and then Pascal stayed there to make the Grasshopper's job easier. Unbelievable!" Liam fumed.

"Liam, Liam... calm down. Think about it. Now Kaella thinks that Pascal is with us on the plane. That was most important to us. That is why Seneca gave us his airplane. So that you could not see on the satellite footage that Pascal did not get into the tube. That is why you waited for me for so long in the VIP lounge under the roof of the hotel. For the three of us to get organized, for it to look like Pascal too left the hotel and got on the plane. Kaella is now waiting to see where we will land, and to send the Grasshopper or some other assassins after us."

"Or he will attack our airplane," said Liam.

Everyone stopped breathing after Liam uttered those words, but no one commented.

"He won't," said Raul. "During the first half hour of our flight not a single airplane took off from any of their airports. In any case, we are being escorted and protected by Seneca's squadron. A ground-based rocket shield has also been created around our airplane."

"Really?" asked Margot. "Liam has got me scared."

"Yes. They are protecting us just in case. Seneca insisted on it, although all three of us agreed that Kaella would not attack the airplane."

"Why?" asked Liam.

"Because, Liam," Jagdish answered instead of Raul, "then it would be clear to the entire world that we had been shot down by Kaella, that is by the State, and he cannot allow himself this. Perhaps one of his snipers might take a shot at Pascal and the inspectors would never find him. Or they might kill him and state that it was some fanatic who hated Pascal... or something similar. If it were clear that Kaella killed Pascal, the entire free world would rise up against him and Kaella would fall sooner or later. This is clear to me now, when I heard this truly incredible percentage of the votes. I am so proud people, I'm so happy because of this..."

"We are all! We all are, Jagdish!" the team shouted.

"Forgive me, Raul, for explaining instead of you... but I'm so excited... I'm certain that this is how the three of you thought."

"We did, my dear analyst," Raul smiled. "And I'm glad that you said it, that we are thinking alike. That you don't hold it against me or Pascal... And you, Liam, what do you say now?"

"You want to hear what I have to say, Raul?"

"I do."

"I can't wait for the Grasshopper to come after us. To get him in our crosshairs. That's what I say."

Chapter 33

When Prince's father started to answer in great detail, and when the red lamp on the camera pointing at Prince did not go for while, he finally allowed his eyes to slide down from Babe's face.

To watch the struggle between her leather jacket and her huge bosom. Babe's breasts tried in vain to expand more, to rid themselves of the large lapels. And the jacket forced them, ample as they were, to get closer to each other and remain tightly fixed.

"You don't have a bra, you don't have one... I see. And you always wear one. You want to drive me mad... that's what you want. Only those buttons..." Prince thought in anger about the two done-up black buttons above and below Babe's bellybutton. "I'll undo them. I'll slowly... I won't even touch the jacket. It will slide off on its own from your... They'll defeat your jacket, because they want me to see them, for me to..."

It was no longer important whether a women's bust was a gift from mother nature or not. Implants no longer meant that breasts became two motionless stone orbs. No, today's breasts shake, bob while you walk, gave way to hands, fingers...

"How I will cuddle them, squeeze them, pinch them... I won't stop! Why doesn't at least one of the lapels shift a bit to the side, it takes just a bit... so that I can see your... It doesn't have to be a whole one, not everything... that will be tonight... But at least part, just a little piece of your nipple? No, the lapel won't budge. It won't, that's the way you did it, set it up..." and only then did Prince notice two discrete Earths on the jacket, embroidered in black thread.

"Exactly in the place... like two nipples! Babe, you... with those wonderful, enormous breasts and such nipples, you symbolize the essence... Earth... fertility... buxomness... nipples, milk... motherhood, birth... new life, new..."

"...generations of Consumers," the old Mr. Kaella completed his sentence.

"Why do you sit so humbly? Why do you clench your knees when in all your shows you cross your legs? I can always see your thighs… and now you won't let me. Why do you have those fishnet stockings, if you won't let me…"

Prince stopped. He quickly glanced at Babe's bare arms beneath the short sleeves of the jacket. He had not paid attention previously because it had been so common. But now he thoroughly studied two dragons tattooed on her upper arms. Then he looked again at her fishnet stockings. Then at the two flowers tattooed on her forearms. Then again at her fishnet stockings. "But…", Prince couldn't believe it. "But, Babe… you… the stockings… Those aren't real stockings! You've tattooed them! Bravo, Babe, bravo! What an idea! What a change! What a business move! That's the type of woman I need! Who will fight with me side by side!"

"What a fight it was," Prince thought. Not a fight but a true war for the prevention of permanent tattoos. Even the law prohibiting them did not help. How many people did they have to arrest and publicly remove, skin, peel their permanent tattoos off. There could be no compromise. No one could be permitted to permanently usurp the most commercial space in existence, the human skin. But it was worth it. It instilled fear. Even today, not even Non-Consumers dared have permanent tattoos.

"And you, Babe, have now shown how women and girls can tattoo stockings, instead of putting them on. Two entire legs, what a huge percentage of the skin's surface! What profit there is to be made there!"

Chapter 34

The first time that mom tried to take Henry out of Liv's hands was at the end of the season when they bought him. Liv was a bit over three years old at the time, so she didn't remember that. When she grew up her parents told her how she cried, held Henry to her chest and hid beneath the dining room table.

That was the first time her dad allowed her to keep anything from last season in the house and not hand it over to the Inspectorate to be destroyed. Her mom told her that because of Henry the house became a place of tension and fear of a sudden Inspectorate search. Because they would surely find him and arrest dad.

A sigh of relief came when quite unexpectedly a law was passed according to which children could keep one favorite toy from any season, up to the age of five.

That is why on her fifth birthday mom tried to take Henry from her hands for a second time. Liv didn't remember that either. But her mom and dad later told her that she never cried as much as she did on her fifth birthday. And that is why dad, whose favorite girl was more important than anything, again allowed Henry to remain in the house.

But Liv remembered very well when she herself, when she was in her sophomore year in high school, without holding back the tears, handed Henry to dad. She remembered how dad stood there completely still and was quiet. And mom told him:

"Take it if Liv is giving it to you. You're not going to sacrifice everything for it, are you? If they find it you'll never have the opportunity to save other children's Henrys. Liv is grown up. Take that penguin."

That was the only time that Liv saw her father cry. He said

"I can't. Henry is… the beginning. Henry helped me understand. I've come this far because of Henry."

Chapter 35

"You see for yourself, Miss Babe, it will not be difficult for me to tell our dear viewers my memories, because for some time now… You know, when a man gets to my age and is preparing for the departure, then…"

"Don't talk like that, Mr. Kaella, please. We common people don't want to even think about that. You are not at all aware how much the Consumers respect you, but also how much they love you, Mr. Kaella," Babe was so moved and passed her index finger beneath her eye, alluding to a tear.

"Yes, yes, I'm aware of that. And I am very happy… and grateful to the people," Kaella looked at the camera. "If I didn't love our people as much as they love me, everything that I have done and created in my life… would not have been possible."

"And you have done the most, created the most, Mr. Kaella."

"Behind everything stands the invincible, unbreakable, carved-in-stone, love for each and every person, every Consumer."

"You have done… not only done… but continue to… even now, at every moment you are doing… something that is the most grandiose, most magnificent in the history of the world, Mr. Kaella. You and your honorable ancestors… and of course, your son, Mr. Prince."

"Yes. Thank you for these words, Miss Babe. I wanted to say that in front of our audience, I would just like to repeat what I have already determined, in summarizing my life… what I have realized."

"Go ahead, Mr. Kaella."

"You see… I would like to mention my ancestors…"

"Of course," Babe encouraged Mr. Kaella.

"My grandfather discovered cosmic energy at a time when fossil fuels were disappearing, during the period of bloody wars where people were destroying each others' few alternative sources of energy. And he created a system of accumulating cosmic energy in space, delivering it through energy beams to cosmic power plants on Earth and transforming cosmic energy into electrical energy. And he offers this pure energy to all mankind, without any concern for the differences between them. And of course people accepted this. That is how our company, the Kaella Cosmic Energy Corporation, grew and developed. And my father continued down the same path, building a state. This process was not easy. At the time not all groups of people wanted to join the integrated human community. But gradually, weakened by previous wars, storms, droughts, floods, landslides, earthquakes, pandemics... without water, without food... without energy, these people toppled their dictators on their own, and joined. My father dedicated his life to creating the State of Earth... and that is why I am so moved, Miss Babe, because a beautiful intelligent young person such as yourself, is paying respect to my father, our family, our State, with her entire appearance, her entire being."

"Not only me, Mr. Kaella, not only me. Today I am just a representative of the Consumers. I symbolize the respect and love of all the people."

"Thank you... truly... thank you very much," Mr. Kaella's eyes were full of tears.

"Excellent moment of sentimentality," thought Babe and looked at the camera.

"And now dear viewers, let us take a look at the messages from our dearest friends, the generous sponsors of the interview with the two greatest men of the present."

Chapter 36

In the dense darkness Pascal sat on the bed and lowered his feet to the floor. "My telephone's gone!" he thought as he searched his jacket pockets. "Of course it's gone. Why am I surprised? Who in their right mind would leave their captive with a telephone? Something soft beneath my feet." Pascal slid his shoes along the floor. "Carpet.. I'll get up." He rose suddenly, staggered and sat back down on the bed. "This drug of Raul's is still... Slowly... It was too quickly..."

He stood up slowly, managing to maintain his balance. He took a step. One step... another... He hit his knee on a hard object. It seemed to him that even that faint sound echoed through the complete silence. He stood there for a while, listening.
"Did someone hear that? Again nothing, silence... No one heard me. Or they did but are not reacting."
He bent over to touch the object that he had hit. He passed the palms of his hand over the flat surface. He spread his hands as much as he could, but he still didn't touch the edge. "It's long. Like a low cupboard... a dresser. Let's see how wide it is," he moved his palms forward, leaning his knees on the object. He immediately touched the end. "A wall", he passed his hands across the wall in front of him. "Wait, wait... bed, dresser, wall. I'll go to the end of the dresser... there'll probably be some door or window with the blinds drawn... something... a light switch. No, no... if this is... and it looks like a hotel room... the light is... the nightstand!"

He stepped back, felt the bed under his knees and sat down on it again. He propped himself up with his hands and moved his body along the edge of the bed. With the outside of his thigh he felt a low hard object. "There it is!" he touched the object with his hands. "It must be a nightstand," he thought excitedly. "And on it a lamp," he concluded as he passed the palm of his hand over its entire surface. But he didn't feel anything. "Then it's a wall-mounted lamp. Above the nightstand." Still sitting, he ran his fingers over the wall and found a switch. He pressed it. The room was lit up by a lamp on the wall, placed slightly above the switch.

Pascal closed his eyes because even this weak light bothered him at first. Then slowly, squinting through his eyelashes, he looked around himself. He was in a typical bedroom. The bed was large, a double bed covered in an elegant silk dark-red cover with a black rose embroidered in the middle. There were two nightstands, on each side of the bed, and along the walls – two dressers made of the same dark wood. The bed practically took up the entire length of the room. Between the end of it and the opposite wall there was just enough room to open the door.

"A door! And how about window?" Pascal wondered. It was only then that he noticed that the room didn't have any windows. "What is this? Some luxurious solitary confinement cell?"

He went to the door and put his ear against it. Complete silence again. He turned the doorknob and the door opened.

Chapter 37

Mr. Kaella's aging prostate held up very well during the interview. But now, during the commercial break, he had to give in to it. Prince knew this very well and waved to the bodyguards to take his father to the toilet.

When Mr. Kaella had left the submarine salon, Babe and Prince got up and approached each other.
"Babe, I'm simply speechless. You take my breath away," Prince openly showed his exhilaration.

"Wow!" thought Babe, very pleased. "We've already lost the 'Miss'. And with my knees clenched."
"Thank you, Mr. Kaella," she answered Prince. "I hope that it is now clear to you why I was in such a hurry today."
"Yes, yes... and forgive me for keeping you. Had I known..." Prince paused, listening to the cheerful, inspired voice in the first commercial.

"Look, dear Consumers, where is it that your Miss Babe has a piercing?""
Prince suddenly turned to the nearest monitor and watched in shock as the camera zoomed Babe's eye, filmed just now, during the interview.
"You were surely wondering, dear Consumers, during the interview with Mr. Kaella and his son Prince," chirped the voice in the commercial, "where it is that Miss Babe attached the two chains with the little Earths. Take a good look..."
Babe smiled when Prince's focus jumped from the monitor to her eyes.
"You see, dear Consumers, but don't believe. Believe it, believe it... Miss Babe has a piercing in her whites of her eyes. Yes in her the whites of her eyes, her sclera! Let's hear what Miss Babe has to say about this new fashion."

Prerecorded footage of Babe appeared on the monitor, as well as on television screens across the planet.

"I was a bit afraid, dear Consumers, I have to admit it. But I have absolute trust in the achievements of our science and technology. And above all – I couldn't resist this piercing. I simply couldn't. Just as I am certain that all the girls watching this cannot resist either. But don't worry, girls. You won't have to wait for next season. Sclera piercings are coming to fashion accessory sector shops already..." here the background music went into crescendo, and then suddenly subsided. "The day after tomorrow!" Babe shouted in the commercial. "And that is why, girls, line up in front of your shop tomorrow evening." Babe blew a kiss to the camera with her full lips and said "Love, Babe."

"It seemed to me... but I didn't believe..." Prince stuttered after the commercial. "Are you at all aware of what you mean to this State? How much you mean to me, Babe..." he whispered hoarsely.

"So, a new piercing means going to first-name basis", thought Babe, shyly lowering her head. "The obstacles are falling faster than I expected."

"All the usual things" thundered the narrator's threatening voice from the monitor during the regular narrative between commercials, while he reminded Consumers of what all they have to hand over to the Inspectorate by the end of the month. "So everything, all clothes and shoes, all fashion accessories, cosmetics, children's toys, pots and pans, computers, telephones, tablets, television sets..."

"Don't Mr. Kaella, please. Don't give me false hope," Babe whispered to Prince in a sad voice.
"False hope?! What false hope? You mean everything to me, Babe, everything..."
Touched, Babe tried to hold back the tears and turned her right cheek towards him.
"I need you, Babe..." Prince suddenly went silent, wanting to take advantage of this opportunity to have a good look at the discrete tattoo behind her ear.

It seemed to him that it was just hieroglyphs, but carefully studying them one at a time he realized they were letters. "Just a little strange," he thought. "Distorted, of different sizes, thickness... overlapping... but they are letters... There that's an r, and that's an h or perhaps an n, and the first one... it's..."
"Prince! You've tattooed my name!" he shouted.
"Quiet, quiet..." Babe calmed him.

"You're driving me crazy..." he whispered feverishly.

"Don't be angry, Mr. Kaella, but I had to..." she looked at him humbly, her eyes begging for forgiveness.

"Be angry? I'm crazy about you! Crazy!"

"I had to show it somewhere. This deepest, most hidden intimate thing."

"Deepest?"

"Yes."

"Most hidden?"

"Yes."

"Intimate thing?'

"Yes."

"My name?"

"Yes."

"I can't go on without you, Babe. You have to be mine..."

"If you truly think that, Mr. Kaella..."

"'Mr. Kaella! Mr. Kaella!' Is that your deepest intimate thing? Is that what you hid behind your ear?"

"Prince..."

"So," thought Babe, "a tattoo behind the ear equals 'Prince' instead of 'Mr. Kaella". Well, we'll see, Prince, what the following advertisement will bring. Just as soon as this guy finishes listing to the Consumers..." Babe looked at the monitor. And Prince continued excitedly:

"Your intimacy... deepest... you say, Babe. And do you know what is my deepest intimate thing?"

"I don't, I don't dare..."

"Princess, my Princess! That's what I'll tattoo! Princess!"

"I was wrong," thought Babe, pressing her chest with her hand so that her heart would not burst. "A tattoo behind the ear equals 'Prince' instead of 'Mr. Kaella' plus 'Princess' instead of 'Babe'."

Chapter 38

Jagdish came up to Raul and Margot and asked:

"Do you know what I don't get, Raul?"

"What?"

"Where did this information about such a high percentage of votes suddenly come from? I mean, we did our studies, locally, in our cities, but..."

"Jagdish, we couldn't get the real picture based on that. We couldn't even guess that so many people from consumer cities, from places we had never set foot in, with censured media, the Internet... that people there knew about us, about Pascal... Not only that they knew, but that they would vote for him. I find something else odd. That's what the three of us mainly discussed yesterday. This informant of Seneca's has been sending him the results of their polls every two, three week, since the beginning of the presidential campaign."

"Why didn't you tell us earlier, Raul?"

"We couldn't. Seneca didn't want anyone to know about this informant of his."

"I understand. And how did the percentages change? They increased in time, right?" Jagdish asked.

"They didn't. That's what's odd. The entire time they were around twenty seven, no more than thirty percent for Pascal."

"And for Xing?"

"Close to forty."

"So how did it suddenly...?"

"We don't know. We can only assume that their pollsters this time falsely introduced themselves as being ours or neutral... I don't know. So the people weren't afraid to say that they would vote for Pascal. Kaella also received all those periodical results of the polls. And this is now a great shock to him, as it is to us. That is why we concluded, just as you did, that they would try to carry out an assassination."

"Raul... alright, we understand now. I mean, the situation changed so suddenly with this information about the certain victory in the elections... But, where does this trust of yours in Seneca come from? As Liam said, how do you know that he didn't immediately hand him over to Kaella?" Margot asked.

"He could have arrested us all and handed us over to Kaella whenever he wanted. At any moment, during all these months. And he didn't do that. So, you tell me, Margot, what is the most important thing to Seneca?"

"Megapolis," Margot said.

"Exactly, Megapolis. And had he arrested us, banished us, handed us over to the villains… what would Megapolis have done to him? What would the students have done - all those educated people, experts, scientists, athletes, artists of all profiles, which Megapolis is full of. They would have despised him. Spat on him. He could rule by force, but Seneca is not like that. He loves Megapolis precisely because of those people. Because of the youths, because of the University. That's all he boasts about. He hands out scholarship, rewards the best students, that's why I… I mean… that's why we trusted him… that's why we trust him to keep Pascal safe."

"I understand, I agree," said Margot, already much calmer.

"People…" Raul said loudly, addressing the entire staff. "Calm down, think it over, talk among yourselves… You'll see that I'm right. And that is only until the elections. We simply moved out of the way. And we got Pascal out of the way. We're calmly waiting for Kaella's move. And that's when we'll decide how to proceed."

"Raul's right," Margot supported him. "He and Pascal have done the right thing. We can be at ease. There, I'm already completely calm."

Chapter 39

Babe and Prince twitched when the old Mr. Kaella returned from the toilet, and they moved away from each other. Luckily the makeup artist immediately rushed in an started powdering the sweaty Mr. Kaella, her body concealing the two of them.

Babe used the opportunity and turned up the volume on the monitor, so that her conversation with Prince could not be heard in the salon.
The voice of the speaker rumbled from the monitor:
"On that day it is time for all the bathroom accessories. That means we change: bathtubs, sinks, toilet bowls, bidets, faucets, showers, tiles, both wall and floor. We're looking forward to the new designs and new wonderful pastel colors, dear Consumers."

And after that came a completely different, joyful and frivolous voice in the next advertisement:
"Our Planet is heating up, dear Ladies. The temperatures are increasingly higher. You're hot in your stockings. But you don't reject them, since they make your legs long and sexy. Unfortunately, you cannot fully enjoy your sexy appearance because you're sweating. Look, dear Consumer, how Miss Babe has solved this dilemma."

Prince swiftly turned towards the monitor and was petrified. Babe was lying on her stomach, in a luxurious pink stand, covered from her armpit to just below her derriere by a pink towel. Two top, publicly well-known tattoo masters were at that very moment doing the lace on her floral stockings.
"What is Miss Babe doing, dear Consumer? Yes! You've guessed it! She's tattooing stockings. Let's hear what Miss Babe has to say, what is her experience with tattooed stockings?"

In the next shot, sitting in a tight miniskirt on a bar stool, with her legs crossed, revealing to the viewers the very edge of the lace on the tattooed stockings, this time with a star pattern, Babe said:

"I will never again put on real stockings... Forgive me, dear Consumer, I didn't express myself properly, because these tattooed stockings are the only real ones. Tattoo them just once and you will see for yourself. You'll confine the old ones to fashion history, where they belong. You can feel comfortable, with cooled legs, and look equally attractive or even more attractive," here Babe moved a bit, her skirt rode up also revealing the skin of her thighs above the lace, "and feel..." Babe winked at the camera. "Girls, you know what I mean."

"Why are you doing this to me, Babe?" Prince panted after the advertisement.
"You mean, Princess?"
"Why are you doing this to me, Princess?"
"What am I doing to you, Prince?"
"Why are you clenching your knees the entire time? The entire world can look at your long, wonderful legs in tattooed stockings, only I can't. And now, when they are fishnets. Why am I not allowed to see them? Why?"
"You'll see them."

"Babe, Mr. Kaella, please sit down. We're live in thirty seconds," the assistant director said.
"When will I see them?" Prince asked.
"Now," answered Babe, and walked towards the couch.

Chapter 40

The students of the fifth and eighth grade, standing in line one after another, took black scarves with a blue Earth on them from one large box, and black hats with a blue Earth from another, which Mitke the janitor had brought from out of storage to the school hall.

The boys from the eighth grade, some of them already young men with thin moustaches and a few hairs on their chin, with their highly changed voices, cursed as rudely as they could, aggressively shoving the fifth-graders, and without having tied the scarves around their necks or placing the hats on their heads, they went out into the yard, strutting as they walked. They were very angry because they couldn't watch Babe's show to the end.

The girls from the eighth grade, some of them blossoming, were a lot calmer. They talked about how much money their parents would give them and which of Babe's wonderful fashion accessories they would allow them to wear.

The boys from the fifth grade were mainly tried to get out of the way of the enraged young men from the eighth grade, and when they had passed, they would smack one another upside the head and kick each other.

The girls from the fifth grade stood around in small groups, muttering something among themselves.

All this together caused a noise that spread through the acoustic hall and disturbed the students from the other grades, who were in their classrooms calmly watching the interview with Mr. Kaella and his son Prince.
Being aware of this and his responsibility, Mitke the janitor kept repeating "Quiet, children, quiet!" without taking his eyes off the large screen hanging from the ceiling of the school hall.

What was in common for both the boys and girls in both the eighth and fifth grades, was that walking through their teachers they all boarded the buses parked in the schoolyard, which were waiting to take them to the prepared, fenced-off space in the middle of Short Street.

Chapter 41

After the commercial break Babe sat at the very edge of the couch so that her head would be closer to her guest, Mr. Kaella. But not only for that reason. She leaned on the couch with her left shoulder so that Prince could see her profile. He saw a cascade of blue hair, long eyelashes, lips...

"Your lips... How the two overhangs at the ends of the upper lip lie on the lower lip. And this leaves that gap in the middle... You can't press them closed, can you? How I will open them, spread that gap with my tongue, tonight... and penetrate... Tonight? What tonight? Now! During the next break!" the impatient Prince decided.

"You know, Miss Babe, before I continue with my recollections, I'd like to say something else to our viewers."
"Go ahead, Mr. Kaella."
"This reminded me... I mean, this between the commercials... Although it sounds kind of coarse... But, dear Consumers, it isn't so. We trust you completely... but... we all know how fast we live today, how many obligations we have. And a person simply forgets to surrender to the Inspectorate... I don't know... a toothbrush... paste... from last season. And then this is discovered and completely unnecessary problems are created.
"So we are reminding you so that you, dear viewers, will be spared such unfortunate situations. And don't be angry at our inspectors, when they go through your houses and apartments. Do you know how many people are employed by the Inspectorate? How many families survive from their earnings? The inspectors are part of us, part of our community and they are working solely for the common good."
"Of course they understand that, Mr. Kaella," Babe said.
"I know, I know that you understand, dear Consumers," Mr. Kaella continued. "I just mention that in passing... to pay homage, to take this opportunity to thank the inspectors for their effort and fervor... Actually," a smile lit up his old face, "I wanted to say something else. I was reminded by this, when the speaker listed everything

that had to be returned, and says 'children's toys'... It reminded me of my granddaughter. I adore her, Miss Babe."

"You do?" Babe uttered with tight lips.

"Yes. I also love my two grandsons. But they are young men... and she... she's grandpa's little butterfly. And these toys... We returned them at the end of every season. I mean, dear viewers," Mr. Kaella looked at the camera very sincerely, "so that you don't think that we Kaella's don't abide by the law. On the contrary – very strictly. To show through action, not only words, that we respect the laws and Constitution of our State.

"And ... what was I ... ah, yes... grandchildren... it is never a problem for them to return the old toys. Boys... as you know yourself..." Mr. Kaella grinned at the camera, "they destroy them the second day, disassemble their toy car...

"And grandpa's butterfly... she had a little pony. And when we were supposed to hand it over to the Inspectorate, my little granddaughter cried and cried. And this son of mine, strict as he is, wanted to take away her little horsy. And I jumped up, dear viewers and shouted 'Well, this won't do!' I picked up my little granddaughter with her pony in my hand, and ran away from my son and daughter-in-law to my chambers, and immediately called the President of the State... I don't remember who it was at the time... and ordered him to change the law, that children don't have to return toys.

"You know how it is... Everything in life is important. What you do, what you have achieved, what you have given humanity... But children, grandchildren... they are the most important and the most beautiful thing of all.

"And then this son of mine, and a bunch of people from the Company, from the Inspectorate, from the university... all kinds of psychologists, lawyers, psychiatrists, sociologists... I don't know who all... started convincing me that it didn't work that way, that it undermined the Constitution, that it fundamentally perverts the young consumer's soul... and so on. But I wouldn't allow them to take that little horse from my butterfly."

"Stop boring with the stories about that granddaughter of yours and that nag, old man!" Babe panicked, thinking that this would discourage Prince. So she slowly raised her leg and glanced over at him.

"And finally we agreed that children could keep only one toy until their fifth year. That is what we said. Anything more than that and the future Consumer would be forever lost in space and time," Mr. Kaella concluded his recollection.

Having seen Prince's lustful gaze, Babe realized that he wasn't at all listening to his father. On the contrary, he had completely leaned over towards her when her blue-black skirt rose up... when she crossed her legs, when the squares on the two fishnets intertwined, when the tattooed black lace on her perfect, smooth thigh eliminated all other thoughts, everything else...

Chapter 42

The staff members, better yet brothers in arms and friends, because they had been roaming the planet for years as part of Pascal's freedom caravan, and diligently, tirelessly, and wholeheartedly carried out their tasks, were gradually calming down on the plane and approving Raul's and Pascal's decision as the most rational one at the moment.

"There, you see for yourself, that now, when you have all the information, that we acted appropriately. Each of you would have done the same, right?" Raul said contentedly.
"I would, undoubtedly," said Jagdish.
"I don't know... I don't know. The only thing that is important to me is for this to pass as quickly as possible. So that I can be at Pascal's side again, all the time. Only then will I be at ease," Liam sighed.

"Can someone finally tell me why Svetlana was devastated? And where did she go?" asked Svetlana's secretary, Jin.
"What do you mean 'devastated'?" the other secretaries shouted all at once.
"I only know what Pascal told me, Jin. And I don't know where Svetlana went. And the fact that she was crying, that she was devastated, that is only their affair. It is not up to us to discuss that."
"I have the right to know what happened to Svetlana. She's my best friend," Jin said unremittingly. "Perhaps last night someone else saw or heard something... or knows something? Someone from security? Liam?"
"We only know that she left the hotel in the early morning," Liam said.

"Jin, what do you mean 'did someone else see'? Who saw Svetlana last night?" anxiously asked Marina, a secretary, looking at her colleagues Phoebe, Eve and Dorika, who, also surprised, shrugged their shoulders and shook their heads.
"Gloria saw her," Jin said.

"Gloria?!" shouted Marina, Phoebe, Eve and Dorika, looking at their colleague in disbelief.

"How could you not tell us?" Phoebe asked Gloria in an excited tone, still not believing that such a thing was possible.

"I'm sorry... How could I tell you when Raul said that she left Pascal?"

"You should have, in any case..." Phoebe was relentless.

"Alright, let it go, Phoebe. Come on, tell us what you saw," Eve said impatiently.

"I was just falling asleep..."

"What do you mean 'you were falling asleep'?!" Dorika exclaimed in shock. "So, you were in our room, and you didn't wake me?! How could you?! How?! Margot, please, I don't want to sleep in the same room as this person... I mean, in the next hotel. Don't talk to me anymore, Gloria! Is that clear?"

"Dorika... forgive me... I'll explain everything in private. I was waiting for something... I can't talk about that right now..."

"I'm not interested! Now you're going to make things up!" Dorika raged on.

"I'm not making anything up, I just didn't want to..."

"Wait! Wait, Gloria!" Raul interrupted. "You girls will go on for days. Now tell me, what did Svetlana look like? Was she really in tears?"

"Yes, she was. She was desperate... miserable. As though it wasn't her, as though..."

"Do you hear, Raul? That's not a girl that left..." Margot said.

"She left someone?" said Gloria. "Pascal? Nonsense! Who could leave Pascal? I'm sorry, Raul, but you are very naïve if you really believed Pascal."

"You think?" Raul asked.

"Of course!" said Gloria with the authority of an expert. "And even if she had left him, she wouldn't be crying because of it. I've left guys... I mean, it's unpleasant while you tell them, but when that moment passes, you immediately forget everything and think about him. I mean, the new one... that you like. Right?" Gloria asked her colleagues.

"Exactly," the girls confirmed.

"Alright, alright... You're probably right," Raul interrupted them. "Svetlana left for some reason of hers. It's not important. What's important is that she is safe. She's neither with Pascal nor with us. No one will be looking for her," said Raul. "Now please return to your seats. I have to think in peace about which city we should go to. Liam, I expect to hear your recommendations."

"Very well," said Liam.

Chapter 43

"You know, I'm getting old... I get sentimental very easily... but let's continue..." said Mr. Kaella. "Yes, dear viewers, that was the state of Earth when I was born. And as a boy, growing up alongside my father, I wondered... what is my mission? What is it that I have to do, to create in my life, to prove worthy of my name?"

"Growing up and pondering, I realized that it wasn't enough that our family, our Company, provides mankind with energy. People also need food and water. When I looked around, I was surprised with what I saw.
"Numerous companies that used our energy, at a very cheap price, were selling food to people at astronomical prices and profiting from the hungry and the thirsty. That is why I increased the price of energy to a level that they couldn't withstand. And I bought them all and merged them with our company. The prices of water and food immediately dropped drastically for all people."

"Then I wondered, what next? What else do people need? What belongs to people? Education, healthcare, protection of lives and properties... Does every person have this? Does every person, to who my family selflessly gives energy, food and water, also have everything else necessary for a decent life? No. And why not? Because not every person can earn enough to be able to put their children through school, get medical treatment... And why not? Because there is no work for them, or they aren't paid enough, or the company that they worked for went bankrupt. Is a person responsible for their company going bankrupt? Is another person responsible for their company not going bankrupt and for being able to educate their children? While their neighbor cannot."

"At one moment, I was nearing forty, it became clear to me what I must do. I have to create an Association of Companies within which all companies will collaborate, and not compete against and destroy each other."

Chapter 44

The elevator doors opened. Bear stepped out into the garage and passed by his colleagues with his head hung low, carrying a role of duck tape. He walked up to the presidential car, opened the passenger door, bent over and said to the dead driver
"Hello, Barney."

He threw the tape on the passenger seat, stood up and went to the rear door, opened it wide and knelt beside them.
The Xings were seated, fastened to the seats and backs by wide gray adhesive tape. Seated on Bear's left were her mom and dad, and across from them, to Bear's right, looking with dead eyes at their parents was she, and next to her - her brother.
Bear reached into his jacket pocket and took something out. He put his hand on her lap.
"I found this in your sheets last night, Liv," whispered Bear, gently laying Henry on her nightgown. "I didn't know... you know, your Bear isn't very smart, Liv... that there used to be birds in tuxedos."

With angry jerks of the fingers and nails of both hands he tore the tape fastening her upturned palm to the seat. He raised the bluish hand to his lips and kissed it.

His colleagues looked on in silence as Bear slowly rose, closed the rear door, took the roll of tape and sat down in the passenger sat.
At that moment Iceman ran up and held the door with both hands, preventing Bear from shutting it.
"What are you doing, Bear?"
"Let go of the door, Iceman."
"Don't, my friend... please. It's difficult for me too. For all of us."
"Move out of the way, Iceman."
"Don't be crazy..."
Iceman was silent when Bear drew his pistol from his belt holster with lightning speed and pointed it at him.
"Move away, Iceman, I'm telling you."
Iceman stepped back. Bear closed the door and locked the car from the inside.

Chapter 45

"And I created the Association around my Kaella Cosmic Energy Corporation," Mr. Kaella presented his life's journey to the viewers. "I sent a public invitation for all companies to join me.

"Dear viewers, don't think that everything went smoothly. On the contrary, it was a lengthy process. I traveled the world and spoke to and begged CEOs and managing boards to hear me out. Some did and some companies joined the Association. But they were a minority.

"At one moment I had had enough of the begging and convincing. I created two prices for my energy: one was for the companies that were part of the Association, and the other, ten times higher, for those that were not.

"In the following months all the companies either joined or simply collapsed. Miss Babe, perhaps your viewers are confused," Mr. Kaella looked at Babe. "I am aware that people call the Association of Companies simply the Company, but this is not a single company, neither legally and formally, nor by ownership.

"My family fully owns only our company, which dear Consumers, provides you with energy, water, food... We later also took over pharmaceuticals, in order to be certain that all people would have access to medicaments, and my son also took over all infrastructural and construction businesses, in order to provide people with new, modern apartments in our planet's green oases.

"For the other things, which are not of vital importance in your lives, dear viewers, i.e. in the other companies, which we today call sectors of the Association, our family has only majority, but not full ownership.

"Well... you yourself know. You all have shares in the sectors for vehicles and transportation, for communication and internet, for consumer electronics, for interior decorating, for retail, for film production... music, for fashion accessories..."

"Miss Babe," Mr. Kaella suddenly said loudly. "Had I known that you would look like this today, I would have bought shares in the fashion accessory sector. Thanks to you they will skyrocket after this show."

The three of them laughed.

Chapter 46

"Forgive me, Liv, for not saving you," Bear said quietly to her, while they sat back to back. "Your Bear didn't save you. And you always asked that Bear protect you and follow you everywhere. To drive you to the university, to wait for you after class... to drive you to the movies... shopping... always Bear.

"Because you knew that Bear would not tell mom and dad about that older student. Nor that you didn't go to class, but rather to the movies with him. And that you didn't go shopping alone... nor that you didn't try on clothes alone in the changing room," stuttered Bear, as though he was weeping, but his eyes were dry and his gaze was empty.

"Forgive me Mrs. Xing, for hiding their love from you. But... I knew that you would get worried because he was older... and you wouldn't let Liv see him anymore... And she would have suffered... But no need, trust me, ma'am. When I noticed it, I immediately checked out the young man. He is an excellent student, his parents are respected experts, decent people. He also has a brother who is much older. Also with a university degree. A good job. Two children. A serious family man. You have nothing to worry about, ma'am. Trust Bear. Do you think that I would allow just any guy to hang around Liv just because she is the President's daughter? I would have chased them away... and then some. But this boy... he loves Liv very much. Sincerely. And our Liv... If you could only see how she glows when she's with him."

"And ma'am, I didn't save her. I didn't save your little Sasha either... I love him too... You taught him well. 'Mr. Bear'... and he always says hello. And an excellent pupil. Who could he take after poorly? Who? You, ma'am? The President?"

"I would vote for you, Mr. President. Iceman also promised that he would vote for you. And the others... they say... what do they care... The Kaella's appoint presidents, no one even votes anymore... And I listened to all your speeches. And excuse me, but I have to tell you where you went wrong. You were like... we'll change things slowly, one step at a time, over the course of several generations... and so on. You say that this Alexander is dangerous... How did you put it? Radical. Well, you were wrong there, Mr. President. The Kaellas and Erivan actually need someone dangerous. To shoot them in the forehead... like the Grasshopper did to you... us. And you paid for this mistake with your life. And your entire family... Liv..."

Bear was silent and passed his hand across his face several times. Then he turned towards the driver.
"But... you play the hand you're dealt is. Isn't that right, Barney?" Bear slapped Barney on the knee. "What's up? You just keep quiet and listen, don't you? And you can't wait to run after your cooks and maids, and tell them that Liv has a boyfriend? Right? Admit it. You didn't even say hello, Barney. You don't see me. They've taped you to the head rest across one eye, so you're just squinting with the other one. And where's that big smile when you see me? And you say, 'where have you been, Bear?' How do you... that hat of yours..." Bear turned towards Barney, gripped the brim of his hat and moved it up and down. "That's it... that's how you greet your friend."

Chapter 47

"And these shares in our companies guarantee you a good life even after you've finished working, dear Consumers. They are constantly increasing... our stock exchange does not have, like there once was... bubbles, and then they burst, and shares lose their value and an entire generation of older people is left without a livelihood. You are certain that your shares will always be at least worth the same."

"That's right, Mr. Kaella," Babe confirmed. "Even average people, thanks to the sale of shares, can extend their lives for months. Here, I am working on a story about a lady, with quite an average income, who fell ill, who isn't able to work anymore, and who managed to live off the money from the sale of the shares for another two and a half years. Do you hear that, dear Consumers?" Babe looked at the camera. "Two and a half years! She paid her bills, bought the seasonal goods and got treatment. Albeit, she did eat every second or third day... but she had money for the medicaments. Well... in the end she didn't have enough for the surgery... but that's normal. Surgery is expensive. I won't tell you any more, dear viewers. You will see my story. We filmed the lady the day before she went to Euthanasia. You'll see, a very positive inspiring human story."

"There, you see all the things that I have provided for the people. And I can't wait to see your report, Miss Babe," said Mr. Kaella, and continued. "It was really funny... You know, some people accused me of being a communist."

"Impossible!" Babe was stunned.

"Yes, yes, Miss Babe. Communist? Me? I, who consider private ownership the greatest sanctity? I mean, not only mine, but that of every person. And when they saw that everything had worked out, that these people were actually the owners of shares in various sectors, then they accused me of being an usurper, an oligarch. They asked why I didn't go public with company on the stock exchange, so that anyone could buy its shares. Can you imagine that, Miss Babe?"

"Ridiculous!" Babe shook her head in disbelief.

Then for a moment she turned towards Prince, smiled at him and with a glance gestured toward her side. His eyes obediently looked down and he saw that Babe, running the tips of her black nails upward from her knee, slowly passed over the haunch, all the way up to the edge of the skirt, and as though by accident raised her skirt even higher, and she tilted sideways even more and he saw... Prince saw... how the black lace ended... and the beginning of her curve... firm and protruding... tanned...

"I can't take it anymore... Don't do that to me... Sit like you were before... Clench your knees... I can't... I can't anymore!" Prince was going crazy, tearing at the leather armchair with his nails.

"...that I take risks," Mr. Kaella startled Babe. "That I don's sleep at night, thinking about whether that day energy, water, food, pharmaceuticals reached every Consumer, their families, children? That this is decided by some managing board of dispersed owners? Come on, please! Our family discovered Cosmic Energy, brought it to Earth, gave it to the people. We have been proving this humanity for generations. This is simply in our genes. That is what we Kaellas are like, the only guaranteed benefactors of all the people on Earth."

"The only one, Mr. Kaella, the only ones."

Chapter 48

Bear heard a knock on the window and turned around. He saw Alpha standing next to the car. He rolled down the window.

"Hello, Alpha," he said.

"Why are you sitting there, Bear? People have been telling me that you're behaving strangely today."

"Probably. And you know best why I'm sitting in the passenger seat."

"I don't understand."

"You don't understand? Didn't you say last night that everything must look normal, as usual?"

"Yes, I did."

"And this morning you killed Barney because of that."

"Bear, that is how it has to be. Everyone understands that, only you…"

"Alpha, I understand it the best, trust me. So, where's the adhesive tape?"

"What tape? What are you talking about?

"Where did you hide it last night? Admit it. Behind some pillar, under a car."

"Why do you think it has to be you, Bear?

"I don't think so. I'm volunteering. It is normal and usual that when the President goes somewhere with his family by car… like today, for example… to hold the election speech… it is normal for one of us to sit next to Barney in the passenger seat. So, I'm the volunteer."

Alpha was silent, and the other colleagues, when they heard this, one by one entered the two cars that would escort the presidential car, or put helmets on their heads and mounted motorcycles.

Only Iceman ran over and shouter:

"Alpha, we can't do it like that! Come on, let's draw straws… rock-paper-scissors. Why does it have to be Bear? Why are you being silly, Bear? Get out of the car!"

"Iceman, please go. It's difficult enough. I've decided. Go."

"Everyone in position, Iceman," Alpha said. "That's an order. It has to be one of us. Bear has volunteered."

Iceman turned and walked to his car, without saying another word.

"Alpha, tell me, who did you have in mind?"

"No one, Bear. I was going to say that someone should check how the driver is taped…"

"Barney."

"Barney. And whoever sat… there…"

"Yes?"

"I'd kill him."

"So, you'd leave it up to chance?"

"Yes."

"And where's the tape? Time's running out…"

Alpha looked at his watch.

"How much time do we have before departure? You have probably planned everything down to the minute, right? There can be no dilemma that the president and his family were killed by Non-Consumers."

"There can't be, Bear. These are historical moments."

"Clearly. That is why I want to be a hero. How much longer?"

"Two minutes."

"Where's your tape?"

"Behind that pillar," Alpha motioned with his hand.

"You don't need to waste time to go to the pillar and back. Here it is. I brought it for you. Hold the tape, Barney," said Bear, placing the roll in Barney's legs. "Take out your gun, Alpha. You also need to tape me up. Time is running out."

Alpha was sweating.

"You're messing around, Alpha. Erivan is at his window, he's looking at his watch and waiting for the presidential motorcade to leave the garage. And if it doesn't leave on time, Erivan will call the Grasshopper."

Alpha swiftly drew his gun and fired a bullet into Bear's head.

Chapter 49

"During the following period of my life I focused on creating the minimal, cheapest possible State," Mr. Kaella continued his life's story. "Why should the Consumers and the Company Sectors have to pay high taxes in order to support some mastodon-like State."

"There really isn't any reason," Babe agreed.

"Of course there isn't. And do you know what else they criticized me for?"

"Is it possible that they criticized you for something more?" Babe was stunned.

"Of course. There are people whose malice knows no boundaries. They criticized me because my company doesn't pay taxes."

"Well, that's something I really cannot believe, Mr. Kaella."

"My company can certainly pay taxes, but it will be then immediately included in the prices of energy, water, food, treatment, apartments... How can the average Consumer pay for that? How can they survive?"

"Impossible."

Babe turned towards Prince, opened her mouth, rolled her eyes, and sighed like it was very stuffy and she was struggling for air. She waved her hand in front of her face as though to cool herself, like she was too hot. She lowered her hand and reached the lapel of her leather jacket. She drew the jacket away from her, that is to say from her ample breasts, because she was obviously getting hot under the reflectors in the submarine salon.

"Yes, impossible," Mr. Kaella confirmed yet again. "That is why I reduced the costs of the state. I abolished these two parliament houses that had existed previously..."

"What was all that about?" Babe was wondered.

Prince leaned his hands on the edge of the coffee table. That was the only thing preventing him from jumping Babe before the million-strong audience. Having seen his reaction, Babe used her other hand to unfasten the button above her bellybutton, concealed from the old Mr. Kaella by the couch armrest, and she opened wide her lapel.

"That was nonsense. You hadn't even been born back then. You know, back then there were like some elected representatives who sat in some seats, talked, quarreled. Like, they would pass laws... and for that they received huge salaries, which the average person could only dream of. Then they formed some sort of government, then the prime minister, and the ministers, and all kinds of agencies, assistants... assistant's assistants, secretaries, assistant secretaries... And then elections every four years. You can imagine how much it cost! I abolished all that nonsense and significantly reduced the costs of the state. I left the President of the State, who has a minimal administration. And the president is elected every ten years, as you know."
"Of course."

Prince stared sideways at the huge breast, scratching with his nails at the surface of the table and barely breathing. Perhaps Babe was only pretending to be hot and that she was running out of air, but Prince was truly gasping for air.
"How big is it? It's even bigger when it's bare... Bigger than in my wildest dreams... with two hands... I'll knead it, squeeze it, slap it..."

"I merged the former military and former police into a single organization, i.e. the Inspectorate. This also cut costs. I stopped weapons production. I mean, we produce a minimum, for the Inspectorate. There are no more wars... I mean..." Mr. Kaella remembered that he would soon be declaring a new war.
"It doesn't matter," he thought. "It's going to be short. I have to explain my ideas, my principles, to the people."
"How can I permit wars, Miss Babe?"
"You can't, of course."

From her protruding nipple dangled another chain with a small Earth.
"You'll pay for this... you'll pay, when I tug at that Earth. You'll squeal..."

"I can't. What does a person spend in war? A bullet. Or an entire group of people spends only one projectile. And then what? We lose Consumers."
"Terrible."

Prince managed to raise his eyes to Babe's face, wanting to appear menacing, to let her know that he would ravage her, seriously punish her for what she was doing to him. And Babe, running the tip of her tongue across the edge of her teeth, studded with silver stars, licking the ends of the upper lips, clearly showed her Prince how intimidated she was.

"Not to go into all these details – I reduced the costs of the state to one third," Mr. Kaella summarized at the end of his exposé.
"To one third?"
"Yes."
"Do you hear this, dear viewers? Do you understand what Mr. Kaella has done for us?"

Chapter 50

Pascal could not believe that the room wasn't locked. "What is going on?" he wondered. He left the door wide open so that under the light of the wall lamp he might see the room that he found himself in. He immediately saw a switch on the wall and he turned on the light.

He was in a long narrow hallway, closer to the left end. In front of him, slightly to the right, was a door. The only one on that side of the hallway. He approached it quietly, listening to hear whether there was something behind it. "Nothing. Quiet," he concluded. When he tried to open it he realized that it was locked and that he was in fact Raul's and Seneca's captive.

The hallway was a bit over a meter wide, and about fifteen meters long. Pascal saw that on the side of the hallway where he had come out of there were three other doors. He went to the one next to his room, on the left-hand end of the hallway, which was also unlocked, and opened it.

There was a bathroom with a two-sink vanity, which ran along the entire length of the bathroom, as did the mirror above it. On the opposite side were a shower, toilet and bidet.

He froze in shock. "Where am I? On another planet? How is this possible?" The entire bathroom accessories, colors, vanity design, lighting, tiles... were not only from some previous season, but were also in some black-and-white combination. There were incredibly old. Years old.

"Well of course. The room too... I hadn't paid attention... the nightstand, lights... it's all ten years old... or more."

He left the bathroom and went down the hallway, past the door to his room, to the next one. He opened it quickly, without pausing or listening, not expecting any room to be locked. It became clear to him that he was imprisoned in some apartment, a suite, and that the only way out was through the locked door that was across from his room.

He switched on the light. This room was narrower than his. It had a bed for one person, a dresser and a nightstand, a lamp and a pink cover. The last room in the row was the same size as the previous one. It had two bunk beds with a light-blue covers, and only one dresser that was the entire length of the room. But there were no windows anywhere.

"This is underground. Some shelter. A bunker. For someone important. For several of them... pink... for a girl... two blue covers... the bunk bed..." he thought. "Two boys... yes, that's surely it. The underground shelter that Seneca had prepared for himself and his family. Nonsense! How could it be for his family when... he has... She gave him... him... Peter and Eir... one boy and one girl... she gave him. And not two boys and one girl..."

"What am I doing!? Thinking about covers and bunk bed! What do I care how many children you gave him? It could have been one or ten! What difference does it make?! You're not mine... and you never will be. And nothing else matters."

Chapter 51

The entire time watching on the monitor the final image that was being aired, in the corner of her eye, Babe saw that the director of the interview and the guy handling the video mixer were keeping to their agreement. She had created a special script – that they must not film when she showed Prince the lace and buttocks, when she bore her breast, when she licked her lips. And to show Prince. And they showed him.

"That wrinkled old lady of his saw how my Prince looked me in front of the entire world, how he leaned towards me, how he was going mad. Pack your stuff you old hag and get out of my palace!"

This deal hadn't been cheap. She had to give the two of them half of the fee she received from the Company sector for fashion accessories.

"It's ok. I don't mind. It wasn't a great expense. That was the best investment that any girl has ever made."

"Miss Babe, do you know what the False Balance was?" Mr. Kaella interrupted Babe's thoughts.

"A False Balance? Of course, Mr. Kaella. Our history teacher made us learn that by heart," Babe smiled.

"Did he? Good teacher. Tell us..."

"A False Balance was a period without serious wars..." Babe hesitated.

"When did this period start?" Mr. Kaella helped her with another question.

"In the second half of the twentieth century, after some war. I guess the Third..."

"The Second. They still counted them back then. Just before the permanent war," said Mr. Kaella.

"And how long did the False Balance period last?

"Less than century, I think..."

"Excellent. What was the False Balance based on?"

"States becoming indebted."

"Bravo, Miss Babe! And how did it end?"

"It burst. The states couldn't even pay the interest. There, I remember everything!"

"Very good, very good!"

"And then there was a war of money..." Babe continued the history lesson.

"Currencies."

"Yes, currencies."

"And what happened next?"

Babe stopped for a moment. Mr. Kaella helped her.

"The collapse..."

"Ah, yes," Babe remembered. "Then came the collapse of the global financial system."

"Bravo. Next..."

"Then protectionism... then isolationism..."

"Wonderful, next... what thin line had been crossed?"

"I know that!" Babe shouted excitedly. "The national social states crossed the thin line and became national socialist states."

"Which led to..."

"To bloody wars..."

"For..."

"In the beginning for raw materials, for natural resources... and over time, with the destruction of the planet's ecosystem, for water, for food, for shelter... for survival."

"The national socialist states..."

"Fell apart."

"Because..."

"Even within them people fought for rivers and lakes that were drying up... they fled from the ocean shores inland..."

"This led to..."

"The great migrations of the hungry and the thirsty..."

"Did hunger and thirst account for the most victims?"

"They didn't..."

"What did?"

"It was skirmishes with nuclear warheads."

"That too. But the greatest number of human lives were taken by..."

"The pandemics!" Babe remembered.

"Because..."

"Because viruses mutated at an accelerated rate due to the climate changes."

"Bravo! Bravo! Bravo, Miss Babe! And what happened to the survivors?"

"I don't know what you mean, Mr. Kaella."

"People..."

"Oh, yes! People melted together"

"They created..."

"New, ad hoc communities around sources of drinking water and fertile land."

"Until…"

"Until your grandfather discovered Cosmic Energy, Mr. Kaella!"

"Miss Babe, you are wonderful, you are a jewel!" the thrilled Mr. Kaella shouted.

Babe, proud and happy, looked at Prince. He was completely stiff in the armchair, with both hands on the armrests, as though he couldn't take it anymore, like he was about to jump up and pounce on her. Having seen this, Babe announced a commercial break.

Chapter 52

The vertical cliff of a tall bare mountain reflected the hot sunrays like a mirror. That was until its two halves parted and withdrew into the flanks. This revealed the secret hangar of Erivan's squads. A silver airplane took off from within the mountain.

This stolen Non-Consumer airplane was piloted by Zodiac, the leader of Z Squad, towards the nearby Capital City. He had on several occasions fired missiles at cars on the shooting range in the desert, and determined that this Non-Consumer airplane could not guarantee the destruction of such a small target with only one rocket. The aircraft's other limitation was that it could carry only four missiles. This is why he and Erivan decided that Zodiac would attack the president's car on Short Street.

This had several advantages. First of all, Alpha's two escort vehicles and four motorcycles would be just alongside the presidential limo, because Erivan told them that the attack would be carried out later, on Cypress Avenue. And that they should only then increase their distance. And not before this avenue, so as not to raise suspicion. This meant that with four missiles Zodiac would surely manage to destroy all the cars and motorcycles. Secondly, the people waving flags will also be alongside the motorcade, which guaranteed a maximal number of casualties per rocket.

"That Erivan really knows how to get the maximum out of every situation," Zodiac thought. "He's truly a top-notch strategist. And on the other hand, it's no surprise. I would be too, if I were vice president of the State and head of the Inspectorate.
"Erivan says that what pleases him most of all is that he will finally be rid of A Squad. The Repentant - that's how he calls them. But not because they have done something that they have repented, but because he regretted recruiting them. And then he removed such repentant from other squads and assigned them to guard the presidents. How did he put it at the meeting. 'You can imagine what the rest are like, if Alpha is their leader,' he said.

117

"Ah, we did laugh... except the Grasshopper. I mean really, what's up with him? There hasn't any word of him in a long time. Is he...? I'm sure he is. Erivan is preparing him for the conquest of Megapolis. Wow... that's not good. We'll all be placed under the Grasshopper's command. Perhaps that's not... It's... What else could it be? We're screwed... if you make any mistake... But... what can I do? Whatever will be will be. It's war. When I clear this Short Street, I'll eject, my guys will destroy the plane, and then everyone back to Erivan's residence. And later... wherever he sends us. That's what this job is like."

Chapter 53

When the jingle for the commercial break rang out over the speaker, Mr. Kaella waved to Prince and nodded towards the toilet.

"Of course, father. You've really held yourself heroically," said Prince, while lifting his father from the armchair.

"Yes, I have… but now I have to… you know, not only… prostate but also digestion… we'll be late for…"

"Don't worry, father. We'll cut the interview short. You take all the time that you need.. I'll talk to Miss Babe."

"Alright, son…"

Prince nodded to one of the bodyguards. "Take my father to the toilet." He ordered the other bodyguard to stay and signaled with a glance towards the cameraman who was the only one that didn't go out for the break, and was looking out through the huge portholes onto the submerged city.

The body threw out the terrified cameraman into the hallway, gripping his neck with iron fingers.

"Stay at the door and let me know when my father comes out of the bathroom," Prince ordered.

"I understand, Mr. Kaella," responded the burly lad, and he stood in front of the door which could not close completely because of the cables. He faced the hallway.

Babe didn't get compliments from Prince about her thorough knowledge of history, because Prince immediately pounced on her, trying, as he had promised himself, to spread that gap in the middle of her lips. He grabbed her firmly with one hand around the waste and thrust his other hand under her jacket. In shock, Babe pulled her head back and held his hand in such a way that Prince's fingers only managed to knead her breast only through the jacket.

"Prince, what's with you? Do you want to mess up my makeup?"

Prince realized that Babe was right. He could not kiss her before the end of the interview.

"Alright, I'm sorry. I was wrong. But why don't you let me…" he was still struggling with Babe, who was gripping her lapels tightly with both hands.

"Why don't I let you?" Babe whispered passionately. "What do you think – that I'm made of stone? That I don't want you?"

"Well then let me…" Prince released his grip around her waste slightly, intoxicated by her words.

Babe took advantage of the moment, broke free from him and ran to the large window.

"How can I let you," she said to him while he approached her with a heavy step and even heavier breathing. "If I feel your hands on my breasts, my back, my nails, behind… down… everywhere, all over me… how will I finish the interview with your father? How? Prince… my Prince… I'm already going mad… when I just think of your hands, your body…" Babe was on the verge of bursting into tears.

Prince approached her and stopped with his hand by his sides. He looked at her with a serious gaze. And Babe was trembling, looking at him with eyes wide open, with the terrified gaze of a doe.

"From now on you're only mine," Prince told her in a firm voice.

Babe quickly nodded her head in compliance.

"I need such a wife. A Prince needs a Princess."

"My Prince…" Babe whispered.

"To fight together, to create together… to give me strength when I am tired…"

"I will, I will, my Prince… Always by your side… always…"

"To win together… to be one body, one soul…"

"Yes, yes… one soul… my Prince… on a white horse."

Being sensitive as she was, Babe completely surrendered to her emotions when her Prince uttered the word "soul". She took his hand into her tender palms.

"Your State needs you, Princess. Even you don't know what difficult times are approaching. To stand by my side during them, to be the model, the ideal for Consumers throughout the world. My Princess, we face a great clash with the Non-Consumers," the determined ruler gave away the greatest state secret to his heart's desire. "That is why I need you. To be my flag, my standard…"

"I will, my Prince, I'll be it… We'll defeat them… I can see it clearly…" Babe raised her visionary gaze towards the ceiling of the submarine.

Chapter 54

Mr. Kaella sat on the toilet. He had urinated, that was alright, but number two was somehow a problem. He wasn't pushing much. He actually welcomed a slightly longer break on the can to calmly prepare for the declaration of war.

"This isn't so easy now," Mr. Kaella thought. "To speak to the camera as though I didn't know anything... as though I didn't know that they would be informing the director that the Xings have been killed, that he would burst into the salon and whisper that to me on camera... And then for me, in shock, to get up out of the armchair and declare war. I'm not... some actor. I need time... to be off camera... for at least a few minute, before he bursts in. To prepare in peace for the declaration."

"I'll tell Babe to let Prince talks about the Balance... Hey, wait a minute... It wasn't my son who created the Balance. It was me. Only me. That is how it must go down in history. Well... my Prince did help a little with the Euthanasias. And he instated mandatory medical checkups and restored the Balance. Yes, he did... That's all true. But those are the details, not the principle, not the philosophy... Let Prince talk about his work, about the poleis and the ice age... and those things... And I'll talk about the Balance even longer, in even greater detail, in the next interview. This today felt really good. From now on I'm going to have frequent interviews with Babe. What a great girl. What intelligence.
"What did she ask Prince? Nothing. That little thing at the beginning. Purely out of courtesy. She knows precisely who is still in charge. She admires me. She understands everything. It's clear to her how great I am. And I'm still not for the scarp yard. No, no. I'm going to live for some time. I'll win this war. History will remember me as the ruler who eradicated the last Non-Consumer. And I will eradicate them! You don't want to spend, do you? But you want water, food and energy, you nits? Well that won't do, you monsters! That won't do!"

"No... I can't get this excited... I can't look like this when I declare war. I have to be calm, dignified... Just a little dark, somber... How did Erivan put it? I have to look sinister. For the Non-Consumers to be terrified when they see me. That's it, of course! Sinister! Sinister!"

"Sinister!" shouted Mr. Kaella and pushed.
As though the Inspectorate drums and bugles were playing a magnificent march, the toilet bowl rumbled with the sounds produced by Mr. Kaella's digestive tract, calling to arms!

Chapter 55

"What do you see?" the slightly surprised Prince asked.

"I see you..." Babe described the scene before her, " somehow magnificent... on a white horse tearing through the Non-Consumer ranks..."

"And? What else do you see, my Princess?" Prince asked excitedly.

"In your right hand you're holding a razor-sharp saber..."

"And?"

"In broad, strong swings you're cutting down the Non-Consumers... I see them... I see them falling... like wheat before the scythe..."

"I'm cutting, I'm cutting... you bet!" Prince was excited.

"And I am in your lap, your Princess, your flag..."

"That's right... that's right..."

"And you... while you're cutting them down... Only you can do it, my Prince..."

"What?"

"At the same time, with your other hand," said Babe, gazing up towards the ceiling, raising Prince's hand towards the lapel of her jacket and placing his hand on her breast "at the same time you are gently fondling your Princess' bosom."

Prince completely lost it. He tried to be gentle, like in her description, but he failed. And how could he not be when he felt that little Earth hanging from Babe's nipple. He squeezed Babe's breast forcefully, wildly, as though it was the hand in which he held the razor-sharp saber.

"Hey, Prince, that's not exactly gentle," Babe laughed.

"It's not, it's not... and you are yet to see... Taunting me the entire time... driving me mad... Driving me mad!!!"

"Driving you mad?" asked Babe, suddenly dropping her hand to his pants.

Prince's eyes opened wide when she squeezed his crotch.

"You have yet to feel what it's like to be driven mad. This is nothing. I'm just starting to drive you mad," she whispered in his ear, while continuously opening and closing her hand.

"Yes, yes... that's what I want... what I need..." Prince grunted, while his hand started going up Babe's skirt.

Babe suddenly pushed him away with both hands, so forcefully that Prince staggered.
"You can't touch that, Mr. Prince."
"What do you mean 'I can't'? Why can't I?" he almost shouted, rushing her again.
Babe stepped back and laughed.
"You can, of course you can, my Prince... you can do everything... but only when I want it."
"And you don't want to now?" Prince froze.
"Not now. I want it to be nice for you..."
"We'll its nice..."
"Even nicer... much nicer..."
"Ah, I know... You want in the limo. Alright, I'll order a limo for the two of us. Father can go back by himself."
"Well..." Babe laughed, "didn't you promise me dinner? Just the two of us, with candles?"
"I did, I did... but I can't wait anymore."
"Well you'll have to. You'll go back with your father, just as you came. And you'll wait for me at the restaurant. I have to prepare for you."
"What do you mean 'prepare'? You can't get any prettier."
"I will be. And let me tell you what I'll look like. And you can imagine it until dinner. Long dress, blue-black, sliding behind me..."
"I'm going to die..."
"Bare back, two strips tied together across my breasts..."
"You're killing me..."

Babe came around behind him, pressed her bosom against his back and rubbed his crotch with both hand. She whispered to him
"And those two strips..."
"Yes?"
"Don't worry... they aren't very wide... just covering the nipples and the little Earths."
"Aaaah!"
"And the slit on the dress..."
"Yes?"
"High above my hip..."
"No..."
"So that it's clear to you that I'm completely naked underneath the dress."
"Naked! Aaaaah!"

While he had been screaming Prince had once again tried to get his hand up her skirt again. And Babe pushed him away once more.

"Why don't you give it up? I just wanted a touch, to see whether you're naked now too."

"Nonsense! What were you thinking? I'm doing an interview with you and your father, and not..."

"Alright, alright... Why do you have to get angry immediately?"

The bodyguard turned around and said
"Sir, your father is coming."

Babe went to the couch. Prince ran up to her and tried to unbutton her jacket.

"What are you doing?" Babe screamed.

"I have to see them. At least that... please." Prince panted.

"I would like to show you my breasts. I was thinking about it. I really was. But I can't."

"Why?" Prince was surprised.

"Because you'd see my bellybutton."

"Ah, the bellybutton... I'll drill it with my tongue... drill it..."

"I'm afraid you won't be able to."

"Why? Does it too have a little Earth?"

"Not a little Earth. Something else... it's not important..."

"What else? What?!"

"Something just for you. Something that belongs only to you, my Prince."

"Tell me, don't torture me anymore. What is that which is just mine?"

"I won't tell you. I want you to see."

"But when? When will I see it?"

"Now," said Babe, turning from Prince and walking with her hands held out, like a caring daughter-in-law, to Mr. Kaella, who was at that moment entering the submarine salon.

Chapter 56

When he saw that Prince had sat down in his armchair, Mr. Kaella whispered to Babe, who was standing next to him "Miss Babe, you know, I'm a little tired. I will talk about the Balance in another interview. Here, next week, for example. You now talk to my son…"

Babe was aghast. "What's with you, old man?" she thought in panic. "How can I talk to Prince?! I have to show him something! Do you want a daughter-in-law like this or not?!"

"That won't do, Mr. Kaella," Babe said resolutely. "This is your interview. The viewers want to hear you. Only you, Mr. Kaella."
"I know that… I'm aware… but…"
"This is what we'll do, Mr. Kaella. I believe that you are already tired. But you have a written text about the Balance."
"Yes, I do…"
"We'll put it up on the teleprompter. You can look at the camera, the text will appear, and you will read it. Without any burden or too much thought. And I won't ask you anything. Do you agree?
"Alright… But next week a new interview. I want to explain everything in greater detail. This was too short."
"Of course, Mr. Kaella. We have received countless consumer messages during the show; people are begging you for more interviews."
"Oh? Is that true, Miss Babe?"
"Yes, it's true," Babe responded briefly and ran to the control room to organize the teleprompter.

"But all that wasn't enough," Mr. Kaella read his text about the Balance, while looking at the camera. "The state didn't have enough revenue for carrying out its most basic functions. I increased the taxes and therefore filled the state coffers, but I also increased the poverty of both the people and the sectors of the Company. People had less money to spend. This is why the sectors' profits dropped. In order to salvage their profits the sectors laid people off. Those that hadn't been laid off worked all day long for the same salary, so that they too would not lose their jobs. This is how the sectors reduced costs and increased productivity. Those that had been laid off did not have money to spend, and those that still worked didn't spend it, but saved it for a rainy day. Therefore the cost-cutting did not help the sectors much, because their revenue dropped faster than their expenses. This is why profits waned. And that is why I could collect fewer taxes. This created a vicious circle."

Chapter 57

Babe again sat at the edge of the couch, next to Mr. Kaella, but her body faced Prince, and she clenched her knees. This humble position was the complete opposite of the great lust that she felt throughout her body. She wasn't at all listening to Mr. Kaella. She was overjoyed, because she had rid herself of that last fear.

No,... not fear, certainly not fear. She wasn't in fact afraid of it... she wasn't. "Why would I be afraid of something that isn't at all important?" Babe seriously contemplated. "Alright, it's true that it isn't important, but it also isn't insignificant. Actually, it is secondary. That's it. That's the right expression. Secondary."

And she wasn't afraid of secondary things. Sometimes, recently, when she would think about it she would just get a little worried. She was a little anxious that she might face the same fate as the secretary of the executive producer of her media company, Capital City TV.

That secretary told Babe that while she was once in the producer's office taking his instructions, he suddenly bent her over his desk, pulled up her skirt and pulled her panties down her legs. While bent over the desk, she listened to the producer unbuckle his belt and drop his pants. When she was pinned down on the desk by the producer's big belly, she realized that he was having trouble getting close enough. Even though she wanted to, she did not come to his aid, because her panties prevented her. However, after a while she heard his chugging, which she thought was a little suspicious. To eliminate any suspicion she asked

"Sir, is it in?"

"It is... it is..." the producer wheezed.

That secretary was a smart girl. Babe also appreciated her. The same moment she started moving her hips and said

"Oh, how big it is!"

"Some of our sectors were already reporting losses," Mr. Kaella read his text on the Balance. "There was a growing number of unemployed people. And what did that mean? That I had to give them energy, food, water, apartments, pharmaceuticals... for free? Well that wasn't possible.

"Then at one moment I realized ... that was the moment of my enlightenment, that I have to create the Balance. This meant that every person must be employed and earn enough to pay all the expenses and buy as many shares as possible, for the greatest possible extension of life.

"And how could we achieve this? It was simple. The produced goods and offered services had to be completely spent in a given period of time, so that production and services would continue uninterrupted. That way people would have constant jobs and enough income. This meant that the basic driver of our most perfect and final form of capitalism is constant consumption.

"The modern information systems have calculated for each type of goods and services the time after which the old must be destroyed in order to produce anew. Today we call that seasons. For clothing this is three months, as we know, two years for cars, seven for apartments, for household appliances..."

"No, no... I won't share her fate!" Babe's soul cried out. "My hand wasn't empty! On the contrary! There is something between my Prince's legs. There is, there is... and that is why you will now see what I promised, my Prince. That thing on my bellybutton!"

Babe unbuttoned the lower button on her jacket and looked at Prince, whose entire body trembled in the armchair.

Chapter 58

Pascal returned to the bathroom. As a well-behaved man he closed the door behind him so that he could urinate, even though he was alone in the suite. While he was washing his hands, he realized that the soaps, gels, shampoos, toothpaste which were arranged in a large box on the dresser – were contemporary. From this season.

"Come on, Pascal," he forced himself. "Come on, play detective. Did you see how you forgot about her for a moment at least, while you were trying to guess where you were. It hurt less, at least for a moment. Come on... you see that the soaps are new. What can you deduce from that, Pascal?"

"I conclude that this apartment was prepared for me by someone," Pascal spoke to himself. He pretended that he was not alone and strived for the other person not to notice that he was only thinking about her.

"Excellent," said the imaginary person and asked "And what do you think, who prepared it, Pascal?"

"What do you mean 'who'? Seneca and Raul."

"Is that right? Seneca and Raul? And where did they get this shelter?" said the counterpart curiously.

"Raul certainly doesn't have it," Pascal answered obediently. "And Seneca... why wouldn't the mayor of Megapolis have a shelter for him and his family? One of the most important functions in the State," Pascal nodded to himself in the mirror.

"Aha! And you're saying that he built it a long time ago?" the counterpart still wasn't pleased with the response.

"Yes. At least ten years, maybe even more."

"Aha! For himself and his wife – the bedroom, one room for the daughter and one for the two sons. Seneca now has one son, and ten years ago or more Senece didn't have any children. Nor was he married."

"He didn't have any children, he wasn't even married. You weren't married either! Where was I then?! What was I doing at the time?!

Why didn't I rush to Megapolis and steal you from your parents' house?! Why?!!!"

Chapter 59

"The Balance in our society functions flawlessly," said Mr. Kaella, without taking his eyes off the text which appeared on the teleprompter. "And that is no accident. This is in accordance with the essence of the human being. This is how Mother Nature created us. As Consumers. We live by consuming air, water, food, energy. When we stop consuming, we are dead... we are no more. Consumption, that is life itself. We were created in order to consume. This is the only purpose of existence of every single person and mankind as a whole.

"The consumer is the center, the foundation of the universe. We are born, study, we work, create, only in order to discover new objects of consumption. Scientists and engineers are constantly working on this. Artists of all kinds create works of art so that people would consume them. When I realized that, I immediately cut all funding for further space exploration."

Babe's bellybutton was covered by a crown made of real gold. From it descended a gold chain, which ended in a fluorescent green broken arrow, like a bolt of lightning. This arrow was the emblem of Kaella's Company and represented a ray of cosmic energy traveling towards the Earth. The arrow pointed downward.

Prince could no longer control himself. "A crown! That's me! That is why you say that it is only mine... you magnificent woman! No one understands who I am! Only you do! And my beam, my lightning, my deadly arrow!" he thought.

"Look, look at your crown and your lightning... look, Prince!" Babe told prince with her fiery stare. "And tonight you will look at my crown! I told you that I would have a backless dress, but what I didn't tell you is what will be on my back. What is already tattooed on it. Something that is only mine. Something that is me! A huge gold crown with rubies. The crown of the Princess of the Planet Earth!"

Chapter 60

"Pascal, hey, Pascal, stop that already! You're a detective. Have you forgotten?" Pascal shouted at himself.

"Yes. I'm a detective. Where were we?"

Pascal didn't move from the mirror, as though his image was the counterpart forcing him to investigate.

"Think, Pascal. Who among the important individuals in the state, among the persons who could build themselves such a shelter, who has three children. Two boys and a girl?"

"Well, I understand what you're trying to say, OK... President Xing has two children..."

"That's right," the counterpart from the mirror responded.

"Erivan is alone. He doesn't have anyone. In the top of the Inspectorate..."

"Leave the top of the Inspectorate. Erivan is the top of the Inspectorate."

"Yes... In the Company... by sectors..."

"Leave the sectors. Who is the Company, Pascal?"

"Kaella... he only has Prince... Well of course! Prince has two boys and a girl. But they are students. They don't need pink covers... the bunk beds, that I understand, the rooms are small... but the light blue covers for adult men..."

Pascal turned around and once again took a look at the bathroom accessories... the tiles...

"But ten... fifteen... twenty years ago, Prince's children were little. And it's... it's Prince Kaella's shelter!"

"It can't be... Raul and Seneca would not hand me over to Prince. Perhaps Seneca, if he was scared... but if he was in cahoots with Prince all this time, if it was all just a ploy, pretend... if they waited for the right moment before the elections... to instill fear."

"No, no... Raul injected me in the arm. Raul would never be on their side. That's for sure. Don't even think about that..."

"Oh my God, Prince killed them! He killed both Raul and Seneca! And he abducted me from them! And now I'm in his shelter... beneath the palace... in Capital City. That's got to be it. I slept through the flight to Capital City. And Prince is holding me. He has some plans for me… Raul! My Friend! My best and only friend! And your people… and our people… you're all dead! All of you!"

Pascal covered his face with his hands and trembled. "And you Seneca. You are dead because of me too. Because of me you too lost your life."

Pascal opened his eyes wide and screamed. He ran out of the bathroom, ran to the exit, the locked door, and pounded on it with his fists and feet, screaming

"Don't you dare touch her, you scoundrels! Don't you dare touch her! Or even look at her! Not even the children! I'll kill you! I'll kill you all! All of you!!!"

Chapter 61

"Why would I spend money on space exploration?" Mr. Kaella wondered in front of the viewers. "It could have paid off if we knew that in some remote corner we would find consumers similar to us. Because we could sell our products and service to them and make a hefty profit.

"But they don't exist. It's only us. What do I care if there is water on some planet out there? Like, life is possible. Let that life transform itself into a consumer, my buyer. Then we can talk."

"You're trembling, my Prince... you'd rush me... take off my jacket... raise my skirt... and I would tuck my hand into your pants..."
Babe was losing control of herself, which was uncharacteristic for her. Her case was the most striking evidence that the sense of power, as the strongest aphrodisiac, acts equally in both directions, on males and females alike.

"My arrow, my lightning... from my crown... from me... from my soul..." Prince's eyes were pinned to Babe's bellybutton. "You aimed the arrow downward... towards your... towards her... That's what you meant! That she is only mine... your intimate thing... You... you are only mine, Princess!!!"

"I cannot stand it any longer either, Prince, I can't... I need you immediately... now. Call a limousine for the two of us... call.... And do you know what I'll do to you? I'll wrap myself around you. I'll squeeze you both with mu hands and legs. And I won't let you go until you pour the last drop of your semen into me, Prince Kaella! And I'll bear you a son! A true Kaella! Not only a Prince of Earth, but emperor of the entire Universe. And my blood will rule this world for a million years! Just watch, Prince... Watch!"

Babe suddenly spread her legs. Prince did not bend forward. An invisible force threw him back into the armchair. He saw what his fluorescent lightning was pointing at.

A gold chain was intertwined with the black threads of Babe's lace thong. Hanging on it was a gold coin, which Babe had commissioned from a goldsmith, in the greatest secrecy. Engraved on the gold coin was a profile of Prince Kaella, crowned with a laurel.

*****

The only state institution for which Prince Kaella did not limit the budget was the Organization for the Protection of the State and the Constitutional Order. The Organization had been formed and was personally commanded by Erivan. It was made up of squads labeled with letters.
The organization was popularly called Erivan's squads, and its members – squires.

Charlie, the leader of C Squad, which Erivan had assigned to protect Mr. Kaella and his son Prince at this decisive, historic moment, put his finger on the Torpedo icon on the dashboard of his submarine. He then chose the Fire command.

*****

Any man would be envious of Prince Kaella on such a death. He died looking at his highness basking in Babe's pubic mound.

Chapter 62

The energy system in space consisted of 96 cosmic energy collectors and the Command. The collectors were actually platforms placed in 12 orbits around Earth. There were 8 collectors in each orbit.

Each collector had 36 so-called cannons. The cannons sent narrow, precise beams of accumulated cosmic energy, which charged the cosmic power plants on Earth. The received cosmic energy was transformed into electrical energy at the power plants. There were no more other energy sources.

The collectors were not geostationary. Each collector could change its position by switching on its engines. In addition to this it could also change the direction of each of its 36 beams. This way the cosmic energy beams covered every inch of the Earth's surface.

There were no human crews on the collectors. They were operated remotely, from the Command Platform, which was simply called the Command. The Command crew consisted of top experts and security.

The Grasshopper was on a spaceship, on his way to the Command, together with five hand-picked members of Erivan's squads.

Chapter 63

Screens across the planet Earth went dark and silent. But for less than a minute. After that they displayed the image from a camera mounted on a crane on Short Street. The unpleasant silence was interrupted by the television commentator of the broadcast of President Xing's last election speech.

"Dear viewers, we have technical problems with the reception of the signal from Mr. Kaella's submarine. While we are waiting to reestablish the connection and the continuation of the interview, let's take a look at how Consumers are greeting President Xing."

The motorcade was just entering Short Street. At the moment when the presidential car passed by fence beyond which pupils from the fifth and eighth grade were waving Earth flags, the screens across the planet again went dark and silent.

"Horrific crime! Heinous!" shouted the shocked anchor from the studio of Capital City TV, after several minutes of darkness. "An assassination has been carried out against President Xing! Here's the footage from our helicopter!"

Short Street was no more. In its place, beneath a cloud of smoke, was a deep crater. In some places, where the wind had cleared the dust, pieces of the surrounding buildings could be seen scattered at the bottom of the crater.

The footage from the Capital City TV helicopter suddenly disappeared, and the screens displayed the text "We are awaiting an address from President Erivan."

Chapter 64

Erivan stood in a black suit, black shirt and black tie, perfectly tailored to his demanding figure. There were no state emblems around him, nor was there any indication of where he was located. Only he was illuminated, and around him was darkness.

Erivan was silent while the camera slowly zoomed in on his bust, until it completely filled the screens. Not a single muscle on his face had moved. Only his tight lips and ironclad eyes reflected the unfaltering determination of the new ruler of the world.

"Less than fifteen minutes ago the Non-Consumers carried out a terrorist attack and killed out former President Xing and his entire family..." he said drearily. Then he paused, looked at the floor, sighed deeply, raised his eyes to the camera, now filled with pain and continued "at the same moment, during the interview, the Non-Consumers also slew Mr. Kaella and his son Prince." Erivan paused, allowing people to accept this horrific news. "On behalf of the State and from me personally, I would like to express the deepest condolences to the Kaella family."

The pain disappeared from Erivan's eyes, giving in to deep and sincere hatred. "The State of Earth declares war on the Non-Consumers," he said menacingly and continued "The State is taking over ownership and management of the Association of Companies. After the war the shares will be returned to the Consumers. They will also be given the stakes previously owned by the Non-Consumers. All civilian courts are suspended and martial law is introduced, enforced by the Inspectorate courts. There is only one punishment for the Non-Consumers: death."

The camera zoomed out. The spotlight on Erivan slowly grew fainter. His silhouette faded into darkness.

Part II: The War

"You have no right to be mad at me, Dorika," Gloria told her colleague and friend. The two of them had sat down alone, Gloria by the window and Dorika next to her, to calmly discuss the newly-arisen problem.

Dorika was silent, staring at the back of the seat in front of her.

"You called me while I was waiting for you at the club and said that you weren't feeling well, that you had a migraine and that you had to go to bed immediately. Isn't that right?"

Dorika didn't answer.

"Isn't that right, I asked you!"

"Yes."

"There, you see."

"But that's not an excuse," Dorika softened up and looked at Gloria. "This thing with Svetlana was so important that you should have woken me up. I would have taken another pill for my head and..."

"I know..."

"Well if you know, why didn't you wake me up?"

"Because... but not a word to anyone!"

"You saw Pascal too?!"

"No... it has nothing to do with them..."

"So?"

"Promise me that you won't tell a soul."

"I promise. Tell me already!"

"Last night, when you said that you wouldn't be coming to the club, I paid for my drink and started for the exit. What was I going to do there by myself, right?"

"And?"

"So I'm already nearing the door when I hear... it was noisy, loud music... you know how it gets there..."

"What did you hear?"

"Well... I wasn't at all sure in that noise. I thought that I had imagined it. I didn't even turn around..."

"OK, so?"

"And then, a second time, much louder. I heard someone shout 'Gloria! Gloria!', and I turned around..."

"Who was it?"

"A young man."

"A young man! Really? Was he handsome?"

"Very handsome"

"Wow, tell me more! How did he approach you? How did you get introduced?"

"Well... we didn't get introduced."

"I don't get it. How didn't you get introduced? Why then did he call out to you?"

"You don't get it, Dorika. He called me by my name. There was no need for us to get introduced."

"You know him?"

"You know him too."

"I know him too. Where do we know him from? What are you trying to tell me, Gloria? He isn't one of our guys, is he?"

"You promised that you wouldn't..."

"Yes, I did! Who?"

"Guess!"

"Guess?... alright. You say he's handsome?"

"No."

"What do you mean 'no'? You said..."

"I said 'very handsome'."

"Could it be...?"

"Yes, yes!"

"Habib!"

"Yes, him!"

"Wow, Gloria! Tell me, tell me everything! So you turn around and you see Habib calling you! My leg would have turned to jelly."

"What do you think, that mine didn't?"

"Come on... tell me..."

"I didn't see who he was with at the club. He never left my side. Whoever he was with didn't interest him anymore."

"You lucky girl!"

"We danced, we talked..."

"What did you talk about..."

"Nothing much... about our campaign, our work... it was too loud in there. And I was keeping a distance, like between coworkers."

"Why?"

"What do you mean 'why'? Well you can't immediately show how much you like him. The guy has to work a little."

"Wow, you know everything. Lucky you."

"I'll advise you, when you find a guy."

"A guy? Me? I'll never find a guy. And where would I find one? We work all day long."

"You'll find one, you'll find one. Now, when Pascal becomes president, we'll work less, get good salaries, buy only the most beautiful things… guys are going to be all over you."

"Eh… you think?"

"Absolutely! You bet… this is what I wanted to tell you. It was because of him that I didn't wake you when Svetlana cried."

"Because of Habib?"

"Yup. I told you. I pretended not to be interested in him. And I saw, I know how to recognize this, that he was really into me. From before, you get it? Not only last night at the club."

"Really?"

"Really. I can read men between the lines. And when we went back to the hotel I immediately told him good night, and went to our room. I was certain that he wouldn't resist and that he'd knock on our door, and take me down to the bar for a drink, and then he'd tell me that he's liked me for a long time…"

"Aw, Gloria… and what would you have told him?"

"I would have said that now, ahead of the elections, really wasn't the time for such talks."

"Would you, really?"

"I would. But only in the beginning, when he first mentioned it. So that he would have to repeat it, to explain why he likes me. To tell me what my hair is like, what my eyes are like, that he can't sleep… that he's constantly thinking of me."

"And what if he didn't repeat it? What if he accepted what you said and actually waited until the elections?"

"He'll repeat it, he'll repeat it. And if he doesn't, then I would pout until he said again that he likes me. You can't really plan it like that. You have to feel the moment, and then either be silent or smile or pout. As necessary."

"I wouldn't know how to. I'd immediately tell him how handsome he is."

"I know, but… this is what I want to say to you. That is why I didn't wake you. Last night when I entered our room, I stood fully dressed near the door for a few minutes. And then I quickly changed, put on my nightgown and lay in bed. So that when I opened the door he would see me in my nightgown. So that he didn't think that I was waiting for him."

"You're really clever. You think of everything."

"You have to, Dorika. Of course, I didn't take off my makeup. Who would put makeup on again? Men really don't get those things."

"Of course."

"So I'm lying there… and I hear Svetlana and all that. And after that I still hoped and waited for him… And that's why I didn't wake you, you get it?"

"I get it."

"So you're no longer angry?"

"I'm not. Actually, I am! Why didn't you tell me this morning about Svetlana?"

"This morning? What's with you, Dorika? We were all in panic. Raul banged on everyone's door and shouted 'Get up! Pack! We're leaving Megapolis!'"

"Yes, that's right."

"I remembered Svetlana only after the plane had taken off."

"What are the two of you doing here all alone?" asked Habib, a member of Liam's team, standing behind Gloria and Dorika.

Chapter 66

Pascal calmed down and stopped shouting and pounding on the door. "I cannot save her and the children this way. By giving away that I'm awake."

He turned off all the lights and closed all the doors in this underground apartment of his. He stood in the narrow corridor with his back to the wall.

"I'll wait for someone to come in, one of Prince's bodyguards. He'll go towards the bedroom door. Probably with a raised hand and holding a gun. And he won't see me in the dark. Then I'll jump him and take his gun. I'll run outside, shooting at anyone who is with him, whoever is waiting for him. I just have to make sure not to kill all of them. I have to force at least one of them to tell me where she is. And where the children are."

"'If they are alive'? They are alive! They are alive!!! I know it! Today I stood at the hotel window and they didn't shoot at me. They also didn't kill me now. Perhaps they still haven't killed Seneca or Raul. They're waiting for something. I'm sure they're waiting for the elections. I'm sure! To kill us all on the day before the elections, for example. And for the people to be afraid and to feel only fear. So that they don't have time for anger and for an uprising. And then they cancel the elections and declared a state of emergency. Or something like that.

"They're alive! I'm sure they're alive! I'm Kaella's greatest enemy. He wouldn't kill others before he killed me," Pascal calmed himself, while lying in wait.

Chapter 67

"We're not here all alone…" stuttered Dorika, when she and Gloria turned suddenly towards Habib in surprise.

"Why are you eavesdropping on our conversation, Habib?!" Gloria erupted. "That's very rude!"

"I wasn't eavesdropping. I was dozing on the seat in the back, and I felt like a stroll… and then I saw… the two of you… alone here…"

"Nonsense!" said Gloria and turned away from Habib.

"May I sit with you a bit?" Habib asked, already sitting down next to Dorika.

"Of course…" Dorika uttered.

"Didn't you say you wanted to have a stroll?" Gloria asked Habib crossly, looking straight in front of her.

"I just wanted to stretch my legs…"

"So stretch them."

"I've already stretched them."

Gloria fell silent and looked out the window.

"So, Dorika, you're really angry with Gloria, because of Svetlana," Habib laughed.

"No… that was just for a moment. We made up immediately."

"Aha. That's nice, such a friendship."

"It is."

"Do you also leave guys as often as your friend?"

"Me? Well, I… no…" Dorika stuttered.

"And that's very nice of you. And Gloria…"

"Gloria – what?" shouted Gloria. "I intentionally made that up in order to convince Raul that Svetlana didn't leave Pascal. If you can't understand that than we have nothing to talk about."

"We do, we do… about many things."

"Such as?"

"Such as how is it that you heard Svetlana in the first place?"

"I'm not deaf."

"Neither is Dorika, are you Dorika?"

"No, I'm not, but I was asleep."

"Aha. And you Gloria, you hadn't gone to sleep?"

"I was reading something, if you're so interested."

"I'm interested, I'm interested... I'm very interested..."

"Excuse me," said Dorika. "I have to get something to Margot... you know, Gloria, what she asked me for... that list..."

"Ah, that... yes..." Gloria was relieved because Dorika understood that she should leave.

"Habib, please, just a little... so I can pass."

"Here you are, Dorika." Habib got up from his seat.

Chapter 68

At that moment Raul was napping in his seat. The telephone in the inside pocket of his jacket vibrated twice and fell silent.

"Who's calling me now?" wondered Raul. He didn't feel like talking on the phone. This nap was doing him well, this semi-sleep after all the stress that he had been under that day. "And everything ended well. The people are calm... and they are happy, because of all that support for Pascal. They are proud... I see, how proud they are... there... there... and they deserve it..."

"But that's not my telephone... mine is at my waist... ah, yes... it's Pascal's. Forgive me, my friend... I know that you'll forgive your friend Raul. I even stole your telephone today... So that Kaella, even if he can locate it... he isn't all-powerful... thinks that you are with us. It doesn't matter... some journalist got a hold of your number, Pascal, and he's being a drag.

"Wait, wait... that's not your telephone. I gave it to Margot... and she placed it in her bag... Yes, I saw her, when she put it in..."

Raul rose up suddenly in his seat and opened his eyes. "Seneca's telephone! With the secure line. Raul, remember what Seneca said when you were going into that tube! He'll call me only in the event of an emergency. Pascal! What has happened?!" Raul panicked.

"Seneca didn't betray him! He didn't! Why would he call me if he did?

"Pascal, you must be causing problems! You're awake and you want to into the street. To be killed. Like, you'll be more useful dead than alive. Tell that to someone else. That won't fly with your friend Raul. But, you were scared today, my poet, so you think that the Kaellas will calm down if they kill you and that they won't take revenge on the people. You can't stand people suffering because of you.

"It's not suffering, Pascal. There's been enough suffering. An entire century. The struggle for freedom is starting. And the people need you, alive. Not just as a symbol. Not as an idea in people's minds, which will be passed on for generations, and which will topple the Kaellas through nonviolent resistance.

"You're wrong, my friend. When people such as yourself disappear, then those around them craving power ride that wave and pervert the idea, transform it into the opposite. They become the same or even worse than those they were fighting against.

"You tried to trick me this morning that Svetlana left you. The secretaries laughed at me. Seneca will put you on the telephone and you'll pay for that, Pascal." Raul looked at his watch.

"Hurry up, Raul. You're getting chatty... What did Seneca say? First two vibrations, and then exactly five minutes later – a call. To give me time to find privacy, to get away from the staff. Where can I be alone? The toilet is... I can't go through the salon, people will get suspicious.

"I'll go to the back, to the tail of the airplane... Hurry up, Raul. The man's going to call."

Raul got up and walked towards the toilet in order to take the Mayor's call and to make it clear to Pascal that he should stop causing problems.

"If need be I'll also put Margot and Liam... and Jagdish on the telephone... The entire staff, each and every one of them... so that they can tell him the same."

Chapter 69

"I thought we were going to have another drink at the bar, Gloria," said Habib, sitting down next to her. "To talk a bit more."

"About what? About work? Like at the club? I've really had enough talk about work."

"No, no... it was noisy there, you can't talk properly."

"Then about what?"

"About you, Gloria... about us."

"Why then didn't you invite me for a drink?"

Habib waited for Raul to pass by them and then said

"How could I when you immediately ran for the elevator? And while you were running... that hair of yours..."

"You could have gone after me, you know where my room is."

"I wanted to... but you are not alone in the room."

"And you visit girls only when they are alone in their rooms, Habib? You can only dream about that. I'm not that kind of girl."

"No, no... I didn't want to wake up Dorika. It wouldn't be right."

"If you really wanted to talk to me, you wouldn't have even considered of. But you obviously didn't."

"I did, Gloria... I didn't sleep a wink all night..."

"Why?"

"I was only thinking of you. Do you ever think of me?"

"Habib, this isn't the time for such talks. The elections are coming soon..."

*****

When he had finished the conversation with Mayor Seneca in the airplane's toilet, Raul placed the secure telephone on the sink, looked at himself in the mirror, turned on the tap, wet his palms and briskly passed them across his face.

"I'll tell Liam to give me a gun. I'll tell him it's just in case, if I get caught... because only I know where Pascal is. So that I don't give him up, if they torture me... or if they give me a truth serum. Liam will give me a gun, he'll give me one... I just have to be convincing."

Raul wiped his face and hands, took the telephone from the sink and put it in his right jacket pocket. He heard the muted sound of the telephone hitting something.

"The syringe. The second syringe… Seneca gave me two. In case one dose wasn't enough… If Pascal didn't go down immediately. I won't need your gun, Liam."

Raul left the toilet and went towards the front of the airplane.

*****

"Raul," Citra called out to him as he passed by her.

"Yes, Citra?"

"Does she know that he eats only spicy food?"

"Does who know? I don't understand."

"Well that woman. The new cook."

"Pascal's?"

"Whose else, Raul?"

"She knows, Citra. I told her that straight away."

"You sure?"

"I'm sure. Don't worry."

"Does she know that she has to add chili to every dish?" Citra burst into tears. "A lot of chilly…"

"She knows, she knows… Come on, Citra, calm down, please."

Raul leaned down and wiped Citra's single tear with his thumb.

"Raul," Liam called out as he passed by him.

"Yes, Liam?"

"I have three recommendations."

"What recommendations?"

"What do you mean 'what'? Three cities that we could land in."

"Excellent, Liam… I too have some cities I was thinking of."

"Well let's talk."

"OK… in a moment. I'm going to see Aslan."

"To who?"

"To our pilot. His name is Aslan."

"Why?" Liam asked.

"To check the weather situation with him. You know… that there isn't a sandstorm somewhere, and that we can't land."

"Ah, smart. It's good that you thought of that."

"Margot," said Raul while passing by her.

151

"Yes, Raul?"

"Margot…"

"What is it, Raul? Are you alright? Has something happened?"

"No, Margot, it hasn't… it's Citra… she's still crying, she can't calm down. Please go be with her a bit… so that she's not alone…"

"I will, of course" said Margot and started walking towards the middle of the airplane.

"Margot…"

"Yes, Raul?" Margot turned around.

"Thank you…"

Margot smiled and continued on her way.

"For everything…" whispered Raul, when Margot had gotten far enough.

*****

"Gloria, do you know that I can't wait for Tuesdays, which is when I'm assigned to your Secretariat?" said Habib.

"I believe you. Five girls…"

"What five girls? Because of you, Gloria. Only because of you."

"Why because of me?"

"Because of your eyes, your hair… at least look at me, Gloria," Habib touched her face.

"Don't touch me, Habib. OK, I'm looking at you. Are you satisfied?"

"Why shouldn't I touch you? Remember how we hugged last night."

"Hugged? I wasn't hugging. I was just dancing."

"Well, I was hugging. Do you feel anything for me, Gloria? Anything at all? Please, tell me," said Habib as he grabbed her hand.

"Let go of my hand, Habib!"

"I won't."

"Well then I'm not talking to you anymore," Gloria said defiantly and looked out the window. But she didn't move her hand from Habib's palm. Not a hair.

*****

"Aslan, hello."

"Oh, it's you, Raul," Seneca's pilot looked over his shoulder, sitting strapped into his seat.

"I'd like to ask you something, Aslan."

"Go ahead."

"Can you already now check the weather situation at the airports that we discussed with the Mayor."

"Here, right away." Aslan bent forward and touched the commands on one of the screens. "Perhaps at this moment I can't for all of them..."

Standing behind the pilot, Raul removed the syringe with the tranquilizer from his pocket.
"...but for most of them we will know already now. You're worried about sandstorms, Raul?" Aslan asked, still leaning over the screen.
"Yes," answered Raul, while removing the sheath from the needle.
"You're right. They're frequent in this part of the world..."

For the second time that day Raul plunged a needle into someone's body. This time it was into Aslan's neck.
"Forgive me... if you can..." he said while locking the bulletproof door to the flight deck.

Chapter 70

Mayor Julius Seneca, standing next to the window of his office, appeared on the screens of the people who were watching Megapolis television. He was a man of medium height with wide shoulders, a square face with a strong jaw, hair the color of ripe wheat, neatly trimmed and parted. The gaze of the light brown eyes was once again calm and poised.

The Mayor always dressed elegantly. His suits, shirts, ties and shoes were always in the seasonal colors, but always the lightest available shade.

Even though he did not intend on emphasizing the contrast to Erivan's black, standing there in front of the cameras in the beige suit, with his physical appearance, it was precisely this impression that he made on the viewers, who he addresses with the following words:

"Dear citizens of Megapolis. I would like to express my deep condolences to the families of all the people who died today.

"The war, which the new president of Earth just declared, does not apply to us, it doesn't exist. Because Mr. Erivan, appearing as the president of the Consumers, has announced war on the Non-Consumers. We, the citizens of Megapolis, don't know what this division means. And we don't want to know. We will defend our city from anyone who dares to attack it.

"The Megapolis region, with the armament, numbers and capabilities of its Inspectorate, represents the largest individual defensive force on Earth. This is why I am deeply convinced that no one will dare come even close to us.

"Dear citizens, I expect you to continue with your daily lives and work. Megapolis, with its water supply, fields of wheat, plantations and farms, with its diverse industry, is completely independent from anyone else. We will survive autonomously for as long as it takes.

"I also want to send a message out to those living among us, and who think that they might take advantage of the moment and impose their ideologies on us, regardless of what they might be – that I will decisively prevent that. Any violence in Megapolis will be stopped and punished.

"And another thing… I'm appealing to the youths, to the pupils and students. Don't allow anyone to lure you onto the path of hatred and conflict. Continue studying, peacefully as you have so far. That is the only way that you can defend your city."

Chapter 71

In the cabin of the spaceship the Grasshopper watched Kaella's interview, the footage from Short Street, Erivan's declaration of war and Seneca's announcement of Megapolis' neutrality. After that he called Erivan, who immediately picked up.

"Grasshopper, is everything alright with you?"

"It is. I just wanted to tell you 'Bravo! Bravo! Bravo, Mr. President!'"

"I knew that you would immediately recognize my signature," Erivan was visibly relieved.

"The end of the Kaellas has finally come! This world has finally gained a real ruler! And what a genial strategy with Short Street, Mr. President!" shouted the Grasshopper with excitement.

"Yes. I had to shed a little blood to boost the fighting morale of our Consumers. You know, you can't expect a Consumer to kill a Non-Consumer just like that. Just because they are wearing last season's shirt. The Consumer would hesitate, right?"

"Of course, Mr. President. And this with the schoolchildren! That was magnificent!"

"You said it – magnificent! People are somehow especially sensitive to children. There were parents with children and the occasional baby, but not enough. And they were spread out. It could have gone unnoticed. But these pupils, all of them on that fence, they really drew attention. Now they're all anyone is talking about. Television interviews with the grieving parents are being prepared. It will be a real success. The Consumers will go crazy. They'll kill Non-Consumers with their bare teeth. You'll see, Grasshopper."

"They will, they will. All thanks to you, Mr. President!"

"I must say that I'm relieved now."

"Why, Mr. President? What was troubling you?"

"I wasn't sure how you would react to these events. You know what all depends on you."

"How I would react? How could you doubt my loyalty, Mr. President?"

"Well... I know how loyal you are to me. You've proven that countless times... But still, you're a Doctor of Philosophy, and I'm always suspicious of them," Erivan laughed.

"You once told me that you had read my PhD thesis, Mr. President."

"Yes, I did."

"Well what does it say, Mr. President? Forgive me for asking you like this, but I'm deeply troubled by your lack of confidence in my loyalty."

"Alright, I'm sorry. Calm down. It says that the purpose of man's existence is to serve the leader. But to this moment I couldn't be completely certain which leader you meant. Who do you consider your leader, me or Kaella?"

"Kaella?! That miserable patsy!? You are the only leader! And not only mine. And not only as president. You, Mr. President, are the greatest leader in the history of mankind. I still cannot believe that I have the honor to serve you. This all seems like a magnificent dream. You are the greatest, most grandiose, most magnificent person that this world has ever seen."

"I too am pleased that there is a man capable of understanding my magnitude, Grasshopper."

"I understand your magnitude more than you do, Mr. President. Because your perception of it is skewed by your excessive modesty."

"You're right, Grasshopper. I am too modest."

"And your declaration of war. It left me breathless. And you... and the darkness around you, all in black. Fantastic!"

"Yes. The film director was excellent. I won't replace him. And I ignited them well, right? When I said that we would seize the stocks from the Non-Consumers and hand them out to the Consumers. They're going to rat them out like crazy."

"Yes, Mr. President. I'm sure they will. Genial, really."

"Well, Grasshopper, Now I'm at ease. Thank you for calling me immediately."

"Did you think that I could hold out any longer to express my admiration?"

"I didn't, I didn't." Erivan laughed. "I have to hang up now. My staff is coming."

Chapter 72

Pascal heard the quiet distant turning of a lock. Someone was unlocking the door. But not in his apartment, not his door. Some other door, beyond it. He stood against the wall. He heard someone's fast steps come towards his door. The steps of only one person. No conversation. Someone was approaching the door alone. This person unlocked the door, opened it, and stepped towards the bedroom, as Pascal had anticipated. The person entered from a lit room so Pascal could clearly see who it was.

"Seneca!" he shouted in surprise.

"Alexander!" Seneca jolted and turned towards Pascal. "You scared me! I didn't expect you... I though you were still..."

"And where is your..." Pascal fell silent. "Shut up, Pascal!" he shouted to himself in his thoughts. "She's safe, if Seneca is here."

"Raul? You mean Raul... He is... They are... well. Come here, Alexander. These aren't your quarters..."

"What quarters?" Pascal asked, entering the large lit room.

"A living room... some kind of armchairs... a couch... my clothes from the hotel..." Pascal's eyes quickly glanced around the room. "It is all together... and a dining room... table... six chairs... a kitchen," Pascal was stunned.

Through the door on the wall left of Pascal, entered the Mayor's son Peter and immediately behind him Manami with little Eir in her arm.

"Manami, Peter, come here," Seneca said quickly. "These are your quarters," Seneca pointed towards the door behind which Pascal had been locked.

"Good day, Mr. Alexander," Peter greeted him cordially, passing by him and entering their quarters.

Manami looked at him, just nodded as a sign of greeting, walked in after Peter and closed the door.

"Alexander, I have to immediately return to my office. Your quarters are over here. Here, take a look," said Seneca, opening a third door and standing in front of it. You have a large room and bathroom...

everything that you need. You can take your clothes from the couch. We brought all of your things from the hotel room..."

Pascal didn't move.

"You don't want to take a look... alright. You can do so later... in peace. You see... there is a kitchen too. My wife will cook for you too... She is an excellent cook, you'll see... I'm really in a hurry... You just settle in... and rest..."

Pascal was silent and standing in the same place where had been in when he saw Manami.

"You can also wait for me here, in the living room, if you wish. I will come as soon as I can. Tonight, before morning... I will tell everyone that I will take a nap in the office, and that I'm not to be disturbed. Ah, yes... I haven't explained this. This is Prince Kaella's shelter. He built it while he was building Megapolis. It is located between the television station and your hotel. It has entrances on both sides. The quarters that you were in were for his family. That is why my wife and children will be there. And the others, which are now your quarters, were for his bodyguards. We brought you from the hotel, and we now came down using the secret elevator in my office. I really have to go now. People will get suspicious..." said Seneca, while going out the shelter door.

"Their quarters... my quarters... The living room... I was lying on her bed... Get it together, man! What are you doing?! Don't you have at least a sliver of dignity left? The man sedates you, drags you to some shelter, he comes... and I? What do I do? I ask him where his wife is? And when I see her I go numb. He tells me about Raul... and I don't even think of asking him. Instead of hitting him. Hey, this man took me captive, deprived me of my freedom... and I didn't say a single word! What will she think of me? What does she think of me? Well that won't do, Pascal! That simply won't do!"

"Alexander, lock the door! The card is on the dining room table," Seneca shouted, quickly making his way to the elevator door at the end of the corridor.

"Seneca!" shouted Pascal while running out of the living room and down the corridor after him.

"Yes?" the surprised Mayor turned around.

"What is the meaning of this, sir?!" shouted Pascal, stopping in front of him. "Release me immediately! Call and open that elevator of yours! Immediately!"

"Back!" Seneca shouted at Pascal. "Return to the shelter! You are my prisoner, sir!"

"What prisoner?! Don't be ridiculous! Open the elevator! Take me to Raul immediately! Where is he, anyway!? Why has he conspired against me?!"

"Raul is not in Megapolis. He has ordered you to remain in the shelter. Go back!" Seneca pushed Pascal.

"Don't do this, Seneca! You know how much I have respected you! And trusted you! Don't make me hit you!" shouted Pascal walking backward, pushing Seneca's hands away from him.

"Raul is dead! They're all dead! All your people, Alexander, are dead!" shouted Manami, running into the corridor.

Chapter 73

Having ended his communication with the Grasshopper, Erivan immediately contacted Sigma, the leader of S Squad. Sigma and his squires, deployed on three fighter spaceships, was following the Grasshopper's ship at a distance.

"Yes, Mr. President?" Sigma responded.

"Return to Earth."

"To Earth?"

"Yes. There is no more need for your mission, Sigma. I'm aborting it. You are needed here more."

"Yes, sir, Mr. President."

*****

The Grasshopper calmly watched three bright dots stop on his screen, then move in the opposite direction from their previous course. Towards Earth.

Chapter 74

Pascal and Seneca froze and let go of each other. Seneca stopped in his tracks, with his head hung low, speechless. Pascal took a step towards Manami, stopped and shouted, looking her straight in the eye,

"What are you saying, ma'am!? What are these lies?! Why do you think you can use them to keep me here?!" He turned to Seneca again. "Take me to Raul! Immediately!"

"It's not a lie, Alexander," Seneca whispered, raising his head. "They are all dead. It's my fault."

"It's not your fault, Julius! Don't say that! None of you knew what Erivan was preparing," Manami shouted.

"Erivan?! Erivan killed them?!" Pascal cried out.

"No... no, not Erivan," Seneca whispered.

"Raul crashed their airplane into the ocean. Or they had all agreed to that. We will never know," said Manami, lowering her voice.

"Raul?! Why? Why?!"

"Mr. Alexander, please. Return to the shelter. We have to tell you everything," Seneca said.

Pascal briskly walked past Manami, entered the living room and turned towards the wall. Seneca and Manami came in behind him, locked the door and silently watched as sobs shook Pascal's shoulders. After a while Pascal wiped his face with his hands, took several deep breaths and turned towards them.

"Alright. I'm listening," he said quietly.

"Julius, Mr. Alexander, sit down at the table. I'll bring you something, let me just see what we have here," Manami passed by the dining room table and into the kitchen.

"A glass of water, ma'am... please," Pascal said while taking a seat.

Seneca sat down in the chair across from Pascal. Manami poured two glasses of water, placed them on the table in front of Pascal and Seneca and sat down next to her husband.

"All three of us were wrong, we misjudged the situation. We were afraid of an assassination attempt against you, Alexander," the

Mayor of Megapolis spoke quietly, looking at his fingers, wrapped around the glass. We thought that the Kaellas were controlling the game, as it has always been. The two of them believed that too."

"What do you mean 'they believed that too'?" asked Pascal. "Did Erivan do something on his own?"

"He killed them, Alexander... both of them. Father and son."

"Killed? Kaella? And Prince?"

"Yes. During the interview. He destroyed the submarine."

"How? Where were the inspectors? The bodyguards?"

"Erivan had obviously prepared all that in advance. He hid the real results of the polls from the Kaellas. And served it to him at the last moment. He forced him to panic. Kaella became reckless. I think Erivan's squads carried it out. He killed them, Alexander. And President Xing too."

"Xing, too?"

"Yes. His entire family. Wife and children. They fired a missile at the presidential motorcade in the center of Capital City... from your airplane."

"What do you mean 'from our airplane'? I don't understand..."

"He somehow got his hand on one of your aircraft... one built by you. From one of your factories... or from an airport."

Pascal was silent.

"I gave Raul and your people my airplane," Seneca continued. "And a squadron to protect them. But that was not enough. Because as soon as Erivan declared war numerous airplanes took off in their direction from several airports."

"Erivan declared war?" Pascal asked.

"Yes. War on the Non-Consumers. He took over the position of President of Earth, in accordance with the Constitution."

"But... you, ma'am, said that Raul..." Pascal looked at Manami.

"That is the only thing we can conclude, Mr. Alexander," Manami answered, "because..."

"When I was informed about all of Erivan's squadrons that were headed their way, I immediately called Raul," Seneca explained. "And I informed him of everything that had happened. About the murders of the Kaellas and the Xings. And the threat against them. I told Raul that I had informed all your closest cities and that your airplanes were taking off too. That my squadron would protect them until they arrive..."

"Don't tell me any more, Seneca. It's not necessary," Pascal whispered through his tears. "My noble Raul... all of them... Margot... Jagdish... all those young people... children, they were still children... My faithful Liam... my Citra..." Pascal fell silent, with his head hung low, covering his face with his hands. "Erivan didn't fire on them?"

"No," Seneca whispered. "Our squadron created a shield around them. He didn't fire on them, he didn't even try."

"He didn't..." Pascal wept. "He sent planes... to force them down. He wanted me alive. And they crashed the plane down because... only so... So that Erivan would think... that I was dead too! You didn't kill them, Seneca!" Pascal shouted. "I killed them! I did! It's because of me that they are dead! They sacrificed themselves for me!"

Pascal jumped from the chair and rushed towards the exit. He turned the doorknob.

"Unlock it, Seneca! I'll kill him! I'll kill Erivan! Unlock it!" he screamed.

Seneca got up from the table but did not approach Pascal.

"As you have said yourself, Alexander, your friends brought down the plane so that Erivan wouldn't learn where you were. So that he would think that you were dead. So that you would be safe. By leaving the shelter you would render their heroic death worthless. Make it futile. The last words that Raul said to me, before he hung up, were 'Save Pascal, Seneca. He is the only hope that this world has.'"

Pascal cried out loud. Seneca went to him, put his hand on his shoulder and said

"Wait for me just until tonight. We have to talk... after that you will make up your mind. If you want out of the shelter, I will get you out of Megapolis. I have to remain neutral in this war. I have to save this city. No one can know that you stayed in Megapolis."

"Yes... I will... I'll wait for you," Pascal said quietly.

Seneca went out of the shelter and locked the door behind him.

"Sir," said Manami. "Do you need anything? I have to go to mu children."

"No... no, ma'am. Thank you. I'll retreat there... to those quarters... until the mayor comes."

Chapter 75

Sayash was a regular dandy. He trimmed short his gray hair, with its M-shape receding hairline and magnificent white beard, a real man's beard that grew far below his Adam's apple and high up on his cheek bones – with a few passes of the trimmer. In the beginning, when he had just found the trimmer, in an alley behind a salon, Sayash used to stand at night in front of a lit shop window to see what he was doing. But that stopped being necessary a long time ago. It appeared that now he could trim his bear even in his sleep.

He didn't touch his eyebrows. He knew that he was more masculine, that he was more intimidating when he let them grow, and hang down over his dark eyes, bristly as they were. And the capillaries in the corners of his eyes were charmingly ruptured, from the wind and the sun. The only thing that he uncompromisingly purge almost daily were the hairs in his nose and ears.

He was especially proud of the white carpet on his chest. When he would wake up and prop himself on his elbow to see where he had spent the night, without thinking, mechanically, by force of habit he would draw the tips of the fingers of his other hand together, as though to take a pinch of salt, grasping the highest hairs on his chest and drew them to the ends of his beard so that they would connect. He was aware of how the continuous whiteness emphasized the beauty of his dark, wrinkled face.

And of course the shoelace around his neck. He always put in his backpack any type and any color of shoelace that he found. He liked to change them a lot. Either a different one every day, or several of them braided, several days in a row. He would tie to the shoelaces the occasional pendant, a bottle cork or piece of glass, if it was striking enough, with a piece of twine. But not very often.

Sayash was constantly moving from one city to another, because when a person is limited to the same dumpsters it means that they are limited to the same people and their tastes. He couldn't get over the fact that some people always wore the same things. They stuck to certain colors their entire lives. He thought that he would die if someone forced him to paint this refined thin body of his in the same colors. That is why he always had many colors. He wore plaid.

When Sayash would first approach a clothing dumpster he would be overcome with excitement. In the last several steps before their direct encounter he wouldn't see the dumpster at all. A kaleidoscope with the most wonderful colors would be spinning before his eyes.

Sayash believed that his greatest gift in life was that he was a dandy. Because if he hadn't been, he would have never met his best friend, Lucky.

Chapter 76

Manami knocked on Pascal's door.

"Mr. Alexander..."

Pascal got up from the bed in surprise, approached the door and without opening them said

"Ma'am... just a moment, to make myself decent."

He soon entered the living room. He saw that Seneca wasn't there and that Manami was very anxious.

"Ma'am, what has happened?"

"Mr. Alexander, forgive me, please, for disturbing you. Perhaps you were asleep..."

"I wasn't..."

"But I have to apologize. To beg your forgiveness..."

"You want to..."

"The two of us have never met. I mean to say... we have, of course, met... but we have never spoken. It is so difficult for me..."

"Why, ma'am? You are too anxious... Sit down, please."

"No, no... I have to get back to the children. So that they don't wake up and get scared... They are very scared... And Eir... She feels that something terrible is going on. I just briefly wanted to... while we were alone... before my husband comes... to tell you, to ask you..."

"Please calm down. There is no reason to..."

"I was the one, I told you the horrible news. My words... the words that I said to you... My first real words... and not our courteous greetings... back at our house... are surely the most horrific words that you have ever heard..."

"Yes... it is horrific... it is difficult..."

"I didn't want it to be... our first conversation... And I know that my husband would have told you the truth in the end, but... you know... Don't be mad at him, please.... He blames himself... He has never wrestled with anyone like this, like with you... He is completely beside himself..."

"I'm not mad, of course... I..."

"But I listened to everything... I heard everything... the two of you... And I was afraid that when my husband told you about Raul and all your friends... that you would... just as you had reacted... leave... And I thought..." Manami stopped, but didn't bow her head. "I thought... if I was present... if I was there... if you saw me... that perhaps... perhaps you wouldn't leave."

Pascal just looked at her. He didn't say anything.
"Because you are not a commander... Forgive me, please, you are not capable of such things. Not only war... but everything... the organization... Do you understand? You had Raul... or he had you... You were successful together. A capable man with both feet on the ground and a dreamer. You are the dreamer, sir. And people need dreams. Because nothing else makes sense anymore. Raul is gone. But now there is my husband. He now understands everything. He knows. Just like Raul knew... and your entire wonderful staff. My husband will use all the strength, all the power of Megapolis to safeguard you... To safeguard people's dreams. I wanted that... I know how difficult it is for you... I know. But stay... stay, please."

Manami quickly turned around and ran to her quarters.

Chapter 77

When Seneca returned, just before dawn, he found Pascal sitting motionless and alone at the dining room table.

"Mr. Mayor," said Pascal, raising his head only after Seneca had sat down.

"Erivan appeared on television once more and announced your death, Alexander. Of course, he said that the Inspectorate's air force crashed your airplane in the ocean."

"What else did he say? Will he still go to war or is this enough for him?"

"Alexander, Alexander..."

Pascal was silent, looking at his hands resting on the table.

"Raul knew the entire time why you wanted to hold that speech. Why you wanted them to kill you. So that you would be the only victim. Did you really believe that would happen?"

"If Kaella were alive, had the old government remained, perhaps that would have been enough," Pascal said.

"It wouldn't have. Nothing can stop your movement now, Alexander. Neither this war nor Erivan will succeed in that. The world will never be the same again. How many sacrifices will this war demand, what will the world look like after it... that I don't know. And the price is high, Alexander. You felt it today... and I felt it. I will never be the same person again. My conscious bears the burden of your people... and my pilot, Aslan."

"Please, Mr. Mayor, don't place such a burden on your soul. During all these months you did for us the maximum that was possible. You asked Raul and me to leave Megapolis. You didn't order us, your inspectors didn't force us. And both of us, Raul and I, accepted it as the best solution for Megapolis. And Megapolis was most important to us, Mr. Mayor. It brought us votes, you brought us votes. In any case, it is pointless to now go back to that meeting of ours. At the time we were expecting an assassination attempt on me, and Erivan outsmarted us all. And Kaella... and Xing. You say he also killed his wife and children... He had a wonderful family... and he was a good man... A good president. Xing, he was the right person to be president, not I."

"That is what I wondered, Alexander... The two of you, Raul and yourself, your first reaction to the high percentages was very strange."

"What do you mean?"

"Well... you immediately started thinking about Kaella's possible move. Not at one moment did you consider that the elections would take place and that you would become president. You never saw yourself in Capital City, in the presidential residence?"

"Never. Neither Raul or I. Mr. Mayor, can you imagine me sitting down with Kaella and trying to change the world in small steps? As president Xing had done? He pushed back the first medical exam one year, he subsidized two percent of medical treatment costs... Can you imagine me in that role?"

"I can't. But what was your goal then? You must have had some concrete goal."

"Concrete? I don't know how concrete it is for you, but my goal was to awaken the people, to spread free thinking... And Raul? He was planning on establishing a parallel government... He was convinced that the people's resistance would increase enough and that Kaella would fall... that the system would simply collapse by itself. But neither of us were interested in the position of Kaella's president. We entered the presidential race just so that we could have a greater opportunity to spread our ideas."

"I understand."

"Tell me, please, how is it that you and Raul decided to sedate me and bring me to this shelter?"

"It wasn't our decision. Raul demanded it of me. I mean, he didn't demand... He convinced me."

"How?"

"The most important thing for Raul was that you are safe until the elections. He believed that you would be safest in Megapolis, but that you had to be isolated and that you should not be allowed out into the street."

"Actually, for me to be locked up."

"Yes."

"As I am."

"Yes. And that no one should know where you are. Not even your staff, or anyone from my surroundings. Just him and me."

"Why did he trust you? And why did you agree to it at all, Mr. Mayor?"

"Wouldn't you trust me, Alexander? Don't you trust me now? Now, that I have hidden my family here, too?"

"I trust you, I trust you... Forgive me, please."

"You're surely wondering why I've sheltered my family, when all the other people, all the other families are in jeopardy?"

"I'm not wondering…"

"I have to save Megapolis. I cannot allow myself to be vulnerable. I cannot allow Erivan's squires to threaten my wife and children… to abduct them and blackmail me."

"Certainly, Mr. Mayor. Only you can save this city. You did the right thing."

"Yes… I hope so. The people, the citizens of Megapolis will judge me for this one day…" Seneca said deep in thought, and continued "And why I agreed to lock you up and safeguard you…" Seneca slightly smiled, recalling his conversation with Raul. "Raul was really talkative… He told me that it was best for me to keep you captive and to simply wait for the situation to unravel. I can always use you to benefit my Megapolis. I could hand you over to the Kaellas if it were necessary to protect the city. You can imagine, Raul teaching me how to hand you over to the Kaellas."

"My friend Raul…" Pascal smiled also, "Typical of him. Once he starts persuading someone…"

"I told him that if I were to hand you over to Kaella, the citizens of Megapolis would carry me out of the city on their hands and throw me in the nearest ditch. When I think about how the students would react… Alexander, do you know that I allowed you into the city only because of the young people. Otherwise I would have refused Raul when he called me up, a year ago. It's been a year, since we've been together, right?"

"Yes, almost a year… but I didn't know that… about the students."

"I had some problems at the University, in the student dorms… and that was very difficult for me to bear. You know, I consider the University the gem of Megapolis."

"I know. I felt that in you, Mr. Mayor. What problems did you have?"

"Well… that's not important now. We'll talk… I'll come by. But… then my wife recommended…"

"Your wife?"

"Yes. She's an artistic soul. An art historian… You know what they are like… and she knows the mentality of the students. She was a teaching assistant at the University. And then, when Peter was born, we agreed that she should stay home and be with our son. Eir came along later… and my wife never did return to the university. It doesn't matter. She is like that. She has a feeling for young people… and I don't. I'm a practical person, a realist. I don't understand these things… and that is why I didn't cope well with the situation. And my wife recommended that I invite you, to visit Megapolis and the University. To speak to the students."

"You were right, Svetlana. The Mayor listened to her. You were right about everything, Svetlana," Pascal thought.

"Alexander, I realized that Megapolis couldn't be isolated from the world. That the entire world must be free so that Megapolis could shine with all its splendor. And only you can change the world, just as you changed my students."

Chapter 78

Off all the things in the world, what Sayash and Lucky loved the most were the movies. In the theater Lucky would sit in Sayash's lap, and Sayash would pet his hairy head, passing his index finger between Lucky's two pointy and unusually large ear, covered in light brown spiky hair, as were his nose and paws, unlike the black, slightly curly hair that Lucky used to cover his small and slender but muscly and tough body from unwanted eyes.

Sayash got all soft. He remembered how the two best friends first met. And he passed the fingers of his other hand beneath Lucky's chin, even though Lucky did not explicitly demand this type of petting in the theatre.

"Come on, Lucky, pal. I had no idea that you were in that dumpster," Sayash repeated yet again the same story to Lucky. That was why Lucky wasn't listening to him at all, but rather was entirely focused on the movie. "How could I know? Right? I'm telling you, it was pure luck that your buddy Sayash came along. I opened your dumpster and what did I see?! Not what, but who did I see! But I barely saw you, Lucky, do you know that? You were a little baby... man, you were... I could fit you in the palm of my hand, that's how small you were. And completely hairless. You were covered with snot and phlegm. A disgrace, but we won't tell anyone about it. And look at how tall you are now, buster! Fourteen and a half centimeters, man! Not only fourteen! But a half, too! And Lucky, you really irritated me... I straightened out your tail to measure you, to see how long my little dude is, and instead of stretching your neck as much as you can, you turned your silly little head and looked at me, puzzled by what I was doing. Oh, I was so angry... but it doesn't matter... somewhere between thirty eight and forty centimeters. Depends on how I cut your hair. That's a good length! You fit in my arms perfectly. You're just right for me, Lucky!"

When Sayash would stop petting him between the ears, Lucky would have some understanding for his friend if there were no finger on his head for a moment. He knew that Sayash wanted to look good in the theatre and that he scrunched his eyebrows, and that he would soon put back his finger and continue petting him. And when Sayash would start jabbering like this, or stare at the screen, and when the finger would remain motionless between his ears, Lucky would smack him with his tail on the leg, without taking his eyes off the screen. And Sayash would resume petting him. And this now, when the finger was motionless and the other hand still played with the hairs beneath his chin, which he neither demanded nor deemed important – that angered Lucky so much that he turned his head, shot arrows out of his eyes at Sayash, and whacked him twice with his tail. On the stomach.

"Oh, sorry, Lucky... I got carried away..." said Sayash, quickly moving his finger back and forth. "And you... you have to get mad immediately? And hit me twice, hmm? I'm asking you a question, Lucky!"

Chapter 79

"The man is a beast," Seneca said to Pascal.

"Erivan?" Pascal asked.

"Yes. He reduced to dust an entire street in Capital City, which Xing's motorcade was going down. He killed hundreds of people. And children, pupils. A monster! He's a monster! And that is why I have to safeguard you. I have to convince you to stay in the shelter. Raul is right. He said…" Seneca fell silent.

"What did he say, Mr. Mayor? Tell me everything. I want to know everything," Pascal said.

"I didn't want to make things more difficult for you tonight, to tell you the details. I'll tell you another time. When some time has passed, when we calm down a bit."

"Tell me now. There are no details more horrific than their deaths."

"When I called him, while I explained that Erivan's planes were flying towards them, Raul was silent - the entire time. He didn't pay attention at all to the fact that your airplanes were taking off, that my squadron was around them… He knew that all of them together didn't stand a chance, that they were too few… He was just silent. When I finally fell finished, he said 'Seneca, in the entire world, only you know where Pascal is.' It didn't occur to me what he would do, so I was surprised. How was it that only I knew, how about him… and all your people knew that you weren't on the airplane. And Raul repeated once again 'Only you, Seneca.'" Pascal bowed his head. Seneca continued. "And he only said that thing… that I must safeguard you, that you are the world's only hope… and he hung up, Alexander. He simply hung up."

"Terrible, terrible…" Pascal whispered.

"Julius, you came," said Manami, entering the living room.

"Why aren't you sleeping, Manami?" Seneca asked.

"Eir is sleeping restlessly. She's excited… she turned over and woke me up. And then I heard you. Can I get you anything? Would you like some tea? Do you want something to eat?"

"I've already eaten. But I'd like a large cup of coffee," said Seneca. "Because when I go back to the office I have to function all day long, and I haven't had any sleep."

"Sleep here a bit, Julius."

"I can't. I don't have any time. I'll have the coffee and leave."

"And you, Mr. Alexander, you haven't eaten anything all day."

"No, thank you, ma'am. I'd like some coffee, too, if it's not too much trouble."

Manami prepared the coffee in the kitchen. The dining room table and the kitchen were separated only by a counter. Manami listened to her husband say

"The only difference between Raul and me is that now that he's gone I cannot hold you here against your will, Alexander. I've already told you, I want you to stay as long as necessary. Raul thought that we would hold you captive only until the elections and he knew that you would forgive him. And now we don't know how long this war will last."

"It's not about how long the war will last, Mr. Mayor," said Pascal. "Even if it lasts only one day, I have to be with the people during these times. I will go to one of our cities, anyone, and I will fight against Erivan. I know that I'm not a commander. Perhaps I am this world's only chance... or a dreamer, as someone told me..." Pascal paused, wanting Manami to hear, to understand why he cannot obey her wishes, why he could not stay. "But I will cease to be that if I hide here like the greatest coward. Come on, tell me, Mr. Mayor, what would you do in my place? What would Raul do?"

"Both Raul and I would think like you, Alexander. And we'd go to the fight. But neither Raul or I are Pascal Alexander. First of all – the two of us would be good commanders," Seneca smiled.

"That's true," Pascal smiled back.

At that moment Manami placed a cup of coffee in front of her husband and stood behind him.

"Thank you, Manami," said Seneca, lowering his head and raising the cup to his mouth.

Manami and Pascal looked at each other, as though it was green tea, as though they were in the salon of her house. She moved her lips silently, and from them Pascal read

"Stay. Stay. Stay."

Chapter 80

Having taken a sip of coffee, Seneca raised his eyes towards Pascal. When he saw that Pascal was persistently looking past him, looking at his wife, Seneca turned towards her slightly and asked

"And the coffee for Mr. Alexander, Manami?"

"Yes, right away, Julius... I was just waiting for you to try... Is it sweet enough?" said Manami, while returning to the kitchen.

"Yes, is good," said Seneca and continued. "I've already told you, Alexander. By leaving the shelter you'll be rendering the your friends' sacrifice, a courageous act – futile. In any case, what do you think, Alexander? That all this that you are saying didn't occur to Raul? That he wasn't thinking about that while he was silent during our conversation? That he didn't think of the possibility that you might come across as being a coward if you stayed? He did, Alexander. You can be sure of that. In such moments, when a person knows that they are about to die and that they will die for you, in the moments of such courage, such determination, Alexander – a person's thoughts are surely crystal clear. And he obviously didn't believe that you remaining in the shelter would represent an act of cowardice."

"Mr. Mayor..." Pascal interrupted him, then paused while Manami placed a cup of coffee in front of him. He continued when Manami had sat down next to her husband and looked at him. "Raul... all my friends made the decision for me. I don't make decisions about my life anymore... about myself. Am I the hope? Am I a criminal who caused the war? The man who created the opportunity for an Erivan to sow evil throughout the world? Am I a dreamer? Am I a coward? I don't know. And I don't care. Others decide that. Someone else..." Pascal briefly looked at Manami and returned to Seneca. "I'll stay in the shelter, Mr. Mayor. And if you don't mind, I'll retire to my quarters now."

"Certainly, certainly, Alexander. I'll be leaving now, too." Seneca took another sip of coffee and got up from the table. "I'd just like for you to lock the door behind me, to see how it works. Here's the key," Seneca held out a card.

"Good night, Julius," said Manami, heading towards her quarters. "Actually, for you a new day is just beginning. And who knows what it will be like. Who knows what all awaits you."

"I'll make it through, Manami. I'm much more at ease now that we've reached an agreement with Mr. Alexander. You get some sleep, until the children wake up." Seneca was already heading out the door of the shelter. "Lock up, Alexander."

Pascal closed the door behind him and locked it. When he heard Seneca's elevator go up he turned towards the interior of the room. Manami was standing in front of her door. They looked at each other for a long time, in silence.

"Give me the key, sir," Manami finally said.

"The key? The card?" Pascal was surprised.

"Yes. The key will be with me at all times. In my room. You are an impulsive man, sir, and I cannot trust you."

Pascal walked up to her and handed her the key. "Here you are, ma'am."

"Am I that 'other' who decides about your life, sir?"

"Yes, you are, ma'am. You decided," Pascal said quietly.

"You're wrong. I didn't. You decided. Good night, sir," said Manami and entered her quarters.

"Good night... my love," Pascal whispered, after Manami had shut the door.

Chapter 81

"Grasshopper, how much longer until reach the Command?" asked Erivan, when the Grasshopper answered his call from the flight deck.

"Another ten hours, Mr. President. Why do you ask?"

"Well... no special reason. Just to complain a bit..."

"What do you wish to complain about, Mr. President? Did someone..."

"The grieving parents are infuriating me!"

"The parents of the pupils from Short Street?"

"Them. Imagine, they don't want to give statements. Like – its difficult for them."

"Doubters!" said the displeased Grasshopper.

"They locked themselves in their apartments and won't let the television crews in."

"Well break down their doors, Mr. President."

"I don't need you to lecture me!"

"I apologize..."

"Of course I sent the inspectors. They drove the parents into the children's rooms... and all around – school charts, toys, posters, pictures of the children on the walls... just as it should be."

"Now I'm relieved," the Grasshopper sighed a sigh of relief.

"And they complained, whined..."

"Wonderful!"

"You'll see it tonight, right after the evening news. A special program."

"I don't know whether I'll be able to watch. I'll be reaching the Command about then. But I'll watch it later. I'm excited about it."

"Well... We can't exactly be excited, Grasshopper. Those are our children, consumers. But, what can we do about it, right?"

"We can't do anything at all, Mr. President."

"In every war you have colonoscopic damages."

"A very adequate name, Mr. President."

"No, no. I meant coronarographic damages."

"Well, you could use that too, if the heart were not just a pump."

"They keep forcing me to have all these tests, Grasshopper, and then that's all that's in my head. I'm not crazy to go for tests, and for them to find something. You really like to be a smart aleck, do you? OK, tell me what it is."

"Collateral damage."

"What?"

"Col-lat…" the Grasshopper pronounced the syllables.

"Col-lat…" Erivan repeated.

"…er-al."

"…er-al."

"Col-lat-er…" the Grasshopper helped Erivan pronounce the entire word.

"Collat-er…"

"-al."

"Collateral!" Erivan said. "There! I'll need that, if anyone asks me. Collateral!" Erivan repeated once again. "Why do I have to know everything? I don't have a PhD in philosophy like you do, Grasshopper."

"You don't… And I know why you don't, Mr. President."

"Why?"

"Because you weren't interested in that. If you had been interested in those things you could have gotten a PhD in any field."

"Of course. You're absolutely right."

"Even in several fields. You would have had five PhDs by now."

"Five? Ten! …if I wanted, Grasshopper!"

"But you decided that you can't waste time on those trifles. Who then would rule the world?"

"That's right, Grasshopper! That's right! You read me like a book."

Chapter 82

The central part of the shelter that Prince Kaella had built for himself and his family consisted of one large space.
It included a kitchen, a dining room table with six chairs, a club table, a commode with a lamp, three dark brown leather armchairs and a large leather couch, fluorescent-green. The color of the beam on the Kaella company logo. There was a door on each wall of the living room area.

The first was located between the kitchen cabinets and it led to the sleeping quarters for Kaella's bodyguards. These quarters, which consisted of a large dormitory, bathroom and toilette, was now occupied by Pascal.

The second door, on the opposite wall, could be accessed between the dining room table and the leather sofa set. It led to the quarters planned for Prince's family. Manami, Peter and Eir now occupied them.

The third and fourth doors, opposite one another, on the remaining two walls, were exits from the shelter. The one next to the dining room table led to the hotel, and the one next to the third armchair led to the television station.

The corridor that led from the shelter to the hidden elevator was wider than the corridor that led to the secret door in the hotel basement.
Behind a thin wall with sound insulation in the wider corridor were a large refrigerator, freezer, washing machine, drier and ironing machine.

Chapter 83

The Grasshopper sometimes went alone on his missions, with a sniper rifle. But more often they were assignments of a wider significance. Then the Grasshopper would put together a team. Erivan allowed him to include members of any squad, for any mission. In some situations Erivan's entire squads, including their leaders, were placed under the Grasshopper's command.

For this mission the Grasshopper chose five squires: Kid, Elephant, Victor, Scorpion, and Cupid, and took them along to the Command.

At the entrance to the Command the Grasshopper handed the guards Erivan's written orders to the head of the Command and the head of its security.
In order to give the orders greater meaning, Erivan wrote them by hand, signed them with his full name and stamped them with the magnificent, embossed state seal. It stated that Mr. Grasshopper was his personal envoy to the Command, that he had full authorization, and that he was to take absolute control of the Command and the entire energy system.

When the chief and head of security at the Command made themselves available to him, the Grasshopper carried out the following steps, the following order:
1. He ordered that he and his men be taken to the operations room.
2. He ordered that the shields be raised around the Command and all the platforms in the energy system, which the system administrator on duty in the operations room carried out.
3. He ordered that all those present in the Command, regardless of their function, including the guards at the door, go to the amphitheatre where he would convey President Erivan's instructions for operation under wartime conditions.
4. After a while he checked on the monitors whether all the other areas of the Command were empty. When he was certain of it, he ordered Scorpion, Kid and Elephant to go into the amphitheatre, to close the doors, and if necessary prevent anyone from leaving the

amphitheatre until the chief, head of security, Victor, Cupid and he joined them.

5. He asked the chief and head of security to approach the command desk, so that he could first explain to them the wartime regime for the functioning of the energy system. Because he expected their full support when he addressed the staff in the amphitheatre.

6. When the chief and head of security approached the command desk, the Grasshopper nodded to Victor and Cupid.

7. While Victor fired a shot into the temple of the head of security and Cupid emptied his clip into the chief's body, the Grasshopper, with truly incredible speed, which completely deservingly represented a significant part of the legend about him, drew his two (also legendary) revolvers from his thigh holsters, throwing himself on the ground and before even touching the floor, firing a single bullet from each revolver, making holes on the foreheads of the surprised Victor and Cupid, who had just turned towards him.

8. He approached the command desk, remotely locked the doors to the amphitheatre and switched off its oxygen supply.

9. He walked out of the operations room into the corridor, opened the first aid cabinet and took out gauze and a bandage. He returned to the operations room, and used a knife, which he drew from the sheath on his belt, to remove a bullet from the chief's body. He placed the bullet on the edge of the command desk and thoroughly soaked the gauze in the chief's blood.

10. He placed the bloody gauze on his left side and attached it with the bandage, wrapping it around his stomach.

Chapter 84

"You're good, Bruce, you're good," said Lolo, the former boxer, while coaching a boy in his basement.
Lolo didn't coach just anyone. The boys had a boxing club for that. His basement was open only to those that Lolo identified as having a love of boxing. Those for whom fists were just a means. Those that boxed from the heart.

"Hey, you!" roared Lolo's wife, coming down the stairs with curlers in her hair. "You are to take the car to the Inspectorate immediately! Do you know that there's a war starting?! Do you know that your car is already two months out of season?! Do you think that the inspectors will look the other way again?!"
"Leave me alone, woman. You and that car... Those are all my people... Excellent, kid... That's it! Hit it! Hit it! That's it!" said Lolo, while Bruce ran around him, punching the gloves he held up.
"Enough with that nonsense! Get out of that basement! First go buy some sour cream, then go return the car!"
"Man, you're such a drag," said Lolo, while taking off his gloves. "Don't ever get married, Bruce. Listen to what Mr. Lolo has to say. Keep hitting the sack, I'll be back in a moment."

Lolo ran up the stairs without looking at his wife, and entered the hallway. He was surprised that his wallet was not on the dresser, next to his car keys. He checked the pockets of his pants, which were lying on the back of the armchair in the living room.
"What are you fussing about there?" his wife asked, having come up from the basement.
"Well... I can't find my wallet."
"You lost your wallet?!" his wife shouted.
"Well... I didn't... I didn't..." Lolo searched around the living room with his eyes. "It must be in the car..." he said, and took the keys from the dresser and went out to the car, which was parked in front of the house on their peaceful street.
"Moron!" said his wife and returned to the kitchen.

Sayash and Lucky were dozing in the shade. Lucky only opened his eyes half-way when he heard Lolo's noisy wife, and Sayash didn't even move.

Chapter 85

The Grasshopper turned on the camera above the command desk and called Erivan.

"Mr. President... Mr. President..." he said with a exhausted voice.

"Grasshopper! What's going on?!" shouted Erivan in a panicked fear, seeing the entire operations room on his screen with bodies on the floor.

"Don't worry... Everything is alright... please, don't worry..." the Grasshopper whispered.

"What do you mean 'alright'?!" Erivan asked hastily, but with a calmer voice. "You're wounded, Grasshopper!" He shouted again when he saw Grasshopper's bandaged body. "Is it a serious wound? Will you survive? Where are the rest?!"

"I'll tell you everything... sir... let me just catch my breath..."

"Alright..."

"I carried out your orders..."

"Did you? Really? Congratulations, Grasshopper!"

"But..."

"But – what? Speak up!"

"I'm trying... I'm exhausted... so..."

"Alright... alright... take it easy, but what?"

"I was attacked by... my..."

"Who? Your people? Why? Impossible!"

"Possible... possible... Mr. Presid..."

"Did you manage to kill them all?"

"I did... don't be angry..."

"All five of them?"

"Yes..."

"And all the rest in the Command?"

"Yes... don't be angry... I was defending myself..."

"How can I be angry? As long as you are alive, Grasshopper! Is it a serious wound? Who will help you? Who will treat you if you are alone in the Command? Will you bleed out?"

"I won't... don't worry... I've already gotten the bullet out..." The Grasshopper moaned as he bent over to lift the bullet and show it to Erivan. "And I've sown up the wound..."

"You operated on yourself? Without anesthesia? You're a hero, Grasshopper!"

"My loyalty to you... my upcoming mission... it gives me superhuman strength, Mr..."

"Grasshopper, Grasshopper!... do you see that it was the right decision to send you up there?"

"I see... Mr..." Grasshopper passed out. In doing so he hit the command desk with his forehead, right on the wrong icon, and he disconnected the link with Erivan.

Chapter 86

Lucky raised his head, opened his eyes wide and looked at the Inspectorate armored vehicle coming around the corner. He rushed towards Lolo's house.
"Hey, Lucky! What's the matter with you?" Sayash shouted. "Lucky, stop!"
Lucky started manically digging up flowers in Lolo's wife's garden.

Lolo didn't find his wallet in the car's glove compartment. He had just squatted next to the driver's seat and was running his hand underneath it, when Sayash rushed into his wife's garden.
"And who are you?" asked Lolo, catching the red-and-yellow squares of Sayash's three quarter pants in the corner of his eye.

"Ah, you peed," Sayash said while catching his breath, having run up to Lucky. "What is this new thing of yours, Lucky? Showing off with your front paws when you pee?"

Lolo had gotten up and was headed towards the house. He saw Lucky digging up his wife's flowers and Sayash smiling cheerfully.
"What now!?!" Lolo shouted, already annoyed because of his missing wallet. "You bum, you're insane!"

"Lucky, where are you going? Wait for me, Lucky!" Sayash panted while running after Lucky, who was sprinting down the street.

"Come back, you bum! You'll pay for this! You and that mutt of yours!" It would have taken Lolo only another step to reach the clumsy Sayash, when the Inspectorate armored vehicle fired a shell and blew up his out-of-season car.

Lolo first stumbled from the explosion, then stopped and turned around. He watched in shock as his car disappeared in the flames.
"Hey, Lolo!" shouted inspector Marlon, peering through the turret of the armored vehicle. "Sorry, buddy, I had to. It's war, no messing around. In any case I spared you the trouble of driving this heap of junk to the Inspectorate. You're buying beer tonight at Legends.

188

See you, buddy!" Marlon greeted his buddy Lolo and lowered the hatch after him.

Lolo didn't say anything to him. He turned around and looked down the street, but Sayash and Lucky were nowhere to be seen. He stood there on the sidewalk for a while, in reflection. And then he ran to his veranda, where standing next to each other were his wife in curlers and Bruce in red gloves.

"Did you see that?" the excited Lolo told his wife. "Do you get what happened? That bum... and his puppy... How did they just disappear? Do you get it? They saved my life! That's why he was digging in your flowers! To make me run after them, to get me away from the car! They saved my life, woman!"

"Stop the nonsense! There's nothing wrong with my flowers," Lolo's wife said.

"What do you mean 'there's nothing wrong'?!" said Lolo looking at the garden where all the rows were perfectly neat. "What do I care?" he shouted, still very excited. "I saw them! And I know that they saved my life! Without them I would have been squatting behind the car and Marlon wouldn't have seen me!"

"Did you find your wallet, buster?! That's what I'm asking you! Tell me that!" his wife interrupted him.

With a short and lightning-fast blow of the fist Lolo hit his wife in the chin, turned around and ran down the street.

"Damn, now that's a direct punch!" shouted Bruce, while Lolo's wife was going down next to him. Bruce knelt next to her and started counting: "One... two..." But it didn't seem that the missus would be getting up and continuing the fight. "Ten!" shouted Bruce, and got up – glowing. "Classic knockout!"

"That's the beauty of boxing, Bruce," thought Lolo while running down the street. "You count to ten and you know exactly whether it was a knockout or not. And not like this: you persistently count the months, years, decades... and it still isn't clear to you that you were knocked out long ago."

"How could they disappear so quickly?" Lolo was taken aback when he reached the Legends café, which the Company sector for catering opened at the sport center nearby, following a written request by the former boxers.

"People! People! They saved my life!" Lolo shouted while bursting into Legends. "And they disappeared! They disappeared!"

"Who did, Lolo?"

189

"How did they save your life?"

"What are you saying, Lolo?" his friends jumped to their feet.

"Oscar, can I stay with you? For a few days, until I find a place?" Lolo asked.

That is how the legend of the Saint and his Dog was born, in the namesake café.

Chapter 87

"Sir," said Manami, sitting after dinner next to Peter at the dining table and holding Eir in her lap.

"Your forehead is high…" Pascal tried to rationalize her beauty, while sitting across from them. To fit it into certain standards, molds. "…oval. You have strong cheekbones. And then it gets narrower towards your cute chin."

"We have to discuss how we will function in the shelter. You will put your clothes in the machine. I will turn it on and wash them," Manami continued.

"Your nose is flat and small. Your upper lip is fuller. Its upper edge dips down in the middle. And your lower lip is smaller. And thinner. Actually, your lips are the shape of a small heart. Which I want to kiss so much. Do you know that, love? Do you know that, darling?"

"I'll dry it and iron it," Manami explained.

"Your eyes are unusually large… for such… dark and slanted eyes. I like it when you let your hair down. I also like it when you wear it up… but more like this…"

"Sir! You are not listening to me at all!" Manami was cross.
"I'm listening, ma'am, I'm listening," Pascal answered
"Well then, will you take your laundry to the machine?"
"I won't," Pascal answered calmly.

"You always speak quietly, Manami. And when you raise your voice, you also raise your eyebrows."

"What do you mean 'you won't'?" Manami was surprised.

"And your eyebrows are not as round as your forehead… They somehow look sharper. And now… now that I've explained it all to you so nicely, explain to me, my love, why do I find your face to be

191

the most beautiful of all? Why do I love you so much? Why is it that because of you I've become the world's greatest coward?"

"Sir…" said Manami, noticing how Pascal was looking at her.
"I just won't. I'll take care of my own laundry," Pascal finally answered.
"Nonsense!" suddenly shouted Peter, who was silent until then. "A man washing his own laundry?! I've never heard of that! My father would never wash his own laundry!"

"You're right, Manami. You didn't decide that I would be a coward. I decided. It's not your fault, you're not responsible for being, for existing" thought Pascal, and then twitched and said
"Peter, your father is a different story."
"What do you mean 'different'? You are the president of Earth, Mr. Alexander! How can you wash your own laundry?"
"Peter, we're in…" Manami tried to explain to her son. "In an unusual situation. Mr. Alexander might be embarrassed. Perhaps dad would be… Do you understand?"
"Dad? What does he care who washes his clothes? He just wants everything to be clean and ironed."
"Sir," Manami was getting uncomfortable, "I rather not discuss this topic any further. You will do as I said. This is the end of this discussion," Manami concluded with a firm voice.
"Alright, ma'am. As you wish," Pascal agreed.

Chapter 88

"Peter looks a lot like the Mayor," said Pascal.

"That's what everyone tells me!" shouted Peter proudly.

"Your hair is a bit darker," Pascal smiled. "And your face is narrower... and your chin is smaller, like your mother's."

"They tell me that I'm exactly like my dad! Eyes, and eyebrows... and everything!" ten-year-old Peter was relentless.

"Yes you are... exactly like your dad," Pascal laughed.

"Both in appearance and in character," Manami smiled, brushing the hair from her son's forehead.

Peter pulled his head back. "Don't, mom!" he said.

He parted his hair on the right, just like his father. But he grew it longer. So that it fell over his forehead, all the way to the left eyebrow. That was the hairstyle that boys at school wore.

"And Eir..." Pascal said, while gazing at the two-year-old girl, who was playing with a doll on the table, while sitting in her mother's lap. "Eir is just like her mother."

"That's normal. She's a girl," said Peter. "Elevator! Dad!" he shouted, hearing the elevator doors open. He jumped out of the chair and ran to the shelter door.

Seneca appeared a few moments later. He silently nodded to Manami and Pascal, who had gotten up to greet him. He stroked his son head

"Peter, take your sister and go to your quarters. Play with her. I have to talk to mom and Mr. Alexander."

"Alright, dad. Come, Eir," said Peter, lifting his sister from their mother's lap.

"What's happened, Julius?" Manami asked frightened, when Peter and Eir had left, looking at her husband's tense face.

"Erivan has killed more than three hundred people. The heads of the Company, Inspectorate... the heads of Kaella's state."

"Awful!" Manami cried out. "Did he also..."

"Yes, Manami. Both of them."

Manami screamed. Seneca hugged her and held her to his chest. Pascal turned around and went to his room.

Chapter 89

"Alexander," Seneca knocked on Pascal's door.

After a few moments Pascal entered the living room.

"Yes, Mr. Mayor?"

"Please sit with my wife," said Seneca. "The children are asleep and I have to go... so that she's not alone."

Pascal locked the door to the shelter and sat on the couch, next to Manami. She was sitting with her hands in her lap, shoulders slumped and head hung low. She was crying. Pascal wrestled with himself not to hug her. He finally wiped a tear with one finger.

"Who are the Levis? The mayor of Capital City?" he asked quietly.

"Yes. Our best friends," Manami answered. "He was like an older brother to Julius. He was the one who recommended Julius, who wasn't even thirty at the time, to Prince Kaella for the mayor of Megapolis. And Sophia... what a woman. What a lady... Noah is upstairs... with Julius, in his office."

"Noah?" Pascal asked.

"Their only son. They wanted him to study here, in Megapolis."

"A student?"

"No. He's with the Inspectorate now. He already holds a high rank. An extraordinary young man... What is he feeling now? He doesn't have anyone anymore... Julius won't let him leave his side... so that Noah doesn't do anything to himself. So that he doesn't go to Capital City... Awful... only now do I understand what you must have felt when we told you... when I told you about your friends. Only now..." Manami looked at Pascal. "You know what, sir?" she raised her voice. "I will tell my husband that it isn't enough that he has switched off all the media and communication in the shelter. When he brings such news, we can't do anything to change that... I cannot pretend in front of the children... when this... hurts so much... I will tell my husband not to tell us anything anymore. And I forbid you to ask him anything. Not in front of me."

"I will not ask the mayor anything, ma'am. Nothing at all," Pascal said.

"You have to know what is going on. So that you are prepared when the moment comes for you to take the presidential office."
"Presidential office? Ma'am, you don't still believe in that?"
"Of course I believe. That's the only thing..." Manami paused.
"Sir..."
"Yes?"
"May I...? Just for a bit... a few moments... rest my head on your shoulder?"

Chapter 90

For hours the Grasshopper did not answer Erivan's persistent calls. In the meantime he had moved the four bodies to the amphitheatre and cleaned up the operations room. He finally called Erivan.

"Grasshopper! You're alive!" Erivan shouted. "I've been beside myself since you crashed like that. And the connection died."
"Forgive me, Mr. President," said the Grasshopper, with a stronger voice. "It wasn't intentional. I passed out."
"I know, I know. Are you alright now? I mean, you can't be alright. But are you better? Or will you pass out again?"
"I won't anymore. At least I think I won't. The wound hurts and I have a slight fever. But nothing much. I'll take an antibiotic, rest for a few days and I'll be as good as new."
"Alright, alright. You rest as much as you need. This first phase of the war is working for me. Do you know how interesting it is to look at maps with the generals. Then we discuss which city to attack. It was awesome! And Consumers need to perish some more. So that they get fired up even more. You just recover calmly. No hurry. But pick up the line as soon as I call you."
"Of course I will, Mr. President."
"Alright, go lie down now... wait, stop," it dawned on Erivan. "You didn't tell me what happened over there. Why did your men attack you? And how did you kill the Command crew so quickly?"
"Simply, Mr. President, I sent them all to the amphitheatre..."
"What's that?"
"It's the largest space here. It's used for meetings, lectures..."
"Alright, and?"
"And their chiefs stayed with me in this operations room, supposedly for me to explain to them the new method of operation."
"And?"
"My men killed the two of them immediately. And I switched off the oxygen to those in the amphitheatre."
"Bravo! It's like watching myself! Why did your men attack you? What was it, they didn't have the stomach for it?"

197

"No, no. I told them back on the ship that we would kill everyone here. That's why I brought the five most brutal men. But... that's what surprised me so much. When these five couldn't take it..."

"What?"

"In the end I told them how it was. What your orders were..."

"And they refused?! My orders?! It's good that you killed them!"

"I killed three in the hallway, and then, wounded as I was, I burst into this operations room, and two of them were on my tail. And I protected the command desk with my body and shot..."

"That's good, that's good!" Erivan shouted. "My generals are at the door. I can hear them already. I have to go, Grasshopper."

Chapter 91

Pascal chose a place at the table for himself. The place from where his view of Manami in the kitchen was least obstructed by the counter.

"That's very interesting, ma'am," he said, while Manami was preparing lunch. "The fact that you wear a kimono."
"That is my family's tradition, sir. I observe it with great pleasure," said Manami, turning towards Pascal. "And this isn't a kimono," she smiled. "It is obvious that you are not knowledgeable about this type of clothing."
"It isn't?" Pascal was surprised.
"This is a yukata. It is thinner than a kimono. It was originally made of cotton soaked in indigo. Today they are colorful, like this one."
"Yours isn't exactly colorful. Neither are the other ones I've seen, which aren't blue."

"It isn't? Well it isn't exactly youthfully colorful, with flowers, etc. But you see that it has geometric patterns on it."
"It does, it does... but they are just a little darker... and they're gray. They don't stick out much. But you know what? I've already forgotten the other name. For me that's a kimono."

"That's what dad says, too," said Peter, while playing with Eir on the floor. "It's a kimono to him, too."
"Peter," said Manami. "You need to start studying soon, son."
"Aw, mom!"
"No 'aw'. You know what your father said. Just like at school. And I'll help you go over the new material."
"If you would permit me, ma'am... I mean, you have plenty of work with Eir... And you're cooking for us, cleaning... I could work with Peter. You know, I'm a teacher."
"Yes, I know. Biology."
"Yes, but that's not important. The two of us will cover all the subjects. To help the time pass. Isn't that right, Peter?"

"Great!" said Peter, jumping to his feet. "I'll go get my tablet. And if the teacher wants to give me a low grade, I'll tell him that that's what the president taught me!"

"Peter!" Manami pretended to be angry. She waited for Peter to leave the room, she looked at Pascal and asked "So, you are bored with us? Something to help the time pass, is it?"
"Ma'am, please... don't joke like that with me."

Chapter 92

"The Mayor told me that there had been some problems at the University…" Pascal said.

"Yes, there were…" said Manami, while putting a cup of tea on the table.

"And that you proposed at the time…"

"Pete'… doggy," Eir placed a toy dog on Peter's tablet.

"I can't study because of you!"

"Forgive me, Peter," said Pascal. "It's my fault. I won't speak any more."

"Peter!" Manami shouted. "What is that behavior?!"

"Mom, I really can't study!"

"Of course you can't! But we too cannot be silent all day because of that! Mr. Alexander explained the new lessons to you. Now go to your room and study. When you learn it, come and he will test you."

"But mom, it's nice here."

"And where did you study at home? You studied in your room, Peter. The sooner you learn it, the sooner you will be able to join us and talk with us. Come on now, go to your room."

Peter reluctantly got up off the couch."

"And Eir? She might fall from here…" he said.

"Sir, I have to clean up the kitchen. Please take Eir," Manami said.

Peter went to his room. Pascal took Eir in his arms and walked around the living room. He finally went into the kitchen and stood next to Manami.

"Eir is exactly like her mom," he said quietly.

Manami turned and kissed her daughter's arm. "Eir has a soul like a fine string," she said.

"Like you… like yours, ma'am."

Manami looked away.

"Eir is an unusually calm child," Pascal continued.

"She is calm… yes," Manami looked at him. "But not as calm as she is now. I think, it seems to me… that Eir, in her own way, feels the atmosphere. That she understands. That is why I said that she has a soul like a fine string. The smallest breeze will play a tone on it. It is because of Eir that it is important that Julius doesn't tell us anything. I might be able to hide my pain from Peter, but not from Eir. Regardless of how strange it might sound."

"It doesn't sound strange, ma'am."

"You say that Eir is like me. And not only in appearance."

"Yes."

"I wish for my little girl to experience everything that her mother did. But on time. That she doesn't inflict pain on anyone because of it."

"You are not inflicting me any pain, ma'am. There is no room for it. There isn't any room for anything else, ma'am," Pascal whispered.

"I wasn't thinking of you, sir."

Chapter 93

The Grasshopper called Erivan.

"I've been thinking, Mr. President."

"Doing a little philosophizing, a?" Erivan smiled.

"I was watching the news last night," the Grasshopper continued in a serious tone.

"And?"

"That report from your office, with you and your generals..."

"Yes?" Erivan murmured suspiciously.

"I didn't like it, Mr. President."

"Why?" asked Erivan in a slightly annoyed voice.

"For several reasons," the Grasshopper continued calmly, not paying attention to that.

"Oh, yes?"

"First of all, you weren't visible, because the generals were in front of you..."

"What was that stupid director looking at?" Erivan got excited.

"You have no business mingling with them, Mr. President. They are generals, but they are far beneath you."

"They are! Of course they are! Everyone is!"

"That's what I've been telling you. You need the camera to show this."

"What do you propose, Grasshopper?"

"I propose that you take the big screen, the one with the map of the world, off the wall and place it in the center of the office, on four legs, like placing a map on the table, get it?"

"Yes. I like that idea..."

"Because this way everyone is looking up, like reading the train schedule at the station. It doesn't look dignified."

"You're right. You're absolutely right!"

"And when the screen is placed at table-height, then let all the generals gather at one end of the table, pushing and shoving among themselves, while you stand magnificently on the opposite side of the table, alone."

"Excellent! Bravo, Grasshopper!"

"One other thing..."

"Yes, tell me…"

"That suit of yours…"

"What's wrong with it? It seems to me that the tailor did an excellent job."

"Yes, he did. It fits you perfectly."

"So what then?"

"Have the same tailor make you a uniform. Also entirely black. With a black shirt and a black tie. And high, black leather, shiny boots…"

"Excellent, excellent… I agree…"

"Because the State is at war. You, as the supreme commander, must be in uniform."

"In uniform! Clearly, of course!"

"People remember wartime presidents the longest. The peacetime ones are soon forgotten. War is the ideal opportunity to go down in history. And in it the throne that has never been reached awaits you."

"Wow, Grasshopper, how well you express yourself. Throne!"

"Pedestal!"

"Wow, pedestal!" Erivan was elated. "I'll call the tailor immediately. Goodbye, Grasshopper."

"Just one more thing…"

"Yes, but say it quickly."

"When you are in uniform, and the generals are squeezing around the table, across from you…"

"Yes?"

"When the camera is recording…"

"Yes?"

"It should also film them from the side…"

"Alright…"

"And let them lean over the table, let their heads peer through…"

"Aha…"

"And they will peer through to be filmed for the news…"

"They will, I know…"

"And they will all try, with all their voice, in their dull gray uniforms, to have you accept precisely their proposal…"

"I know, they try…"

"And you, on the opposite side… in the wonderful black uniform. Pants tucked into the boots, which have been impeccably polished, shining under the spotlights…"

"I can already see it… wonderful…" Erivan gargled.

"…with one hand, clenched tightly into a fist, bent over slightly, leaning on the table, and with the other bent at the elbow, placed

204

on your back; one foot slightly forward and wisely nodding, while they are running around, showing their proposals in the map…"

"Yes! Yes! Hand behind my back!"

"And finally… I think at the end of the news report, you turn your head, looking resolutely at the camera, that is to say into the heart and soul of every Consumer, and you place your hand on the map, anywhere. It doesn't really matter."

"Fantastic!"

Chapter 94

"My husband wanted to make Megapolis the most advanced city in the world," Manami told Pascal, after the children had gone to bed, explaining to him the problems that had occurred at the University.

"That is why he paid the greatest attention to youths. He wanted the University to provide top experts and scientists, but also respectable, polite, moral people. Young people with a genuine conservative system of values. He invested great efforts and means into this. He requested and received a special budget for this from Prince Kaella. He provided scholarships, financed research and development projects. He developed two new elite student dormitories, one men's and one women's, in the park next to the square, as motivation for young people to achieve better grades. For them to get rooms in that dorm, based on them."

"How is it possible that Prince approved a budget for such things?" Pascal wondered.

"Because it was advantageous. Megapolis was gaining respect and significance. Apartments and office rent went up. Parents tried to work more and make more money so that they could send their children to Megapolis to school. There were numerous benefits."

"I understand. And what problems appeared?"

"Like everywhere: hopelessness, pointlessness. The initial hope, which lasted for the first several generations, faded, disappeared, because the best graduates, Masters and PhDs, ultimately faced the reality of Kaella's society. You only do what generates money for the Kaellas. And whatever you make, regardless of how much it is – you spend. You don't create anything. You don't leave anything behind you. Neither spiritually nor materially. In any case, why am I telling you this? This is why you mobilized the people against the regime."

"Yes. The Mayor said that you proposed…"

"And that is why the results of the next several generations of students were poorer. They didn't go to class. Alcohol, drugs, parties and depravity were widespread. It was especially hard on Julius when this happened in the two student dorms. It also bothered Noah a lot."

"Your Noah? Levi?" Pascal asked.

"Yes. He wanted to quit Public Administration studies and transfer to the Inspectorate Academy. His parents and we tried to talk him out of it. He was an excellent student. We all thought that he would succeed his father as Mayor of Capital City. Or Julius here. But he was adamant."

"Did you really propose to the Mayor that he invite me? To talk to the students?"
"This entire time, sir... you were only interested in whether I was..." Manami fell silent.
"Yes. That's all I'm interested in, ma'am."
"I don't know... perhaps. The only thing I know for certain is that I had to meet you."

Chapter 95

"Mom, when will dad come?"

"I don't know, Peter. You know that your father is busy. Let's get you to bed."

"I don't want to. Dad comes at night. And you don't wake me."

"He also comes during the day. And you can't interrupt children's sleep, son."

"What difference does it make? Why do we care whether its day or night?" Peter still protested.

"Peter, we can't allow ourselves to not care. We have to keep our natural rhythm. Even under artificial conditions. Like Eir, you see..."

"Eir! But she's just a baby, mom!"

"You're mom's baby too," Manami kissed her son's hair. "Come on, let's get you to bed."

Peter silently got up from the armchair.

"OK, I promise you," said Manami when she saw how sad her son was. "If dad comes tonight, I'll wake you up. But just tonight."

"Really?" Peter was overjoyed.

"Really. I see that you want to be present when Mr. Alexander speaks well of you to your father. How smart you are and how you know everything."

"I want to," Peter smiled. "But also the other thing we agreed to ask him."

"Alright, alright... we'll ask him," Manami smiled. "Now off to bed."

"I'm going. Good night."

"Good night, Peter," said Pascal.

Manami got up from the armchair and sat across from Pascal, at the table.

"You've really won over my son," she said. "You're very good at that, sir."

Pascal silently looked at her.

"You have nothing to say, sir?"

"Ma'am, that red cover with the black rose... in the middle..."

"Yes?"

"You..." Pascal stopped and looked down.

"What about it?" Manami asked.

"It isn't important. Forgive me... and this... what you were joking about. I will really tell the Mayor what a brilliant boy your son is."

"What about the cover?"

"You sleep in that room, I assume? In that bed?"

"Yes. With Eir. And Peter is in the room with the bunk beds. He says he doesn't want to be in a girl's room. He sleeps on the upper bunk. He finds it interesting. And I fear that he might fall down in his sleep..."

"I slept on it..."

"On the red cover?"

"Yes."

Manami was silent.

"I mean, I wasn't really sleeping... when Raul and the Mayor drugged me. I guess it was easies for them to put me down there... I don't know."

Manami was still silent.

"That red cover... it's made of silk?"

"Yes," said Manami.

"When I woke up... it was dark, I didn't know where I was... but I felt its smell... It was stale..."

"I immediately washed it. It smells nice now."

"Do you also sleep on it? Or do you cover yourself with it?"

"No. I don't use it. I put it away in the dresser."

"Not even once... You've never laid on it?"

"I'm sleepy, too. Good night, sir." Manami got up and went to her quarters.

Chapter 96

"There, you see, Peter, dad doesn't come only at night," said Manami.

"Dad! Daddy!" shouted Peter, when Seneca entered the living room. "You'll let me, won't you? Mom says it's ok."

"Don't make things up, Peter!" Manami laughed. "I told you to ask your dad."

"Ask what?" Seneca smiled, caressing his son's hair.

"Dad, Mr. Alexander wants me to call him Pascal, to be on a first-name basis."

"That's out of the question," Seneca got serious. "I'm so grateful to you, Alexander, for helping my son in his studies..."

"Allow him, Mr. Mayor. It will make it easier for me too. I demanded that of all my students. I always had a friendly relationship with children. And I had excellent results."

"What do you say, Manami?" Seneca asked.

"Say it's alright, mom! Say it's alright!" Peter pleaded.

"I'm alright with that, Julius. Peter is doing very well. If Mr. Alexander believes..."

"Alright, alright..." Seneca smiled. "I see that you've already decided."

"Pascal!" shouted Peter

"Yes, Peter?" Pascal smiled.

"Tell my dad what kind of a student I am!"

"This is tearing my eardrums," Seneca whispered to his wife.

"Let them, Julius... if they want."

"You have a brilliant son, Mr. Mayor. Intelligent, hard working, responsible, well-behaved... in every way."

"Ts, ts, ts," Seneca smiled. "Peter, how did you bribe your teacher to praise you so much?"

"I really think that, Mr. Mayor. Your son will succeed you. He is similar to you in every way."

"Thank you, Alexander, for those words. They mean a lot to me in these times," Seneca bent over and kissed his son.

"Julius," said Manami. "You've come at the right moment. Let's all have lunch together."

"Dad…" Eir called out. She was leaning forward and stretching her hands towards her father.

Seneca took her from her mother's arms.

"How is daddy's girl?" he asked, kissing her hair and sitting down at the table.

After lunch Peter went to his room, to study. After Manami put Eir to bed in their bedroom, she returned to the living room.

"Manami, it's nice that you covered up that fluorescent-green color of the couch. Not only does it remind me of Prince, it's also an eyesore," Seneca said.

"Yes," said Manami. "It's too irritating."

"And this is a nice cover. Raul and I placed you on it that day, Alexander." Seneca looked at Pascal. "I still didn't know that I would be bringing my family to the shelter. I thought it best if you slept in that room. It's the most comfortable one."

"I know," Pascal bowed his head.

"Forgive me for reminding you of Raul," Seneca apologized.

"Yes. I'm trying not to think about my friends. And then I have a guilty conscious. You thank me for working with your son, Mr. Mayor." Pascal looked at Seneca again. "But it means a lot to me, too. It sidetracks my thoughts."

"I understand." Seneca nodded and got up from his chair. "Thank you for lunch, Manami. I have to leave," he said while going towards the door.

"Julius," Manami called out to him, while getting up from the table.

"Yes?" Seneca turned around.

"The next time you are buying food for us, buy a few packages of chili."

"Chili? For Mr. Alexander?"

"Ma'am, please don't burden the Mayor with that," Pascal protested. "That really isn't important."

"Everyone knows that you like spicy food, Alexander. Of course I'll get some," Seneca laughed and walked out of the shelter.

As soon as he heard the elevator go up, Pascal sat down on the couch covered with the red cover with the black rose.

"Could you sit on the couch for a moment, ma'am… on the other end… please," Pascal whispered.

Manami looked at him for a while. Then she approached him and stood in front of him:

"I won't sit now, sir. I will sit tonight… when the children are asleep. And I won't sit on the other end. I will sit next to you and place my head on your shoulder. And I will sit like that... for a long time, a very long time."

Chapter 97

Pascal sat on the couch, waiting for Manami to check whether Peter and Eir had gone to sleep.

"Don't turn around, sir," said Manami, while entering the living room.

"Why?" Pascal asked with a surprised tone.

"Because I'm in my nightgown," said Manami as she turned off the light. She walked over to Pascal in the dark, sat next to him and put her head on his shoulder.

"I could die right now," Pascal thought. "Do you know that, my love? I don't need anything else."

Pascal took a deep breath. He simply slowly placed his cheek on her head. "Darling, I have to... just that... to touch your hair. To smell it. Only that."

"You know, my husband had come already twice at night and found us sitting at the table. I mean to say that we weren't sleeping. That is a bit odd, you must admit."

"I'm aware of that ma'am. But I cannot leave first. I simply cannot. Until you go to bed."

"That is why this is how we will do it from now on: I will be in my nightgown, and you will be dressed. When we hear the elevator, we will have enough time to run to our rooms in the darkness. Do you agree?"

"Yes."

"And if Peter wakes up, we will hear the door to his room. I will run to my quarters and tell my son that I was in the kitchen, that I was getting something from the freezer. Some meat. To defrost it for lunch tomorrow. That I suddenly woke up and remembered it. That's a logical explanation, isn't it?"

Pascal occasionally moved his cheek across her hair.

"This cover means a lot to you, sir?" Manami asked after a while.

"A lot. It means a lot to me. You know, that day, when I was preparing to go into the square... I wondered... why isn't there something..."

213

"What?"
"A room… our room… and now… it exists."

Chapter 98

"Why won't you have dinner with us tonight, Julius," Manami asked her husband from the kitchen. "Dinner will be ready in half an hour."

"I can't Manami, really. I don't have time. I came just for a bit... to tell you something."

"Julius!" Manami raised her voice and looked at her husband, who was sitting at the table and holding Eir in his lap. She gestured towards Peter, who was sitting with his back towards her.

"Don't worry, Manami. Everything is alright, just... obligations are piling up. I won't be able to keep it up like this. I mean, I've been coming almost every day. And I actually have to go to our house. The house is being guarded by inspectors as though my family was in it. I have to stay the night there sometimes. Noah will provide and bring food for you from now on."

"Noah? Does he know that we are here?" Manami was surprised.

"Noah is great, Pascal!" Peter shouted out. "Colonel! He has a black belt in karate! He taught me a kata!"

"Alright, Peter, alright..." said Seneca. "I had to tell someone, Manami. I can't provide for you on my own and lock the office. It's too intense. Do you understand? I have to be available, to make decisions at every moment. A huge number of people are calling, coming... day and night... events are sudden, unpredictable..."

"I understand, Julius, it's clear to me. Does Noah also know about Mr. Alexander?"

"He does," Seneca looked at Pascal. "I had to tell him everything, Alexander. He will bring you food, cosmetics... perhaps you will also need clothes. He will realize that there is also an adult male in the shelter."

"Mr. Mayor, please, don't trouble yourself with that. You know best who you can trust."

"I have absolute trust in Noah, especially now that..."

"Julius!" Manami was afraid that Seneca would mention the death of Noah's parents in front of Peter.

"Peter," Seneca turned towards his son. "You won't see Noah. He will just bring the supplies down to the corridor and immediately return to my office. And mother will distribute them later."

"Why?" Peter was disappointed.

"Noah doesn't have time. He is now head of my personal security. He has to be with me at all times. Those are the Inspectorate rules."

"That's great, dad! That Noah is protecting you!"

"It is," said Seneca. He got up, kissed Eir and put her on the floor. The little girl ran off to the armchair full of toys.

"Peter, help Eir get up," Manami said.

"I have to go," Seneca said goodbye. "Son, you just keep on studying."

He stroked Peter on the head and started towards the door. Then he remembered something and turned towards them.

"Alexander, do you know who turned up at my office yesterday?" Seneca smiled.

"Who?" Pascal wondered.

"Your assistant, Miss Van Andel."

"Svetlana?" Pascal shouted.

"Yes. She left your staff a day earlier. That's what Raul told me."

"Yes, she did. But I thought that she had left Megapolis."

"She didn't. She's here. We also thought that she had left... I was just telling my wife that Miss Van Andel was wrong..." Seneca looked at Peter. "If you understand what I mean?"

"Yes... I understand," said Pascal. "Why did she come to you?"

"To ask for a job. She has no income."

"And?" Pascal asked.

"I immediately gave her a job in my secretariat. Miss Van Andel is educated and a very capable young woman. That is the impression I got when you came to our house. I need associates. It is especially important that I can have full confidence in her. That is of the utmost importance at times like these."

"It is. I'm glad for Svetlana, I truly am. You won't regret it, Mr. Mayor. Svetlana is exceptional," said Pascal.

Chapter 99

"Did you watch the evening news, Grasshopper?" Erivan asked as soon as the Grasshopper picked up.

"Yes, Mr. President. You were fantastic."

"Hm? Was I?" Erivan chirped. "Here, I'm playing back the recording. I can't stop. And the hand on the back? What do you think?"

"Unique."

"And one foot a bit back, straight, sharp like a sword, a?"

"Phenomenal."

"The most phenomenal, Grasshopper! Had I not stuck it out, the spotlight would not have shined on the boot."

"No, it surely wouldn't."

"And like this it gleams!"

"It gleams."

"You're not exactly thrilled?"

"Of course I am. I watched it many times."

"Really?"

"Of course... Nevertheless, I'm watching events in different cities. Everywhere... across the Earth. I'm zooming in the images from our satellites..."

"Why?"

"Because such things interest me. I zoom in on people's faces. It's a pity I don't have audio."

"You are a strange one, Grasshopper."

"I've been thinking."

"What? You have a proposal?"

"No, no... I see... in one city Consumers and Non-Consumers are mixed together."

"Yes, that's the case in most cities."

"They've set up barricades in the middle of some street."

"Yes, they're doing that everywhere. The city is split into the Consumer and Non-Consumer part, and each flees to their own."

"I see. But not everyone makes it across. In this street, the one I mentioned, they fell a man behind the barricades, and they're kicking him. And he hasn't moved in a while. He's probably dead."

"What does that have to do with me on the news?" Erivan was curious.

"And behind the other barricades, on the same street, in the same city, the same picture. They are kicking another man. The only difference is the clothes. Ones have t-shirts with vertical stripes, and the others have t-shirts with horizontal stripes. Then I thought how lucky these people are today that they can clearly differentiate between themselves. The seasons have provided people with uniforms, already in this initial phase of the war. For all of them. There will be no civilians in this war, Mr. President."

"Excuse me?" Erivan asked without any interest, stopping the recording at the moment when he banged his fist on the map and looked at the camera.

"All those wretches in past wars…" the Grasshopper spoke contemplatively, "… went into the street and had no idea who was on their side and who was the enemy. They differed only in the invisible. In what was in their heads."

"What heads, Grasshopper? Man, do you see this gaze of mine? Do you see it?"

"But that's man. That's how he was created. Experience doesn't play a role… only instinct. Here, look at this generation of ours. There were other such generations in history, when the lulls lasted several decades. I mean… periods without wars. These children think that wars serve only to torment them in history class. There were other such generations that thought that wars were the thing of their past, stupid, primitive and undeveloped ancestors. And that they were developed, civilized, humane… and then a war would break out, like this one… after an entire century… and people immediately, instinctively start kicking."

"Ah, they're funny," said Erivan, watching the generals push and shove on their side of the table.

"I'm thinking about our season clothes. What's wrong with that? Nothing. People have found all kinds of excuses to kill each other throughout history. So why should this one, with the t-shirts and different stripes, be any less worthy than the previous ones? Perhaps it isn't as dignified as the pervious ones? It's really a pity that I don't have audio so that I can hear one of the heroes, bare-chested, carrying a staff with the t-shirt hanging on it, charging the enemy barricades, shouting 'Horizontal stripes!' or 'Vertical stripes!', just before being cut down by a hail of gunfire."

"Are you still running a fever, Grasshopper?" Erivan asked, going back to the story from the evening news.

"No. I'm just very content. I would sometimes wonder… doubt myself… for a moment…"

"Did you notice at all how I approached the table, Grasshopper?! Did you see that stride!"

"I'd think about whether the Balance has actually been achieved. Is that the final answer? Has the killing come to an end? Although, Kaella did kill the old and the sick to keep the Balance..."

"Yes, he did. What a scoundrel he was. Here, I'm slowly making a fist..."

"...in those hospital of his, Euthanasias."

"Yes, the hospitals are full. They're constantly pestering me with that, Grasshopper! They say, 'what should we do, Mr. President? There are many wounded, then there are these epidemics... we don't have drugs...' I'm sick of them... Look, look! Are you watching my footage at all, Grasshopper? I'm placing the fist on the table, leaning on it..."

"But that was systemic, regime killing. That is why I wondered what happened to the basic human urge... and now I'm at peace, content. That is... always the same, just with a new excuse. And those striped t-shirts of ours, that is probably the cutest excuse in history."

"Cute? You think that they're cute? I think they're really funny!" Erivan laughed loudly, watching the generals stretch their necks.

"And now I'm certain. Now I know... Now that I'm finally here, in this room, I know that I was right all along, that my effort wasn't in vain... that my life has a purpose..."

"Grasshopper, that's..." Erivan was laughing so hard that he struggled for air.

"To serve you, Mr. President," Grasshopper jolted back from his thoughts.

"I'm going to die laughing, to die... Hmm? What did you say?"

"I say, to serve you, Mr. President."

"And you're lucky to have me, Grasshopper," said Erivan, watching himself wisely nod his head over the map of the world.

Chapter 100

"Move it! Move it!" shouted the commander of the firing squad while his men were taking their positions. "Come on!" he continued. "Don't disgrace yourself! You see the large audience we have today!" he pointed to the group of Consumers from the nearby city, who stood on the side and watched their fellow-citizens, the Non-Consumers, lined up in front of the firing squad.

"Lucky, what is this horrible movie?" Sayash asked Lucky, while holding him in his arms. "I'm getting the creeps. You're not afraid of anything, are you, Lucky?" Sayash bowed his head and looked at Lucky. "You don't even blink, do you? How are you going to fall asleep tonight?"

"Get the bum back in line!" shouted the commander, when he saw Sayash and Lucky in front of his firing squad.

"What's that, Lucky? It's started to rain, is it?" Sayash asked, looking up at the sky, when Lucky's first tear fell on his arm. "It isn't rain, Lucky," Sayash concluded. "Everything is dry," he turned Lucky towards him. "There, I knew it! You're crying! This isn't the movie for you, Lucky! Let's go to another one."
Lucky turned in Sayash's arms away from the Non-Consumers, lined up to be shot, and looked towards the gathered Consumers.

"Mommy, look! The dog is crying!"
"What dog? I don't see it."
"In that man's arms!"
"Give your other hand to your father," said the Consumer, when she saw Lucky's tears. "Let's go," She took a step towards the Non-Consumers and took her son and husband with her.
All the Consumers followed them and mixed with their fellow-citizens, the Non-Consumers.

"Let's go home, neighbor, for a chess match. What do you say?"
"I'm white."

"Today dinner is at our place."
"That's out of the question, neighbor. It's our turn."

"So, when are you going to pay back that money?"
"I knew that was going to be the first thing you ask."

"So, you put on last season's clothes because of your daughter-in-law?"
"Don't mention it. We barely found them. Can't you see that I have on this season's shoes?" the father answered his colleague.
"She still isn't our daughter-in-law," said the mother, "but she will be. What else could we do? Our son doesn't want to live without her. Isn't that right, son?"
The son didn't answer. He just hugged his girlfriend.

"Mommy, where are that man and the dog?"
"I don't know. They're around here somewhere."

"People! People! It was them!"
"Them who? Why are you shouting?!"
"The Saint and the Dog! They bring good luck and then disappear!"
"What Saint? That plaid bum? You've already started drinking, but you're not sharing, are you?"

"Dad! Dad!"
"Wait a moment. Don't you see that I'm talking to our neighbor?"
"Dad, we will all be playing in front of the building! All of us, dad! Do you know how long it's been since we all played together?!"
"Alright, alright, but only until dark."

"Get in the vehicles! Let's go! These people have completely lost it!" the firing squad commander said with a terribly annoyed tone.

"People! How long are we going to keep standing here in this wasteland?! Let's go back to our city! To hide it! So that one will ever find it!"

Chapter 101

"What's wrong with you, Mr. President? Why are you so pale?" the Grasshopper asked Erivan.

"I haven't been sleeping enough... problems..."

"What problems? The war is going well, as far as I see. And I'm looking at these snipers in the cities. Are those our boys?"

"Both ours and the others. Everyone has a sniper these days. And I released from prison all the killers, rapists, pedophiles... let them terrorize the Non-Consumers a little."

"There, there. But I'm curious about these snipers. I wonder, how do they choose who to kill?"

"Well you've killed people so many time with a sniper, Grasshopper. What's strange about it?"

"That's different. Those were targets that you identified for me, Mr. President. And I wonder, how do they...? Sitting in a window, watching the people in the street through their scopes... I can't grasp, what is their criteria? I see them kill both men and women, young and old, children... I really don't get it. I guess depending on whose face they don't like. I couldn't do that. All faces are the same to me."

"You wouldn't kill anyone until I gave you a target?"

"No, no... I'd kill them all."

"You can't do that with one sniper, Grasshopper. You kill one, and the others run from the street. Then you have to move to a different skyscraper. It isn't easy for them. Its hard work. Especially if the elevators don't work. By the way, do you know that Consumers have started to protest?"

"Why?" the Grasshopper was surprised.

"Because I said that we would seize the Non-Consumers' shares..."

"I know."

"And the Non-Consumers immediately started selling them on the stock exchange. And the prices dropped, so the Consumers started to panic. And they too started selling. Within a few days the Company lost ninety percent of its value. And everyone is blaming me."

"Well that is a great opportunity, Mr. President."

"What do you mean?"

"Well, buy now, when the price is so low."

"What can I buy it with? My salary?"

"Who said anything about your salary? Do you know how much money Prince Kaella has in the vaults beneath his palace?"

"That's right! Why didn't I think of that?"

"But, I was thinking about something else."

"About what? Tell me."

"Kaella's family is still in the palace?"

"Yes."

"Throw them out, and move in. Those presidential quarters aren't really that nice."

"Well, they aren't... I too was thinking about moving, but after the war. Here I have communications and logistics."

"You're right. But then don't move into their palace."

"Why?"

"Because the colonnades are too low. For them they were even too high, but for you, Mr. President, they have to be at least a meter higher. To make it clear to everyone who is the new ruler of the world."

"A meter? Five meters!"

"I agree. First get the money from the vault, then tear down Kaella's palace, the whole thing, not only the colonnades. And build yourself the most lavishing edifice that has ever existed on Earth."

"I will! The most lavishing!"

Chapter 102

"When will we start the blackouts, Mr. President?"

"Well we could gradually, Grasshopper. Are you sure you know how to control that?"

"I trained for that for five months. Do you doubt me?"

"I don't doubt you. OK, start switching if off."

"I will, but I don't know which cities to turn off the power to."

"What do you mean 'which ones', Grasshopper? To the Non-Consumer cities."

"I know that, but where should I start?"

"First black out Megapolis."

"Megapolis?"

"Yes."

"Is that what the generals said?"

"No. They still don't even know that I'm going to switch off the power."

"They don't know? So that's why you think that they will immediately propose that you switch off the energy to Megapolis. You are absolutely right, Mr. President. That is exactly what they will propose. Because they envy and hate you. And that is why they don't want you to leave Megapolis for the end of the war."

"You're right, Grasshopper. They envy and hate me. I don't trust them at all."

"That's right. That's why you won't listen to them. And you will wait until the end of the war, when the entire world has already surrender and bowed before you. Only then will the two of us switch off the energy to Megapolis. They are all spoiled wimps and they will surrender quickly. And then you will arrive in the center of their main square in a gold chariot pulled by sixteen white horses. There at the table the defeated Seneca will be waiting and before you he will sign the capitulation of Megapolis."

"That is wonderful! Fantastic! That's all I'll dream about from now on!"

"So, what should I switch off first?"

"Switch off whatever you want, Grasshopper."

"Yes, sir, Mr. President."

Chapter 103

"So what don't I understand?" wondered Pascal, while sitting at the dining room table, with his back turned towards the kitchen.

"Pascal," said Eir. The little girl raised her head, while sitting in his lap, offering him a doll that she had just put a dress on.
"Yes, Eir?" asked Pascal, accepting the doll. "Well that is a very pretty dress. Now put this one on her," Pascal pointed at a floral dress. "So we can see which one is prettier."
"Oki," said Eir and took the doll from Pascal.

Pascal's eyes went back to the white sheet which had been covering the couch for the past two weeks. "How long will I stare at that sheet? What am I waiting for? A fairy godmother to turn it into our cover? To turn this room into ours? I have nothing to wait for. Nothing to hope for. I have experienced the pinnacle of my life. My five minutes are passed. They're passed, Pascal!" he shouted at himself. "Accept it. It's over, finished, caput, no more, the end!"

"...my husband doing now?" he heard Manami behind him. "He's been gone for days. He'll defeat Erivan. If you can say that anyone is truly exceptional, then it's my husband."

"There, Pascal. Did you hear that? You did, you did. That's all you hear. That's all you listen to all day long. 'My husband, my husband!' Your Mrs. Seneca has made up her mind. That night, your only night, Pascal, she sat next to you in her nightgown and she saw that you're nothing special. That she doesn't need that. You probably stumbled upon her during a small marriage crisis. The young woman, whose husband is never at home, longed for a little attention, a little adventure, a break from monotony. And she slipped into her nightgown, put her head on your shoulder and that was it. For such a conservatively raised woman that was more than enough. She ended her adventure and went back to her family. After that she 'accidently' spilled tea on your cover and she said that she had to wash it. And she still hasn't washed it. And she will never wash it. Regardless of how much you stare at that sheet."

"There, I'm done in the kitchen," said Manami, taking Eir from Pascal. "The two of us are off to our quarters. Thank you very much, sir, for looking after her," said Manami, without looking at him.

Chapter 104

"You had your hopes up again, Pascal?" Pascal asked himself when Manami took his plate after lunch. "Your hands tremble every time that you raise the spoon to your mouth. You think, this time, for sure... Well, it wasn't this time either! And it never will be! She didn't put chili in your food once! Sober up! Get out of here! Go already, man! It's over! Over! You heard the lady, what she's telling you the entire time? My husband this, my husband that! No more Julius! Only my husband! So that you will finally understand who she is and who she belongs to. To get you off her back once and for all."

"You're not saying anything, sir? How was lunch?" Manami asked from the kitchen, with her back turned.
"Excellent, ma'am, thank you," Pascal answered, with his back turned to her.
"Excellent? Only excellent? So it wasn't exceptional?"
"Yes, ma'am, it was exceptional."
"That's alright. I'm just joking with you, sir. Only rare things are exceptional, right?"
"That's right, ma'am."

"Make up your mind once and for all!" Pascal returned to his dark thoughts. "Don't desecrate it! Don't desecrate your night any more. As soon as you hear that Noah bring the food, or if Seneca... no, not Seneca – the lady's husband! Please, Pascal, express yourself correctly! So, if the lady's husband appears... That's right, Pascal! Bravo! Even you are learning some manners! Then nicely, say goodbye to Mrs. Seneca..."
At that thought, with that image before his eyes, Pascal sighed deeply. He waved his head. "I can't... I can't imagine it... That moment... I hold out my hand... and see her for the last time... I can't... I can't go on without you, Manami! I can't!!!"

"Pascal, do you want to test me now," said Peter, when he too had finished lunch.
"Alright. Bring the tablet."

"Leave the gentleman be, Peter. He might want to have a little rest after lunch."

"No, no ma'am..."

"When you're finished testing Peter, Eir will wake up, then she will want you to play with her. That's not your responsibility, sir." Manami stood next to Pascal. "You know what? From now on the three of us will be in our rooms. I will work with Peter. So that you can have a rest from all of us, sir."

Pascal bowed his head.

"What are you saying, mommy?" Peter shouted. "I want to study with Pascal."

"And I want to test your knowledge myself, Peter. To see whether it is truly as exceptional as the gentleman claims. Peter's knowledge is exceptional, isn't it, sir? That is your favorite expression it seems to me, sir!"

"Yes, it's exceptional," whispered Pascal, without raising his head.

Chapter 105

"You have to get through that moment, Pascal. This moment is the price that you have to pay for that night. You just squeeze her hand... Who says that you have to look her in the eyes? Look past her. And you just turn around and run to the elevator.

"Noah will probably come tomorrow. He hasn't been in a while. Tomorrow! Surely tomorrow! Only that one moment and the end. You go to one of your cities... I won't go to one of our cities. I won't. I'll ask Seneca to explain to me the war situation. Then I'll go to one of Erivan's cities. Perhaps even to Capital City? No, not to Capital City. It is entirely controlled by him. I will go to one of the cities where our people are surrounded, where they are losing the battle. Yes, that's it. Somewhere where I will certainly be killed, already on the first day. I will take a weapon and immediately rush the inspectors. Let them mow me down in an instant. And what if Noah appears now? If I hear the elevator now, in the middle of the night?

"And she's asleep. How will I say goodbye? How will I see her at least one more time? I cannot... I cannot leave. Let her drive me out! That's it! I won't decide anything. I won't think about anything any more. I don't have the strength to think. I can only look at her. Only love her."

"Sir, why are you not sleeping?" asked Manami, entering fully dressed into the living room in the middle of the night.

"I can't, ma'am," Pascal kept his eyes pinned to her.

"I feel like tea. I thought of making some, but now I won't. I don't want to bother you."

"You are not bothering me, ma'am. You never..." whispered Pascal.

"Alright, if you say so," Manami passed next to Pascal and went into the kitchen. She poured water into the kettle. "I'll make some green tea. It is my husband's favorite. Actually my husband is exceptionally fond of green tea..."

"My husband! My husband! My husband!!!" Pascal exploded. "As though no one here understands that! It is as though someone here doubts that! That he is your husband, ma'am! The Missis has a husband! Nothing is more important than that! That is the only thing that should be discussed! That is the only thing that should be constantly repeated! My husband! My husband!!!"

"How dare you!?" Manami shouted.
Pascal didn't pay attention to that; he didn't listen to her nor did he control himself. He continued to shout.
"Does that husband of yours have a name, perhaps?! As far as I hear, you call him Julius! And when you talk to the children you call him dad. Only when you speak to me, then he is 'my husband'!"
"What insolence!" Manami shouted, trying to outdo him.
"What do you tell him? 'Do you want some lunch, my husband? Here you go some green tea, my husband!' Is that how you speak to him?!"
"You should be ashamed of yourself, sir! What gives you the right!? You are the last man in world who has the right to say something like that to me!"
"The last?! I know that I'm the last one for you, ma'am! You don't need to explain that to me! What do you tell him?! 'Come to our room, to our bed, my husband!' Is that how you call him?!"
"Shame on you! Shame on you!" screamed Manami, as an uncontrolled rage came over her.

Pascal suddenly fell silent. He awoke from a trans. Only then, when he had gotten it all out of him, did he realize what he had told her.
"Forgive me, ma'am... forgive me, please..." he passed by her, on his way to his room. "As soon as your husband comes, I will leave... Forgive me, please... You will never see me again... forgive me..." He was already near the door.
Manami ran after him, around him, opened his door, grabbed him by the hand and pulled him strongly into his quarters.
"Close the door and turn on the light!" she said angrily, sharply, with a whisper. Pascal did as she said. "Where is your room?!" she asked, louder.
"Here... over here," Pascal said.
Manami burst into the middle of the large dormitory, turned to Pascal and ordered him
"Close the door and turn on the light in the room!"
Pascal did so.
"I won't let you wake my children, sir!" Manami was now shouting as loud as she could.
"Forgive me... forgive me..."

Manami rushed at him and pushed him.

"At least I have one husband!" she pressed her hands against his chest and pushed him. "And you, sir?!" she shouted. "How are you surviving in bed alone, for so long?! Without all those women of yours?! How?!"

Pascal watched her lips twitch and ever muscle on her face tremble.

"I know how! You have your memories! You have so many of them that you can remember a different woman every night!"

"I don't remember…" Pascal whispered.

"If this were to last another hundred years, you wouldn't lack the memories! You won't, sir!"

"I don't remember anyone. Anyone…" Pascal took her clenched white fists in his hands.

"Let me go!" she said, pulling back her hand. "Don't touch me! I'm not one of your women! I'm not! Tell me one thing, which one do you think of most often? Which one do you dream of the best?"

"No one… only you … only you…" he whispered.

"That Svetlana of yours!? The youngest, isn't she? If even she is young enough for Mr. Alexander?! Not one is young enough for the gentleman, isn't that right?"

"There is no one… only you…"

"And the gentleman thinks that I'm to blame! He accuses me! Of course! It's easier that way! Offense is the best defense!"

"Forgive me… forgive me…"

"And I've been waiting to see when you will tell my husband… there it is! My husband! My husband! And there's nothing you can do about it! Nothing!!!"

"It's alright… forgive me…"

"I've been waiting to see when you will tell him to bring your Svetlana here!"

"I won't…"

"Your exceptional Svetlana! Isn't that so, sir?! Exceptional, isn't that right!?" she pushed him away again.

"Manami, my love… love… Love!!!" Pascal shouted overjoyed. "You silly, you're jealous! I'm so overjoyed! Overjoyed!!!"

"I know that you're overjoyed! I know! Because your Svetlana didn't leave Megapolis! That's why you're overjoyed, sir! Now she can come to you here! To this dormitory of yours!" Manami spread her hands. "Because you cannot survive without her! Because the nights are too long!"

"My love! My Manami!" Pascal cried out, trying to hug her.

231

"Let me go!" Manami pushed his hands away. "You will tell him to bring her to you, because you've had enough of this prison with me!"

"I haven't had enough, Manami! I will never have enough! That's all I want, my love! Just to be locked up with you! Do you know how much I have suffered? I thought that you don't love me anymore, but you were only jealous of Svetlana! You silly..."

"Don't say that name any more!" she pushed him all the way to the wall. "I prohibit you! I prohibit!!!" she screamed.

"I won't, Manami! I won't! Anyone's name! Only yours! Manami! Manami! Manami! Do you hear, Manami? My Manami! Are you mine? Tell me! Tell me that you're mine!"

Pascal tried to hug her. Manami fought back wildly.

"What do you need me for, sir? She is yours! She is!"

"She is not mine, my love." Pascal lowered his voice, realizing that he had to explain it to her, that he must calm her.

"She's not?! And whose is she!? Whose!?"

"I don't know... She knew from the first day how in love I was with you, Manami. From the first moment that I saw you. My love, my life... You cannot understand that; how much I love you. There is no me, Manami. There is only my love for you."

Manami started crying aloud and ran out of Pascal's quarters.

Chapter 106

"Peter, please wake Mr. Alexander. Tell him that lunch is ready," Manami said the next day.

"Finally," Peter shouted. "He can test me."

He got up from the couch where he had been sitting with Eir, painting something on the tablet. He knocked on Pascal's door.

"Pascal, wake up! Lunch!"

"I'm coming, Peter. Let me just wash my face."

Pascal entered the living room area and stopped dead in his tracks. Then he rushed towards the couch which was covered in their red cover. He sat down next to Eir.

"What are you drawing?" he asked, passing his hands across the red silk.

"A bunny," said Eir.

"What's wrong with you, Pascal?" Peter was puzzled. "Sit at the table."

"I will, Peter... in a moment..." He touched their cover as though he was touching her.

Manami placed a plate in front of her son, looked at Pascal and smiled.

"There, there, sir. You've been sleeping all day. Peter has been waiting for you to test him."

"Mom saw that I know everything, and now she wants you to test me again, Pascal."

"That's good... Has Eir eaten, or..."

"She has. The child can't wait for heavy sleepers," Manami was radiant.

"I sincerely apologize. But I haven't slept a wink in two weeks."

"Why?" Peter asked.

"I had constant headaches," Pascal got up from the couch, approached the table and stood behind Peter. He was looking at Manami. "And last night the pain went away. It disappeared. Never again to return. Isn't that right, ma'am?"

"How would I know, sir? You have to take care of your own health," Manami laughed.

233

"Come on, Peter," Pascal tapped Peter on the shoulder.

"Come one, what?" Peter was surprised.

"Well… go to your seat."

"What's wrong with you, Pascal? This is my seat. You sit across the way."

"That is where I sat while I had a headache. You've forgotten that I used to sit here before."

"Whatever," said Peter and moved. "I don't care."

"I do," Pascal sat in his place, with a view of the kitchen.

"Bon appétit!" said Manami.

"Thank you," answered Pascal, and started eating.

"Chili! Finally you've put it in, my love!" he said with his eyes. Manami didn't touch the food. She just watched him and smiled.

Chapter 107

Peter did not leave the living room area the entire afternoon. Manami and Pascal were left alone only late in the evening, when Peter finally got tired. Pascal rushed to Manami, clutching her shoulders and feverishly whispering

"Do you love me, Manami? Tell me! Tell me that you love me!"

"Peter isn't asleep, sir!" Manami was glowing.

"Tell me! Tell me, my love!"

"I was brought up in a conservative family, sir," Pascal went silent and let go of her shoulders. "Where marriage is a sanctity."

"I knew it! I knew it!" Pascal shouted and ran towards his room.

Manami rushed after him, grabbed his hand and turned him around. "What is the matter with you, sir?" she laughed. "Why are you so impulsive? One cannot explain anything to you completely."

"You love me! I know that you love me!" Pascal shouted, when he saw Manami looking at him lovingly and smiling.

"You fixate on something," she ran her fingers through his long wavy hair, "and you don't notice anything else. It took you two weeks to realize how jealous I am."

"My love... My Manami..." Pascal whispered while hugging her.

"I was angry at you for two weeks, and you didn't get it, my darling!"

"Well, I thought... alright, alright," said Pascal holding her by the shoulders again and looking her in the eye, "you said yourself that you consider marriage a sanctity."

"Yes, I did. And you only know how to go crazy. You didn't let me say that I'm not a saint. And that I'm madly, madly in love with you!"

Pascal moved towards her lips. Manami pressed her head against his chest.

"Let me kiss you! I have to kiss your lips, Manami!"

"I won't let you. We cannot. We have to behave like nothing has happened."

"How, Manami, how? I can't go on like that."

"You have to... We have to. Promise me."

"I can't..."

"If you love me, promise me."

"Alright… if you wish so. I don't want to force you to do anything, my love. Everything will be as you wish."

Manami wriggled out of his embrace and said
"I'm going to see whether Peter is asleep. And to put on my nightgown. I want us to sit on our cover until dawn. In our room. That's all I've been dreaming of, Pascal."

Chapter 108

"The generals have turned against me, Grasshopper," Erivan moaned. "They say that they want no part in this and that they will not be held accountable for crimes against humanity and for gecide."

"Genocide."

"Yes, that's it. They say that they convicted you, without any mercy."

"So you are also a doubter, Mr. President?"

"Me, a doubter?!" Erivan was in shock.

"Well, if you doubt our victory."

"Me doubt victory?! Be careful of what you say, Grasshopper!" Erivan rumbled.

"Of course you have doubts. Have the defeated ever judged the victor?"

"Well, that's true. You're right, Grasshopper. That has never happened. We will try them for gecide."

"Genocide."

"Yes, that."

"And what did you tell the generals to that, Mr. President?"

"Nothing. Charlie killed them all."

"That's good. How is my friend Charlie?"

"He is well. They are all well, and I haven't slept in nights, Grasshopper."

"Why do you permit yourself this, Mr. President? You do your office hours, your eight hours, then to bed. Or a casual stroll around the residence. You have to think about your health, above all."

"I do, but it's no use. I'm always swamped by people."

"By whom?"

"Everyone. From all sectors of the Company. They complain that they can't deliver goods to shops under these conditions. That the few that they do deliver are not selling at all. That is why the workers are not getting paid. Then they don't want to work. They go on strike. No one is paying for energy anymore. Even in the places where you haven't switched it off. They're a wanton mob, Grasshopper."

"What salaries? There's a war. Introduce labor duties."

"I've already tried that, Grasshopper. It doesn't work. The inspectors have created a labor union and even they won't work. Neither to arrest the Non-Consumers nor to take them to the camps. They are demanding regular pay and an increase of 30%. Where do I get the money for that?"

"What happened to Prince's money?"

"Its all gone. I bought cheap shares for all the money in the vault, and the price started to go up. But now the sectors are not producing. They're on strike. The stock is worthless. It's a disaster, Grasshopper. Even I received only one quarter of the salary for this month."

"What do you care about your salary? You can have whatever you want."

"I know… I'm just saying, so you can see that the situation is difficult."

"I really don't see any problem there."

"Its easy for you up there, Grasshopper. That's why you can talk like that."

"What is money, Mr. President?"

"What do you mean 'what is it'? Money is…"

"Its just printed paper. That's what money is."

"Yes, Grasshopper, but…"

"Print it, Mr. President, as much as you need. For our squads, for the Inspectorate, for weapons production."

"I don't need it for the squads. I told them that all the war booty is theirs. Some of your colleagues are already very rich. They could buy both you and me, Grasshopper."

"I believe you. But I'm telling you, print money for everything else."

Part III: The Apocalypse

Chapter 109

"What did you do to the entire city, Grasshopper?" Erivan asked anxiously.

"I vaporized it. That's easy. You increase the strength of the cosmic energy beam to the maximum and you reduce the entire city to atoms. You vaporize it. That's what I call it. Because the city makes a 'puff' and that's it."

"But why the 'puff'!?!"

"I saw that in that city the bandits were preparing a secret weapon for the destruction of your residence, Mr. President. I'm merciless in that respect, when your safety is in question, Mr. President."

"Wow, thank you, Grasshopper. What would I do without you? Who would defend and protect me? By the way, do you see how bloodshot my eyes are?'

"I do. They're really red."

"I'm still not sleeping. It's getting worse and worse."

"How is that?"

"I printed the money. I gave the inspectors their salaries. And I increased them 100%, not 30%, like they had asked..."

"And?..."

"And they started working normally, but then they came and said that I had tricked them, that the money was worthless."

"What do they mean worthless?"

"It isn't worthless, but they said that all the prices had gone up. That they can't buy even a kilo of potatoes for their monthly salary."

"Print more and increase their salaries again."

"I did and I gave them a raise, as a reward in the middle of the month. And they said that they can't buy even half a kilogram of potatoes. So I asked them 'how much do these potatoes cost?'. They said a million. No problem. I added six zeroes and printed their new salaries. And they came back. They said that potatoes now cost a thousand billions or a billion billions, I've already forgotten. And that's where I realized that they are only greedy and that they were lying to me. Even Prince Kaella didn't have that much money."

"And?"

"Nothing. Charlie killed those from the union and now all the inspectors have turned against me. You can probably see from up there how they are tightening the noose around my residence. And you're playing dumb and asking me why my eyes are red and why I'm not sleeping."

"I see. Who's defending you? The squads?"

"Nope. Only Charlie's left. Everyone else has stolen as much as they wanted, killed as much as they wanted, each one created their own army... Now I hear that they're killing each other."

"Don't worry, Mr. President. I'll defend you. I've been working on that for a while now. Just hang on a little longer."

Chapter 110

"Where have you been, Grasshopper?" Erivan shouted in panic, when the Grasshopper finally picked up. "Can't you see that they're almost in the residence?! Charlie's barely holding on!"

"Calm down, Mr. President. I've completed my procedure. Everything is in place now," the Grasshopper calmed him.

"What procedure of yours? What is in place?"

"Are you seeing how I'm vaporizing cities across the Earth?"

"Yes. And they say that I'm to blame for sending such a butcher up there."

"Butcher? Cute. Now listen to me carefully. My procedure automatically controls the energy beams targeting a ring around the entire region of Capital City. When it detects that someone has entered that ring, the beams go online and vaporize everything that is in it. Do you understand, Mr. President?"

"I understand..."

"So no one can enter or leave Capital City."

"Alright..."

"You're not pleased? I'm providing you with absolute protection and you..."

"Can't you create that ring around my residence? What use is the region. You probably see..."

"I cannot create such small beams. And I also don't want to. You'll see, Capital City will adore you."

"How, Grasshopper, how?!"

"You will immediately appear on television and explain to the people everything what I've told you. And tell them that if anyone gives you the eye, I will vaporize all of Capital City."

"They won't believe me... you have to tell them, Grasshopper."

"Me?"

"Yes."

"Alright. I'll call the television station."

Chapter 111

Dr. Palladino never cared about anything. Except for on two occasions. The first time was on that day, when he was the only one not to appear at his wedding. Not that something was wrong with the bride. Brides will be brides: she cared about children, a home, furniture... etc. That is why Dr. Palladino remained alone his entire life.

Dr. Palladino had become a doctor because his father, Dr. Palladino, wanted it. He chose psychiatry on his own, because the job didn't require him touching people.

Humane Capitalism suited Dr. Palladino. As soon as he got a job at a psychiatric hospital in Capital City, he asked an elegant older colleague where he dressed.
Honored by such a question, the older colleague explained to him in detail how the location and size of the apartment, the car and clothes were very important for psychiatrists like them. Because that way they emphasized the high standing of their clinic, and they assumed the respectable social ranking, which, by the way, they fully deserved.
That is how Dr. Palladino learned where he would live in the future and in which shops he would be buying his car, furniture and clothes. He immediately created a special contact with the vendors and asked them at the end of the season to immediately hand over all the old things to the inspectorate, and to bring and install, assemble, put in all the new things... as it was supposed to be.
Humane Capitalism allowed Dr. Palladino to relieve himself of all great burdens, in one move, for his entire life. But he didn't know how to wear all that. He spent all his time in the smallest room of his large apartment. He didn't drive his car but rather he took the taxi. All the elegant clothes, in the right sizes, hung loosely on him. And because of the loose knot, his silk tie draped diagonally.

Humane Capitalism also suited Dr. Palladino in the professional sense. Because Prince Kaella had placed the highest prices on drugs for the treatment of psychiatric conditions. That way Dr.

Palladino's patients quickly spent their meager savings, if they had any at all, and quickly ended up at Euthanasia. The Balance, which Mr. Kaella had created in society, could not support such a burden for long. The high frequency with which patients changed allowed Dr. Palladino not to get overly involved with them.

Dr. Palladino did not care much for cigarettes, whiskey or poker. He considered all three to be implied. This way of waiting for death started reflecting on Dr. Palladino's physical appearance. His hair had gone white at an early age, as decided by his genes. But nonetheless, its thickness led to envious looks by many young passersby. Dr. Palladino didn't care to tame it, which is why occasionally a lock would reach his ear or fall on his forehead, unobstructed. His skin got wrinkled, with sacks under his eyes, and his green eyes matured.

Such an appearance on the part of Dr. Palladino, without any intention, changed the traditional dress code at the psychiatric clinic. The male colleagues noticed that the female colleagues found Dr. Palladino to be a very interesting man, which is why they created a new doctrine according to which the psychiatric clinic cannot establish its identity by imitating the style of stock brokers, but rather through the lucid development of its own style. And the own style of every serious psychiatrist must be wacky. That is why the staff, before entering the clinic in the morning, loosened the knots on their ties, ruffled their shirts and crumpled the line on their pants. Despite the efforts, the original remained interesting to the female coworkers. That is why some of them discretely offered Dr. Palladino their bodies. And he didn't care to turn them down.

That is precisely when that other occasion happened in Dr. Palladino's life, when, now for the second time, he cared about something. Namely, an Inspectorate captain asked Dr. Palladino to help him in his enduring and unsuccessful hunt for a serial killer, who left numerous victims in his wake, with a specific mode of operation.
The psychological profile of that serial killer, which Dr. Palladino created based on the extensive documentation that he received, was of crucial importance for the apprehension of the criminal and bringing him to justice.
For more than a decade, the collaboration with the Inspectorate and the creation of profiles of serial killers had been something that finally brought some meaning to Dr. Palladino's life, something that

he truly cared about. While on the hunt Dr. Palladino did not drink whiskey or play poker. He only smoked.

At the beginning of the war the Inspectorate was concerned with more important things. That is why Dr. Palladino went back to poker and whiskey. On one occasion, when he was a little late for a game, one of his fellow poker players said that his wife was leaving him because of poker and taking their children. And that that night was his last game. The other players at the table said that they were very sorry and that they understood him completely. Although none of them really understood why he was quitting poker now, when he could now play unimpeded.

A week later the news spread that this player had committed suicide. And ten days later the reliable information at the poker table was that he had done so by playing Russian roulette.

Chapter 112

Like every night, Manami and Pascal were sitting in the dark on their cover. Manami raised her head from Pascal's shoulder and got up. Then she knelt on the couch, turned towards him. He sat leaning back, motionless, with his hands in his lap. Manami took his face in her hands and turned him towards her. She caressed him.

"Why don't you love me, Pascal?" she asked.
"Don't do this to me, Manami," Pascal answered.
"Why don't you caress me like this? Why don't you also run your fingers through my hair, my love?"
"Manami..." Pascal said painfully. "Don't torment me..."
"I'm overjoyed, my dear! Overjoyed! That's why I'm teasing you. Because the most impulsive Don Juan is behaving like this. He won't even touch his loved one until she tells him to. And he trembles with love. I'm not an adulteress, Pascal, because I allowed myself to be seduced, because I allowed you to seduce me, because you spoke sweet words to me. I am an adulteress only because I'm so in love with you. And only because my love is so big and strong. And that is why I have the right to caress you. If anyone were to see this now, they would later say that I caressed your cheek... your hair. They would not be able to say that you caressed my hand with your cheek. That you seduced me."
"Manami... I want to touch you... I can't... I can't take it..."
"Talk to me," said Manami.
"I love you! I'm crazy about you! I want to kiss you! I have to kiss you!"
"Not like that" Manami laughed.
"What then?"
"What kind of a world will you create?"
"Me? I'm not going to create any kind of world, my love. I'm not interested in that anymore. I just want to be with you... Only you exist for me. And do you know what, Manami? Those stories of yours, whether you are an adulteress or not. This way or the other... You can tell them to someone else. You are just a selfish creature."
"Is that so? So that's what you think of me?"

"Exactly."
"Well, now you'll see how selfish I am, my love!"

Manami got up, sat in his lap, covered his lips with her hands and kissed his hair, forehead, eyes.
"There. That's how selfish I am, my darling!"
Pascal moved her hand from his lips and tried to kiss her, but Manami sat up, pressed her hands against his shoulders and said "Don't you dare!"

"I won't. I won't, Manami. Forgive me..." said Pascal, trying to calm himself. "I'm aware of how much it means to you... that I... didn't seduce you allegedly. Because, as far as I understand, that would be a sin. And the fact that you fell in love with me on your own, that allegedly isn't a sin."
"Of course it's not a sin. My soul is pure. My love is pure. It's like a mountain stream from ages ago. That is how pure my love is, Pascal."
"Your love is pure, Manami. As is your soul. You are wonderful... wonderful, Manami. But my love is pure too. And powerful. And I cannot go on like this anymore. I must caress you, touch you, kiss you... Don't torture me any more, please. In any case, you're just deceiving yourself and me for no reason."
"What do you mean?"
"Well, I seduced you with my eyes, when you were bringing the mayor tea."
"You seduced me?" Manami exclaimed. "You're really talking nonsense, Pascal. I seduced you with my eyes! In any case, I looked at you first. And you were puzzled by that look for days. Only later did I succeed in seducing you, in forcing you to look at me that way."
"You looked at me first?! I looked at you intently the entire time that you were brining the tea. And you felt my gaze, my seduction, on yourself. And that is why you even looked at me in the first place. To see what was so powerful, who loved you so much."
"Just you keep deceiving yourself, my darling, if it makes you feel better."

Manami got up from Pascal's lap, sat next to him and placed her head on his chest.
"So kiss my hair... So what? I'm a lonely sad woman in a shelter... in the middle of a war. And you are a good friend who's comforting me... who is hugging me and kissing my hair, in difficult times. That is completely understandable and acceptable."

Pascal kissed her hair in silence and stroked her back.

"I want to kiss your lips so much, Pascal... But I can't. The one who is watching would then say 'He kissed her.' That's what they always say 'he kissed her,' and not 'she kissed him.' Right?"

Chapter 113

"Is everything alright, Mr. President?"

"Yes. Everyone is as calm as a toad in the sun. No one's coming near the residence. I've finally had some rest and my blood pressure is stable. Thank you, Grasshopper. You are truly a man of your word."

"Are you thanking me, Mr. President? Tell me again, what did I write in my PhD thesis?"

"That you want to serve the leader."

"Not only do I want to - that is the purpose of my life. Which leader, who do I consider the greatest leader in history?"

"Me."

"That's correct. And why then are you thanking me? I exist only to carry out your orders."

"Thank you... I mean... I'm pleased with you, Grasshopper."

"Thank you, Mr. President. It means a lot to me. But, may I ask you, how do the people get paid now? Are you still printing money?"

"No, no. They're not getting anything."

"So they're not working? The Inspectorate is not working?"

"No, no.... everyone's working."

"How? How do they pay for food? Alright, I provide the energy for free. Your waterworks are running..."

"They don't pay... They've organized themselves. You know that we produce enough food for the city here. And they distribute it somehow... according to the number of household members. They negotiate... There are also pharmaceuticals, doctors are working... how do I know..."

"Excellent, that means that no one is pestering you with that nonsense."

"No... they are settling it all on their own."

"Perfect. There is bread, the games are coming."

Chapter 114

"Hey, Grasshopper. Don't accidentally vaporize Megapolis," said Erivan. "I need to go to their square, and for Seneca to sign the capitulation. We have a deal."

"Don't worry, I won't. I guess you see what I'm doing. People are afraid that I'll vaporize their city too, so everyone's fleeing to unpopulated areas. And I'm waiting for them to become thirsty and hungry and to move on Megapolis and Capital City. Those are the only two regions that still have energy, water, food, production... everything. They are the only two oases on the planet."

"No! What's the matter with you? What should I do with all these people in Capital City?" Erivan was aghast.

"They can't enter your area. Have you already forgotten about my ring?"

"Ah, yes..."

"And let them flock to Megapolis. I'm interested in how Seneca will react, what his decision will be. However, let's leave that aside... There's time for that. I wanted something else. I was just getting ready to call you, when I got your call."

"What did you want? Tell me, Grasshopper."

"Your Imperial Majesty!" the Grasshopper suddenly shouted.

"What?" Erivan was baffled.

"You are no longer President. You are now, Your Imperial Majesty!"

"What does that mean?"

"Presidents are elected in elections, and Emperors are chosen by God."

"God? Me too?"

"Of course. You are his final choice."

"What should I do now, Grasshopper?

"I'll explain it to you. Capital City is your empire."

"Alright..."

"Barbarians will gather around my ring, but they won't be able to threaten the empire."

"I know that."

"So, you don't need to worry about wars. You can just have fun and enjoy yourself."

"Well, alright…"

"But you must also provide this for your subjects."

"For whom?"

"Your subjects, the citizens of the Empire, of Capital City."

"Ah… I understand. But how will I entertain them, Grasshopper?"

"I will tell you. But first take off that uniform and let us make you a toga."

"What is that?"

"No, not a toga. Just a tunic. But it has to be short. Tell that to your tailor. And have them make you a wig. Long hair which will blow in the wind. And a pedestal with a magnificent throne. And have it all done in black. We won't change the style. Call me when you are prepared," the Grasshopper said and hung up.

Chapter 115

"Pascal, did you see how angry Julius was today?" said Manami, as soon as she sat down next to Pascal in their room.

"Angry?" Pascal was puzzled. "At whom?"

"I don't know, Pascal. At us? At himself? I don't know."

"Why was he angry? How did you notice it?"

"Pascal, you don't notice anything! When he picked up Eir, she immediately held out her hands towards you and called you Pascal."

"Manami!" Pascal shouted out. "I am in love with his wife. And I can tell him that at any moment. But I'm not taking away his children. Peter and Eir are yours and his children. In any case, that is normal. We are closed up here, I play with Eir, he rarely comes…"

"Yes, it's as you say. The child connects to the person that plays with it. I think that Julius is angry at himself, because he never found time for the children, even before this war."

"That's not my issue. I'm not to blame, Manami."

"Of course you aren't…"

"Listen to me now, Manami, please," said Pascal in a determined voice. "I've been wanting to tell you this for some time…"

"Tell me what, Pascal? Don't scare me, please," Manami was surprised by the change in the tone of his voice.

"Manami, you are struggling because of me! I'm harming your wonderful soul! You're split between your family and me. Between your children and me. I am destroying what you are.

"Your dignity, your convictions, your being. Where do I get the right… No, no… it's not about rights. It's about me not wanting to pain the woman that I love more than anything. The being that I love more than anything!

"And what will happen when all this ends one day, Manami? Think about it. Your husband, the mayor of Megapolis, will come out as the winner in this war. He will be, and he should be, President of Earth. He deserves it.

"You say that I'm a dreamer, that I offer people dreams. And for years I was just visiting cities, with my friend Raul, and telling stories. And the entire time that I was telling stories, your husband was making them happen in Megapolis. He created the elite University, he motivated creative young people, he developed science, art, sports. Exactly what I was talking about – that's what the mayor created. And that is why he will win. Because he created an invincible Megapolis.

"And what will happen when one day the mayor opens the door to this shelter and says 'The war is over. We've won Alexander. You can come out of this hole in the ground.' What will you do, Manami? Give up your husband, perhaps even your children, and stay with the greatest coward that ever existed? With a man... not a man, you cannot say that of me anymore... with the coward who spat on the sacrifice of his friends. The best and only friends that he had in his life.

"I curse myself for being, for you falling in love with me, for destroying your life. Love is very selfish. It wants the loved one just for itself. But not mine, Manami. My love is unearthly, unimaginable, almighty. It isn't interested in me. It just loves you. It wants you to be happy, at peace. To again assume your position in your family. To be you again."

Manami didn't say a word. She quickly got up from the couch and turned on the light in the room. She stood in front of Pascal, dressed in a lilac sleeveless nightgown. Pascal sat in silence.
"You're right, Pascal. I'm torn, shattered... and those several hours when we lie down I can't sleep. My stomach is in knots, Pascal."

Manami closed her eyes and squeezed them tightly. Her entire body was trembling. Then she swiftly raised her nightgown to her chin. She wasn't wearing anything underneath it. She stood in front of Pascal, completely naked.
"Look, Pascal!" she shouted with her eyes shut. "Why would you need this body?! You're used to the young beautiful bodies of girls! I won't seduce you with my eyes any more! I won't lie to you! Because there is nothing behind that! Just an ordinary woman, nearing forty!" Manami exclaimed.

Tears ran down Pascal's face. He got up slowly, walked up to her and loosened her constricted fingers. The nightgown slid down her naked body. He pulled her towards his chest and kissed her hair.
"You're crying, Pascal!" Manami shouted. "I don't need that! I don't need your pity! That's only my concern! Only my pain, Pascal! If one of your sexy women had shown herself to you, you wouldn't be crying, Pascal! You'd jump her body full of lust and make love to her!"

Pascal knelt down, grabbed her beneath the knees, fell her onto his arm and picked her up. He took her towards his room.

"Manami, I will now make love for the first time in my life."

"Don't you dare!" Manami shouted.

Chapter 116

They decided never again to sit in the dark. They turned on the light on the dresser. Manami sat in Pascal's lap. She pressed her hands into his cheeks, and quickly kissed his lips, then retreated. Pascal stroked her neck and back.

"I'm the happiest!"

"No, I'm the happiest!"

"I'm the happiest! And shut up, I tell you!" She kissed him again.

"Alright, I'll shut up, but I'm the happiest!"

"I want to hear it! Tell me again! Come on, tell me – whose body is the most beautiful in the world?"

"Your body, Manami, is the most beautiful in the world."

Manami giggled.

"You should be ashamed of yourself for lying! I would be ashamed."

"I'm not lying, my love. The most, most beautiful!"

"It's all my fault. For loving so much when you lie to me."

"The most, most beautiful! You are the most beautiful! The most wonderful, Manami! And it is the most beautiful body, which I could barely see through the tears. Let me look at you again, now that I'm no longer crying."

"Don't be cheeky, Pascal. Get serious. It's out of the question!" Manami moved slightly away from Pascal and looked him in the eye. "Now tell me that thing."

"Manami, with you I will make love for the first time in my life."

"It is true? Is it true, my darling? You have never before made love?" she kissed his lips.

"It's true, my love. Absolutely true. It's the greatest truth of all. And that expression is silly. I don't understand how can I make love? It makes me. It makes me belong to you, only you, my dearest being."

"Pascal, my Pascal!" Manami giggled. "My love, my joy, my darling, my everything, everything! Only mine! Are you? Only mine? You are only mine?"

"Only yours! Only yours!" Pascal pressed her against his chest and kissed her hair.

They were silent for a while, touching and cuddling.

"I'm not sure that I heard everything that you told me," said Manami. "I only thought about what you would say when you saw my body. But now I want to talk to you. To talk to you until the morning. About what you said or didn't say, it doesn't matter. And you to only listen to me. I am much smarter than you, I guess you've realized that up to now?"

"I know," Pascal laughed.

"And you're again imagining something in that head of yours and you don't understand at all what is tormenting me. Everything needs to be explained to you, Pascal. Like to a child. But what can I do? That's how I have it. First of all I'm not split between you and my family, my upbringing and my convictions. You and my children are my family. And my love is my only conviction. Don't you see that the four of us here are like in a house. Julius comes, like the father, to see us and say hello to his children. And to drink tea with us, have lunch. Everything is as it's supposed to be. He brings us food and supplies... That's like paying alimony to me."

"You're being silly," Pascal laughed.

"I'm not being silly, Pascal. That's how it is now, that's how it will be when we get out of here. Do you know that every time that Julius comes through our door I want to rush to you, to take you by the hand, to put my head on your shoulder, and tell him... him and Peter 'Pascal and I are in love. We cannot live without each other. Julius, I want a divorce immediately and I want my children.'"

"Manami..." Pascal whispered.

"And why can't I tell him that? Because the two of us, Pascal, don't know what's going on above us. I can't know what we will face when we get out. Will some powerful force separate us? Will Julius take my children and will the two of us will be powerless to prevent it? We don't know whether there is still a civilized world up there. And that's why I remain quiet. That's the only reason, Pascal. I have here what I want. You and the children. I couldn't take it if we were not together, for any reason. If we had to be separated even for a day."

Pascal raised her face and gently gave her a kiss on the lips.

"And secondly, Pascal, I very much want you. I want your body. It is truly the most beautiful thing in the world. And that's why I don't let you kiss me. Because if you were to really kiss me only once, I would lose it. And we would make love. And after that I would never be able to keep quiet, Pascal. Neither in front of the children, nor in front of Julius. Even if I didn't say anything, he would see it as soon as he looked at me. Anyway, he is already noticing..."

"What is he noticing?"

"What do you mean 'what'? My looks, your looks... our body language... When I serve you, how close I get to you, how you thank me, how you smile at me, how you love me with your eyes... we can try with the 'sir' and the 'ma'am' as much as we want..."

"You're overreacting, Manami. I don't believe..."

"Believe me, it's true. I know Julius very well. I was his real wife. I tried to understand each nuance in his mood, his behavior... Not to anger him, to please him... There is a seed of doubt in him, Pascal. Perhaps he still isn't aware of it. He still hasn't uttered it to himself. But even the smallest detail could change that. Like when Eir infuriated him. And then what will be will be. I will hug you and nothing will be able to separate me from you. Not anyone and not anything!"

Pascal held her to his chest.

"And another thing, Pascal" Manami continued. "You say that Julius is the mayor of Megapolis. He created everything that you only talked about. It's true that he created Megapolis and the University – but for his own reasons, in his own way. Within a given theme. He took part in and won Kaella's competition.

"It is true that he offered everything to young and talented people. But he couldn't understand that those scientists and artists became unhappy when they grew up. Because they had to focus and use their talents and their knowledge to increase production efficiency, reducing costs and increasing Prince's profit.

"Prince had the greatest respect for Julius because the scientific institutes in Magapolis developed materials and tools for tearing down skyscrapers and building new ones, in the same location, in only a month. Your apartment's season is over, folks! You now have a new apartment, folks! And your rent is higher, too!

"Artists had to create only odes to Humane Capitalism or to solely commercial products. Literature, fine arts, music, theatre, film... they all created the ideal of the super-consumer, which younger generations would admire and mimic.

"Julius didn't question that at all. That was a given for him. He acted, with exceptional success, within such a system. He could never understand the hopelessness and desperation of young people. And their escape into depravity. Even now, after everything, after your arrival and the talk to the students, when you told them that they should dream, when you gave young men and women hope, when they listened to you and returned to themselves, even now, when the war started – Julius still does not understand that.

He only understands that Megapolis and the University will be able to function only in your world, not in Kaella's or Erivan's.

"But Raul understood that, Pascal. And the fact that you stayed in the shelter and that you will safeguard yourself so that tomorrow you can help people create a new world, that is an expression of your greatest admiration, your deep respect for your friends' sacrifice.

"And understand that already! A hundred Juliuses and Levis could not create a better world. Only my Pascal can do that, my dreamer," Manami said and kissed him.

"I am a dreamer that has seen his dream come true," said Pascal. "I'm living my dream. You were my only dream this entire time, Manami. Everything that I dreamed of in life, everything that I did in life, was all a dream about you. I realized that the first moment that I saw you. When the light that reflected off of you first reached my eye."

"What are you saying, my love? Why are you torturing me so, when I can't kiss you?" Manami touched his face and looked him in the eye. "Who are you? A biology teacher or a lovesick poet? Tell your Manami – who are you?"

"I don't know. I know only that I am yours. And that nothing else matters."

Manami couldn't hold back anymore. She kissed him passionately. Pascal was still caressing her back.

"Cuddle my breasts... just my breasts..." she whispered in a moment when she separated from his lips.

Pascal gently cuddled her breasts through her nightgown.

"Not like that!" Manami screamed. She raised herself from his lap, lifted her nightgown and placed Pascal's hands beneath it. "Just my breasts, Pascal! Don't you dare..."

Manami and Pascal could barely part, standing in front of her door. They had to get a few hours sleep so that they could function normally in front of the children.

"I'll tell you this, my dear. You're not a coward. You're the bravest man there is... who has ever lived."

Chapter 117

"Wow, Your Imperial Majesty! It looks so good on you!" shouted the Grasshopper when he saw Erivan in the black short tunic, wearing a wig.

"I don't know... it's a little strange... but at least its comfortable..." Erivan stated his opinion.

"It's perfect, Your Imperial Majesty. But, do you remember that reality show before the war? The one where the competitors killed each other, and whoever survived won money?"

"I do, how could I forget it! I loved it! I kept sending messages. I spent a bunch of money, but I have no regrets."

"You should now organize the same show, but at a stadium. Let the people watch them live as they kill each other."

"Wow, that would be great! Even I would go watch that."

"Of course you will go, Your Imperial Majesty. In the central box. And your throne will be carried in by hand."

"Will they do that?"

"Only if they want me to vaporize Capital City..."

"So, that's what I should say..."

"It's clear to the people, Your Imperial Majesty. You just give the orders and don't worry about a thing."

"I will. I've really missed that show," Erivan finally relaxed.

"When the show is over and one survives, you get up in your box, you slowly raise your hand..."

"And?"

"And then if you give the thumbs up – the survivor gets the prize, and if you give the thumbs down, Charlie's boys will kill him."

"That's great! I can't wait!" Erivan was excited.

"That's only the beginning. I have many things to teach you, Your Imperial Majesty."

Chapter 118

"Today I was definitely convinced that you will tell Seneca about the two of us one day, Manami," Pascal smiled.

"I couldn't leave you with that bad haircut. I don't know what was up with Peter. He's always cut your hair nicely. I guess his hand trembled for some reason."

"And you pounced like a lioness. You grabbed the scissors from his hand. Peter was shocked."

"Really?"

"Yes. It was really strange. I was watching in the mirror. I was watching you, my love. How silly you were. You were all red. And you, the missus, took the scissors to cut my hair in front of your son. You won't let me be ugly."

"Well I won't! I won't let you, my handsome man," Manami kissed him.

"Really kiss me, Manami," Pascal placed his hand on her breast.

"Not now, Pascal. The night has only begun," Manami grabbed his hand, but she didn't move it away. "Alright... two minutes, but through the nightgown... We mustn't... you know how it would end. We always have to leave that for the end of the evening, my love. Two minutes before bedtime. Kissing and cuddling breasts beneath the nightgown. That's our agreement."

"Yes. But these two minutes now, through the nightgown," Pascal caressed both her breasts, "can it also be with kissing?"

"Alri..." Manami was already kissing him, not to waste time.

"Alright. Now you tell me," said Manami five minutes later, when the agreed two minutes were up.

"What should I tell you about?" Pascal asked.

"I want you to tell me what kind of world you will create."

"I won't. I've already told you."

"Yes, you will."

"Alright, I will. Whatever you say."

"Well, then it will not only be the law of the jungle that applies in the struggle for survival in your free market."

"It isn't my free market, Manami. It doesn't belong to anyone. That's why its called a free market. Those are its rules. As powerful as nature's laws. Like evolution. Whoever opposes it will lose. Sooner or later."

"Evolution created life, Pascal. All life. Including man. And human life, regardless of whether it is strong, young, full of energy, triumphant… or weak, ailing, old, incompetent, a loser… whatever it may be, it is the greatest value there is. You will create a world that will bow to life… and protect it."

"Whatever you say, Manami."

"Pascal, as your wife, I will warn you."

"My wife!" Pascal shouted. "My wife, my beloved wife!" He kissed her passionately.

When they finally separated after a while, Manami continued:

"I will tell you when you must interfere. When you must stop the torrent of the free market and protect the people. Protect the little nature that we still have left. To defend life. And you will listen to your wife."

"I will. I will obey my wife. I will always, always listen only to you. I will do everything that you want."

Manami kissed him gently and placed her head on his chest.

"Manami, do you have a gold kimono?" Pascal asked.

Manami raised her had and gave him a puzzled look.

"I do. How do you know that?"

"I don't know how I know. Perhaps the mayor mentioned it during one of our conversations. I really don't know. But I dreamt of it that day… before the war."

"Of my kimono?"

"I dreamt of the two of us… in a huge ballroom… I dreamt of it while I was putting on that dark suit and the shiny black shoes… like dance shoes. And a white shirt. I wanted to be shot in the heart. So that you could see on TV how my heart bleeds for you."

"Don't say that! I don't want to hear that, Pascal!"

"Forgive me. I won't. I won't let anyone shoot at me. I want to live every moment with you, Manami. I dreamt of just the two of us being in that ballroom. Hugging… and you, my love, were in a gold kimono. Beautiful!"

"That's my great-grandmother's kimono," Manami said. "My family gained artwork status for it. So that the Inspectorate wouldn't destroy it, as outdated. Perhaps you saw that kimono somewhere on the Internet. There are pictures of it. It says that I own it."

"Possibly."

"The kimono is my family's prized possession. That's why I brought it with me to the shelter."

"Manami!" shouted Pascal. "Go put it on! Immediately! Please!"

"Not now, Pascal. I didn't know that you knew about my gold kimono. And that you imagined us dancing alone."

"Alone, Manami. Just the two of us, in the whole world. Why won't you put it on?"

"Because, Pascal, this entire time I've been having my own dream about the kimono."

"What is your dream, my love?"

"When we first make love, I'll be in the gold kimono. And you will take it off of me slowly and gently."

"Well that's what I'm telling you. Go, put it on," Pascal said with a smile.

"Don't torture me, Pascal, please. Alright, alright… as a reward for dreaming about my kimono you'll get two extra minutes under the nightgown…"

Chapter 119

"Are you comfortable, Your Imperial Majesty?" the Grasshopper asked.

"Comfortable? Fantastic, Grasshopper!" Erivan exclaimed. "Like in the nicest dream!"

"I'm glad for you, Your Imperial Majesty. And what do you like the most?"

"Everything. I like everything! The reality show at the stadium... Wow, how quiet it gets when I raise my thumb. And when I give the thumbs down – ovations! How my subjects adore me! How they shout when they carry me through the streets... You see that, I guess?"

"I do, I do, but I don't have audio. And I like it when you tell me. I'm the happiest if you are happy."

"I'm overjoyed! And the orgies! Phenomenal! Live, at my residence. And not like at Kaella, only in porn movies. But do you know what's bothering me, Grasshopper?"

"What's bothering you?"

"I get stuffed to quickly, I'm about to burst. I want to eat more, I want to eat all the time... all the goodies that they make for me... and I can't."

"That's no problem, Your Imperial Majesty. As soon as you feel that you can't eat anymore, just vomit."

"Yes?"

"Yes. Make some room in your stomach, and then go at it."

"Great idea! How didn't I think of that?"

"That's because Kaella first made his money from food, and later on teas, pills and therapies for losing weight, and he covered up this best method for continuous eating. And I see that you also have interesting events in the streets and squares."

"We do, we do. I do all that for my subjects. And I love them."

"Of course."

"I have something for them every day... a firing squad, a hanging, guillotine, impalement, crucifixion... and then they make an offering to me. And I eat a young heart. You have no idea how healthy it is! I come alive! Hey, do you know what my subjects love most of all?"

"What?"

"Bonfires! I do them twice a week. They all cry out in excitement."

"You've spoiled your subjects. It's no surprise that they adore you."

"They adore me terribly! Terribly!"

"I see that you've opened to them the two sports arenas, Kaella 1 and Kaella 2."

"I have. So that they too can organize binge drinking, drug consumption, feasting and orgies. And they aren't called Kaella anymore."

"No?"

"I'm not sure. They gave them some odd names."

"Sodom and Gomorrah."

"Yes! How did you know?"

"From now on demand that they address you as 'Your Highness the Human Being'. And you, Your Highness, have truly deserved that title."

"I will! Great name! I'll immediately call the television station to tell them..."

"No, no... wait a bit. Throw off that stupid tunic that conceals your beautiful human body. From now on, let them carry you naked, standing up."

"What will I do naked, Grasshopper?"

"Alright... have them make you a thong with your image."

"Well... I can't do that either..."

"Why?"

"I have a boil on my ass."

"Don't worry. It will be a wonderful fashion detail."

Chapter 120

"Doctor?" Erivan called his psychiatrist in the middle of the night.

"Yes, Your Highness the Human Being?"

"Should I take a double dose? I can't go to sleep."

"No, don't. It won't help you. And it can damage your liver."

"So what should I do? I can't go on like this . I'm not getting any sleep. I can't even enjoy myself properly."

"You have very rare condition, Your Highness."

"Me sick? You'd better be careful what you say!"

"No, no. You didn't understand. You're not sick. Mr. Grasshopper is sick."

"The Grasshopper? What do I care about him?"

"It's a strange condition. Its called the cosmic syndrome. When someone spends so much time alone in space, like Mr. Grasshopper, then they develop ..."

"Let him develop..."

"They develop it but the condition is transferred to the person that they communicate with. And that's you, Your Highness. He doesn't have any symptoms. It's a very strange condition. He needs to be treated, not you."

"Very well. I'll tell him. And you can treat him."

"I can't. I don't know this disease. There is only one doctor who treats it."

"Alright. Let him treat him. It makes no difference to me."

Part IV: Hope

Dr. Palladino sat in a chair set up between Erivan's desk and the office door. Charlie stood behind him.

"You will now call the Grasshopper and ask him this question," said Dr. Palladino to Erivan.

"It's a stupid question, Doctor," Erivan hesitated. "It isn't at all for the Grasshopper. He does what I command him."

"That's clear to me. But this is the magical question which cures the cosmic syndrome. After that you will sleep like a baby."

"Really? Great! I'll call him immediately."

"Why will you kill all the people, Grasshopper?" Erivan asked, as soon as the Grasshopper picked up.

After a few moments of silence the Grasshopper said

"Widen the camera angle, Your Highness."

Erivan looked at Dr. Palladino, who nodded. He then showed the entire office to the Grasshopper.

"You are...?" the Grasshopper asked when he saw Dr. Palladino.

"Palladino."

"Why is it that it was precisely you, Mr. Palladino, who got the opportunity to ask me this question?"

"My colleague asked me to do so, Grasshopper."

"Colleague? From which field?"

"Medicine."

"Psychiatry, I presume."

"Yes."

"Why didn't your colleague ask the question himself? Why did he ask you, Dr. Palladino?"

"Because I create psychological profiles for serial killers."

"Aha. So your colleague believes that I'm a serial killer?"

"Yes."

"And you?"

"I believe that you are an absolute killer."

"Absolute? I will do everything in my power to justify your confidence, Dr. Palladino."

"I believe you will."

"I've noticed that you are on a first name basis with me, Dr. Palladino."

"Yes, I am. Does that bother you?"

"No, but I'm interested why you decided to do so?"

"Because in my practice I'm always on a first name basis with killers."

"Because you despise us?"

"It helps me create a profile."

"To create a profile or negotiate with a killer?"

"I've never negotiated nor have I communicated in any way with serial killers. I've only talked to them in my head. I would ask them questions and imagine their probable answers."

"I am the first killer to whom you have actually spoken?"

"Yes."

"Have you studied me?"

"Yes. I looked over the recordings of yours and Erivan's conversations."

"Erivan's? You're a bold man, Dr. Palladino. How dare you call His Highness by his name?"

"I call Erivan by his name because I believe that you are wrong."

"You don't believe that Erivan symbolizes His Highness the Human Being".

"No, I don't."

"Do you perhaps believe that I represent His Highness the Human Being?"

"No, I don't."

"Alright, Dr. Palladino. Ask away."

"I've already asked the question."

"Why will I kill all the people?"

"Yes."

"Because I can."

Chapter 122

Having heard the Grasshopper's answer, Dr. Palladino lowered his head, placed the palms of his hands on his knees and stayed in that position for several moments. He then got up from his chair and without looking at the Grasshopper he started for the door. Charlie stepped in front of him and placed a hand on his chest.

"Where are you going, Dr. Palladino?" the Grasshopper asked.

"I'm leaving," answered Dr. Palladino, looking at Charlie's hand.

"Did my answer anger you?"

"No."

"Disappoint you?

"No."

"Did you expect it?"

"Yes."

"And now you think that talking to me no longer makes sense?"

"Yes."

"And you do only meaningful things?"

"Mostly not. Only when I work for the Inspectorate," Dr. Palladino turned towards the Grasshopper.

"You're not afraid that Charlie will kill you? You're not afraid of dying?"

"No."

"I see," said the Grasshopper, looking Dr. Palladino in the eye. "You're eyes are red, Dr. Palladino. You haven't had enough sleep. You've been working hard, studying my file, I assume?"

"Yes."

"Charlie, are your men in front of the door?" the Grasshopper asked.

"Of course."

"Have them take the Doctor to another room, to get some sleep."

"Here you go, Doctor," said Charlie, having opened the door.

"Grasshopper, did the doctor cure you?" Erivan asked. "Hmm? Are you better? It seems to me that I'm a little drowsy. I'll try to have a little nap..."

"Charlie, kill the idiot," said the Grasshopper, when Charlie returned.

Chapter 123

"Are you rested, Dr. Palladino?" the Grasshopper asked.

"Yes. Erivan's gone?" Dr. Palladino sat down in a chair.

"He won't be bothering us anymore," said the Grasshopper. "Do you still think that talking to me doesn't make any sense?"

"Yes, I do."

"Aren't you at all professionally curious to create the psychological profile of an absolute killer?"

"I don't create profiles to learn whether the killer had an unhappy childhood, but rather to help inspectors find him and lock him up; to prevent new killings. Creating your profile will not contribute to that."

"Probably not, but you cannot be absolutely certain of that. Or perhaps you can, with your knowledge and experience?"

"I cannot."

"So you do allow for the small possibility that you could convince me to stop killing?"

"Anything is possible, but I do not see that possibility."

"Doctor, you are the only person in the world that I am talking to. And you don't want to even try to make out this possibility and take advantage of it through our conversation. What then is the difference between the two of us? You are therefore my accessory."

Dr. Palladino looked out the window in silence.

"Charlie told me that he found you... in a very delicate situation. But this is not about your life, Doctor, but about..."

"You're right, sir," Dr. Palladino said, looking him in the eye.

"We are no longer on first name basis?"

"Yes."

"Why?"

"Because I've decided to talk to you for as long as you will permit it. And I cannot use my usual methods and ways of thinking."

"In addition to what you said, perhaps you feel that a first name basis is not appropriate? Perhaps you have started to respect me?"

"Respect you? Certainly not. But you leave such an impression on a person, that first name basis is not acceptable."

"Tell me, Doctor, I'm certain that you thought everything through, what do you think why am I talking to you?"

"Because you are bored. Am I right?"

"You probably are. Also, I've been given this unexpected opportunity to talk to an intellectual, for the first time since I finished my education. I'm also probably interested in what my psychological profile would look like."

"I've told you that I'm putting aside my method of work; that I have to have a completely different approach."

"Different in what way? Do you already know that or do you need time to think? We can end this conversation now…"

"We will not interrupt it. I don't want to think, because the usual patterns will prevail. I will ask you everything that I think of. And then I will see where it leads. If it leads anywhere at all."

"Go ahead, ask."

"OK… What would be the conclusion of your true, sincere doctoral thesis?"

"What do you think, Doctor?"

"The purpose of my life is the destruction of all living things."

"I wouldn't agree with that… entirely. First of all, Doctor, 'destruction' is not the right word. Non-living things are destroyed. Life is exterminated. I would put it like this 'I would exterminate all life, if I had the opportunity.'"

Chapter 124

"Hey, Lucky, what's with you? Why are you biting my thumb? You're silly," Sayash told Lucky, while they rested in the shade of an olive tree, on a knoll by the roadside. "I know why! Your mother didn't breastfeed you as a baby. That's alright… I don't mind."

Their conversation was interrupted by the sound of a truck engine.
"Let go of my thumb, Lucky. The movie's started. Come sit in my lap so we can watch. A truck is coming down the road, Lucky. I've seen many such movies. An empty road, and a vehicle appears. This could be interesting, Lucky."

Lucky let go of Sayash's thumb and sat in his lap. Sayash stroked him between the ears.
"Look… the truck has stopped. Has it broken down? Another one will come now, and they will connect themselves with a giiiiaaaant shoelace, and the second one will pull it. I know, I've seen this movie… Wait, wait, Lucky, it's not that movie… this is a different one… this truck is carrying some children. I haven't seen this one. I really haven't…"

The driver came out and lowered the side of the truck.
"Is the actor going to wake the children? Lucky? Do you see them; they're asleep like angels."

The driver returned to the cabin. A piston raised and tilted the trailer.
"What is this nonsense?" Sayash commented excitedly. "What does the truck think, that it's an amusement park ride, or what? Hey truck, don't you see that the children are asleep? They don't want to play and be jerked around now!" Sayash was annoyed while the children's bodies fell by the road. "Lucky, do you see how stupid this truck is?!"

Sayash looked at Lucky who shed tears incessantly.
"Hey, Lucky, it's not you that should cry because the truck is stupid! What do we care about it! I guess you see that the children are still

asleep... Hey, Lucky, stop!" Sayash ran after Lucky. "Don't you wake them up now!"

The driver raised the side and returned to the cabin. The truck went on its way. To pick up some new load.

Chapter 125

"You've strived the entire time to find yourself in such a situation? I've concluded this from your biography," Dr. Palladino said to the Grasshopper.

"That's right."

"When did you realize that the opportunity was that room that you are in and that command desk?"

"Very early on. As soon as I understood how the energy system was organized. Back in high school."

"And at that same moment you wanted to sit at the command desk?"

"No. That developed within me over time. I cannot tell you the exact moment... Somewhere half way through university, I guess. That's when I understood that the urge to kill would overpower sexual urge."

"Eros and Thanatos?"

"Eros, yes, but only as libido. Everything around it is noise. As far as Thanatos is concerned, I agree that we can call it the primal instinct of death, but solely at the collective level."

"What do you mean?"

"At the level of mankind. As humanity's unique urge for self-destruction. At the individual level Thanatos is the drive to kill other people. It doesn't represent man's desire to return to inorganic matter, but to transform another living being into the non-living state. Our aggression does not appear because Eros has pushed Thanatos out of us and directed it towards other people. Our drive to kill is primal, seminal, basic. When we cannot satisfy it, when we are not in a situation to kill, that is when self-destruction emerges, the desire for one's own death. As the just punishment for our incompetence, our failure."

"This could be argued..."

"Certainly. But all that doesn't matter, that was in the days when I was a student. It simply seemed to me that the urge to kill was so strong that it couldn't be only the reflection of the urge for self-destruction. It was precisely then," the Grasshopper continued, "as a young man, that I thought about the causes. But actually I haven't been interested in them for a long time. I'm only dealing with the consequences. Just as you said, Dr. Palladino. You aren't interested in whether the killer had an unhappy childhood."

"I understand. Let's go back to the beginning. You said that you understood that the urge to kill would overpower the libido."

"Yes. The sexual act leads to the creation of new life. And killing represents the act of ending an existing life. People consider the satisfying of both urges to be immoral and sinful. The difference is that sex, unlike murder, is not persecuted and punished. This is why it took only one excuse for people to have sex: the birth of their progeny and survival of the species, so that..."

"Excuse me. I have to interrupt you..." said Dr. Palladino.

"Yes?"

"In your opinion, why is murder punished and sex isn't?"

"Because of morals, ethics, God's commandments..."

"And where did people get all that, if the killing instinct is so strong?"

"The Eros in people came up with that. It is that noise around the libido that I mentioned. It is the result of people's fear that they will be killed. Fear for their own lives. And that fear was the only thing postponing the inevitable end of all life."

Chapter 126

Lucky was jumping manically, spinning around, falling down and getting up, all over the children's sleeping bodies. Until a tear of his fell on the face of each child. Brandon was the first to awake.

"Hey! It's Lucky!" he shouted all glowing. "Wake up!" Brandon called out to his friends, shaking the one nearest to him. "Lucky's here!"
"And Mr. Sayash!" said Melek, who was now also awake.
"Lucky! Lucky!" the other children shouted, while waking up.

"Do you see what you did, Lucky? You woke the children!" Sayash was worried.
He waved his finger angrily, standing on the side and watching the children's hands jostling to pet Lucky.
And Lucky... he was all warm with pleasure.

"It's OK if he woke us, Mr. Sayash," Gala said. "Don't be angry at Lucky."
"How can I not be? He doesn't listen to a thing I say..." Sayash answered, with a smile.
"It was time to get up, wasn't it?" asked Kimo, winking at his friends.
"It was! It was!" They all answered at the same time.
"And why was it time? You have to go to school, do you?" Sayash wanted to know everything.
"No, no..." Kimo was confused.
"We don't have to, Mr. Sayash, it's recess!" said Sara, who got a hold of Lucky and held him in her hands.
"Recess, is it?" Sayash looked at them suspiciously. "So where are you snacks?"
"We ate them!" said Matic. "That's why we were sleepy."
"Aha! So you had your snack, you had a nap... That means that recess is almost over. Doesn't it?" Sayash asked.

All the children fell silent for a moment, disarmed by Sayash's ironclad logic.
"Actually, it isn't..." Tai stuttered.

277

"What do you mean 'it isn't'? Don't dilly-dally!" Sayash said angrily.
"Well… it's not recess. I mean, it's over…" Tai continued, frantically looking for a solution.
"Of course its over! Who knows when it was over?! Its all clear to Mr. Sayash! You got on that truck and skipped school!"

Chapter 127

"At this moment it is all insignificant," the Grasshopper continued. "I want to talk about consequences, about these moments, about the end."

"Forgive me. I won't interrupt you any more. Please, continue," Dr. Palladino said.

"I will. It is important to understand that people had to find various excuses in order to kill with impunity."

"Yes. You said that the excuse for having sex was the survival of the species."

"Exactly. But in the case of killing, people had to be much more creative in finding excuses. All ideologies in history were created only as an excuse for killing. Certain ideas, membership in a certain group, are placed above human life and serves as the excuse for killing with impunity. You saw the conversations between Erivan and me, and you saw what Erivan did..."

"Yes. I watched your satire live on the Capital City stage. You were the screenplay writer, director and prompter for the main actor."

"Satire? I'm not a satirist, Dr. Palladino. I, in the role of the trustee, only took inventory of a bankrupt civilization."

"And you say that you were aware of this bankruptcy even as a student?"

"Yes."

"And you wanted to liquidate the bankrupt firm?"

"I asked myself why shouldn't it be me, knowing that this room represents the tool with which I could do it."

"And you never wondered why the Kaellas or Erivan hadn't done it?"

"Because I beat them to it."

"What do you mean? The Kaellas could have done it half a century ago, when they completed the energy system."

"I'll explain it to you. The Kaella's didn't find the excuse that would allow them to use the energy system as an absolute weapon. That is why they used it to sell energy to the Consumers. And while that functioned, they used a different, more selective excuse for killing."

279

"What killing?"

"What do you mean 'what killing', Dr. Palladino? The killing of the old, the ill, the inappropriate, the misfits, the helpless, the homeless… The killing at Euthanasias.

"The third Kaella saw himself as the greatest humanist, who created the Balance in human society. Just like all other rulers in history, he used his ideology as an excuse to kill.

"He placed the Balance and Humane Capitalism above life. And he could neither create it nor maintain it without killing the sick and the elderly people, who didn't have an income to pay the bills, and who only represented an expense for the balanced state. And his ideology didn't permit that."

"That is why, in order to save the Balance and Humane Capitalism, he introduced mandatory medical checkups, with complete ideological justification. And at these checkups potential parasites were identified in a timely fashion. Following the medical checkup the information system predicted the likely course of the disease for each examined person, the costs of their treatment and the expected date when their revenue would cease to cover the costs.

"Every morning the information system sent the tax administration a list of people for whom this critical period had started. Then they carefully monitored every financial transaction of such an individual. They waited for the person to sell their shares, if they had any, and to pay the bills and treatment for a while, using the money from the sale. And when that too was spent, the person would be taken to Euthanasia and put to death.

"The descendents of the deceased would be pleased with this. The tax administration would notify them on time that their father, mother, grandmother, grandfather, uncle, brother, sister… would be left without the necessary financial sustenance within a month. They would be asked whether they wanted to take over financial responsibility for their relatives. As a rule the answer was negative."

"Why would people in their prime want to spend on the sick and the elderly the little money that they were left with after they paid their bills to Kaella and the mandatory purchase of goods from the new season? They too deserved to live a little, to go out to dinner, to travel, to take a ride on a submarine."

"I understand. It's dreadful, what has become socially acceptable," Dr. Palladino said.

Chapter 128

"We didn't! We didn't skip school!" the children shouted at the top of their voices.

"We were on a fieldtrip!" it dawned on Babette.

"On a fieldtrip? Children that small? All by themselves? I don't believe it," Sayash shook his head.

"What do you mean 'alone', Mr. Sayash?" Enzo asked him. "We're going on a fieldtrip with you."

"With whom?"

"With you and Lucky" Enzo took Lucky from Zuri. "Isn't that right, Lucky?" Enzo asked Lucky, holding him in front of his face and rubbing noses with him.

It looked like Lucky was about to take off, that's how much he was wagging his tail.

"Oh, Lucky, you're so gullible. You fall for it," Sayash was still serious.

"Our mothers and fathers told us 'kids you can go on a fieldtrip, but only if Mr. Sayash and Lucky take you,'" Kaya said.

"Did they, really? I don't believe you!" said Sayash scrunching his eyebrows. He was on high on elation.

"Really! Really, Mr. Sayash!" all the children shouted.

"Well, alright… if that's the way it is… What do you say, Lucky?… I do ask silly questions," Sayash laughed while looking at Lucky, who was running around in circles with joy.

"Alright, if your mothers and fathers said so… And what did they say, where should we take you on the fieldtrip?"

"Where you and Lucky were headed, Mr. Sayash," said Mona.

"I don't know if that's smart…" Sayash reflected.

"Why not?" asked Edwin.

"Well… the two of us were on our way… we saw it in the movies. A huuugeee city, the largest in the world…"

"Megapolis! Great! Let's go!" the children shouted.

Chapter 129

"On the other hand, Prince's greed for increasingly greater profits," said the Grasshopper, "which he called the organic need of the economy to constantly grow, was eating away at the Balance. It was necessary to constantly increase consumption, quarter over quarter.

"That is why they created the labor camps where they took the Non-Consumers, and carried out experiments on them, with the goal of creating a Super-Consumer, a being that would have an intensive and increasingly frequent need for new models.

"They tried to copy the sexual drive. And in time they succeeded. The problem emerged when they realized that the Super-Consumer must have that much more income to be able to afford all the new goods that they wanted, at least three times per week. They must earn a lot more, i.e. they have to work that much more.

"That is why at the camps they designed state-of-the-art maximally automated and robotized plants with excellent productivity and the minimal need for human labor. They trained the most successful specimen of the Super-Consumer to work and employed them at these plants. The calculation showed that their appetite for new models could be financially covered only if they worked sixteen hours per day at these most automated plants. And they worked.

"The next problem occurred when the Super-Consumers, having seen the first pieces of the new model on the assembly line, would jump onto the conveyor, steal the piece and run around the factory with it, already trying it on. When they would change, they would see the next piece on the line. They would again steal it and take off the piece from a minute ago, even though it was the same model. But this piece was a minute newer. And so on indefinitely.

"It turned out that the Super-Consumer was unusable, that their desired passion for consumption, which the Kaellas had finally developed, at a huge cost, prevented them from working and earning to satisfy their super-consumer needs. They shut down the labor camps and killed all the people."

"Dreadful."

"Nothing new, Dr. Palladino. It's always the same, all throughout the existence of mankind. All the Kaellas and the Erivans of this world, regardless of the level of development of the civilization or its social organization, under the excuse of expanding its ideology, territory, wealth, power... they killed with impunity. Killing was always the only goal and death was the final outcome.

"It was by mere chance that these historic individuals, who we are familiar with, gained the oportunity to kill. Had they not killed, someone else would have. The problem of ordinary people was that they didn't get the opportunity. And the problem of those that had the opportunity were the instruments. They had to use one group of people as the instrument for killing a different group of people.

"Through history the development of science and technology changed the structure of the killing instruments. In each subsequent epoch an increasingly smaller group of people were needed for killing an increasingly larger other group.

"This was labeled the increase in the number of civilian casualties. The need for subjects or followers was decreasing. The instruments were becoming more advanced and the killing was simpler."

Chapter 130

"Well, I don't know if that's great," Sayash hesitated. "It's a very large city. I'll lose you."

"No, you won't, Mr. Sayash, we promise!"

"We won't leave your side, or Lucky's!" the children shouted out.

"What grade are you anyway?" Sayash suddenly wondered.

"First, Mr. Sayash," Larisa said.

"First? Well then the big city is out of the question!"

"Why?" they shouted all at once.

"What do you mean 'why'? You're too small. You don't even know the alphabet. You'll need to read all the signs... you know which ones... and all that..."

"We know how to read!"

"And write, Mr. Sayash!"

"Aha! And how do you know?" Sayash didn't believe the children.

"Well, we know. We learned in preschool," said Sib.

"Hmm... You have an answer for everything, don't you?" Sayash smiled, already giving in to the children.

"What can we do - we're smart!" Ekene smiled.

"Well, even if we didn't know how to read, you'll read the signs for us, Mr. Sayash," said Mariam.

"Me?" Sayash was shocked. "Oh, children, you're so naïve! You think that when you are as old as Mr. Sayash you'll still be able to keep all the letters in your head. You won't. They fall out... For example, the letter L is still in my head. I mean, in addition to the letter S. That's why I named Lucky - Lucky; in case I had to sign our names somewhere. So that we are not embarrassed..."

"So how would you read the signs in Megapolis, if you didn't have us, Mr. Sayash?" Milan asked.

"I wouldn't read them. Lucky and I don't need that. The two of us aren't interested in where we are... or where we're going. No... we never part..."

"We'll do the same, Mr. Sayash! We'll never part from you and Lucky! We too aren't interested in the signs. Here, the letters have already fallen out of my head!" Flavia said out loud.

"Oh, you're so nice…" Sayash was getting soft. "OK, so let's get going. This is how we'll do it. Now listen to me very carefully. I'll go at the head of the group. You follow me, in pairs. And hold hands. I'll hold Lucky in my hands, but backwards. He won't look forward but back at you, over my shoulder. As soon as someone lets go of their pair or leaves the group, Lucky will whack me with his tail. And if I turn around…"

"No one will, Mr. Sayash. We'll be good. We'll listen you!" said Nirmala.

"And if someone did let go, Lucky wouldn't give us up, would you, Lucky?" asked David, holding Lucky to his chest.

"You've really grown close, haven't you?" Sayash smiled.

Chapter 131

"I realized that the end of the epoch of Humane Capitalism was coming to a close," said the Grasshopper. "The appearance of Mr. Alexander and the unstoppable growth of his movement had shown me that the system would collapse in my lifetime. And that entire time, up there, above all of us, the absolute killing instrument has been suspended. And I wondered, what would Kaella do when the system started to collapse, when he saw that he was losing? What do you think, Doctor? What would Kaella have done his last moments, when he realized that there were no more buyers?"

"I know what you mean."

"He would think 'if you're not my Consumers, then you have no more reason to live.' And Kaella would finally find his excuse to use this absolute weapon."

"Probably," Dr. Palladino agreed.

"Or imagine Prince, sitting in my place, at the command desk, watching live satellite feeds. Watching Non-Consumers taking out wads of money and gold bars from the vault beneath his palace. Or David from his garden, or The Night Watch from his hallway, or the Mona Lisa from the wall over his bed. What do you think, which buttons would Prince press at that moment?"

"All of them."

"And..."

"Forgive me for interrupting you, but what happened to all those masterpieces? Erivan demolished the palace..."

"Yes, he demolished it. And he tried to build higher colonnades. As though Kaella wouldn't have done so, if the construction could support them. Charlie removed the artwork to a safe place on time. In the underground depots of Erivan's squads. I wouldn't allow anyone to lay a hand on them. Only I can destroy such beauty."

Dr. Palladino sighed a deep sigh and lowered his head.

"Why don't you light a cigarette, Doctor? Charlie tells me that you are a heavy smoker."

"I myself don't know why," said Dr. Palladino, taking out a pack of cigarettes and lighter from his jacket pocket. "I guess because this is the presidential office." He lit the cigarette and took a drag.

"That is how you still perceive that space? And you're still sitting in that uncomfortable chair, as you did on the first day. Why don't you sit in the armchair?" the Grasshopper asked.

"I don't want to." Dr. Palladino took a small silver dish from the stylish dresser and sat back in his chair. He lay the dish in his lap and put his ashes in it.

"May I continue, Doctor?" the Grasshopper asked.

"Yes, yes... of course..."

"Thank you. Consider any ruler in history who lost the war. And at the ends of the epochs every ruler lost it. Imagine the enemy capturing his castle or city, his residence... and he's sitting at this table. What would the ruler do? Any of them?"

"The same. They would all do the same."

"And don't you think that the Kaellas were aware the entire time of the weapon that they had at their disposal? Their last interview reminded me of that. Did you watch it?"

"I didn't."

"Kaella said that he had reduced the State's expenses by merging the army and police into a single organization – the Inspectorate. And he didn't merge them. He abolished the military, in the classical sense. The inspectors spent their entire time searching people's apartments and preventing petty crimes. Or they would stifle an uprising or protest. That is why he stopped producing weapons. He produced minimal quantities, and only conventional weapons. Why? Because he knew that no one could do anything to him, that he could ultimately come and sit down at this table."

"You're right. It all fits. They were aware of what they had in their hands."

"Exactly. Just like all rulers, the Kaellas lived in their own world. And that's why they didn't sense the threat on time. That is why they allowed the unintelligent but wily Erivan to mislead them and outmaneuver them. And I clearly saw the course of events and the end of civilization. The destruction of the planet. And I wondered, why would the Kaellas have to do that? Why wouldn't I do that?"

"Because you didn't want to be their victim? Because that would be an insult to your intellect?"

"No, because I wanted to be the executioner. Because I wanted to lower the curtain. And I will be a victim. I told you that I would kill all life. And as you can see, I too am alive."

"Unfortunately."

Chapter 132

"In that largest city in the world..." Sayash told the children sitting around him, during one of the breaks on their voyage.
"Megapolis," Hideaki reminded him.
"Yes... there are many streets..."
"We know that!" the children shouted.
"Pssst! You'll wake Lucky!" Sayash hushed them.

Lucky was lying on his back in Sayash's lap, and Sayash was stroking his stomach.
"Well, you know that..." Sayash continued with a whisper. "But you don't know what there is in those streets."
"We know that too. Shops...
"Monuments..."
"Advertisements..."
"Cars..."
"Stoplights..."
"Newsstands..."
"Crosswalks..."
"Cafes..." the children went on.
"Yes, yes... there is all that. But that's not important."
"I know what's important, Mr. Sayash," said Zita.
"What?" Sayash asked.
"There are many dumpsters."

"Bravo, Zita!" Sayash shouted out, waking Lucky, who was on his feet in an instant. Sayash immediately took him in his arms and stroked him with one finger between the ears.
"I'm sorry, Lucky. Please forgive me. But they made me so happy! These children of ours are really smart."
Lucky looked at the children and wagged his tail. It seemed that he wasn't angry at all.

"Mr. Sayash will change your clothes. We'll find all kinds of things in those dumpsters. You'll take off those stained shirts. What class did you have before the fieldtrip? Art, wasn't it? You got it all over your shirts. And all of you the same color. What kind of art is it if they give you only one color? I have a bone to pick with your teacher when we get back from the fieldtrip. Hmm, art with only one color... although it is bright red... but still..." Sayash wouldn't stop bickering.

Chapter 133

Seneca had spent the previous night in the shelter with his wife, for the first time since the beginning of the war. The following morning Pascal didn't come to breakfast.

"Sir, breakfast!" Manami said loudly, standing in front of the door to Pascal's quarters.

"I won't be having breakfast!" Pascal said from behind the closed door.

"Why?"

"I'm not hungry."

"Alright, sir, as you wish. Peter, you'll have two eggs, right?"

*****

"Sir, lunch!" Manami said loudly, standing in front of the door to Pascal's quarters.

"I won't be having lunch!" Pascal said from behind the closed door.

"Why?"

"I'm not hungry."

"Alright, sir, as you wish. Peter, help Eir get into the chair."

*****

"Sir, dinner!" Manami said loudly, standing in front of the door to Pascal's quarters.

"I won't be having dinner!" Pascal said from behind the closed door.

"Why?"

"I'm not hungry."

"Sir, you haven't eaten anything today. Are you ill?

"No."

"Peter's anxious because you haven't left your quarters all day."

"I'm not ill."

"Peter thinks that you're angry at us."

"I'm not."

"You hear that, Peter? The gentleman isn't angry at us."

"So why doesn't he come out? He doesn't have to eat," Peter whispered to his mother.

"Peter asks why you don't come out to the dining room? He says you don't have to have dinner."

"I won't be coming."

"Sir!" Manami said even louder. "Peter has been thinking about your strange behavior all day. The child might even think that you have an argument with his father last night. And perhaps you are angry at him, since you say you aren't angry at us. Do you understand?"

After a few moments Pascal opened the door, came out into the dining room, passed by Manami without looking at her, and sat down at his place at the table. He stroked Eir on the head, raised his eyes towards Peter and smiled at him, unsuccessfully.

"I'm not angry at anyone, Peter. Why would I be? I've just had enough of all this. I'm a bit nervous... and I don't want to spread it to you. Do you understand?"

"Well... I understand. And when will you be over that?"

"Leave the gentleman alone, Peter. Eat your dinner. It will get cold...," said Manami, placing a plate in front of Pascal.

"I won't be eating," said Pascal.

Chapter 134

"You call me an absolute killer, which is certainly true," the Grasshopper said. "but above all, I see myself as the only honest killer. I have removed from my face the masks of all of their excuses and I didn't put on a new one. I have announced the end of the masquerade and asked the courtiers to leave. My honesty and the chance circumstance that I remained alone and untouchable at this command desk have made me the absolute killer."

"Chance circumstance?" Dr. Palladino was surprised. "But you told me that you strived to get to that room."

"Yes, that is true."

"It is interesting that you didn't choose a technical vocation, so that you would be hired there."

"I didn't because I was already a philosophy student. And not only because of that. I had to train myself to kill. How could I, as an engineer in the Command manage to kill the entire crew?"

"I understand."

"That is why I decided to impose myself on Erivan. For him to recruit me into his squads. I started actively doing track and field, I wrote papers celebrating Humane Capitalism, ratting out Non-Consumers to the Inspectorate, and so on. And he bought it. It later turned out that I was an excellent squire. With my Ph.D. I finally gained Erivan's trust. Of course, in direct communication with him I constantly catered to his ego."

"Where do you see the chance circumstance?"

"There were a number of them. It could have happened that despite all my efforts I was not recruited, or that I was average, an unnoticed squire. There were countless dangerous situations where I could have been killed. It could have happened that Erivan didn't trust me entirely, that he didn't send me to the Command."

"You could have taken a spaceship on your own and come to the Command under some pretext, even earlier. Wasn't that feasible? You didn't have to wait for Erivan to kill the Kaellas."

"Without his letter of authorization I wouldn't have been able to get past the Command's shield. It is impenetrable. Erivan has sent ships against me in the meantime. Of course, I destroyed them as soon as they took off, but even if they reached the Command or any of the collectors in the energy system, they would not have been able to penetrate the shield."

"You didn't talk about the ships with Erivan. At least not on the recording that I saw." Dr. Palladino was surprised.

"We both pretended that it wasn't happening. And that was in the very beginning, when I started switching off energy to Consumer cities too.

"It became clear to him then that he had lost. And just like any ruler who had lost, who was powerless, Erivan too escaped into his own world. He hid in his image of himself.

"These images actually represent the rulers' last excuses to kill. Because of them they killed in the most demented fashion, using the means that were still available to them.

"And I helped Erivan decorate his image with jewels from the abundant treasury of the history of mankind."

Chapter 135

"I told Julius last night to go to bed immediately," Manami started, as soon as Peter had gone to sleep.

Pascal got up from the dining room table and started for his door.

"Come back!" Manami said in a commanding manner.

Pascal stopped for a moment, then slowly turned around and sat in his place, eyes fixed on the table.

"I returned to the kitchen and did some more work. After that I went to the bathroom and stayed there for a while. Much longer than usual."

"Why are you telling me that? What do I care?" Pascal muttered, without raising his eyes.

"When I finally went to my room, Julius was fast asleep."

"And when he woke up?" Pascal whispered, looking at his fingers, intertwining them nervously.

"I don't know when he woke up and left. I was sleeping and I didn't hear him."

"You're not lying?"

"I'm not lying."

"How... how can I believe you? How can I be sure? How can I go to sleep?" Pascal said in a fast whisper.

"I know how," Manami said calmly.

"How?"

"Look me in the eye and you will be sure."

Pascal finally raised his eyes and saw her two magnificent honest eyes looking back at him. He smiled.

"Do you believe me now?" she asked.

"Yes. Thank you, Manami. Thank you very much."

"How did you survive it, Pascal?"

"It was horrific! I was going mad, mad I say! Had you not cleverly warned me that Peter would tell his father how I was behaving, I wouldn't have come out of my room until he came around again. And then I would have left here for good. Because, Manami, I couldn't survive another night like that."

"I didn't mean that," Manami smiled.

"No?"

"I asked how you survived without seeing me all day?"

"Manami... my love..." whispered Pascal, caressing her with his eyes.

"Well, for that look you deserve dinner. You'd better eat while I look in on the children and put on my nightgown."

"And what will happen next time, Manami?" Pascal asked as soon as she sat down next to him. "He hasn't spent a single night here so far. I guess that's why I've convinced myself that he never will. And that's why I'm asking you now, Manami, what will happen the next time that he lies next to you?" Pascal jumped off the couch. "What do I care if you didn't make love! I won't let him lie in your bed! I won't let him touch you! I won't let him even look at you anymore!"

Manami got up and tried to hug him.

"Let me go," Pascal pulled out of her arms. "What use do I have from your hugs? Answer me, Manami!"

"Pascal, this is too important to discuss this way," said Manami in a serious tone. "It will be the way that the two of us agree on. When the two of us make up our minds."

Pascal sat down on the couch.

"So, we have to discuss it," he said. "You won't tell him that he can't sleep in your bed."

"I'll tell him, if the two of us agree on it."

"There it is again! If the two of us agree on it! As the two of us agree! I have nothing to discuss with you! I've clearly said what I have to say! I won't let him enter your room!"

"Alright, Pascal. Then that's settled. There, you see how quickly we reached an agreement?"

"What did we agree on?! We didn't agree on anything!"

"Yes, we've agreed. The next time that he sits here at this table and when he says that he will spend the night here, I'll tell him in front of the children that I won't permit him, because I'm in love with you and that only you can sleep with me."

Pascal didn't say anything.

"Why are you silent now? That's what we've decided and that's it. We won't talk about it any more," Manami concluded.

"And what will happen then?" Pascal asked quietly.

"I don't know. Whatever happens will happen. We'll think about it then," Manami said in a calm voice.

"It can't be like that, Manami. I can't do that to you; for him to take the children because of me; to separate you from them... that's out of the question."

"My darling, my darling..." Manami caressed him. "I didn't want to have to convince you. I wanted you to think for yourself. And why didn't you sleep all night, silly? Why did you pout all day? Didn't you hear Julius say at the table how tired he was? Don't you know, my love, where Eir sleeps?"

"I thought that you moved her to the other room."

"I didn't. She slept between us."

"Really?"

"Really."

"And what if he comes once and... wants to be with you... I can't even say it!"

"Then I'll tell him everything, Pascal."

Chapter 136

"How then did you get name Grasshopper?" Dr. Palladino asked. "Because you stalked your victims and waited unnoticed for days, until the right moment? And then you pounced like a grasshopper from the grass?"

"Grasshoppers are herbivores, Dr. Palladino," laughed the Grasshopper. "Its not because of that. That's what people say. Erivan called me Grasshopper because I held the record at the Megapolis University for the high jump. He was keen on giving squires the names of animals."

"But it's true that you enjoyed completely surprising your victim?"

"Enjoyed? I wouldn't put it that way. I did that whenever it was possible, so that I could see the victims eyes the moment that they saw me."

"Why?"

"Because at that moment, which is very, very short, you see true, genuine, primeval, original fear. That is the moment when reason becomes aware that the end of life has come. The next moment the fear is gone and it is replaced by horror, disbelief, powerlessness, sorrow, despair, begging, prayer, anger, defiance, hatred, panic, hysteria... something else. But never sadness. People aren't capable of being sad. Have you ever been sad, Dr. Palladino?"

"I don't know. In that sense, and it seems that you have somehow isolated sadness, that you give it special meaning – I think I haven't."

"You certainly haven't. No one has. But let's put that aside. I'd like to ask you something else, Doctor. Why were you playing Russian roulette? Charlie told me that he found you in the middle of a game."

"It just happened," Dr. Palladino answered. "A poker partner had disappeared. After a while I learned that he had died playing Russian roulette... When the war started... when snipers appeared in every block, firing squads, widespread raping of women and girls... when my job became pointless... when the only thing that gave my life meaning disappeared... I went to play Russian roulette."

"And why did hunting killers mean so much to you?"

"You'll laugh at me. Because of Hercule Poirot."

"The Agatha Christie character?" the Grasshopper was surprised.

"Yes. I read her books countless times."

"Really? Isn't it boring when you know who the killer is?"

"No. Even when I read one of her books for the first time I wouldn't try to discover the villain. I would simply let the lady take me wherever she wanted to. I enjoyed the atmosphere of her novels."

"And what influence did Hercule Poirot have on you?"

"He simply said 'I do not approve of murder." And that was the only thing that was truly important to me, my entire life. The only thing that I care about."

"And you know why?"

"I know. I admire people who appreciate, who love life, who rejoice it, enjoy it. I consider this to a gift that I do not have, and that is why I do not approve that the lives of such people be taken."

"You are an interesting man, Dr. Palladino."

"On the contrary, I'm very dull..."

"I've remembered something else... something I've wanted to ask you several times, Mr. Grasshopper."

"Ask away."

"Have you read Tolstoy?"

"Of course. Are you thinking of his thoughts about the importance of individuals in history? If he were with us today he would know that the role of the individual sitting at this desk is crucial."

"Certainly. But I was thinking of Anna Karenina."

"Anna Karenina?" the Grasshopper was surprised.

"Yes. Tolstoy's introductory statement, that all happy families are alike and unhappy ones are not, seemed monstrous to me."

"Why?"

"Because in it he suggests to the reader that they should be unhappy."

"How did you come to that conclusion?"

"Why would someone seek happiness if it is dull? Always the same. Like your neighbor's. And now I'm certain that the claim is incorrect. At least in its second part."

"Why?"

"Look at the Earth, Mr. Grasshopper. Misery is dull. Pain is dull. The same for all people, endless."

"And you wish to test the truth of the first part of Tolstoy's claim on my case?" the Grasshopper raised his voice. "Because you think that I am happy now. And you want to hear from me that my happiness is equal and dull this entire time. And that I will stop what

I am doing and kill myself because of the dullness. And with Hercule Poirot you tried to make me empathize with the people that love life. Dr. Palladino, I do not know how to feel, nor empathize. I only know how to think. I feel neither happiness, nor sadness, nor satisfaction, nor dullness, nothing. I only know how to read the feelings in the eyes of other people. To understand and classify them. To draw conclusions from them and form opinions. And to act based on those opinions. I'm a little disappointed in you, I must admit."

"It's all clear to me, Mr. Grasshopper," Dr. Palladino said loudly, getting up from his chair. "But I simply have no ideas, I don't! My greatest problem is that... I want to tell you that with Tolstoy and dullness I made a desperate attempt, but not with Poirot. You asked me why hunting killers meant so much to me, and I answered you honestly and precisely."

"It's alright, Doctor," said the Grasshopper in a calm tone again. "Continue. You wanted to say something else. What is your greatest problem?"

"It's that I find no faults in your opinions. Your actions based on these opinions are horrific. But I cannot change that. I was hoping, this entire time, that I would find a crack... some inconsistency in your thinking. That I would point it out to you, that you would change your mind, at least in some detail, that you would act differently because of it... you would do that, I'm certain."

"I would."

"But I can't find it... I'm not educated enough, I wasn't interested in all that... You probably wouldn't accept to talk to other experts... historians..."

"My last conversation is with you, Dr. Palladino."

"That's clear to me... Alright, like this... Tell me, what do you think about Pascal Alexander? You mentioned him only once. And the strength of his movement, which would topple Kaella, right?"

"Yes, I did."

"So you know how he thinks? His conclusions?"

"I do."

"Can you tell me what you think of them? They are the complete opposite of yours. They are full of life energy, optimism, hope. Can you tell me why they are wrong?"

"I can."

Chapter 137

"First of all, I'm immensely grateful to Mr. Pascal Alexander. Without him I would never have had the opportunity to sit at this desk. Someone else would have appeared, undoubtedly. But not at the right moment. Not at the moment when I was ready," the Grasshopper said.

"So, Pascal made it possible for you to kill? That is a very unfair claim, Mr. Grasshopper!" Dr. Palladino said angrily.

"That's the way it is, Dr. Palladino. Mr. Alexander made it possible for me. Had he not, someone else would have done the same for the Kaellas, another Erivan… another Grasshopper. The absolute weapon is there. The only question is who would pull the trigger and when. Like in the theater, when there is a rifle hanging on the wall. Everyone knows that it will go off by the end of the play."

"Your logic is horrific! Awful! I simply don't accept it, Mr. Grasshopper!" Dr. Palladino got up from the chair and angrily paced around the office.

"It's not my logic. I'm not original in any way," the Grasshopper continued in a calm voice. "My answer, that I will kill all people because I can, also isn't original. Everyone killed because they could. Or at least because they thought that they could.

"And all the groups of people strived to create opportunities for themselves to kill, just as I have done. To be stronger than other groups of people. To have better weapons, a larger and better trained army.

"And when they achieved that, when they could kill other people, it was easy to come up with an excuse: they hate us, they are a threat to us, we have to expand our territories, we have to ensure resources for ourselves, they believe in something else, we have to get revenge, we are superior… a million excuses.

"You've seen history shows on television. No one wastes time explaining why one group of people killed a different group, why did the groups fought in the first place. They don't explain that because wars and killing are implied. They only talk about who was more skillful, which king, tsar, general or admiral outsmarted the other one, how a certain war, a certain battle developed. When you watch at those shows you get spattered by blood and death.

"I'm not original in any way, Dr. Palladino. I only asked myself why I would kill only the members of this group or the other group of people, when I have the opportunity to kill all people."

Dr. Palladino calmed down. He returned to his chair. He looked at the Grasshopper and said

"Would you please continue the discussion about Pascal Alexander?"

"As you wish, Doctor. I know more about Mr. Alexander that can be deduced from his speeches," the Grasshopper continued. "Because we had him under surveillance on several occasions."

"And? What did you hear? I'm interested in Pascal's intimate thoughts."

"Mr. Pascal Alexander was an utopist. One of many. With the exception of being the last one, he differed from his predecessors in that he did not offer anything new. His goal was the restoration of the old. Restoration of democracy and the free market.

"He wanted... and this needs to be said in the beginning: Mr. Alexander saw a link between evolution – he was a biology teacher – and the free market.

"His thesis was that creation of companies that would compete between themselves in the free market, companies that are constantly developing, changing and adapting to market conditions – is a next phase in evolution. Just like different life forms changed through evolution and struggled for survival.

"And that in this same way, in the free market the strongest survive, and the weaker, unadjusted, incompetent – die out."

"What do you think of that, Mr. Grasshopper?"

"I didn't go into that. I'm not interested in the market, free or not. Or evolution. I'm not interested in whether man was created by evolution, God or something else. I'm also not interested in whether man's instinct to kill was imbedded by the creator intentionally or by accident. I only understand what has been created. And if this unknown creator truly had the intention to create sustainable life, life capable of surviving – then his project is failing, he's become perplexed, like a pupil solving a math problem for a test. And I will help him. I will do what is most sensible in such cases. I will tear out the piece of paper with his scribbling, crumple it up and throw it in the trash. Let him start solving the problem from the beginning, on a blank piece of paper. If he has any time left until the school bell rings."

Dr. Palladino got up and went to the window.

"You have nothing to say?" the Grasshopper asked.

Dr. Palladino didn't answer. He lit a cigarette and looked out the window.

"In any case, don't you think that this is quite alright, that a Grasshopper is sitting at this desk, Dr. Palladino?"

"What do you mean 'alright'?" asked Dr. Palladino moving in heavy steps back towards the chair.

"Don't movies depict Earth and mankind under attack by monsters from outer space, with many arms and legs?"

"I don't watch such films, Mr. Grasshopper," said Dr. Palladino while taking his seat.

"I believe you. These movies differ only in the number of hands and legs that the monsters have. There was a competition between the moviemakers in who would have the most limbs. And it turned out that it functioned only up to a certain degree. Up to an optimum. After that it was counterproductive; every limb that the author added to his monster only increased the movie's financial loss. So I've been thinking, perhaps it is optimal for mankind that it be killed by a Grasshopper. Six legs is perhaps the optimal number?"

"I'm surprised by your cynicism, Mr. Grasshopper."

"It wasn't my intention to be cynical, Dr. Palladino. I'm just surprised by the level of dishonesty among people. They don't want to admit that the greatest monster in the universe has only two hands and two legs."

"I think you've been kidding yourself the entire time, Mr. Grasshopper," Dr. Palladino said.

"What do you mean?" the Grasshopper was surprised.

"Because you consider yourself an honest killer who doesn't need an excuse."

"That's right, Doctor."

"It's not true. Your excuse is your disappointment in people, Mr. Grasshopper."

"No, it's not," the Grasshopper answered immediately, without a second thought. "I'm not disappointed. In order to be disappointed in something one must first have some expectations. And I don't have any. I never had any."

Chapter 138

"Manami, do you see how much I love Peter and Eir?" Pascal asked.

"I see, my darling." Manami sat in his lap, straddling him. She ran her fingers through his hair. "And I'm overjoyed about it. I also see how the two of them have accepted you... alright, for now as someone they are living with, but even there you would be able to see any animosity, any antagonism. And there is non, my love. Not even a speck. I know that my children will also accept you as my husband. Perhaps there will be some initial resistance in Peter. Not perhaps – there surely will be. But so many people get divorces, and the children adapt, don't they? The children grow, they get interested in children their age, their generation. It will be alright. I know it. It's clear to me. I stopped worrying about that long ago."

"And I will always love them like that. Even if..." Pascal fell silent and dropped his head.

"What? Even if what? What could happen?" Manami was frightened.

"Nothing, it's not important..." Pascal looked at her and smiled.

"Why are you smiling, Pascal? What are you scheming?" Manami relaxed when she realized that Pascal was teasing her. "Tell me, even if what?"

"Well that... I mean, it isn't unusual... actually it happens to other people at our age. When a married couple agrees, what and how..."

"I do, my love, I do! I want it! The children also won't mind if they get a baby sister or a baby brother. You'll see, my love! You're wonderful! Wonderful!" Manami kissed Pascal ecstatically.

"Do you really? I was sure that you wouldn't. You already have Peter and Eir..."

"I also want our child! How could I not want it?!"

"And for it to be beautiful like you, and smart like you, Manami."

"Stop kidding around, Pascal! Kiss me, please. The two minutes start earlier tonight."

"That sweet tongue of yours has gone wild, Manami" said Pascal, when they stopped for a moment to catch their breath.

303

"Don't be sassy," Manami laughed. "What do you mean 'wild'? It's like it always is during the two minutes."

"No, not like always. I mean, yes, it's always wild, but not exactly this much. This is a bit too much for such a lady, Manami."

Manami thought about it.

"Perhaps you're right. But that's only now. Because I'm so happy."

"So in your case, like with me, happiness causes physical excitement," Pascal said.

He left one hand on her breast, and for the first time, he gently lowered his other hand down her stomach.

"Don't you..."

"Dare," Pascal ended her usual command. "I know that and I'm getting tired of it."

Manami kissed him.

"Hey, darling, slowly," Pascal laughed. "I'm afraid."

"What are you afraid of? Don't play around with me any more, Pascal," Manami laughed too.

"I'm afraid that your tongue might get free," Pascal teased her and sighed deeply. He was running his hands over her thighs and buttock for the first time.

"Well, that's not right!" Manami shouted and got up from his lap. "That's very inappropriate, Pascal, taking advantage of my moment of happiness! I'm angry! I'm very angry! You won't get even two minutes any more! Remember what I said!" Manami shouted.

Pascal got up and tried to hug her. Manami moved away and held her hands on his chest.

"Don't you dare touch me again, Pascal!"

"My love, why are you angry? You know that I'd never do anything you didn't want me to."

"You wouldn't? And what were you doing just now?"

"Only what you wanted."

"Well I don't want it! Not now! I made it clear to you! When I am..."

"What you want so much, my darling! You're very excited!"

"I'm not excited!" Manami pushed him away.

Pascal stepped forward, towards her.

"Actually I am! I never expected to be able to fool such an expert!"

"Don't start with that again. I told you..."

"I'm excited! I am! Very much so! Unbearable!" Manami was jumping up and down and stomping her feet on the floor.

"And what do you propose, ma'am? What should we do?" Pascal smiled at her.

"That's only temporary bodily excitement," she tried to calm herself. "It just happened... this situation. You're so cheeky!" she shouted suddenly. "You created it! You planned everything! That's why you started telling me how much you love my children. So that I would relax, be happy and carefree, and for you to jump me and take advantage of me! We'll that's not going to happen, sir! I've seen right through you! Your tactic has failed, sir!"

"I didn't plan it, my love, I didn't. I just wanted to ask you, to beg you to have our baby. I was afraid that you wouldn't want to. And now I'm so overjoyed!"

"I am too. But it doesn't help."

"I love you too much, Manami, to allow you to be so excited, and..."

"I am a woman of flesh and blood, Pascal!"

"Yes, you are, my love. The most beautiful, most wonderful woman. A real woman!"

"Don't say such nice things, Pascal. I can't take this anymore."

"I love you so much, Manami! So much! I won't do anything if you don't want me to. So you tell me, how do we get out of this situation. This has to end somehow. You have to be calm and satisfied, my joy," Pascal said seriously, watching upon his beloved being struggling with herself.

"I don't know," Manami whispered in heat.

"Well, think about it. Because the excitement will not just go away. On the contrary, it will only grow."

"I know."

"Here, I'm selflessly offering to help you," Pascal smiled.

"I don't doubt that. I want it, I want..." Manami paused for a moment, then continue. "Here, this is what we'll do. We'll go to your room now. And we'll lock the door. There will be four doors between us and the children. They won't hear us."

"They won't hear me for sure, and on the other hand, I never thought that you were that loud, Manami, that you need four doors to stifle your..."

"How dare you?!" Manami shouted.

"...sighs," Pascal finished his sentence.

"You can't talk to me like that, Pascal! I won't let you!"

"You'll let me, you'll let me. And you want me to. I'm just trying to enhance your excitement, my love."

"There's no need to try. It can't get any greater. I'm going mad, Pascal!"

"Well, alright... so we lock ourselves behind four doors, and what then?"

"Don't fantasize too much, Pascal!" said Manami, going toward the door to Pascal's quarters. "You won't get anything out of it! When I tell Julius how much I love you and that I want a divorce, when I am free, that is when I will give myself to you. And nothing before then! That's how I was raised! I'm the only daughter of an Inspectorate general, sir! A long-standing head of the Inspectorate Academy! The only daughter of the famous general..."

"I understand, selfish ma'am. Who cares about me? But what will we do about you? We have to find a solution," Pascal approached her.

They stood in front of his closed door.

"You will... We won't even lie on any bed. Don't you dare think of pushing me on the bed... or anything similar."

"You mean - pick you up in my arms, and gently place you on the bed?"

"Stop already! Don't you say another word!"

"Alright, I won't. I'm silent. I'm just looking at you. Do you see how I'm looking at you?"

"You're impossible! Impossible!"

"Alright. We won't lay down. So we'll sit down. Probably on one of the chairs."

"Don't provoke me! We'll stand."

"Stand?"

"Yes, stand! And you won't hug me or kiss me. Do you understand?"

"Yes, of course. The two of us standing, without hugging, without kissing, and all that until we drop out of exhaustion."

"Well that does it! No one has ever mocked me like that! I'm going to bed. Good night, Pascal."

"Good night, my love."

Manami didn't move. Pascal only grinned and consumed her with his eyes.

"Good night, my love," he repeated, already laughing out loud.

"You'll pay for this!" Manami screamed.

"But not now?"

"Take me to your room already!"

"I can't, Manami, until you tell me what we will do. Because if you don't define that clearly, then I will decide. And if I decide..."

"Shut up! I'm going to go insane! Well, like this… and don't interrupt me any more."

"I won't."

"You will stand away from me…"

"Away?"

"No, not away… you won't hold me. Just with your hand stretched out… and I will lean against the wall… in that place… You understand?"

"No."

"What do you mean 'no'? With one hand, stretched out, you'll touch that place. Are we clear? Don't pretend…"

"It's clear to me what you want, but what's not clear…"

"What?"

"Well… you can do that on your own. What do you need me for?"

"On my own?! How dare you think of me like that?!"

"I'm sorry, I'm sorry." Pascal laughed.

"But only that place. So only outside, not inside… Clear?"

"Clear, clear. I didn't think…"

"You didn't think?... Who am I trusting? Who am I giving myself to? Manami, Manami, why are you doing this?"

"You need it? A lot?"

"A lot!"

"And what will I do with my other hand?"

"On the side, Pascal. I mean, at your side."

"And what will you do with your hands?"

"Also at the side."

"Also at my side?"

"No! My side! And stop torturing me!"

"And the gold kimono? I mean, what is our interpretation of this? Is it making love or… ."

"What kimono now?!"

"Alright, alright, no kimono… But Manami…?

"What is it now? Take me in!"

"Alright, immediately. Just one more question."

"What?"

"How long will this last? Because I won't be able to stay long in such a silly pose."

"Just a fraction of a second. As soon as you touch me…" said Manami, while opening the door herself.

Chapter 139

"Mr. Grasshopper, can we go back to Pascal Alexander? You said that he didn't offer anything new, that he only wanted to restore something that had existed previously?" Dr. Palladino asked.

"Yes. He wanted to restore the human community which would offer every person equal opportunities. A society that in his opinion had the most correct value system."

"What values are those?"

"Freedom, human rights, democracy, free entrepreneurship, progress, success, material prosperity... work, efficiency... scientific development. He believed that such a society is capable of once again finding itself and moving forward after each development phase, after each cycle. In his opinion such a society would represent an ecosystem, an incubator, which would produce the Third Renaissance."

"The Third Renaissance? I didn't know that there had been two," Dr. Palladino was surprised.

"Mr. Alexander claimed that there were. He claimed that the first renaissance was created after the Dark Ages in Tuscany, and that the second renaissance was after the even darker first half of the twentieth century, in Northern California."

"In Northern California?"

"Yes. He was delighted by the fact that some young men created companies in their garages, which in turn changed the world; that by teaching people to think differently, one young man created a company that had the largest market value in the world; that something created only using gray cells and sand from the Californian coast, was more valuable than even the largest energy company at the time.

"When the man died, his President and First Lady said that he not only changed the world, but was one of the rare persons who changed people's views of the world. Mr. Alexander was fascinated by the story of two young men who created a machine for searching the Internet. He was excited by the fact that it was possible to get uncensored search results."

"Uncensored?"

"Yes. There is very little information about all that. The Kaellas hid that part of history. Because the Internet was free. The regimes couldn't lie to people for very long through controlled media. And not only that. There was an Internet encyclopedia which people continuously created and updated, in all languages. The story is that there was even a social network with free communication. With communication that no one controlled. The users on this network were mainly young people. But they were from all across the planet.

"According to Mr. Alexander, a new generation of youths was growing up throughout the world, under the influence of the second renaissance. This was a generation that didn't hate and wasn't evil. A generation with open hearts, Mr. Alexander called them.

"But it wasn't given an opportunity to take the world in the direction that it wanted to. They were remembered as the lost generation. What Mr. Alexander felt worst about was Kaella's bragging that the ultimate result of the False Balance was the lost generation."

"Why was that generation lost?" Dr. Palladino asked.

"You didn't watch Kaella's interview. Babe explained everything very nicely. These young people lost their future.

"They had finished school, but they couldn't find jobs. They didn't have any income, they didn't get married, have children or create families. In certain groups of people their unemployment exceeded fifty percent even before the over-indebted states collapsed.

"Their parents had taken away their future, by providing leisurely and carefree lives for themselves through decades of loans and by destroying the planet's ecosystem. And they extinguished their children's second renaissance."

"And this Third Renaissance? What will that be?"

"Mr. Alexander didn't know that. Nor did he claim that he knew. He believed that when he restored democracy and free market, the Third Renaissance would come on its own; that its time will come because that is the nature of historical cycles. That this is what must come after the darkest of all centuries. After Kaella's century. That is why he believed that the Third Renaissance would be the most magnificent. That it would bring about something that we cannot even imagine today."

"Of course, you don't agree with that."

"No."

"Will you tell me why?"

"Dr. Palladino, you fail to find arguments against my theses and you want Mr. Alexander and I to cross swords in front of you. It seems that he is your last hope. And the same goes for these people on Earth. Have you seen what people do?"

"I have."

"They pray to him, asking him to return to Earth from heaven, and to save them. They are improvising his temples. At the very end mankind is summoning a new messiah. Like always when people realize that they are only victims and nothing else. That's when they turn to religion, to God. They swore to him that they would not sin, that they would respect His commandments. And during periods when they were powerful, when they had the opportunity to kill their victims, then they did exactly that – and in his name."

"I agree. I admit that I can't find any argumentation against your claims. I want to hear your comment about Pascal's thinking. I admit that it is my last hope. Will you tell me, please?" Dr. Palladino asked the Grasshopper.

"I will. Even if Mr. Alexander is right," the Grasshopper explained. "even if this third, most magnificent renaissance occurs, if something that we cannot imagine were to be created, even then the collective ancient urge to kill would use it to its advantage.

"The achievements of the human mind always created newer and more effect deadly weapons. That is how this command desk, the one that I am sitting at, was created. If it didn't exist, the Third Renaissance would only postpone the agony.

"Think about it. What did the second renaissance create? It created technologies that the Kaellas used for their information systems, systems that control every person, from birth to death. At every moment they know where each person is, who is communicating with whom, what they are looking up on the Internet, what their affinities are, what they could additionally sell them... They erase and change people's identities, biographies...

"And that was all made possible by the technologies from Northern California, Dr. Palladino."

Chapter 140

"Dr. Palladino, it was precisely Mr. Alexander, and especially the unstoppable growth of his movement, that finally confirmed to me that I'm right," the Grasshopper said.

"How is that?" Dr. Palladino asked.

"Because he wanted to restore democracy. He often repeated Churchill's thought that democracy is the worst form of government, with the exception of all those other forms that have been tried from time to time. He claimed that this was valid in Churchill's time and that it's also valid today."

"And you agree with this?"

"I don't know whether one form of government is better than another. I don't know the criteria based on which I would make this assessment. But I do know that democracy is certainly the most deadly form of all forms of government that we have learned about so far."

"I don't understand," said Dr. Palladino.

"I'll explain it to you. In all other non-democratic social communities the rulers, dictators and a few people around them had the opportunity to act on their instincts to kill. During the entire duration of the regime, both in war and in peace. Their subjects could act on their instincts with impunity only during wars."

"I think I know what you're trying to say. That in democracy the instincts of all people come into play equally."

"That's right. The strength of one person's instinct or that of a few people, regardless of how strong these instincts are, cannot be compared to the sum of mediocre instincts, sometimes numbering in the billions. Which, by the way, were suppressed in non-democratic regimes.

"This is why they exploded with all their might when democracy gave them the right of vote. Then people circle the name on the ballot that told them that they were the most beautiful, smartest, most superior. The name that told them that their hour has finally come. That they are now prepared. The name that promised them that they would plunder, banish, conquer, kill the other group of people."

"You say that you are not interested in the causes," said Dr. Palladino, "that you draw your conclusions from the consequences. I don't see that democracies conducted more wars that dictatorships. On the contrary. And these were wars for defending democracy, and for freedom."

"Every excuse for killing is a good excuse. And you, Dr. Palladino, place pluses and minuses in front of excuses. Like every person does. In front of their convictions, in front of the values that a person believes in, they place a plus sign. And in front of the values contrary to theirs, they place a minus sign.

"For example, you consider democracy to be positive and dictatorship negative. This means that you believe that democracy would be quite an acceptable excuse for killing.

"Or for example... remember what the world was like for most of its existence. It consisted of a finite number of various groups of people. Now imagine a person X who was born into one of the groups, let's say group A, and became its member by birth.

"Person X places membership in group A above life. In this membership he finds his excuse for killing. And he places a plus sign in front of membership in group A. When group A wages war against group B, person X uses his membership in group A as an excuse for killing members of group B. Do you follow?"

"Yes."

"If that same person X, coded with identical genes, or created completely identical by God, if you like, were to be born in group B, placing membership in group B above life, it would mark this with a plus sign, and would use it in that same war as an excuse for killing members of group A.

"This applies to rulers, commanders, soldiers and civilians alike. Group membership is an excuse that is very democratically distributed.

"People place group membership even above the lives of their progeny. Because of it they send their children to their deaths. Do you understand that?"

"Yes, I do."

"What I said here was not my answer to your question, why democracy is the deadliest form of government. Here I just wanted to explain the irrelevance, pointlessness of your, i.e. everyone's, pluses and minuses that you place in front of excuses. The excuse for killing that a person will use in their life is decided by chance: the time and place of their birth. The only absolute category embedded in the foundations of every person is the primal instinct to kill. Everything else is relative."

"I understand. According to you all wars are the same. Tell me, what is this more deadly thing that has been carried out by the sum of a billion average instincts?"

"This sum, which was finally made possible by democracy, actually represents the collective self-destructive instinct, the Thanatos of humanity."

"Give me an example from history, show me a consequence of collective self-destruction."

"Look around you, Dr. Palladino. Look at the ecosystem that you spent your life in. Do you know what nature used to look like?"

"I do."

"The vast democratic majority, within all the previously existing groups of people, chose to kill the planet. The planet was killed by people through the sum of their deadly instincts.

"Their collective excuse also represented the sum of small greeds for small prosperities, small envies, small lazinesses, small disinterests, the sum of small carelessnesses, conformism and comforts… the sum of small indifferences for the future of their own progeny.

"Mankind's Thanatos defeated life long ago, Dr. Palladino."

Chapter 141

"When did you first recognize your instinct to kill?" Dr. Palladino asked the Grasshopper the following day.

"A day before my fifteenth birthday. At 7.10 p.m."

"That was a strong, impressive feeling if you so clearly recognized it and remembered the date and time."

"Yes, it was," said the Grasshopper and continued. "There's something different about you, Dr. Palladino."

"How did you come to that conclusion?"

"From your question. When did I first feel the urge to kill? Isn't that one of your usual patterns? Your usual method of operation?"

"Yes, it is."

"At the beginning you said that you were dropping all of that, that you were approaching me unconventionally."

"Yes. I am intentionally returning to traditional methods, because you fit the profile of a serial killer. I've had such a case. And that is why I have to thoroughly prepared for our next conversation."

"Do you? And how long will that take, Dr. Palladino?"

"As long as it takes."

"You think that I will allow this?"

"Yes, I do. And during that time you will switch off your deadly rays and charge the power plants on Earth that you still haven't destroyed."

"The two of us are quite different, Doctor."

"In what way?"

"I kill on an industrial level, efficiently. And you apparently enjoy the anguish of the victims, and you want to give them a moment of hope. Let them relax a little, have some water, eat something. Let them gain some strength for the long and painful death."

"I'm not listening to you. I know that you will do as we have agreed."

"Agreed?"

"Yes. Tell me now, what happened on the evening before your fifteenth birthday?"

"I was on my way home from basketball. I took a shortcut, a narrow alley between some warehouses and garages. And I heard the excited shouts of three boys…"

"What were they doing?"

"I recognized them, they were from my school. Two years younger than me..."

"What were they doing?"

"They were passing a cat between them, holding it by the tail and smashing it against the garage wall."

"You had the desire to join them?"

"No. I had the desire to kill them."

"Alright, Mr. Grasshopper," Dr. Palladino got up from the chair. "I will now retire and prepare for our last conversation. I will call you when I am ready. Goodbye."

Dr. Palladino reached the door and looked at the Grasshopper one more time.

"Turn the people's power back on," he said and left the presidential office.

Chapter 142

"How you tricked me, Pascal. I'll never forgive myself for trusting you," said Manami, sitting in their room.

"I tricked you, my love? What are you talking about?"

"You promised that you would only touch me... not..."

"Me? I did exactly what you said. I only touched you. And you, Manami, immediately jumped on me and started kissing me. It's your own fault."

"I did, I admit it. But you knew that it would be like that. You're the experienced one, not me. How could I know that I would lose it like that?"

"My sweet darling. You lost it, did you?"

"Yes, completely."

"And now you'd like to do it again, admit it."

"I would. I mean, I would never leave your bed. But perhaps I'm not interesting to you. My body might not be... You're used to..."

"Shut up! I really mean it! Once and for all! For me there is only your body. Only you, Manami."

"And you too would never leave my bed. Tell me that, please... Lie to me."

"Lie to you? Stop being silly! I would never leave, but not your bed or my bed. I will never leave our bed, my love. For days... weeks... our bed."

"Oh, that was so nice. The best! How you... I still don't know what you did to me... I wasn't at all aware how time passed... And that's why I'm angry with you, Pascal! Two hours! And you knew that and you didn't care about..."

"Let's go to my room. I can't take it anymore," Pascal took her by the hand.

"We have to endure it, love, we have to. We cannot do that here anymore. The children could wake up, Julius could come in at any moment."

"Alright, Manami. I won't caress you or kiss you... I won't do anything anymore, if that's how you are."

"Shut up... shut up, please. We cannot talk about it. We cannot think about it. It is as though nothing happened. That is how we have to behave."

"You shut up! Because, if I see that you are that excited again, I won't ask you anything. I won't listen to you at all, Manami. I will pick you up in my arms and carry you to my room."

"There! I knew it!" Manami shouted.

"So know it! You should know!" Pascal shouted back at her.

"When you see that I'm excited! Me! And you're never excited? You are, of course you are, but not because of me! I'm not sexy enough to excite Mr. Alexander!"

"Stop it!" Pascal shouted. "I'm not excited?! I've been burning with desire for your body! I'm mad about you, Manami! And I won't take this any more! I keep quiet, I keep it in, I burn up, I suffer so as not to upset you! Not to pressure you! I only think about you! Well, I can't do it anymore!" Pascal got up from the couch, violently pulled her by the hand and picked her up in his arms.

"Tell me! Tell me, are you crazy about me?!" Manami was overjoyed.

"I'm not going to tell you anything more. You'll see for yourself," he said while opening the door to his quarters.

"Don't, my love, please don't! Really don't! What if Peter comes in!"

Hearing her words Pascal stopped.

"Alright, Manami. But if you say once more time that I'm not excited..."

"Well, I'm so afraid..."

"What are you afraid of, my dearest darling? I don't want you to be afraid of anything! Don't you see that? Why don't you understand how much I love you? How much I want you? Ever part of your body! Your beautiful breasts and your back... your arms and your shoulders ... and your legs, refined, perfect. Your thighs, your hips... and your buttocks, my dearest buttocks. It is because of it that I can't take it anymore. You haven't let me get to know it at all, to love it, and caress it and kiss it. And your rose. My most beautiful rose, which opens its petals only to me, which loves only me, which is only mine. Only mine!!!"

"I'm all only yours! Forever only yours!" Manami hollered, finally certain that Pascal wanted her.

Pascal was holding her in his arms the entire time.

"I don't care about anything!" he shouted and opened the door.

He ran into the room, placed her on the bed and lay down next to her. He raised her nightgown.

"Pascal…" Manami whispered in heat. "Just this now, please. And quickly. Just to calm ourselves. Please, my love…"

Pascal got up, locked the door to the living room, closed the door to the dormitory and said

"I will make love with you until morning, my goddess. I'm no longer in a hurry anywhere. I will first kiss every inch of your body for hours. For hours, do you hear me?"

"Pascal, don't talk that way. You know I can't resist you. My son could come in. Please, Pascal…"

"He can't come in. I've locked the door. And if he wakes up, you will come out from here and tell him that I have a high fever and that you put that meat for lunch, which you supposedly defrost every night, on my forehead to cool me down," Pascal laughed.

"What meat? What are you talking about… Ah! You're so shameless!" Manami remembered her fictional alibi.

"And if Julius comes, let him come. Let him find out. I want him to learn, as soon as possible. And what do I care what the world is like up there? Only we exist! Only the two of us, Manami!"

Manami didn't say anything anymore. Pascal took off his clothes and lay next to her. He slowly raised her nightgown and stroked her legs.

"Now just that little problem, Manami," he whispered in her ear.

"What problem? I knew it, I knew that something wasn't to your liking!"

"Well… we were behind four doors, but I still had to cover your mouth with my hand."

"You're so shameless!"

"You're really loud, Manami."

"Apologize! Immediately!"

"I apologize," Pascal smiled.

"So what if I'm loud? It's your own fault," said Manami and started kissing him wildly.

Chapter 143

The following evening Seneca stayed the night in the shelter with his family for the second time. When he and Manami wished Pascal goodnight and retreated to their room, Pascal went to his door with a heavy step. He entered the corridor and started towards the bathroom. He stopped halfway.

"You won't make love to him, Manami. I know that. You promised me. You promised that you would tell him how much we are in love. And I believe you, Manami. Because I know that you love me as much as I love you. I only have to make it through this night. Eir is between you. You won't take her anywhere…" Pascal turned on the light and went into the bathroom. He raised his head and looked at his eyes in the mirror. And they were wild. "What do I care that a child is between you! I don't allow him to lay in your bed. Or kiss you goodnight! I won't allow it!!! Not even on the cheek! I won't allow him to touch you! To look at you! I won't allow it! I won't allow anything anymore!!!"

Pascal burst into the living room and rushed toward their quarters. And then he stopped dead in his tracks. At that same moment Seneca came out and quickly walked towards the entrance to the shelter. He didn't even look at Pascal. He hurried out and slammed the door.

Manami, with her back to Pascal, carefully closed her door. And then she turned around and ran into his arms.
"I told him, Pascal!" she shouted. "I told him everything!" Her entire body was trembling.
Pascal held her and didn't say anything. He didn't interrupt her.

"When we went into the room," Manami continued excitedly, "he told me to take Eir away. So I took her to the other room. So that we wouldn't wake her if we argued.
"When I came back he wasn't in bed. He was still standing in the same place, next to the bed, looking at me. I stood near the open door and waited to hear what he was going to say. And he said

319

'You probably aren't in the mood for this. You satisfy your needs regularly with your Pascal.'
"And I immediately, without thinking, instantly, Pascal, told him that it wasn't a need, that it's a great love, that we're crazy in love and that we can't live without each other. I was preparing to rush into your room and get you, but he was faster. He didn't say a thing. He just turned around and left."

Chapter 144

"It's not only that I can't survive without the children, Pascal. They need me, too. And I don't mean only my physical presence," said Manami, when they calmed down and sat down on their cover. "Not only to care for them, provide for them, look out for them: they need me spiritually too.

"I give to them and I have to give to them until they grow up, something that Julius cannot provide. Something that he doesn't have. I don't know how to describe it. But I feel it. I know it. I'm certain of it. And it's something that both of them need in order to develop their personalities.

"Not only Eir. Peter needs this from me, too. He is like his father in appearance and in intelligence, the way that he thinks... And his character takes after Julius, mainly. I mean mainly in span, in quantity...

"But I have a corner in Peter. And that corner is very important. You see yourself that he is actually a sincere and cheerful child."

"Yes, Manami. You're right. I'm delighted when he is so joyful. And when I see how happy it makes you."

"That's right. And that's why Peter needs me. To defend and safeguard that joy, that merriness, as you put it, from the world."

"Don't worry, darling. We won't allow Julius to take away your children. He also isn't that type of person, Manami. He wouldn't take children away from their mother. The mayor is a good man."

"He puts family above all other things, Pascal. No... perhaps that isn't the right word. Perhaps we aren't more important than anything else. He has his... mission. The way that he sees it. And the family, the faithful wife and good, well-behaved children – he considers them a given. He never would have thought, never would have considered that it could be any differently. If it had crossed his mind... only once... only one fleeting thought... he would have never left me alone with you."

"And what now, Manami? Will we wait for his move or will we leave this place on our own?"

"We won't leave our shelter until we have to, Pascal. Here the four of us are together. I didn't even think it through seriously until now. I kept postponing, waiting for it to happen. And now that it's happened..." Manami suddenly raised her head from his shoulder. "Now I don't even need to think, Pascal!" She said loudly. "Now I know! I probably knew the entire time, I'm sure I did..."

"What, Manami? What did you know?"

"But I didn't want to admit it to myself, didn't want to say it..."

"What? Tell me."

"Because I would have a guilty conscious and I wouldn't be able to completely give in to my love. Yes, that's it. I'm sure it is!"

"What didn't you admit to yourself? Well, tell me. Stop torturing me."

"Julius won't throw us out of the shelter, Pascal."

"He won't? Then what?" Pascal asked.

"He'll do something to himself."

Chapter 145

"Thank you for turning on the energy and stopping the vaporizations," Dr. Palladino said at the beginning of his last conversation with the Grasshopper.

"You're welcome."

"You asked me at the beginning what I thought was the reason why you were talking to me. And I said because you were bored. Do you remember that?"

"Yes."

"You responded that you were talking to me because you were bored, because you longed for a conversation with an intellectual and because you wanted to see what your psychological profile was like."

"Exactly."

"No. None of that is true."

"No?"

"One serial killer that we were looking for wrote to the Inspectorate begging them to catch him, to stop him."

"And? Did you catch him?"

"That same moment. Because he wrote that in an email from his workplace, from his office."

"So, Doctor, you didn't get much glory in that case, did you?"

"No, I didn't."

"Dr. Palladino, you think that through our conversation I have actually been asking you to catch me and stop me?"

"Yes, the entire time."

"Well, then catch me, please, Dr. Palladino. I'm waiting for you. You know where I am, at my workplace."

"It's not funny. On that first day, when I heard your answer that you kill because you can, I wanted to leave this office."

"I remember."

"I told you that I was leaving because I believed that I couldn't persuade you to stop killing. Do you remember what you told me then, Mr. Grasshopper?"

"I remember."

"You claimed, correctly, that I cannot be completely certain of that."

"Yes. And I still think so."

"Now let me ask you, Mr. Grasshopper, can you be completely certain that Pascal Alexander's Third Renaissance will not bring something that is presently unimaginable to us now? Something that might enable life to defeat the collective Thanatos?"

"Of course I can't be completely certain. A person cannot be absolutely certain of anything. But what does that change, Dr. Palladino?"

"You told me that by leaving I would become your accomplice. And I stayed."

"I really don't see any parallel. The fact that I'm not certain whether anything would develop from something that doesn't exist at all, does not make me your accomplice."

"I agree. It doesn't make you my accomplice. It makes me your accomplice. And this time I agree to it."

"I admit that I don't understand you, Doctor."

"You understand, you understand. I agree to be your accomplice in your transformation from an absolute killer to a man who sent a warning to the world. A warning that people will never forget."

"A warning? You've come to the conclusion that I only warned mankind and that now I will stop this?"

"Yes. And that is why I expect you to kill yourself."

"I will. In the end."

"No, not in the end... soon, as soon as possible. You didn't only warn people, Mr. Grasshopper. You did much more than that. You saved them from certain death. You saved the world from an apocalypse. You prevented Erivan from taking over the command desk."

"Doctor, according to that logic Erivan can also be considered a contributor because he prevented the Kaellas from reaching this position. It's just history repeating itself, Dr. Palladino. Everything remains the same. The typical struggle for domination between a few strongmen. Outmaneuvering, undermining, intrigues, assassinations... And the victims don't care which one of them will kill them in the end. The victims are always only victims."

Chapter 146

"What are you saying, Manami? You're probably overreacting. You're too excited now. Let's talk about something else, and we'll come back to this later. When we calm down."

"Julius knows how much everyone respects him," Manami continued, without listening to Pascal. "He knows that he is a great man. And that's what's most important to him. He is a proud man. And he thinks... he's probably right, that he would lose that respect if people learned that his wife cheated on him. Not only cheated – but left him. He cannot allow that. He will not allow that! I'm sure he won't!" Manami raised her voice.

"Alright, my love, alright..." Pascal tried to calm her.

"I don't know how he'll do it, Pascal, how he'll disappear from this world, while being remembered as the great, undefeated, untainted Julius Seneca, the Mayor of Megapolis."

"He is great, Manami, and he will go down in history as such," Pascal said.

"Yes, yes he is... of course. Don't get me wrong. I'm not ridiculing his pride. I only understand it. Such people like Julius, such as my late father, the general, I understand them best. I grew up beside them, lived... my entire life. Julius is now thinking... but he is not thinking about us, Pascal. Nor is he thinking about the children, trust me. He has already accepted the fact that he is a cheated husband and now he is just looking for a solution how to come out of that without being humiliated. And Julius always finds a solution. Always. And the only solution that I see... It can be only his... or my... or our death."

"Manami, please don't talk that way. It's not the end of the world..."

"But not murder... or suicide," Manami wasn't listening to him. "Some type of death, I don't know... in a traffic accident... I'm talking nonsense! There's a war out there! Countless opportunities for death. A death that conceals everything, erases everything... like nothing happened."

"Manami, please stop. Don't say anything more. You're in shock, my love... you're out of your mind. Let's sleep on it..."

"That's the way it is, Pascal. You don't understand it. You're not that type of man. You're not interested in your public image or your place in history."

"You're the only thing that's important to me, Manami."

"I know that, my darling. But you weren't interested in those things even before you met me."

"I wasn't, you're right. I just wanted to be free."

"Think about it. What would you do if I left you?"

"How can you say that to me, Manami?! I would never say something like that to you!"

"I know. Forgive me... but answer me. What would you do?"

"I'd kill myself. That very instant. A bullet to the hearth. In front of you."

"There, you see how simple it is. And you tell me that I'm exaggerating. I'm not exaggerating. Julius too will kill himself... or he'll kill us... but for his own reason."

"I won't allow him, Manami. Here, I know what I'll do. I'll go out of the shelter and talk to him. Man to man. We're not the only adulterers in the world, right?"

Chapter 147

"Let's put that aside, Mr. Grasshopper. You've explained what this world is like. You've sent your warning. You're aware that your mission has been successfully completed. And that's why you're begging me to stop you somehow," said Dr. Palladino.

"And Doctor, you now expect me to raise my revolver and shoot myself?" the Grasshopper laughed.

"No. I know that's not how it goes. I have a different proposition."

"Do you? What is it? I've been wondering all this time what you will come up with. Where do you get such self-confidence? This order of yours to turn on energy for the people was quite cute. I barely kept myself from bursting into laughter."

"But you switched it on nonetheless."

"Because I can switch it off again at any time."

"I know."

"And decisions that there is no turning back after require a much stronger reason than my temporary sympathy."

"Or an excuse," said Dr. Palladino.

"An excuse?"

"Yes. I hear your cry, Mr. Grasshopper. 'Come, Dr. Palladino, stop me!' but I can't come to you and kill you. Instead of that I can give you an excuse to kill yourself. The entire time you have been expecting a good excuse from me. You can admit that much to yourself."

"Perhaps. Do you have it?"

"Perhaps. You've been claiming the entire time that throughout the history of mankind only the excuses for killing have changed."

"Exactly."

"And that they themselves are not important. That it isn't at all important whether it is an idea, membership in a group, greed…"

"Yes. Completely irrelevant."

"It is important to exercise the instinct to kill? Any excuse is good?"

"Precisely."

"So, if every excuse for killing is good, then every excuse is good to stop killing, Mr. Grasshopper."

"You were very cunning coming up with that," the Grasshopper smiled. "Let's accept that. But these excuses for killing are in fact notions. They have their names, they have meaning…"

"The excuse to stop killing which I place in your hands has both a name and a meaning."

"And that is?"

"Luck."

"Luck?" the Grasshopper was surprised.

"Yes. Do you remember when you told me how you strived and what all you did to get to the command desk?"

"I remember."

"You imposed yourself on Erivan as the logical choice for his squads, won over his trust, wrote your doctoral thesis…"

"I know what you're saying."

"What?"

"That in the end it was luck that decided. Because I told you that it could have happened that I wasn't recruited, that I was killed in action, a number of factors… and that's true. I still think that."

"You're a smart man, Mr. Grasshopper, a man who knows that despite all the effort, knowledge, abilities, in life it also takes luck to achieve goals. You are a man who is reduced to sitting at a command desk thanks to yourself and to luck."

"That's right. I agree."

"That's why you are a man who will allow the world to try its luck one last time. You will allow for the die to be cast one more time."

Chapter 148

"First of all, you're not going anywhere, Pascal. Second, you're not listening to me at all or you're not understanding what I'm saying. I'm not in shock, Pascal. I've known the entire time that this moment would come. I'm just thinking intensely right now."

"Alright, Manami, if that's what you want, let's think together. Let's say that the mayor decides to kill only me. That's emotionally the simplest for him. Do you agree?"

"I don't agree," Manami said firmly.

"Why? Explain it to me," said Pascal.

"He won't raise his hand against us. He would never threaten the life of another person. That's what I think. But the two of us cannot rely on my opinion, because Julius was never in such a situation. Humiliated like this. Now I'm thinking about what he could do. What are the options that he has available?

"He cannot bring the inspectors to our shelter to arrest you and take you away, because he knows, he's aware that... but even if he wasn't sure of that, he cannot dismiss that possibility... that I'd jump on the inspectors, pull you from them, scream... in front of the children... in front of Peter.

"Such a scene in front of his son could destroy Julius. He cannot take such a chance. Even if he were only to send Noah... or come himself... the same thing would happen in front of Peter. No... he would never allow that, for any reason. To be humiliated in front of his son.

"He doesn't have any choice... Julius is powerless, Pascal, while we are in the shelter. He must find a way to get us out of the shelter, all together, all four of us... and then to somehow separate us... to get you away from us... or you and me, together, away from the children."

Manami sat up on the couch and looked at Pascal determinedly.

"Listen to me very well now, Pascal! When the time comes that we have to or want to leave the shelter, the four of us must not be separated even for a moment.

"Don't you dare be a hero, defy anything, feel sorry, feel sorry for someone, because of some guilty conscious, because of some regret... anything.

"I won't permit anything! I'm forbidding everything! You can't think anything! Or feel!

"You must constantly repeat to yourself that the four of us must not be separated. At any cost! For any reason!

"That's the only thing you must think about. And listen to what I tell you. And do what I tell you. Is that clear, Pascal?"

"It's clear, my love," Pascal whispered.

"What's the first thing that I told you, Pascal?"

"I don't know what you mean, Manami."

"What's the first thing that I said? What was my first thought? I said that Julius would do something to himself. Julius... and my father... the two of them would raise their hand against themselves if that meant that they saved face. The two of them... that's how they are... that's what they are made of... That's the type of people they are."

"And me? What am I made of, Manami?"

"You, Pascal? You're not made of hard materials."

"So, you think that I'm soft," Pascal smiled.

"You are... made of... of love for me."

Pascal didn't say anything. He just ran his fingers across her hair, her face and her lips.

"Pascal, I couldn't change any of that even if I wanted to. I have no guilty conscious. Why would I? Am I to blame? I'm not to blame. You simply appeared and I fell in love.

"I too was no stranger to love before that. No, Pascal," Manami said thoughtfully. "I learned about different kinds of love. For my parents, cousins, friends... I loved Julius, too. And the children, of course. You know very well how much I love them...

"Julius and I, we had... not only the two of us... all of us, our family, we had wonderful moments... not only nice moments... everything was nice... our entire life... organized, decent... our luxurious ship anchored in a calm port.

"I tell you, Pascal, I knew very well what love is, even before you. But that love... all those loves... somehow they... how can I say... they... as my late father would say, they came with the territory. Do you understand what I'm saying?

And now this... this is... You're an impulsive man... you can explode in an instant, become wild... But this, what I feel for you,

330

how much I love you... Well, that love, Pascal, is the truly wild, wildest, crazed, strongest storm! It washes away everything in its wake! The ship, the port... even the coastline!... It washes everything away!"

"My love..." Pascal whispered.
"Don't think that I'm trawling for titles. I want that to be clear to you. Like, the Mayor of Megapolis isn't enough, and I need the President of Earth."
"Manami, really..."
"I thought about that too, Pascal. I asked myself whether I'm that kind of woman. Are titles important to me? But I concluded that it isn't so. That you could be working in a grocery shop or as a clerk... Anywhere, anything... and the first time that I saw you I would have fallen in love."
"Manami... what are you saying, my love..."
"I would come every day to your shop to get a glance at you... to force you to fall in love too..."
"Silly, I would have fallen in love long before..."
"Pascal..."
"Yes, my love?"
"I can't talk any more, I can't think..."
"I know, my darling... Don't worry... Everything will be as you said. The four of us will stay together."
"I'm tired, Pascal, of all of this. I need you... Kiss me, please."

Pascal moved towards her lips. Manami gently stopped him by placing her hand on his chest.
"But not that way, Pascal."
"I don't understand, Manami."
"Don't kiss me that way now."
"What way?"
"Shamelessly."
"Shamelessly?" Pascal laughed.
"Stop pretending! You know very well how shamelessly you kiss me."
"Alright, I won't kiss you shamelessly. So tell me, how should I kiss you?"
"Well... like... gently... just affectionately."

Chapter 149

"And what would you like, Doctor?" the Grasshopper laughed. "That we just throw the die or coin, heads or tails? Tails – I kill myself and the world lives, heads – the two of us say goodbye and I continue with my work?"

"No," Dr. Palladino said calmly.

"So?"

"Russian roulette. The two of us will play. I will play on behalf of mankind."

"Why? What's the difference?"

"First of all I don't believe that if tails fall that you will actually raise the revolver and kill yourself. And as a participant in the game you will pull the trigger. And the second thing is only important to me. I couldn't bare staying alive after our talks and watch you continue killing."

"I understand."

"When do we start? You have your famous six-shooter revolver. Charlie, who is in front of the door has a similar one."

"Doesn't it seem to you, Dr. Palladino, that your self-confidence is turning into arrogance? That you might anger me?"

"No. I know that you will agree to Russian roulette. It is such a logical ending. Whoever invented that Russian roulette, invented it solely for this moment."

The Grasshopper was silent.

"Don't think. It's not something to think about. It has to be an impulse. When do we start?"

"I have to think about it. I'll get back to you."

"No!" Dr. Palladino jumped up from his chair. "I won't permit it! It's not a rational matter, Mr. Grasshopper! It is a matter of your entire being! It must now say whether it is an absolute killer who will kill all life or the greatest serial killer who is begging me to stop him. Which are you? Tell me – which are you?!!!" Dr. Palladino shouted.

"I'll let you know in four, five days, Dr. Palladino," the Grasshopper said calmly.

"In five days? What does that mean? What do you need those five days for? Don't you dare even think about shooting at Earth again!

Is that clear to you?!" Dr. Palladino threatened the Grasshopper with his finger, putting his face in the camera.

"You've become quite delightful, Doctor," the Grasshopper laughed. "We'll play Russian roulette."
"We will?" Dr. Palladino stopped breathing.
"Yes, Doctor, we'll play."
Dr. Palladino placed both hands on the desk, lowered his head and sighed deeply.

"But you will be in Megapolis."
"Why do I have to be in Megapolis, Mr. Grasshopper?" Dr. Palladino again put his face in the camera. "It's complicated! How will I get to Megapolis safely? If something happens to me, nothing compels you to…"
"Dr. Palladino, calm down, please. That's my concern. I will arrange it with Mayor Seneca. He, in cooperation with Charlie, will provide you with safe transport," the Grasshopper said calmly.
"But why Megapolis? And why do you need four, five days?"
"Megapolis is my city," said the Grasshopper, lowering his voice. "My University. When I went to school there… it wasn't like it is now. I was one of the first generations of students at the new University. Mr. Seneca became mayor at that time. He introduced uniforms, emblems, an anthem, manner… We were full of enthusiasm, pride…
"For a while… no, not only for one period… it happened several times… Megapolis, the University managed to shake my intentions. Megapolis was the only thing that managed to do so.
"In the meantime I was recruited. And I met Erivan. I haven't been shaken since.
"That is why I will give Megapolis one last chance. Giving the world a chance without Megapolis means nothing. It will quickly turn out new Kaellas and Erivans. And if Mr. Alexander's Third Renaissance ever materializes, it will be in Megapolis.
"Dr. Palladino, Megapolis is the only excuse that I will agree to."

"So Megapolis was important to you the entire time. That is why you never switched off its energy supply. So that people would swarm to it, and then… Capital City, too."
"No, not Capital City. It means nothing to me. My plan was to direct the beams towards the oceans, once I destroyed Megapolis. And to lock the energy system in that position," the Grasshopper fell silent.
"And?" Dr. Palladino whispered.

"And?" the Grasshopper smiled. "And then, Dr. Palladino, I would calmly watch from here as the oceans heated up and storms ravaged the Earth.

"I would regularly measure the increase in temperature on the planet, but I wouldn't get too excited about it. How could I prove that the temperature was increasing because of my beams if I didn't have enough historical data? What could I compare it to? I would know very well that it was only a claim by vicious tongues and that such an increase in temperature was actually a regular cycle in nature... I'm joking, of course...

"I would direct the beams towards the oceans, lock the energy system and kill myself. The evaporation of the oceans would do the rest. I would kill all life. The collective Thanatos would triumph."

"And that's exactly what you will do, if Megapolis loses against you."

"Precisely."

"And five days?" Dr. Palladino was persistent.

"That is approximately how long it will take me to redirect the beams towards Megapolis. When I'm finished, only then will I call Seneca and inform Charlie. I want you to be in that residence as long as possible, safe. Because I won't play Russian roulette with anyone else, Dr. Palladino. So please don't tell Charlie anything. I will communicate with him."

"I won't, of course," said Dr. Palladino.

"And then I will see what Seneca and Charlie will say. How much time it will take them to get you safely to Megapolis. Then we will set the exact time of the Russian roulette."

Chapter 150

On the fourth night after Seneca had left their shelter, Eir, Peter, Manami and Pascal heard the elevator doors open.

"Noah," said Eir.

"It might also be dad, " Peter was hopeful. "Yes! It's dad!" He shouted when he heard the shelter door unlock.

"Dad!" shouted Eir, sliding off the chair and running with her brother towards the door.

Pascal rose from the table and looked at Manami. She just calmly nodded to him.

Noah entered the shelter for the first time. He was a very handsome shapely young man, wearing an Inspectorate colonel's uniform.

"Noah!" Peter ran up to him.

"Hello, Peter," Noah said and put out his hand.

"Noah, what are you doing in the shelter? What has happened?" Manami asked.

"Madam Manami, Mr. Alexander, the mayor has said that the four of you should immediately come to his office."

The shelter fell silent. Peter stood in silence in front of Noah, and Pascal stared at the floor.

"Why, Noah?" Manami asked after a few moments.

"You have to leave here, Madam," said Noah. "This shelter is no longer safe."

"Why isn't it safe?" Manami asked. She walked over to Eir and took her in her arms.

"The Mayor has not authorized me to give you any information, Madam Manami. He told me to remind you of your agreement, according to which he would not trouble you with information from the outside world."

"But that no longer applies," said Manami. "You are now taking us into the outside world. I have to know what's going on."

"I'm not taking you. You are just relocating to a different shelter. There's a helicopter waiting for you on the roof of the television station, which will fly you out of the Megapolis region. You will be put up in a hanger that is deep underground."

"And what if we don't want to leave this shelter?" she asked.

"Madam Manami," Noah said calmly. "The mayor assumed that you would be scared. That is why I am to tell you that you have nothing to worry about and that everything will be as you wish."

Manami looked at Pascal.

"Does that mean that Mr. Alexander is going with us to the new shelter?" she asked.

"Of course. The safety of Mr. Alexander is crucial for the future of this planet. People are worshiping and glorifying you as their savior, Mr. Alexander. Didn't the mayor tell you?"

Pascal said nothing.

"No, Noah," Manami replied instead of him. "That was the agreement. Julius didn't tell Mr. Alexander anything. We didn't want to transfer the apprehension to the children. And only now do I see how right we were."

"Madam, Mr. Alexander, we really have to leave immediately. Every moment is precious. Leave everything here. I will have your things brought to you later."

"Alright, Noah," Manami agreed. "Eir, the gentleman will carry you," she handed the girl to Pascal.

"Mommy..." Eir fought back.

"Listen to mommy, Eir... Be good..." Manami said.

"Eir, come to Pascal," said Pascal while taking the girl.

"Don't leave my side!" Manami whispered to Pascal. "Not for a moment!"

Noah and Peter went down the corridor towards the elevator.

"Wait!" Manami shouted.

The two of them stopped and turned towards her.

"The elevator is very small," said Manami, when she, Pascal and Eir reached it. "This is how we will go up to Julius. First Peter and I, then you, Noah, and Mr. Alexander and Eir at the end." She looked at Pascal. "You and Eir at the end, sir."

Chapter 151

The windows in Seneca's office on the last floor of the television station building were draped. The large aquarelle of Megapolis was shifted to one side, at an angle. The elevator doors opened behind it. When Manami and Peter came out they didn't see Seneca from the front behind the painting. And he didn't come to them, but stood in silence at the office door.

"Dad!" shouted Peter, when he and Manami came out from behind the painting. He ran towards his father and hugged him around the waist.

Mayor Seneca stroked his son on the head and looked at his wife. And Manami looked breathlessly into his empty eyes.

"Julius…" she whispered when she approached him.

"Don't worry, Manami. Everything will be alright. You're going to a safe place," said Seneca quietly. He knelt next to Peter and took his face in his hands. "My son," he said and kissed his forehead.

He got up when Noah came out of the elevator and entered the office.

"There, Mr. Alexander will now come up with Eir," Noah said.

"Noah, take Manami and Peter to the roof, and I'll come with Alexander and Eir."

"No!" shouted Manami, squeezing Peter's hand and stared directly at her husband.

"Alright, Manami, alright… we'll all go together," Seneca said calmly. "We'll wait for Eir… Noah will provide you with large quantities of food and water… you'll also have electricity… it will be alright… like here," said Seneca. "Noah will explain everything to you. Don't worry about a thing… and you, son," he looked at Peter, "should study hard…"

"And you, dad?" Peter asked with a trembling voice, looking at his exhausted, worn out father.

"I'll be alright too, Peter. Everything will be alright… Don't you worry about me. I have Noah to take care of me. You know how he…"

Seneca rushed to the elevator when he heard the doors open. Pascal stepped out of the elevator with Eir in his arms and stopped in front of Seneca. The two men looked each other in the eye.

Manami couldn't see what was happening from the large aquarelle. She let go of Peter's hand and ran towards them. "Stay there, Peter!" she shouted.

When she reached the elevator she saw Eir in Pascal's arms, leaning, towards her father.

"Daddy, daddy," she said.

Knowing that Peter and Noah couldn't see them, Manami grabbed Eir by the shoulders.

"No, Eir! Stay with Pascal!" she whispered fervently. And then her arms dropped to her sides when her husband whispered

"You've gained a wonderful family, Alexander. Take good care of them."

Mayor Seneca took his daughter's stretched out hands and kissed them. Then he turned around swiftly and was the first to leave the office.

Chapter 152

Seneca stopped when he went out onto the roof.

"What is this, Noah?" he asked angrily.

Noah stood next to him and saw what the Mayor meant. In the dark night, next to the aircraft planned to take Seneca's family and Pascal out of Megapolis, was a silhouette of another helicopter, with a large television screen and powerful speakers attached to its side.

"I thought that they had already taken off, Mr. Mayor," said Noah. "I'll tell them to take off immediately." Noah stepped out onto the roof.

"Not you!" Seneca shouted and held him back. "You stay here with them. You're armed. I'll tell them."

The door to the aircraft was open. The pilot was surprised and frightened when he saw Mayor Seneca running towards him from out of the darkness.

"Mr. Mayor," he stuttered, nervously unbuckling his belt to get up and salute his commander.

"Sit!" Seneca shouted. "You are to take off from here immediately!"

"Yes, yes, Mr. Mayor, just as soon as the technician finishes…" the pilot calmed down when he saw that this was the only problem.

"What technician?!" Seneca asked. "As soon as he finishes what?"

"The screen is loose, Mr. Mayor. He's tightening it."

Seneca ran around the aircraft and reached the technician who was standing between the screen and the aircraft fuselage.

"Leave that now!" Seneca shouted. "The helicopter has to take off immediately!"

The technician stood in attention.

"The screen isn't firmly attached, Mr. Mayor!"

"That's not important! You don't have to go on the mission now. Just get out of here. Land at the airport… down in the square, wherever – just get out of here!"

"Yes, sir, Mr. Mayor. The arm will hold until the airport. And even if it's a little loose … the viewing angle isn't important now…"

"Come on, come on, less talk!" Seneca was angry. "Get in the chopper!"

The technician got in and closed the door. The pilot immediately switched on the engine and the helicopter started lifting vertically.

Seneca ran to the other aircraft, waving to Noah.

"Bring them! Quickly!" he shouted.

Manami ran first, because she felt so bad. She felt bad because of the way that she had treated Julius, because of his dignified and painful reaction, because of his parting with the children. "You're not saying goodbye to your children, Julius," her thoughts raced while she ran across the roof. "They are your children. You are their father. They love you. You will always be with them, Julius! Whenever you want. Just let us leave now! To hide again! To calm down!"

The second helicopter was still hovering above them. It couldn't keep its balance and could not fly away, because the arm of the heavy screen was coming off of the fuselage. The next moment the arm detached and the screen fell onto the roof between Seneca, who was already standing next to their helicopter, and Manami, who was still running towards him.

The impact with the concrete shattered the screen. One shard from its glass surface, in the shape of a very sharp triangle, flew through the air towards Seneca and jammed itself deep into his body, across his stomach. Seneca dropped to his knees, grabbed the glass, cutting his hands, and dropped to his side without a sound.

Manami was injured by smaller shards of glass. One had cut her forehead, another was stuck in her shoulder, a third in the palm of her hand.

Noah, Peter, Pascal and Eir were still far enough that none of them were injured.

Manami ran to Seneca and knelt next to him.

"Julius!" she grabbed his shoulder and turned him on his back.

Only then, through the darkness, did she see what had happened. The blood from his gut was gushing all over her.

"Pascal!" she looked up and shouted. "Get the children out of here!"

Pascal realized that something horrible had happened. He had to get Peter and Eir away. They had only seen the silhouette of their father go down, but even that was enough. They both screamed, calling out for their father.

Pascal grabbed Peter around the waist, lifted him and carried him on his hip. He ran towards Seneca's office, carrying both children.

Noah rushed over and knelt next to his Mayor, but he didn't say anything.
Manami lifted Seneca's head from the concrete.
"Julius, Julius…" she wept quietly.

Seneca opened his eyes for a moment. He saw Manami, covered in his blood.
"No, Manami, no…" were the last words of the Mayor of Megapolis.

Chapter 153

During the war, Seneca had created an improvised hospital on one of the top floors of the television station building, in the administrative offices. Eir and Peter were sleeping, heavily sedated, each in their own bed in a four-bed room at this hospital. The on-call nurse sat on a chair next to them, paying careful attention.

The cuts that Manami got on the roof were shallow and harmless. The on-call doctor quickly clean and bandaged them. Manami didn't want to take any sedatives.

She and Pascal sat next to each other in the conference room of the improvised hospital and listened to Noah explain what was going on.

"As soon as he finished his call with the Grasshopper, the mayor ordered the helicopter and sent me to get you from the shelter... He wanted you to immediately leave Megapolis. But it's still not too late. I can call a helicopter this moment..."

"That hangar, is it deep enough that the Grasshopper's beams can't reach it?" Manami asked.

"No," answered Noah, after a brief pause. "But it is located near a city that the Grasshopper has already destroyed. This is why the mayor believed that he would not strike there again."

"So that would mean," Manami said calmly "the Grasshopper defeats this Doctor in Russian roulette, destroys Megapolis and continues to destroy the entire world. And the four of us sit there waiting for our end in that basement. In the meantime the electricity generators run dry, we're left without food and water..." Manami turned to Pascal. "I won't accept that, Pascal!" she said in a raised voice. "I don't want that! I won't watch my children die! We'll stay in Megapolis, Pascal! In this hospital room, until that roulette game. And if the decision is such, we will all disappear in an instant. My children don't need the agony! I gave birth to them and I now decide for them! And for you too, Pascal!"

Manami took Pascal by the hand and placed her head on his shoulder. She looked at Noah, who was seated across from them.

"Noah, you've probably noticed my strange behavior," she said in a calm tone. "When I was arranging the order in which we would take the elevator, when I insisted that Pascal carry Eir... when I ran after Julius, so that he wouldn't do anything to Pascal... behind that large painting."

Noah was silent.

"Pascal and I are in love. We love each other, immensely. Julius knew that. I told him, Noah. If we survive, if the Grasshopper loses, we'll immediately get married. Immediately!" she shouted, then lowered her head and sobbed.

Pascal put his hand around her. Noah didn't say anything. He stared at his hands, laid down on the table. When Manami's moans had calmed down, Pascal asked:

"Noah, can you tell me, how did the mayor manage to preserve Megapolis? If I understood you correctly, people from all corners have been coming to this city."

"Yes, that's right, Mr. Alexander," Noah replied. "Because the Grasshopper switched off power to the other cities. When he saw what was happening, that columns of people were moving on Megapolis, the mayor sent helicopters with screens and loudspeakers..." Noah paused.

"Like the one that caused the accident?" Pascal asked.

"Yes. Those aircraft were our media. At night they flew over those thirsty, hungry, desperate people. In the silence of the night they could hear and see the screens better. We informed them that we would not allow anyone to enter our region. We openly told those wretches that we would protect our water works, our fields, our food production... at any cost. Whoever tried to enter would be liquidated without warning. In return the citizens of the Megapolis region introduced drastic restrictions. Families received food and water according to their size. In minimal quantities necessary for survival. All surplus was shipped to the people beyond our borders. Medicaments too. We called on them to forget their mutual conflicts, to organize and establish their stations, where we would airlift humanitarian aid."

"And did work?" Pascal asked.

"In the beginning it did. But when the Grasshopper started destroying cities, the situation became unbearable. The number of people around the region increased to such a level that the closest ones were simply being pushed across our borders. The Mayor was in agony for days. He didn't give us any orders. People surged into our fields, trampling them, destroying them... our wells, irrigation systems... The food and water production and distribution

343

chain started to fall apart. That is when the Mayor decided. He ordered us to save Megapolis, regardless of the cost in casualties. So that at least some people might live, if everyone cannot... and we pushed back this mass of people. We reestablished our borders... at the terrible, terrible cost in casualties, Mr. Alexander. At one moment the Grasshopper switched on the power to the remaining cities. And the pressure on Megapolis lessened. Now these helicopters of ours are flying over the people in the surroundings and showing footage of the Grasshopper speaking about the Russian roulette..."

"I don't want to listen to this anymore!" Manami suddenly said loudly. "What can I do? I can't even save my children! I'm going to lay down next to them and fall asleep, sedated!" She got up and started towards the door. "Pascal, you're coming with me, too!"

Pascal got up and turned towards Manami. She opened the door and stepped through it. She then stopped and turned.

"Noah!" she shouted.

"Yes, Madam Manami?"

"Does that Svetlana still work in Julius' cabinet?"

"Yes," answered Noah. "Svetlana Van Andel."

"You're the mayor of Megapolis now, you say?"

"That's what your husband wanted, Madam."

"This is the television station!" Manami raised her voice. "City Hall is on the other side of the square. That's where the Mayor's office is! That's your secretariat, Mr. Mayor! I don't want to see that person in the building that I am in! I don't want to see her anywhere!" She grabbed Pascal by the hand and pulled him down the corridor. "Come here, Pascal!"

After making a few steps towards the hospital room with Pascal, Manami suddenly stopped, let go of Pascal's hand, and ran up to Noah, who was closing the door on his way out of the conference room. Manami hugged him.

"Forgive me, Noah!" she said. "Forgive me! I never even told you how sorry I am about your parents! Your mother and father. How much I loved and respected them," Manami started crying again, stepped back from Noah, held his arms and looked him in the eyes. "How proud they would be of their son right now. Julius couldn't have had a better successor, Noah. Megapolis couldn't have a better mayor... Don't be angry with me... Forgive me..."

"Thank you, Madam..." answered Noah. "I'm not angry, of course. You're in shock... These are horrible things that you knew nothing about. And the mayor is gone. Go to your children, please, take something to calm yourself. Its been too much…"

Pascal came up to Manami. "Come, my love, lay with your children," he held her to himself and took her down the corridor. "So that you may sleep, my dear…"

The Grasshopper had called the television secretariat the previous day and briefly informed them that he would establish a video connection the following day at 10 o'clock, Megapolis time, and that he would play a game of Russian roulette with Dr. Palladino.

Manami did not allow for Eir and Peter to wake up during the five days since their father had been killed. She demanded that the doctors keep them sedated because she couldn't bear to look in their eyes, knowing that they might die soon.
She also didn't allow any device for communication with the outside world or accessing the media to be brought into their hospital room. "What will be will be," she told Pascal. "I won't watch that."
Pascal wanted Manami to also be sedated, but she wouldn't agree to that. "I want to feel you until the very last moment," she told him.

That morning she said that no one could enter their room anymore.
At half past nine she moved Eir to Peter's bed and told Pascal to sit on the edge of it. She lay down in his lap and held her children's hands.
Pascal caressed her back and kissed her hair.

Chapter 155

Dr. Palladino sat alone at a table in the middle of the square. In front of him, installed on a tripod, was a camera that was filming him. He had earphones in his ears and a microphone in front of his mouth. He held his sweaty palms on his knees. Dr. Palladino looked at the small monitor in front of him, next to which lay a revolver and one bullet.

Noah stood behind him. The table, camera, Dr. Palladino and Noah were protected by inspectors, with their bodies. They stood in a perfect circle, with their backs turned towards them.

A huge screen was installed along the entire width of the television station building. The people that had flooded the square watched it in silence.

The Grasshopper placed a revolver and one bullet on the command desk. He watched the satellite image of the square in Megapolis. At precisely ten o'clock he switched on his camera and microphone, and established communication with Dr. Palladino.

When the participants in the Russian roulette appeared on the big screen, split into two halves, the entire square gasped.

"Good day, Dr. Palladino," said the Grasshopper.

"Good day, Mr. Grasshopper."

"Dr. Palladino do you see my revolver lying on the command desk?"

"Yes, I do."

"That means that the command desk is locked. In the event that I lose this game of ours and if my head hits the desk, it won't cause any change in the energy system."

"I understand," said Dr. Palladino.

"In that case, the shields from all the platforms and the Command will be automatically lowered at noon exactly, your time. This means that specialists will be able to enter this room and take over control of the energy system."

"I understand," Dr. Palladino repeated.

The Grasshopper took the bullet, placed it in the revolver and spun the barrel. Dr. Palladino did the same.

"Who will go first, Doctor?" the Grasshopper asked.

"You."

"No, I won't. We'll flip a coin. Tails – I go first, heads – you go first."

"Alright," said Dr. Palladino. He pulled out a coin from his shirt pocket, spun it in the air, caught it with one hand and placed it on the table. "Heads. I go first," he said quietly.

At that moment the Grasshopper noticed something unusual on the satellite image of the square full of people. Near the television station building, under the large screen with his and Dr. Palladino's images, was an empty space, with a colorful border.

He zoomed in.

The border was made up of children dressed in shirts of different colors, holding hands.

He zoomed in.

They stood around a funny gray-haired old man, whose colors were even more vivid than theirs.

He zoomed in.

The old man was holding a dog in his hands. And the dog was crying.

Dr. Palladino raised his revolver. At that moment he saw the Grasshopper place his right hand under the desk.

"Why are you putting away your revolver?! Where is your revolver, Mr. Grasshopper?!" shouted Dr. Palladino in panic.

"I'm changing the rules of the game, Doctor," said the Grasshopper, returning the revolver to the holster on his right thigh.

"What do you mean?! You can't do that! The game has started! We had an agreement, Mr. Grasshopper!"

"I'm going first, Doctor."

Dr. Palladino couldn't see what the Grasshopper was doing under the command desk. But he saw Grasshopper's shoulder drop slightly when he took the revolver from the holster on his left thigh.

"You took the revolver with the full cylinder?" Dr. Palladino asked quietly, having realized what the Grasshopper had done.

"Goodbye, Dr. Palladino." The Grasshopper placed the barrel of the full revolver against his temple. "It's been a pleasure," he said and pulled the trigger.

When the Grasshopper's head fell on the command desk, everyone sighed in relief. And then nothing. They just stood in silence. All as one.

Dr. Palladino took out a pack of cigarettes and a lighter from his jacket pocket. He tried to open the pack, but his trembling hands wouldn't obey him. Noah walked up to him, took out a cigarette, lit it, and placed it between the Doctor's lips. Dr. Palladino closed his eyes and took a deep drag.

Chapter 156

"We're saved! We're alive! The Grasshopper killed himself!" shouted a nurse running into the room. "I have to get out into the square! I have to!" she turned, ran out of the room and slammed the door.

Manami got up from Pascal's lap, bent over and kissed the sleeping Eir and Peter on the cheek, straightened up, offered Pascal her hand and pulled him towards her.
"Kiss me! Kiss me!" she cried out.
When their lips separated, she shouted out in joy:
"My darling, my president!" She bent over again and loudly kissed Eir and Peter, stood up, and took Pascal's hands in hers.
"My love... my wonderful love," Pascal whispered.
"I apologize, Mr. President," Manami smiled, "for taking up your precious time..."
"What president, Manami..."
"The best! Smartest! Handsomest! My President! Only mine!" Manami shouted.
"Let it be, darling. We'll see. What's important now..."
"What's important now, Mr. President is that you address these people, who have suffered so much. The people, for whom you were the only hope. Not only their hope – you were their faith. People believe in you, Pascal!"
"Alright, alright... there's time..."
"There's no time! The people need you immediately, now! Go to the studio and address them. No, no... find... have them bring Noah to you. He knows the situation best. Discuss with him what you should say first, for the people to calm down, to organize food and water... Primarily for the children, Pascal! Come on, there's no time to waste! Go to the studio, have them dress you, put on makeup. You're all wrinkled and pale. You must listen to your wife, Mr. President!"

When Pascal heard her words he hugged her tightly.
"My wife! My wife!" he shouted and kissed her.

"Come on, come on..." Manami laughed, gleaming with joy. "Why are you getting all soft? I'll wait for my children to wake up... their mommy will explain everything to them. They will always love and respect their father, but they will live normally. They will be mommy's happy children. And yours, Pascal. You are to love them and cuddle them like you did in our shelter! Do you hear?"

"Yes, my love! I will, darling, I will!"

"And we have to hurry up with our baby, Pascal! It's your own fault! Why did you fall in love with an old woman, and now you have to hurry!"

"We will, my love, we'll hurry it up. Already today. Now! Let's go to a room, while the children are still asleep!"

"You really want me very much, sir?"

"Very much! Very much!"

"Well nothing before marriage, sir," Manami smiled. "As soon as Peter and Eir wake up, we'll take them to our house. And you and I will get married. You will marry me already today! Is that clear, sir?"

"Clear, clear! Today, immediately, my wife! My wife!" Pascal shouted.

Manami kissed him. After that she stepped back and said in a serious tone.

"Pascal, I really want to get married today. As soon as possible. Please, find Noah, address the people... so that they see that you're alive, that you're here, that you are thinking of them, that you love them... do you understand?

"And then we'll get married in secret. Noah will be our witness. No one else will know. We mustn't even burden the children with that. Peter and Eir have to have time to mourn the death of their father, to get used to their house again, to normal life..." Manami paused and thought. "The only this is that you have to come with us immediately... to live with us.

"I'll tell Peter that you have nowhere to go. That you will be with us for a while. We'll think of something. And I cannot... I won't allow you, Pascal, to be gone all day long!" she raised her voice. "That you are at some presidential office!

"You will do everything from our house. We'll make you an office there.

"That's it! We'll say that its for your safety. So that its easier for the inspectors to protect you. There, that's what Noah will say as the official explanation. That he, who is responsible for your safety, demands that.

"And Peter will accept that, Pascal! He adores Noah!"

Manami lowered her voice and touched Pascal's face.

"That will be the official reason. And my reason is you. For anything, for everything. Just you. You can't be away from me for a moment. Because I can't live without you anymore, Pascal."

She gently kissed his lips and ran the fingers of both hands through his hair. She smiled, took him by the hand and led him to the door. She opened it and pushed him into the corridor.

"Find a studio, tell them to fix you up and fetch Noah. The two of you discuss what should be done next. Go now, go already..." The smiling and overjoyed Manami shut the door.

Chapter 157

Pascal stopped after several steps. "What's with you, love?" he thought. "What studio of yours? Alright... I'll find Noah. He also claims that people believe in me... It seems that my friend Raul was right... Raul, my friend... my friends... Do you resent me for not thinking of you, for being so happy? Forgive me... but I can't help it, I'm overjoyed!"

Pascal only then realized that the corridor was completely empty and that there wasn't a sound. He continued down the corridor looking in the rooms, through their open doors. All the rooms were empty.
"What's this? Where are the patients? Where are the nurses?" he thought to himself. "Did the Grasshopper actually kill himself or..." dread came over Pascal. And then on the television set in one of the rooms he saw the image of the dead Grasshopper. "Yes, he did!" he sighed in relief. "You're dead!"

"Pascal!" managed to shout a man who was lying in bed with his raised leg and arm in a cast, in one of the rooms that Pascal had just passed by.
"Sir," Pascal was happy to have found someone. "Where has everyone disappeared?"

"Pascal..." the patient whispered.
"Yes, it's me. Tell me, please..."
"Everyone rushed out..." the man was coming to. "Outside... to the square..."
"How could the patients..."
"Everyone... however they could... look in the ICU... there must be a nurse there, Mr. President! Our President! We knew that you were alive! We knew!" the patient shouted.
"Yes, I'm alive," Pascal smiled. "Excuse me, sir, where is the intensive care unit?"

At that moment the nurse that cared for Peter and Eir ran into the corridor.

"I'm sorry, Mr. Alexander, but I had to go down into the square. Here, I'll go immediately to the Madam and the children..." she ran past Pascal.

"Wait please, nurse..." Pascal grabbed her by the hand and stopped her. "Tell me please, do you know where Noah is?"

"The new mayor?"

"Yes."

"I don't know. Probably upstairs... in his office. Try there, I'm sure there is someone. They will tell you."

There was no one in the secretariat or in Seneca's office. "What should I do now? Manami will be angry if I return immediately. I have to tell her at least that I talked to Noah... I'll go to the square, like everyone else. I'm sure he's there."

Pascal took the elevator down to the magnificent hall of the television station building and walked towards the door. As he passed a group of inspectors, a captain who had noticed him stepped out in front of him.

"Where are you going, Mr. Alexander?" he asked.

"Captain, you sure must know where Mayor Noah is," said Pascal.

"He's in the square. But we had to stay here to prevent you from leaving the building."

"Why?" Pascal was surprised.

"Those were the mayor's orders. The situation is presently unpredictable. He said that you must return to your room and wait until he comes to you."

Pascal turned around and ran to the elevator. He chose the floor of the improvised hospital. "This turned out great! You won't be able to drive me away, my love!"

He came out of the elevator and rushed down the corridor. He opened the door to the hospital room and was surprised to see a nurse sitting next to Peter and Eir, who were still asleep.

"Where is the Madam?" he asked.

"She first told me that she didn't need me, that she would call me when the children are awake," said the nurse while getting up. "Then she ran past the nurses' station, I didn't even get a good look at her... and when I came into the corridor she just shouted to me 'Have the gentleman come to our room!' And I was surprised, why should I tell you that if you are here, in your room..."

Pascal turned around and rushed to the elevator.

Chapter 158

"To our room! To our room, my love! And you said only after marriage! After marriage, right? And now you can't wait even until tonight?! My excited darling! You're on fire! Do you know what? We'll make love for hours! For hours! Let the children awake with the nurse. So what? Who knows how long they'll be drowsy?"

Pascal rushed into the Mayor's office and saw that the painting had been moved. He called the elevator. "That's why you sent me away, you little fox! Like, I should address the people. Like, it can't wait until tomorrow, or the day after. It has to be immediately. So that you could go to our room before me and put on your gold kimono! The gold kimono! My love, my wife, my goddess!"

He rushed into their shelter and was stunned. Manami stood in front of their cover, in their room, wearing the gold kimono.
"My beauty! You're wonderful! Gorgeous! You're even prettier than in my dreams!"

Then he looked at her face. He saw that from a small split in the middle of her upper lip, at the top of that small heart that he loved to kiss so much, like the thinnest strand, in silence, without any gurgle, flowed the first trickle of her blood.
He bit down hard on his lower lip and when he felt the taste of blood he rushed towards Manami.

"Don't Pascal! You can't! Because of the children!" shouted Manami and ran behind the couch. She stayed there, her back turned towards him.

Pascal was completely stunned. He didn't say anything. Only tears poured from his eyes.

Chapter 159

None of the numerous mutations of the XZW virus were transferred by airborne droplets. Only by blood. And there was plenty of blood in the case of people infected with any version of the XZW virus.
The first symptom, without any warning, was the sudden appearance of dry cracked skin throughout the patient's body. This is what created lesions on the skin, which with the occurrence of internal bleeding, transformed the dying into geysers of blood.
This is why people called death caused by the XZW virus – the Bloodbath.

The XZW-851 mutant of the XZW virus was special in one way. The infected person would first develop cracks on their lips, and soon after the ruptured capillaries in their eyes.
Several hours into the process of dying the person infected with the XZW-851 would not feel any pain, only a stream of blood would flow unstoppably from their lips, and it would seem as though the person, aware of their impending death, was crying tears of blood.

Death by the XZW-851 virus was generally no more horrible than death caused by any other mutation of the XZW virus.
Except for the people whose loved one was dying this way. Because it was most terrible to watch someone you love bleed precisely from the eyes and lips. The things that you love most of all to look at and kiss.
That is why people call the XZW-851 virus the Love virus, not out of ridicule, but as a description of that immense pain.

The survival rate for people infected with this virus was a zero.

Chapter 160

"Turn around, Pascal" said Manami. "I don't want you to remember me like this. I won't look at you either."

Pascal turned away from her. Between them, on the red silk, was an embroidered black rose.

"Julius infected me," Manami said quietly. "I told you that he always found a solution. This virus would have provided him a honorable way out. He didn't want to kill me, Pascal. Just himself. He infected himself.

"He didn't stage the accident on the roof, because he couldn't have known where the glass shards would fly. He couldn't know where each of us would be at that moment. He couldn't have known that I would run to him and get cut. Because if I hadn't been, I wouldn't have been infected. Julius couldn't have known where Peter and Eir would be standing.

"When I got to him and raised his head he was still breathing. He opened his eyes and looked at me. He said 'No, Manami', and his eyes were full of dread. Because he saw that I was covered in his blood. He didn't mean us harm. He respected our love. He was a noble man. He was a great man.

"And that is why I will ask you something, Pascal. Hide the truth. No one must know that Julius was infected. Tell Noah to make something up. That I was infected at the hospital. By some bloody bandage that I had found and pressed against my cuts. There is no need for my children to bear that horrible burden. And that's why, for Peter's and Eir's sake, I ask that you bury me next to Julius."

Manami was silent. They still stood with their backs turned towards each other. They didn't move. They didn't make a single move. That is why only Pascal's sobs broke the silence.

"And why shouldn't we hide our love, Pascal?" she asked. "Who cares about it? In any case, who can understand it? God only gave us a love this great. So don't cry, Pascal. Don't cry, my love, please. I'm leaving calm and happy. Because of the gift that I was given. Because I experienced it. Because it existed."

Pascal stopped crying. But not because Manami told him so. But because he had nothing more to cry. Because his tears had run dry. Because Pascal Alexander had died.

"You now have Peter and Eir," Manami continued. "You will say that you will take custody of them as a sign of gratitude to Julius, who took your freedom but therefore protected you. He safeguarded the people's president, who will create a better world for them.
"Peter and Eir are now your children. Everything that was mine is yours, my love. Don't let sad tones resound from my little girl's strings. And foster my corner in Peter. Create a better world, Pascal. For your children. For all children."

Manami had told Pascal everything that she had. She still wanted to hear whether Pascal had something to tell her. And he didn't say a single word. That is why Manami decided that they should go their separate ways.
"Go now, Pascal," she said. "I want to be alone."

Pascal went to the door but he didn't open it. Without turning towards her he said
"Alright, Manami. You're leaving now. And I have to stay here for a while to create a better world. Because that is what you want. And because I always do what you want. I will, I will create a new world for your children. And when they have grown up, when I am certain that you, my love, are at peace, then I will put on my dark suit and shiny black shoes. And I will come to you, Manami. And you will wait for me in our chamber. Beautiful, in the gold kimono. I will come up to you and give you my hand. You will place your warm palm in it. I will hug you, hold you to my chest and kiss your hair. And we will be alone. Just you and me, Manami. Just the two of us. In the whole world."

Pascal opened the door and left the shelter.

Chapter 161

Manami went to her room. She took a pair of scissors from the dresser, returned to the living room and cut out the black rose from their cover. She then put back the remaining red silk as it had been. She went to the kitchen and took the largest knife.

Pascal got off the elevator in the lobby of the television station building. He approached the inspectors.
"Where are you going, Mr. Alexander?" the captain asked him. "The mayor still hasn't returned. You know his orders."
"That's not important. I am your President. Take me to the square," Pascal said.
"Yes, sir, Mr. President!"

Manami went to couch and knelt on it. She bound her knees with the black rose and raised the knife.
The first bloody tears ran down her face and dripped onto the gold kimono.
And with her beautiful eyes she was looking at Pascal's image.
"My love," she said, and slit her throat with one powerful cut.

Pascal, accompanied by the inspectors, came out through the large doors of the television station building and stepped out onto the top of a granite staircase.
A whisper spread through the square. "Pascal… Pascal…"

Some people remained standing. Some fell to their knees.
But everyone's hands were reaching out to Pascal.

The Grasshopper
Copyright © 2014 by Saša Mihajlović

Author: Saša Mihajlović
Design: Dragan Grozdanić
Translator: Vuk Tošić
Second Edition, 2014

CIP - Cataloguing in Publication
National and University Library, Ljubljana

821.163.41-32

MIHAJLOVIĆ, Saša, 1963-

The Grasshopper / Saša Mihajlović. - 2nd ed. - Maribor : self
published, 2014

ISBN 978-961-283-017-5

273473792

www.sashajm.com